D1589447

STONE RULES

samantha christy

Books Publishing Group

Saint Augustine, FL 32092

Copyright © 2016 by Samantha Christy

All rights reserved, including the rights to reproduce this book or any portions thereof in any form whatsoever.

This is a work of fiction. Names, characters, places and incidents are either the product of the author's imagination or are used fictitiously, and any resemblance to actual persons, living or dead, business establishments, events or locales is entirely coincidental.

Cover design © Sarah Hansen, Okay Creations

ISBN-13: 978-1539037132

ISBN-10: 1539037134:

For everyone who's had something to overcome.

And for everyone who has yet to do so.

STONE RULES

PART ONE

CHARLIE

PROLOGUE

I feel nothing as I watch them lower her into the ground.

Actually, that's not entirely true. While most of those in attendance are grieving—or at least putting on award-winning performances, considering many have made their living on the big screen—I can only think of one thing.

Ding dong the witch is dead.

My best friend squeezes my hand in support. She's the only reason I'm here. Piper Mitchell is the one person in this world I would do anything for. So when she called, begging me to fly home for the funeral, I could hardly refuse.

'Closure,' she called it. *'Maybe now you can start to heal,'* she said.

I know she means well. After all, she got her happily-ever-after with Mason. I sneak a glance at the two of them. Even here, surrounded by corpses in a graveyard, they look hopelessly in love. He caresses her shoulder with his thumb, holding her tightly against him as she stands between us.

Piper thinks my story can end like hers. But even though we have similar pasts, we are so very different. She grew up knowing love. The love of parents who would do anything to protect her. The love of sisters who would give their very lives for each other.

Hers is the only love I've ever known. The love of a soulmate sister, bound by horrific events no child should have to endure.

Piper's mother, Jan Mitchell, tried to take me under her wing. She tried to show me what the love of a real mother felt like. And she did a fabulous job. But it's not the same. It's not the same as having the love of the woman who birthed you, raised you, cuddled you when you were hurt—then ripped your heart out.

As people take their turns throwing dirt onto the casket, I think back on the service. How could such a terrible person draw that kind of crowd? How could people speak about her as if she were a wonderful, caring, giving individual? My skin crawled as a few of the mourners told tales of her philanthropy. Jan and Piper flanked my sides, each holding one of my hands. Not because I was grieving, but to keep me from jumping out of my seat and telling everyone the truth. The truth about the monster who was my mother.

But I didn't stand up. I didn't say a word. I couldn't draw more attention to myself. Especially since I knew *he* was probably there.

I haven't seen my father since I was twelve. That was ten years ago. I know he's alive. Piper ran into him last year. She said he looked old. Haggard. Broken. Serves the bastard right for leaving his daughter the way he left me.

I don't know if he's here. I haven't bothered to look around. The reality of what else, or more specifically, who else, I might see here sickens me. So I've gone through the motions hoping to remain invisible. I'm here for one reason and one reason only. To see for myself that the bitch is gone.

"Charlie?" I look up to see that people have disbanded and are walking back to their cars. "You coming?" Piper asks.

"Give me a minute please."

She nods before Mason escorts her through the maze of headstones. I watch them walk over to where the rest of the Mitchell clan is standing. None of them knew my mother. They all came for me. Piper's older sisters, Baylor and Skylar, accepted me as part of their family long ago when I started escaping to their house in Maple Creek, Connecticut, where we grew up.

I look back over at the hole in the ground. I shake my head as I lower my eyes to the frozen February grass in front of me. What kind of twisted person feels happy when a parent dies?

The kind of twisted person my mother raised me to be, I guess.

"That could be you," a man says behind me, making me jump out of my skin.

"Excuse me?" I ask in disgust.

"Sorry." He laughs. "I meant you are the spitting image of your mother."

He steps closer to me. Too close. He reaches a hand up under my hair, placing it suggestively on my neck. His dark eyes rake over my body as a sick familiarity washes over me. Bile rises in my throat as I try not to become the helpless girl I once was.

His hand tightens on me. "You've grown," he says.

I maneuver myself out of his grip like I was taught in self-defense class. I hold his surprised eyes with mine. "Don't you ever fucking touch me again or I'll kill you."

He laughs again. It's a cold, devious chuckle. "You're a little firecracker, aren't you?" He reaches into his pocket and pulls out a small baggie of white powder. "I'll make it worth your while. Just like I did for Mommy Dearest." He nods to the grave.

Flashbacks of the scumbag in front of me bombard my thoughts. All of a sudden I'm a scared and naked fourteen-year-old focusing on the mural painted on my bedroom wall as this man pleasures himself while staring at me.

Was I really naïve enough to think none of those perverts would have the balls to show up here?

Dewey, I think was the name Mom called him. He used to hang around the house a lot. He's older now, skinnier and obviously strung out. At least he wasn't one of the ones who touched me. He only liked to look. But that was bad enough.

"What do you say, honey? Now that you're old enough, we can both have some fun."

"Fun? You call what you did to me fun, you sick bastard?"

"What's the big deal, doll? I never touched you."

He puts a cigarette between his lips. Then he searches his pocket for a lighter. He doesn't even see my knee coming. And because I have those extra few seconds, I'm able to lunge forward and grab his shoulders for more leverage.

When he doubles over, grabbing his junk that I'm certain won't work for a good while, I ball up my fist and deliver a blow right in the nose, where I know it will hurt the most. I hear a crack when I connect. I'm just not sure the sound came from his nose breaking, or my hand.

I get my answer when I watch blood gush from his nostrils as his hands can't figure out whether to cradle his face or his groin.

I turn and walk away, watching my friends race towards me. And all I can think is how great that felt. It was exhilarating. Cathartic.

It was closure.

What do you know. Piper was right.

CHAPTER ONE

I stare at the piece of paper in front of me, sure there has been some massive mistake. I look at the salt-and-pepper-haired attorney sitting across the large cherrywood desk. "Mr. Slater, I don't understand."

"This is just an estimate, Ms. Tate," he says, his voice laced with a hint of apology. "This is only what we have discovered so far. It's possible your mother had some other holdings we don't know about yet. I'm sorry it's not more."

"More?" I look up at him in confusion. Then I blink twice, trying to clear my eyes before I look down and focus on the seven figure number. "I didn't know there was *any*."

"Um . . ." Mr. Slater looks around as if there were other people in the room who would understand what I said. "It's my understanding you've been out of the country for some time now, Ms. Tate. But your mother was Caroline Anthony. You must know what that means, right?"

I give him my best *I'm not stupid* look. "Of course I know she was famous, but that was a long time ago. As far as I know, she hasn't done anything for years. And please, call me Charlie."

"Well, Charlie, residuals can produce a lot of income. Especially considering the quantity of films she starred in before you were born. Then there was the life insurance."

"Insurance?" I give him another crazy look. My mother didn't seem the type to plan for the future.

"Yes. She had a few paid-up whole life insurance policies that were purchased around the time you were born. Funny thing though, she never changed the address on them. They all still bear the Maple Creek address. It's almost as if she forgot they were even there. They hadn't been updated in over seventeen years."

"You are aware of how my mother died?" I ask.

He shuffles around some papers, reading one of them. Then he nods in understanding. "Drug overdose. I'm very sorry."

"No need to be sorry. She was an addict. A drunk. A shit mother. She deserved every bad thing that happened to her." I think of what Piper told me about how my mother was found. Alone and decomposing as her body went undiscovered for a week until the neighbors in her building complained of the smell. Nobody she knew cared enough to check on her. Nobody missed her. She dug her grave. Now she gets to rot in it.

Mr. Slater's eyes go wide in surprise. I imagine as a probate attorney, he's used to family that is actually upset over their loss.

I shrug a casual shoulder. Then I roll up one of my sleeves and lay my arm on his desk. "My mom didn't win any Mother of the Year awards."

His face contorts with disgust as he takes in the small circular burn scars on the inside of my forearm. He shakes his head and gives me a look of pity. "I'm s—"

"You're sorry. Yeah, I got that. So, what now?"

"Well, you are Ms. Anthony's sole heir, so you get everything. The will she made when you were born was never updated. The portions of the will that gave property to your father are revoked because of the divorce. And since the apartment she lived in upon her death was in her name only, that will pass on to you as well. You may live there if you wish."

"Live there?"

"Yes. It's very common. It will take months, probably eight or nine, for everything to get through probate. And we all know insurance companies tend to drag their feet as long as possible. However, we can have you appointed executor within a few weeks. That will give you control of her assets until we can get them properly transferred to you. You will be able to pay any of her outstanding debts and use estate funds for the upkeep of the apartment until you decide what to do with it." He pushes some papers my way. "You just need to sign these and I'll get the ball rolling."

I sign what seems like a hundred documents and then get up to leave. Before I reach the door, I turn around and ask a question. "Mr. Slater, if she forgot about the policies for all those years, how did you find out about them?"

His head bobs up and down and his lips form a thin line. Then he sighs like he's about to tell me something I don't want to hear. "It was your father. He contacted the lawyer who drew up their wills all those years ago. And that lawyer found out that I was assigned to handle her estate."

"Of course he did." Anger seethes in my bones, crawling up my spine like rungs of a ladder. "He wouldn't want to miss his chance to get whatever money she didn't snort up her nose. Guess he shouldn't have divorced her if he wanted to be a gold digger."

"You misunderstand, Ms. Tate . . . er, Charlie." He rises out of his chair and comes around his desk, perching himself against the front side of it, his eyes softening so that he looks less lawyerly and more fatherly. "He wanted to make sure you were taken care of. He didn't want you to know and I wouldn't have said anything if you hadn't asked. But I'm all about transparency."

When I don't respond, he continues. "He was at the funeral, you know. He kept his distance so he wouldn't cause a scene. He understands you're upset with him. For what it's worth, he seemed genuinely sorry for whatever happened between you."

"Sorry?" There's that worthless word again. "Well, Mr. Slater, my father can take his apologies and shove them up his ass—the same place his balls lived during my childhood."

His mouth turns upward into something that resembles a grin and I realize what I hadn't before. His greying hair and lined forehead speak to his age, but now that I see him standing, out from behind his desk, I can see he's kept himself up nicely. He's quite handsome. Distinguished-looking. And from the looks of his office—very well off.

You don't need to be taken care of, Charlie. Not anymore.

I continue my perusal of his tall body, my eyes halting when they fall just below the waist of his tailor-made Armani suit. He shifts uncomfortably and my eyes snap up to his to see that he didn't fail to notice the fact that I was mentally undressing him.

He looks at me as if he's scolding a child. "I'm twice your age."

"That never bothered any of the others."

He sighs and shakes his head. "I'm married, Ms. Tate."

"Charlie," I remind him, giving him my best *fuck-me* eyes. "And that never bothered any of the others either."

He forcefully pushes off his desk and strides over to me. He grabs my shoulders and I'm certain he's going in for a kiss when instead, he turns me around, directing me towards the door. "I'll call you when the order comes through. Until then, this is New

York City so you might want to be a little more careful whom you proposition."

Although my ego has taken a bruising, I laugh off his rejection. "Old habits die hard I guess."

"Maybe it's time to find new habits, Charlie. You know, start fresh?"

CHAPTER TWO

My head is still spinning as Piper and I take the elevator up to the fourteenth floor of the modest Manhattan building that houses the one-bedroom apartment my mom bought when she moved to the city. As horrible as she was, at least she kept us in Maple Creek after my dad left. If it weren't for that, I'm not sure what would have happened.

Yes, I am. I wouldn't be here. Piper and her family saved me. She kept me from ending up exactly like my mom. Drugs were everywhere. Lying around our house like an old pair of socks. It would have been so easy for me to just end it. I thought about it a lot back then. And when I was sixteen; when I was at my breaking point and was a handful of pills away from escaping my nightmare, Piper entered her own personal hell. She needed me. And I wasn't about to leave her, not even to escape my own pain.

So, ironically, it was Piper's misery that saved my life.

I turn to her, wanting to tell her. But I can't. I could never validate her horrific experiences that way.

"What?" she asks. The inky-black tips of her hair skate around her collarbone as her head shakes back and forth. "Are you having second thoughts?"

"Nope. I'm just glad you're here with me, that's all."

The elevator doors open to let a woman and her child out. When they close, I find myself staring at my mother in the shiny chrome finish. I've often thought of cutting my long wavy red hair, or maybe dyeing it. But I refuse to give my mother the satisfaction. And I refuse to think of the horrible day that started it all.

Most kids probably remember the way their mom kissed a finger when they pinched it in a drawer. Or maybe they remember the way she rubbed their back when they were sick. Not me. The only thing I remember when I look in the mirror is my mother complaining about how I ruined her life. I can almost see her lips moving in my reflection. *From the minute your dad knocked me up, you sucked the life right out of me.*

"Ready?" Piper startles me and I realize the doors have opened and she's holding them, waiting for me to exit ahead of her.

We pass by a few other apartments before reaching my mother's front door. Apartments that have welcome mats, flower pots, or nameplates. But her front door is exactly how I'd expected it to be. Empty and cold. Just like she was.

I use the key the manager gave me, and the lock clicks open. The first thing that hits me when we cross the threshold is an overwhelming stench of flowers. It's like we walked into a damn garden show, minus the live greenery. The next thing I notice is the obvious absence of a couch. The couch she died on. The couch that was burned by the biohazard company the Mitchells hired to sanitize the place. I wish they wouldn't have spent that kind of money. But I guess it's better than the alternative; the sickening smell of death.

"Please thank your parents for having the place cleaned up," I say.

Her green eyes smile at my hazel ones. "Thank them yourself. They've offered you a room at their house on Long Island if you want it." She laughs. "Of course, they'll have to fight me for you. You could stay with Mason and me. Hailey would love to have another *playmate* around." She raises an accusing brow.

"Playmate?" I shrug an innocent shoulder.

She smirks at me. "I didn't know you could become a centerfold overseas."

"First of all, *Melons Magazine* calls us *Cup Cakes*, not *Playmates*. And it was easier than you think; they have tons of magazines for men over there." I narrow my eyes at her. "How did you even know about it?"

"Really?" she asks. "My fiancé is on a football team, Charlie. Do you know what kind of smut circulates around those locker rooms?" She swats my arm. "Why didn't you tell me? What happened to the sisters' code?"

I let out a deep sigh. I feel terrible that I withheld information from her. We've always told each other everything. The years we spent abroad, even though we were both running away from our pasts, we relied only on each other to get through each day—and those days became some of the best of my life.

When we parted ways last year; when I took off, leaving her with no other choice but to return home to the man she loved, I had to up my game; find more means of making money. Had Piper been able to find me, I know she would have sent some, and for that reason alone, I never told her where I was.

"I didn't want to embarrass your family," I lie. *I didn't want to ask your family for money.*

She puts down the vase she was examining and crosses the room towards me. "You could never embarrass us, Charlie. You *are* family. Don't you know that by now? And the pictures were actually very tasteful. You're beautiful."

"Yeah, well, airbrushing works miracles," I say, glancing down at the many tiny scars on my arms.

Piper touches my arm. "No. You're beautiful even with your scars."

My face twitches with a half-smile before I look around the small but quaint apartment. "Anyway, thanks for the offer, but I think I'm going to stay here."

"Here?" Her eyes widen in surprise. "Are you sure about that?"

My eyes take in the tiny kitchen off the living room, the sparse furniture, and the almost bare walls. "I've never been here. I have no memories of this place. It means nothing to me. So, why the hell not? I only have to stay in town for a few weeks. Just until I get the official executor papers and then I can put it up for sale. Will you help me get rid of her shit?"

"Yes. Of course," she says. "I'm here for you. Whatever you need." Her eyes meet the floor and she sulks. "But, do you really have to leave again? I just got you back. We have so much to catch up on."

We walk through the apartment to the far side of the living room so we can check out the sole bedroom. "You mean so I can hear all the sickening details about how much you love the hot football star and his adorable daughter? Or so you can hear about all the hotties I shagged while you were back home putting it to him?"

Her mouth falls open. Then she closes it and rolls her eyes. "Well . . . yeah."

"I can't stay here, Pipes." I walk through the doorway into the bedroom of the total stranger that was my mom. "I already ran into one of her perverted friends at the funeral. I can't risk that happening again."

"So you are choosing to live in her apartment? That makes total sense," she says sarcastically, as she shakes her head and opens the closet to peruse my mother's belongings. She gasps, reaching up to the shelf overhead and pulling down a shiny metal statue. "What are you going to do with this?" She holds her arm out to me, offering me the Best Actress Oscar my mother won twenty-four years ago.

It was the last award she ever won. I know that all too well. I instinctively rub the back of my head, remembering how much it hurt to have the heavy statue meet the back of my skull from time to time. "I don't know. Sell it? Throw it out? Melt it down and pour it over her grave? Maybe we should have buried it with her since it was the only thing in her life that really mattered."

Piper places the award back where she found it and closes the closet door. "There are others in there. I wonder why she didn't display them, since they were so important and all."

"Mmmm," I mumble in response, staring out the large picture window that overlooks a bustling street. The skyscrapers that line the view are breathtaking. I didn't realize how much I missed it until just now. Even though we didn't live here, my mom was always hauling me to the city for one reason or another. A screening. An interview. Lunch with a producer. Dinner with her dealer.

My mother refused to give up what she thought was her destiny; A-list roles portraying young, vibrant women. She was offered dozens of roles after I was born. Supporting roles. The best friend. The quirky aunt. The mother. She thought they were beneath her so she was always holding out for that next Oscar-winning part. The part that never came. And the longing for it drove her slowly insane.

"Maybe this will tell you." Piper reaches into a bedside table drawer.

"Tell me what?"

"Why she didn't display her awards." She holds out a leather-bound book. "It looks like a diary."

I take it from her, but my hands hesitate before opening it. Do I really want to do this? Delve into the innermost thoughts of the person I despised most in this world? But curiosity gets the better of me and I flip open the cover, revealing the very first page.

August 30, 2000

My throat burns and my eyes sting with bad memories. I know most six-year-olds aren't good with remembering dates. But this one—it would be burned into my memory for all eternity. It wasn't my birthday. It wasn't the day I got a new puppy. It wasn't my first day of school.

It was the day she turned into a monster. It was the very first day she hit me. And she decided to record it for posterity.

I put the journal down and race to the bathroom to lose the contents of my stomach.

Piper runs after me. "Oh my God, Charlie. Are you okay? What is it?" She wets a hand towel and offers it to me as I close the lid on the toilet and sit down on it.

"I'm fine. Just bad memories." I wipe my face while looking around the bathroom.

On her vanity sits every anti-aging product known to womankind. Creams, gels, masks. There are even needles and small vials of what looks to be Botox. I didn't even know one could do those injections on oneself. But what makes me want to throw up again is a picture taped to the mirror. I know it's not a picture of me, but it might as well be. She looks a little older than I am now. Only the clothes she wears dates the photo. She looks young and happy and carefree. More like the mother I remember when I was very little.

I rip the photo off the mirror, leaving the edges torn under the weathered tape that has probably been holding it there for several years. I crumple it up and throw it into the trash. Then I pick up the trash can, hold it to the edge of the counter and sweep everything from the vanity into it. Jars crash together and break, spilling liquid and goo.

I yank open the drawers and pull out bucket-loads of makeup to add to the growing pile of garbage. I open up the cabinet under the sink only to find more clutter that was all part of her quest to regain her youthful appearance. I don't know what she looked like before her death. But I can imagine. She was forty-eight when I left home. Forty-eight going on sixty. Drugs had taken their toll and taken it quickly.

What a stupid, stupid woman. All she had to do was give up the smack. She wouldn't have needed any of this crap.

I look down at the overflowing trash can. Then I look back into the bedroom. "I want to get rid of everything. All of it. Even the furniture. Nothing stays. It all goes to the dump. Right now. I have to do it now."

In the mirror, my eyes find Piper's. If anyone can understand wanting to purge the past, it's her. She gives me a knowing look. "I'll call my sisters and the guys and get them over here. And I think I saw a UPS Store around the corner, so they can pick up boxes on the way. I'll go look for some trash bags in the kitchen. Will you be okay for a few?"

"Yeah. I'll be fine. Thanks, Pipes."

"No thanks necessary. It's what we do for family." She turns to walk through the door and I hear her summoning the troops faster than she can reach the kitchen.

I wander back into the bedroom and I stare at the diary I dropped on the carpet. Nothing but pain can come from it. There is nothing that woman could write that holds any interest for me whatsoever. The bound leather journal should be the very next thing I throw in the trash.

I sink down to the floor, my back against the hard metal frame of a dead woman's bed. *She can't hurt you anymore.*

I pick up the book and reopen it to page one.

August 30, 2000

He's an idiot. I'm only 36. And I don't look a goddamn day over 29. How dare he try to put me in a mommy role. And for a commercial that my 6-year-old was auditioning for. Asshole. Stole my looks, he said. Well, maybe if she weren't so pretty it would be easier for me. I never should have taken time off after she was born. I never should have given my fans a chance to forget me. I shouldn't have even had a kid. Why did I ever let George talk me into it?

I snap the diary closed when Piper walks in the bedroom carrying a box of trash bags.

"I'll start in here," she says, pulling one out. "Why don't you take the kitchen? Less personal."

My friend knows me well. I nod my head and pull on the bed frame to help me up. Then I walk out to the kitchen and with my best basketball longshot, I deposit the diary into the tall garbage can next to the pantry.

I start emptying cabinets, stacking dishes and glasses on the countertop. Too heavy for bags. I'll have to wait for boxes. Some of the things are pretty nice. Maybe I shouldn't throw them out. Maybe I should donate them. To a shelter for abused teenagers perhaps? The thought of it causing her to roll over in her grave gives me a wave of unexpected pleasure.

Piper peeks her head out of the bedroom and sees my growing piles on the counter. "What'll you do if you throw all that stuff away?"

"Eat off paper plates, I guess. I don't want anything left. It all goes. I'll sleep in a sleeping bag if I have to."

"You'll do no such thing. We'll figure something out." She retreats back into the bedroom and I rifle through the kitchen drawers. I pull one of them out and attempt to dump it into the trash can, right on top of the diary, but I miss my mark and end up sending the ketchup packets and take-out menus toppling over onto the floor.

"Crap," I mumble to no one. I fall to my knees and gather up the junk. When I go to throw it in the trash, I glance at a name on the page the diary fell open to.

Dewey.

My stomach rolls. And despite my better judgment, I pick the damn thing up and page through it. I don't read any of her hateful words, but I skim several pages wondering if they hold what I seek. Adrenaline courses through me when I find what I'm looking for—when I think back to the funeral and how good it felt to deck that asshole.

And now I know.

I know why I'm here and what I have to do.

CHAPTER THREE

I look around the reception area. In each corner of the room, there are tall vases with ornate fake flower arrangements. The clean lines of the art on the wall complement the opulent area rug in the center of the room that sits under the white leather couch and chairs.

The woman, who greeted me moments ago from behind a glass partition that reminds me of a bank, fits in well with the high-end décor. Her hair is pulled back into a sleek and severe ponytail. Her makeup tasteful and flawless. Her clothes tailored.

Off to one side of the room, almost as if deliberate and not to attract attention, is a display of personal photos. One picture is of a very attractive couple. A man and a woman in formal attire. A wedding photo. Young, in their early twenties, perhaps not any older than I am, they look deliriously happy, and for a brief second, I envy them.

Based on their hair styles, it's an old picture. But the man is gorgeous. Dirty-blonde hair that's a little long and roguish. And the way he's smiling at his bride brings out a dimple in his cheek.

My eyes wander to some of the other pictures. Most are men who share similar features. His brothers, perhaps. Or his children.

One boy in particular looks vaguely familiar and I wonder where I've seen him.

Before I can finish my examination of the pictures, the stunning platinum-blonde behind the thick partition startles me. "Mr. Stone will see you now." She slides a heavy glass window to the side and leans over the counter, displaying cleavage that she clearly intended for me to see. "You can come through that door."

She points toward a door on my right, her gesture revealing long manicured fingernails that have me wondering how she manages a phone or keyboard.

Her eyes follow me as I cross the room to where I'd been directed. I can feel her sizing me up. Maybe she's even been doing it the entire time I've been waiting.

I reach the door and pull on the handle, but I'm met with resistance and it fails to open.

I look at Barbie, raising my brows at her in question.

"Oops," she says. "Sorry." She reaches over to push a button on the wall next to her. I hear a click and then the doorknob turns when I try again.

I look back at the thick glass partition where she's watching me. I guess in this kind of work, they probably have more than their share of scorned spouses that might be pissed at them. I've seen one or two in my time. Scorned women, that is.

I walk through the heavy door and am met by the man in the wedding photo. Well, it's him, but it's not. This guy is even hotter than that one, if that's even possible. His hair is longer than the man's in the picture, touching the collar of his clean and pressed white button-down shirt. The way it curls up at the ends begs for female fingers to grab onto it.

His eyes are dark. A chocolate brown that is accentuated by the midnight-black skinny tie that is so expertly tied, you know it's not just worn for special occasions. Suddenly, I feel the urge to grab that tie and drag him back onto that white leather couch.

I'm sure Barbie would have an issue with that, however, based on the way her eyes are shooting daggers at me right now. Maybe she's his girlfriend. Or wife. Shame.

I'm tall by women's standards, five-foot-eight to be exact, but I still have to crane my neck when he comes close enough to extend his hand.

"Ms. Tate, I'm Ethan Stone. Nice to meet you."

Oh, hell. Even his name is hot. And although I usually hate being called Ms. Tate, the way his deep voice drips of sultry sex, I can almost envision him screaming it as he pumps into me from behind. Or on top. Or underneath. Doesn't matter to me.

Confidently, I place my hand in his and allow his large fingers to envelop my small ones. And even though his hand doesn't linger any longer than is professional, I don't miss the fact that his eyes do.

Apparently, neither does Barbie. "Hmmpf," I hear her disapproving grunt from behind. I turn my head and catch a glimpse of the back of her stiletto heel before it disappears around the corner.

"Nice to meet you, too. Thanks for working me in on such short notice. And it's just Charlie."

"Not a problem, Charlie. And I'm just plain old Ethan." He gestures for me to follow him down a hallway.

"Nothing plain or old about it," I mumble, staring at his broad shoulders that taper down to a slim waist covered by grey linen pants.

"Sorry?" he asks, stopping in a doorway, motioning me through.

"Oh, nothing. I was just saying how much I like your office."

The left side of his mouth lifts into a smile like he knows I'm full of shit. And, holy God, there is that dimple. The one from the photos. I have a sudden urge to put the tip of my tongue into it.

"Is she your wife?" I nod in the direction of reception.

"Gretchen?" he responds in an *are-you-kidding* tone.

"Girlfriend?"

"Neither. Please have a seat." He walks around a large rectangular glass desk that is pretty much empty with the exception of a laptop and a file folder. It's strange, but the desk—the entire office—looks like he does. Sharp. Clean. Crisp. Well, except for his unruly hair which is a contradiction to the rest of him.

"Does *she* know that?" I ask.

He sits in a high-backed brown leather chair that further complements his eyes. Did he choose that exact color on purpose, I wonder?

"Gretchen is" —his eyes search the room for words— "an old friend."

Friend my ass. She wants under him if she hasn't been already. And if she has, she wants more. I should know. After all, it takes one to know one. Sluts. Dirty mistresses. Home wreckers. She may dress the part better than I do, but I'm sure she perceived the same about me. We all have that sense about each other. That radar that warns us of the competition. That passive-aggressiveness that comes off as bitchy to other women, but allows us to manipulate unsuspecting men.

I don't see a ring on his finger. And there weren't many pictures of women displayed on the wall out front. Not that it matters, but I ask anyway. "Is there one? A wife or girlfriend?"

He lifts a brow. "Aren't I the one who's supposed to be asking the questions here?"

I shrug, not in the least bit embarrassed about my curiosity.

"So why don't you start by telling me why you think you need the services of a private investigator, Charlie."

"To find out if you're single, for one." I smile at him but he cocks his head, unamused. I roll my eyes. "I need to find some people."

"Okay." He opens up the file folder and pulls out a piece of paper. "We're very good at that. Who is it you need to find?"

I open my purse and pull out the list. I unfold it and try not to cringe as my eyes drift across the names.

When he takes the list from me, his fingers brush mine. I'm sure he felt it too—the pulse of electricity that passed between us. He clears his throat, not hiding it as well as he thinks he is.

His lips move in silence as he reads the names to himself. My gaze zeroes in on his mouth as I watch it form each syllable. A chunk of hair falls across his forehead and he absently pushes it back. My breath comes quickly and I reach down to grip the sides of the chair so I don't start squirming. The man is hotness on steroids.

"These are all men," he says, narrowing his eyes at me. His thumb and forefinger rub across his faint stubble, meeting at the base of his chin as he studies me.

"And that's a problem because you only enjoy tracking down women?" I deadpan.

"Just making an observation, Charlie."

As my first name rolls off his lips for the third time – *why am I counting?* – I realize I want him screaming that, too. First name, last name, hell, he can even scream his own name as long as he's deep inside me when he does it.

"A few of these men are famous," he points out.

"Yeah?"

He silently appraises me. He reminds me of the one and only shrink I saw a few years ago. Except better looking. And more fuckable. The guy would just stare at me and occasionally spew out some existential shit that was supposed to get me talking.

Stone, though, makes me want to open my mouth for a far different reason.

He jots down a few notes and it doesn't escape me that he's a lefty. Like me. Damn, even the way his pen flows across paper is sexy. I shift in my seat and his knowing eyes find mine.

Becoming oddly uncomfortable at the piercing silence, I say, "Uh, my mom died."

His stubborn expression softens. "Yes. I heard. I'm sorry."

I shake my head. "Don't be." Then I clamp my lips together before I reveal anything I don't want him to know. I don't think private investigators fall under the same rules as say, attorney-client or doctor-patient privilege. And since I don't yet know what I'm truly capable of . . .

Brows lifted, his dark eyes study my face. I shrink a little in my seat.

"So, the list. My mom was kind of a" —I try to think quickly— "um . . . she liked her men. And I thought I owed it to her to find them. I have something for each of them."

"That's nice of you," he says, making more notes.

"Yes. I thought so."

More silence.

"You're not much of a talker, are you, Stone?"

He puts down the pen and leans back in his chair, crossing his arms as he stares at me thoughtfully.

"It's my job to read people, *Tate*. And I'm very good at my job."

A shameless grin stretches wide across my face. "Well then, Mr. Private Eye, tell me—what are you reading right now?" I ask, looking at him through lidded eyes. "Angsty drama? Exciting thriller?" I lean forward and rest my elbows on his desk, suggestively leaning my head onto my hands. "Steamy romance?"

He's good at hiding his emotions. Better than most. But that doesn't stop me from noticing how he shifts around in his chair. "Why do I get the feeling you are a bit of all three?" he asks.

I laugh. "So, you *are* good at your job," I say. I look around his office again and then let my eyes rake over him slowly. I watch his pen come to his mouth and trace a thoughtful line across his lower lip. "And you—you're a bit action/adventure, crime documentary, sullen mystery."

"Sullen?" he asks, his lip twitching in amusement.

"Yeah," I say. "Don't get me wrong, Stone. It's hot. But you have this moody, ill-tempered, melancholy feel about you."

He lifts a judgmental brow.

"Kinda crazy," I say, flashing him a mocking smile. "Having someone read you so well, huh?"

He looks at me. Hell, he looks *through* me. Nobody looks at me the way he does right now. Like he sees more than the pretty daughter of a washed-up actress and model. Like he knows I'm full of shit.

"Ahem." He clears his throat and shakes his head as if ridding it of unwanted thoughts. "So my cousin tells me you're a friend of the family that owns the Mitchell's restaurant chain. What do you think of him? Of Jarod?"

"I haven't met him yet," I confess, removing my arms from his desk. "Piper Mitchell—that's my best friend—she's the one who told me his cousin was a private investigator. She got your contact information from him."

"I see." He twirls his pen expertly between the fingers of his left hand. "Well, since you're a friend of the family so-to-speak, if you want to hire me, I'll give you a discount off my regular fee. I charge by the hour so the total cost will depend on how difficult it is to find them."

My confidence wanes for the first time since walking through his office door. "Yeah, about that. My inheritance won't come through for a while, and I'm not sure the court would look kindly on me spending estate money on this."

He nods in understanding. "I can offer you a payment plan. Also a perk of knowing someone who knows someone." He winks and a hot shiver crawls down my spine. All the way to my center. "That is, if you have a job. You have a job, right?"

"Duh." I roll my eyes dramatically. I'm not sure why, but I don't want this guy to think I'm dead weight. "Of course I have a job. At Mitchell's."

He raises an argumentative brow. "And yet you've never met Jarod."

"Well, I haven't started yet. I just got back to town a few days ago."

"Mmmm," he mumbles, as if my shit is clear as mud to him. "Do you like tattoos?"

My mind goes crazy thinking about what ink he has and where. "Very much," I say.

"Then you'll love Jarod."

My mouth curves down into a pout when he chuckles and shakes his head alerting me to his sarcasm. He breaks into a smile. One that reveals his hidden dimple. One that melts me like ice cream in the desert.

"What about you?" I ask. "Do you like them?" *Please say yes.*

He shrugs. "They're okay."

"Do you have any?" I bite my lower lip awaiting his reply.

"That's kind of a private question, Tate."

"Just brushing up on my P.I. skills, Stone."

He laughs. It's a deep, throaty, intoxicating laugh. But for some reason, I get the idea he doesn't do it very often. "I may have one or two."

"I'll show you mine if you show me yours," I say, my gaze sliding casually down his body before rising to meet his again.

His eyes close and he slowly inhales then lets out a deep breath. He's thinking about it.

"Charlie," he says, like he's my fifth-grade teacher, and I know the answer is no. But that doesn't keep me from trying to change his mind.

"Ethan." I look up at him through my lashes. "Mr. Stone," I say in my best seductive voice. "Do you ever date clients?"

"No. I don't." The authority in which he says it makes me know it's true.

"Oh." I get up from my chair and walk over to the door. But instead of opening it, I go to lock it. But I can't find the lock. *Oh, screw it, who cares?* I turn around to face him, quickly whipping my shirt over my head before I throw it on the floor of his clean and tidy office. "Well, do you ever fuck them?"

CHAPTER FOUR

I'm sure as a private investigator, he's seen it all. But the look on his face tells me he's never seen this.

Surely women throw themselves at him all the time. Gretchen at least.

"You really didn't need to do that," he says, calm and collected as if I hadn't just put my tits on display for him.

For a moment, I almost have a feeling of remorse. Shame even. I'm about to pick up my shirt when he stands up and I see without a doubt how affected by me he really is. The front of his pants are tented so much, I question if he's even sporting underwear.

"I mean the door. I can lock it from here." He pushes a button on the wall behind the desk and I hear the electronic click of a bolt on the door.

His long stride narrows the gap between us in only a few quick steps. His eyes have further darkened and look almost black as his intense stare freezes me into place. His arms come up and his palms loudly meet the door behind my head as he cages me in.

This close, he towers over me and I crane my neck up until our eyes meet. He grabs me on either side of my head, moving his fingers into my hair, pulling it up and away from my face.

His gaze falls briefly to my bare chest before returning to focus on my lips. I can't help the victorious smirk that crosses my face. He doesn't miss it, but answers it with a roll of his eyes as his face breaks into a slow, sexy smile.

Yeah. He knows I've won this game. I almost always do. Along with my red hair and hazel eyes, I also inherited the art of seduction from my illustrious mother.

"I don't normally make a habit of this." His face moves closer to mine. "But there's something about you." His mouth hovers over my mouth, breathing in the air that's coming in quick spurts from my lungs. "I can't think straight." His lips brush across mine and hold there. "This is probably a bad idea," he whispers right before he crushes his mouth onto mine.

He doesn't waste time lingering. His tongue pushes through and devours my mouth like it's searching for air. I've kissed my share of men. So many I've lost count. But I'm not used to kisses like this one. Powerful. Demanding. Passionate.

Passion is not exactly an emotion I'm comfortable with. I need to take control of this situation so I grab onto his shoulders and jump up, latching my long legs around his waist.

He cups my behind, walking me over to his desk. I suck on his neck along the way, eliciting deep growling noises from his throat.

He holds me with only one hand, the other leaving my body to find the keyboard of his laptop, typing away while I continue my assault of his neck. "Multi-tasking?" I ask.

He nods to the ceiling where there is a small, dark, glass globe. "Just turning off the video."

Shutting the lid to the laptop, he sets me on the edge of his desk, not even having to clear a space because it's so sparse. I look at the vast emptiness of it and frown.

"Too hard?" he asks.

"It can never be too hard," I joke, grazing the front of his tented pants with my fingers. "But, no. It's just that . . . well it's probably every girl's fantasy to shove all the crap off a desk before she gets screwed on it. But yours is just too clean."

His brow arches in amusement. "I never knew being organized was an abhorrent offense." He quickly shifts his laptop over to the credenza on his left. "Go for it," he says.

I turn around and dramatically sweep my arm across the expansive glass desk, catapulting the sole file folder and pen across his office. We both watch the papers flutter through the air before settling onto the floor. It wasn't nearly as fulfilling as it was in my dreams.

"That was so much better in my fantasies," I tell him.

He laughs and the sexy sound has my belly flipping over. I grab his waistband, pulling him between my legs, trapping him with my thighs. I untuck his shirt and then as I undo each button, my eyes drink in the pure male perfection that is underneath. I push the sides of his shirt off his shoulders to reveal the result of what is surely hundreds of punishing hours at a gym. I feel like I've hit the lottery and am claiming the biggest, best prize of all.

I blow out a long, steady breath when I eye the tattoo over his heart. I don't know what it means, and I don't dare ask, because it's probably some chick's name. But the Chinese symbol is more than a little bit sexy.

I trace my finger around the edges of his ink and then across the ridges of his steely abs. Shudders wave across his body at my touch. For some reason, I want him to kiss me again. But for some reason, he doesn't. I'm not usually a fan of kissing. It's too personal. Too intimate. But there's something about him.

There's something about you. His words replay in my mind.

His hand comes up from where he was holding me steady. It stops before he touches my breast. His eyes meet mine and question me as if he's asking for permission. Nobody has ever asked me for permission. Not ever. I grab his hand and press it to my chest, hoping it feels as good as I think it will.

My eyes close upon his touch as his strong yet gentle hands discover my breasts, squeezing and pinching my sensitive nipples.

When I'm about to explode from his expert manipulation, his hands fall away. I audibly protest his retreat, but surrender to his plan when he goes a step further, hiking my skirt up all the way to my waist. He removes my panties, hooking his thumbs on either side, dragging them down my thighs slowly. Seductively. Almost painfully.

His eyes follow the motion of his hands, taking in every curve of my legs as they pass over me. He stops when they land on the unicorn tattoo on my inner thigh. He traces it with his finger, sending shockwaves right through me.

When my panties have made their way to the floor, he slips a finger inside me, groaning at the awareness of how wet he's made me. He coats my clit, gliding his thumb easily across it in slow, tantalizing circles.

I reach for his belt buckle. "You have a condom, right? Please tell me you have a condom."

He smiles, retrieving his wallet from his back pocket. "I have a condom."

There is conversation in the hallway as people pass his office door. Then, as if he just realized where we are and what we're doing, he glances at the clock on the wall. "If we're going to use it, we'd better be quick. I have a two o'clock."

I check the time. *1:54.*

"Just the way I like it," I say, making fast work of unbuttoning his pants. I push them down until they drop around his ankles, my eyes following the movement.

I see what looks like a garter belt strapped around his calf. I look closer to discover he's got a gun secured to his leg, down by his ankle.

I question him with my eyes.

He shrugs. "For protection," he says.

This guy. This virtual stranger is about to fuck me with a weapon strapped to his body. Holy hell, that's freaking hot.

I snatch the condom from him and roll it on, his cock twitching from my touch as he works his skillful fingers inside me. I give him a few long strokes before I guide him to my entrance. He sucks in a breath as he glides into me. The sound makes me look up at him, our faces inches apart. I could swear the air crackles between us, like static electricity, and for some reason, I can't look away.

I *never* look at them as they fuck me. A habit from long ago I suspect.

I put distance between us, leaning back on the desk to give him better access to my clit and breasts. He doesn't need an invitation to use both of them to bring us to a quick and simultaneous orgasm.

Holy God. It's only been thirty seconds—a minute max—but damn . . . it's the best thirty seconds of my life.

We both shout quietly. I could almost swear my name was whispered among his incoherent declarations of ecstasy. And I might be mistaken, because it's never happened before, but I'm pretty sure I murmured his.

His office phone buzzes and Gretchen's nasally voice comes over the intercom. "Your two o'clock is here, Ethan."

"Thanks, Gretchen. Give me five," he responds as if his dick isn't still balls-deep inside me.

"Sorry," he says, looking guilty as he pulls out.

"For what? That was great, Stone." I shimmy off the desk, looking down in amusement at the sex-smudged glass.

He shakes his head. "That shouldn't have happened, Charlie. I'm usually not that unprofessional."

I make quick work of putting my clothes on. "Don't sweat it. I still have every confidence you can get me what I need." I nod to the list of names lying among other papers on the floor. "You are totally hired." I punctuate my words with a playful wink.

He zips up his pants, looking at me in utter disbelief. "What? No. I can't work for you now, Charlie."

"Well, why the hell not?"

He gives me an *are-you-crazy* kind of look as he ceremoniously wraps the condom in a tissue and throws it in the trash.

I giggle. But then I realize no other private investigator would give me the good deal he offered. He's my only option. "Shit," I say, handing him his shirt. "What if I promise not to take my top off again? Will you work for me then?"

He rubs a hand over his erupting stubble. "It's a conflict of interest. Rule number one of P.I.s – don't get involved with clients."

My face distorts with disgust. "Involved? Who said anything about getting involved? This was just sex. Fucking. A quick lay." But as I say the words I know to be true, I get a funny feeling in the middle of my chest. I push it down. "Plus, I can't afford anyone else." I plaster my best innocent smile on my face. "Please?"

His eyes close as if I'd said something hurtful. As if maybe he'd had a funny feeling in the middle of his chest as well. When he opens them, the intense dark eyes are gone, replaced by cold, distant ones. "Fine." He bends over to gather the strewn papers. "But this can't happen again. I'm not in the business of *servicing* my clients."

I sigh with relief. "Thank you, Ethan."

His eyes soften at my use of his first name. "I'll be in touch in a week or so with what I can dig up. Would you mind letting yourself out?" He nods to the ass prints on his desk. "I have a bit of cleaning up to do before my next appointment."

I giggle. "Sure thing. Bye . . . Stone."

He gives me an eye roll before hitting the button that unlocks the door.

I walk down the hallway towards reception when I hear him call out behind me. "Hey, Tate?"

I smile before turning around. "Yeah?"

"Why the unicorn?"

I open my mouth to feed him whatever bullshit I've told every other guy who asks about my tattoo. But what comes out surprises the hell out of me. What comes out is as close to sharing a truth about myself as I ever have with a man. "For protection."

He studies me for a second before disappearing back into his office.

CHAPTER FIVE

My body slices through the water almost effortlessly as my arms and legs gently propel me from one end of the pool to the other. I've always loved swimming. It's not as punishing on my body as running, and the water offers a layer of protection. A bubble no one else can penetrate. It's quiet. Peaceful. Serene.

Today, however, my protective bubble is being infiltrated by my mother's awful words from the journal entry I read yesterday. I kick my feet harder, quickening my pace in an attempt to leave my thoughts in my wake.

It's a futile effort. No matter how hard I swim, I can't keep the demons away and my mind wanders back to the horrible day I lost my mother. Not the day of her funeral; not even the day I found out she died—those were just circumstances of her pitiful life. The day I lost my mother was that dreadful day in August of 2000.

"Mommy, why do I have to do it again?" I whine, tired of pretending like I'm spilling a glass of milk for a paper towel commercial.

*"Because the nice man wants you to do it, Charlie."
She pulls me aside and whispers sternly to me. "Did you
see all those other pretty girls out in the waiting area? We
didn't have to wait out there like they do because Mommy
is a star. You want to be a star, too, don't you baby? Well,
here is your chance. But you have to do as the man says."*

*"Okay, Mommy." I kiss her cheek and walk back
over to the fake kitchen in the studio. I glance back at the
woman I love. The woman I idolize. I would do anything to
be like her. Everywhere she goes people want her autograph.
They want to talk to her. Shake her hand. They want to be
her. And this is my chance. Anything to make her and
Daddy proud of me.*

*The man telling me what to do gets a look on his face
like someone gave him a double-scoop of chocolate chip ice
cream with extra sprinkles on top. "Ms. Anthony, how
would you like to play the child's mother? I could guarantee
her the gig."*

*I watch my mother's mouth open. And close. And
open again. And little do I know, what happens after this
will change the course of my life. "Her* mother?" *She
laughs haughtily, straightening her pencil skirt. "I'm barely
thirty, I could hardly pass for her mother."*

*The man laughs, along with another man standing
next to him. But they cover their mouths so that it's not
very loud. But I hear it anyway. I think Mommy does too,
because she gets that look on her face like when I leave the
refrigerator door open.*

*The man clears his throat. "Uh, sorry, ma'am. I just
thought it'd be great to actually have the mother and child
share a resemblance. And if I do say so, this little one*

should be put in jail, 'cause she downright stole your looks."

Mommy balks at the man, saying words that normally she would cover my ears before saying. Grown up words that sound mean and even make her pretty face look ugly as she says them. Words she is yelling at the man, but then she turns her head and it seems like she's yelling them at me. Her fierce hazel eyes burn into mine as she becomes someone I've never seen.

Then she stomps across the room and grabs me by the elbow. "Come on, Charlie. We don't have to put up with this shit."

In the bright yellow cab on the way home, I cry. I think I've done something wrong. Something bad that made Mommy yell at those men. At me. I hug her and tell her I'll do better next time, but she says there won't be a next time. And she won't look at me. She just stares out the window.

Back at our house, she makes me sit in a chair while she goes to the bathroom. When she comes out, she has flour on her nose and I wonder why she would have flour in her bathroom. She also has a pair of scissors. "Turn around," she demands. "I'm giving you a haircut."

"No, Mommy!" I squeal. "Then I won't be pretty like you."

"Charlie, turn around," she says again with distant eyes.

"No, Mommy. Please don't cut my hair." I put my hands over my head to protect my hair from the shears coming closer to my long locks.

She reaches out and tugs my hair from my clenched fists, ripping it from my tiny clutches. "Daddy!" I scream. "Daddy!"

"Daddy isn't here," she says coldly. "And if I tell him what a bad girl you were at the audition and now again for me—if I tell him all of that, he won't love you anymore either."

I shake my head from side to side, dodging her hands as they try to grip my hair. I turn my head away from her and pull my knees up to my tummy, scrunching as tightly into a ball as I can get. I wish and pray it will all just go away. That it is just a bad dream. A bad dream where mommies don't love their daughters and where daddies fail to protect them.

"Turn around and sit still. Right fucking now," she yells as her open hand hits the side of my face.

It stings badly. Like the time I skinned my knee when I tripped over my feet running through the park, only worse, because this time Mommy doesn't kiss my owie, she caused it.

I erupt from the water to find myself gripping the edge of the pool, gasping desperately for the air that I had deprived my lungs. Thinking back on that day, I guess I forgot to breathe.

As my body replenishes itself with oxygen, I see a welcome face peek around the corner.

"I was hoping I'd catch you here," Piper says, walking around the edge of the pool in her running clothes with a small towel draped over her shoulder. "Isn't this place fantastic?"

I guess it does pay to know people in high places. Piper's fiancé, Mason, owns the gym along with her two brothers-in-law,

Gavin and Griffin. I would never be able to afford a membership. Not for eight or nine months anyway.

"Oh, good. Maybe you'll save me a trip to the restaurant." As I talk to Piper, I walk my hands along the wall until my feet can touch the bottom of the pool. Then I squeeze the water from my hair. "I was going to head there right after my workout to see if I could catch you or Skylar."

"You need a girls' night or something? You know we're always up for it."

"That sounds great, but that's not why I was going to find you. I need a job, Piper."

Piper tilts her head suspiciously, staring at me like I've sprouted a third arm. "I thought you were leaving in a few weeks."

"Nah. I think I'll hang around for a while."

A slow smile creeps across her face. "Are you kidding? Are you messing with me, Charlie? Because I've missed you so damn much these last six months and if you're screwing with me, I might have to hurt you."

I laugh. "I don't know if it'll be forever, but for now, yeah, I'm staying. No joke."

Her squeals of delight bounce off the walls so loudly I have to cover my ears. But then the sound stops suddenly and she studies me. "Wait. Does this have anything to do with why you needed a private investigator? You never did give me details on that, by the way. You took off as soon as I gave you Jarod's cousin's number."

I can't lie to Piper. She'd see right through it. But I know she'd try to talk me out of my plan, and I can't have that either. A half-truth will have to do. "I just want to find out some stuff about my mom. That's all. No big deal."

She nods in understanding. "And private investigators are probably expensive, so you need a job."

"Not just any job. I need a job at Mitchell's NYC, like now. I told the guy I work there so he'd give me a payment plan."

"Not a problem," she assures me. "You can take my shifts. I've been working there until they could find someone good enough to replace me. Skylar would love to have you."

I breathe a sigh of relief. "Thanks, Pipes. But if you give me your shifts, what will you do?" I look through the expansive glass wall that separates the pool from the rest of the gym. The opulent fitness center that is owned in part by her fiancé. *Duh.* "Right. You're marrying the next starting quarterback for the Giants. You don't need a job."

"Oh, I'm going to work," she says. "I was just thinking of trying something a little different. Like maybe get involved in community theater."

Now it's my turn to squeal. "You're kidding!"

Theater was always Piper's one true passion when we were young. But she gave it up after her attack. I never thought I'd see the day when she'd give it another go.

She shakes her head, her excited eyes telling me she's dead serious.

"Oh my God, Piper Mitchell, you've really changed."

"I'm still me," she pouts.

"Yes, you are. Only better."

We share a smile only best friends can share. Then Piper's eyes focus on something behind me. "That guy who just walked in. He looks familiar."

I turn to look before quickly spinning back around and sinking my body into the water up to my chin. "Oh, shit. That's Ethan Stone. He's the P.I. I met with today."

"*That's* Jarod's cousin?" she says too loudly, her voice raising a full octave in disbelief.

"Shhhh," I scold her, worried her voice will echo in the large aquatics room. "Would you please keep your voice down?"

"No wonder he looks familiar. He's probably come into the restaurant before. And what's the big deal if he hears me?" she asks, eyeing me skeptically as I try to get the pool to swallow me further. "Oh, Charlie, you didn't."

I shrug an innocent shoulder under the water, looking up at her with doe eyes. "I may have."

Her eyes close and she lets out a small sigh. But she doesn't bother reprimanding me. She never does. She understands me. How I work. Why I do the things I do. And she never ever judges.

"And now you're avoiding him?" she asks.

"Well, he said he couldn't work for me if we were *involved*." I use air quotes to punctuate the word.

"Sounds like a smart man." She studies him behind me. "With good taste in women."

"Ha!" I roll my eyes. "You should see the one he's fucking at the office."

Her eyes narrow at him with that protective judgment of an overbearing sister. "Okay. Maybe not so smart."

I shrug. "He claims he's not doing her, but I don't buy it. She's possessive as hell and a certifiable bitch."

"Wow. You must have been there a long time if you got to know her that well."

"I didn't actually talk to her," I confess. "Other than checking in when I got there."

A smile breaks across her face. "Oh, *she's* the possessive one?"

"Shut up."

She laughs. "I've got to go pick up Hailey, but I'll make the call to Skylar later and tell her what's going on. Meet me at work tomorrow before my ten o'clock shift and I'll show you the ropes."

"Thanks, Pipes. You're a lifesaver."

"Okay then" —she starts to walk away— "I'll see you at work tomorrow, Charlie," she says loudly, putting extra emphasis on my name.

I splash her before she makes her getaway. Then I look over my shoulder to see that yes, the hot and off-limits P.I. did in fact hear her.

Before I have a chance to see his reaction, I return to my bubble, pushing off the wall and gliding under the water as long as I can before my lungs force me to come up for air. I break into a punishing freestyle stroke so I won't hear if he tries to get my attention.

A few minutes later, I question why I'm avoiding the guy. I mean he did just give me an earth-shattering orgasm. And he is all kinds of hot. Greek god Adonis hot. Gun strapped to his ankle during sex hot. Mysterious tattoo guy hot.

But hey, I can be friends with a hot guy I'm not sleeping with. *Right?*

A few weeks. That's what he said. After that, I'll have the information I'm paying him for and then—*then* we can have a torrid affair. Gretchen be damned. I'm already planning all the shit I can put on his desk to make it more satisfying when I sweep it off. Or maybe the credenza. And there's always the white couch in reception.

"It's not going to happen." Masculine words pry me from my fantasy and I realize I've completely stopped swimming and am staring directly at Ethan Stone.

Beads of water fall in a steady stream off the ends of his hair, that when weighted down with pool water, makes it appear even darker, longer and more unruly than before.

And his tattoo. Holy hell, it's sexy. I find myself wanting to trace the outline of it again. With my tongue.

I snap myself out of it. "Uh, what are you doing?"

He looks around the room and then back at me. "Do you mean what am I doing here at the gym that I've belonged to for the past three years? Or what am I doing in the pool that I swim laps in every night? Or maybe you mean what am I doing talking to the woman who seduced me mere hours ago? Which is it, Tate?"

I smile. I've only known the man for one day, one hour even, but I can already tell his mood by the choice of the name he calls me. "Oh, so you swim?"

"Every day. What—did I fail to mention that earlier?" he asks sarcastically.

He barely talked during our meeting and he definitely didn't say anything about his personal life. I don't know thing one about him. That's normally the way I like it.

Normally.

Without thinking much of it, as if I'm drawn to him by some kind of force-field, I dip below the water and swim underneath the three lane dividers that separate us. The closer I get to him, the more electrified the water becomes. Tingles flutter across my body as the water rolls across me.

I pop up next to him, needing to tread water even though he is able to stand.

"You should really stay in your own lane." He raises a disapproving brow. "It's just common courtesy."

"Are you going to fire me as your client if I don't?" I let my head sink into the pool until the water rests just under my nose. Then I look up at him through my lashes.

He shakes his head, giving me a frustrated smile before grabbing my shoulders, turning me around, and pushing me back under one of the lane dividers.

I squirm out from under his hands and quickly swim around the back of him. I push off the bottom of the pool, catapulting myself up and out of the water so I can push down on him and dunk him under.

He shoots out of the water, shaking out his hair by rapidly snapping his head from side to side. I swear, in my head, I see it all happen in slow motion. And I watch like a bitch in heat.

He grabs me, cradling me like a baby in his arms. He holds me tightly against him as he ducks under each lane partition, never letting me go as he walks us to the side of the pool. He lifts me out of the water with little effort and sits me on the cold hard tile.

"I need to finish my workout," he says.

We stare at each other as the water settles. I look down and see his erection clearly straining his well-fitted swim trunks. "I can help you with that." I nod at it. "And I promise it'll be a good workout."

"I can deal with that later, Charlie. By myself." He sinks into the water and pushes off the wall with strong, muscular legs that torpedo him back into the middle lane.

I don't miss the fact that he called me Charlie. I guess playful, salacious Ethan Stone has left the building.

He swims a perfect butterfly stroke, not even once bothering to look over in my direction as I watch him swim length after length of the pool.

Refusing to believe I'm at all pouting, I finally decide to get up and head towards the locker room. I don't look back. But that doesn't stop me from fantasizing about all the ways he might '*deal with that later.*'

CHAPTER SIX

Getting into the swing of things at the restaurant has been easier than I anticipated. Piper's older sister, Skylar, manages Mitchell's NYC, one of three establishments her parents own, and there are definite perks to knowing the owners—like getting higher starting pay than other new hires.

I guess technically, I'm not a new hire. Growing up, I spent summers waitressing at the first restaurant they opened in the small town of Maple Creek, Connecticut, just thirty minutes outside the city.

While most teenagers dreaded work, I couldn't wait to go. Not only would I get to see Piper and her family, but it got me away from *her*. Even if only for a few hours at a time. I used any excuse I could find to be away from home. My mother would often call the restaurant to see if I was there. And after a while, it didn't matter if I was actually within the four walls or not, whoever answered the phone claimed I was.

They all knew I hated home. They all sensed something was wrong. They all tried to help. But my pride got in the way and I couldn't bring myself to tell them. Even Piper didn't know how bad it really was until we left the country after graduation. Prior to leaving, I finally confessed to Jan Mitchell that my mother abused me. She was livid at me for not telling her. At herself for not paying enough attention and noticing. She blamed herself. And because of that, I didn't have the heart to tell her everything. It would ruin her. She'd already been through so much with Piper.

A few hours into my first shift, it gets busy. Not Maple Creek busy. Not even Barcelona busy. It gets New York City busy. Fucking busy.

Thankfully, Piper is still training me, so she's here to help out when I get slammed trying to juggle eight tables.

Jarod skirts by me with a full tray of drinks he raises over my head at the last second, right before I almost collide into it. He winks at me to let me know the maneuver was purposeful.

Even through the long sleeves of his white button-down work shirt, I can see the bulging of his arm muscles under the weight of the heavily loaded tray. His short, dark, manicured hair is incongruent with the gauges in his ears and his full sleeves of tattoos that I've only heard about, but not seen.

His complexion is quite a bit darker than that of his cousin, and every so often, he curses in Spanish, making me think he's got a Mexican or perhaps Colombian heritage.

He passes me again, shooting me another wink. It's not a *go get 'em* wink. It's more of a *want to hook up after work?* wink. It's hot. He's hot. A bit younger than me, but still legal. My eyes follow him over to his table and I watch his backside while he deposits drinks in front of the patrons. I can't help but wonder if he's as good in bed as his older cousin. Or should I say as good *on desk*.

"Excuse me, miss. I only have an hour for lunch."

I whip around at the familiar voice and my stomach does the jig when I see said cousin sitting at one of my tables. "Sorry. Be right there," I tell him, trying to look all professional and not at all like I'd like him to bend me over the edge of the table after closing.

A half-smile threatens to show the dimple in his left cheek. Yeah, he's onto me.

Jarod swats me with his order pad on his way by as I finish refilling the water glasses at the table next to Ethan. I ponder Ethan's curt remark. Maybe it was meant to be sarcastic, but the scowl on his face tells me otherwise. He's staring at Jarod over the top of his menu. Oh, of course, he must come here to see his cousin. He's probably mad he got seated in my section.

I head to the drink station to grab some sodas. Seeing Jarod there, I ask, "Do you want to take table nine?"

He cranes his neck around me to have a look. "Nah, you go ahead. He's a pain in the ass. Do not put a lemon in that man's water or you'll never hear the end of it."

"But he's your cousin," I state the obvious.

"Yeah. And he's a great tipper." He loads drinks onto his tray. "Still. Pain in the ass." Then, despite the fact there's more than enough room for both of us at the drink station, he brushes up against my arm as he passes me.

I turn around to see that Ethan was watching our little exchange. I decide to add a water to my tray. No lemon.

I drop off the sodas at table twelve and a check at table seven. Then I ceremoniously place the glass of water, sans lemon, in front of the mercurial man at table number nine. "Is this acceptable, or did I put in one too many cubes of ice?"

Air comes in short spurts from his nose in a quiet laugh. "You must have talked to my cousin. He's a pain in the ass."

"Ha! He says the same thing about you." I pull a paper coaster from my apron and put it under his glass. "Actually, Jarod's been great. He's been a huge help today."

"Yes, I can see that." His eyes dart over to Jarod and back to me. "So you finally met him."

"Well, I haven't met *all* of him yet. If I recall, you said I would love his tattoos. But, sadly, his shirt covers them all when he's at work."

He shrugs a careless shoulder. "They're really not all that great now that I think about it. You may not even want to bother."

"Is that so?" I bite my lip in an attempt to keep from smiling. "Will anybody be joining you today? Barbie maybe?"

He furrows his brow. "Barbie?"

"Sorry. Gretchen."

"It's just me," he says, shaking his head in amusement. "Rule number two—never take out a woman who won't eat in front of you."

"That's a P.I. rule?"

"No. That one's a Stone rule."

Hearing the hustle and bustle around me, and not wanting to screw up on my first shift, I nod to his menu. "Have you decided what you want? And can I bring you anything besides the water? Extra lemons perhaps?"

His dimple finally makes an appearance. "Just the water, thanks. And I'll have a Reuben with a side of fries."

"Great. I'll put that right in for you. I know you're in a hurry." I give him an obligatory smile before I spin around and walk away.

"Take your time. I know you're busy, Tate."

A shiver runs through me and it takes all my willpower not to turn back around and look at him.

~ ~ ~

Walking back to the apartment, I think of how Ethan's eyes followed me around the entire time he was there. Even when I couldn't see them, I could feel his dark-chocolate gaze on me. Like somehow his eyes had a direct connection to my senses.

It was so busy we didn't exchange more than a few additional words. And Jarod was not exaggerating when he said his cousin was a good tipper. He all but doubled the cost of his meal.

I smile wondering if he tips everyone that well or just women who like to grab his dick.

When I enter the apartment, I have to double check the number on the door to make sure I'm in the right place. I am. And upon further inspection of the fully-furnished living room, I come to recognize the couch as being the one from the Mitchell's basement that they later gave to Baylor; a chair from Skylar and Griffin's; and even the very same television I admired at Piper and Mason's place a few days ago.

Big balls of tears balance on my lower lashes as I look around the rooms that were bare just this morning, with the exception of the borrowed air mattress I slept on.

On the kitchen table is a note. The tears finally spill over when I read it.

Welcome Home!

It's signed by everyone. All the Mitchells and their significant others.

Skylar and Piper were with me at the restaurant the entire time. They didn't even bat an eye. It must've been the guys and Baylor who did everything. I take it all in. They not only furnished the entire place with pieces of their own, they decorated it too.

Jan. I'd bet my life she had a hand in this. She was always redecorating her girls' rooms when we were growing up.

I never realized how much I missed all of this for the five years I was away. I mean, it was great traveling the world with Piper, but this—this is a support system. A faction thicker than blood. They are my family.

CHAPTER SEVEN

At the end of each lap my eyes do a quick sweep of the other lanes to see if he's here. It's late, but there has been a pattern developing over the past few days. The first time I ran into him here, he said he comes for a workout every day after work. I took that to mean he leaves the office and heads to the gym. But this week he's been showing up later and later, and it makes me wonder if that has anything to do with my late-night swims.

Most days, I work until the dinner rush is over, about nine o'clock. By the time I get here, the pool is practically deserted.

On Tuesday, Ethan wasn't here when I arrived, presumably because he was long gone after his workout. On Wednesday, he was walking out when I was walking in. Yesterday, our workouts overlapped and he even asked me if he could hang around and walk me home.

I declined of course. I don't need any man looking after me. I've looked after myself since I was six years old. Granted, I did a piss poor job of it, but still. It's been me and Piper against the world. And now she has Mason, so it's just me.

In hindsight, maybe I should have taken him up on it. Maybe it was just his way of getting a booty call, even though it would break rule number one.

I get the feeling he'd very much like to break rule number one again. *Again?* Technically he never broke it since I wasn't actually his client when we had sex. Okay, so I was five minutes later, but whatever. I'll give him a pass on that one.

I find myself wondering about the man who is Ethan Stone, and it pisses me off. I don't wonder about men. I never wonder about them. I don't give a shit about personal details. I could care less about their jobs or their cars or what movie they saw last Friday night. The only thing I ever cared about was if they could keep Piper and me off the streets. A warm bed. A hot shower. A decent meal.

Even after her college fund that she never used for college, ran out, the Mitchells always sent a small stipend each month. That would only go so far, and even combined with the money we made from odd jobs, it wasn't enough to keep a decent roof over our heads. Anyway, we never stayed in one place for very long. We lived the lives of gypsies, bouncing from one town to another dragging all our worldly belongings in one suitcase apiece.

Barcelona had become our unofficial home base. There was a guy there who would take us in whenever we were around, no questions asked. Well, no questions except *'do you want it from behind or on top?'*

I didn't know anything about the guy other than his name and, eventually, his credit card number since he let me use it from time to time.

So, why then, as my arms and legs glide through the water, am I wondering who Ethan's favorite band is? And what he likes to do for fun. I already know what his favorite food is. He orders it every time he comes in for lunch. A Reuben with a side of fries. Every time.

It occurs to me that he's been to Mitchell's for lunch three times since I started working there last week. It also occurs to me that his office is four subway stops plus a five-block walk from there. Not exactly convenient. If he were coming for free food, courtesy of his waiter cousin, I could see what the hassle was all about. But he's not getting free food, and he sits in my section every time. And he tips me like he's got a money tree growing out of his ass.

I find myself smiling under the water. Yeah, he wants to break rule number one alright. He wants to fucking shatter it.

I reach the end of the pool and do my visual sweep. But at this late hour, the only person here is Mrs. Buttermaker. She's as old as the hills and swims the breaststroke at a snail's pace, not making a sound as her wrinkled arms glide through the water. I made her acquaintance a few days ago. She said she likes to come late so she doesn't get bothered by those pesky kids who make too many waves. And by kids she means anyone under the age of fifty.

I make sure to choose the farthest lane from her as she is usually finishing up her swim as I arrive. Best not rock that boat. She's an old frail woman, but I get the idea she could chew the ass off a Kardashian. Yesterday, she didn't seem all that pleased that Ethan also decided to join us, disrupting what I'm sure she had hoped was going to be a peaceful swim.

Butterflies do flips in my stomach when I see strong, muscular legs walking towards me. But they're instantly stilled when I look up and see the face of a man who is not Ethan Stone.

Not that the guy towering over me isn't hot. He is. He's hot into next week. He's tall and dark, his sweat-dampened body ripped to perfection. He wipes his face with the gym towel casually thrown over his shoulder.

He crouches down and extends his hand to me over the edge of the pool. "I've been wanting to introduce myself all week. I'm Devon Totman. And you're new here."

I lift my dripping hand out of the water and put it into his. "Charlie," I say, purposefully omitting my last name. Not even the Barcelona guy was privy to that. "Nice to meet you, Devon."

"You look familiar," he says, studying me.

I get that a lot. A lot, a lot. Many people my age have seen my mother in one old movie or another, but most can't seem to place me. Lately, however, her face has been plastered over the news because of her death. It makes it even harder to remain anonymous. After a few patrons at work recognized me as her lookalike daughter, I started wearing my hair in a severe bun, and I even purchased a pair of black-rimmed glasses to help camouflage my face.

I shrug. "So I've been told. Is that a standard pickup line here in New York? Do they train you to use that one in college or something?"

He laughs. "I wouldn't know. I never went to college. I'm a self-made man."

"And clearly you didn't need higher education to acquire your cockiness."

"It's not cockiness. It's confidence," he says. "So you aren't from New York then?"

I simply shake my head, not willing to acknowledge his question in further detail.

In my periphery, I see someone walking around the pool. My skin prickles before he comes fully into view. My body is aware of him even before my mind is.

I ignore the pull of him on my eyes and keep my focus on the man before me. I'm not the least bit interested in Mr. Self-Made. Maybe I would have been a few weeks ago. Hell, he'd have been a shoo-in back then. But things are different now. I don't need them to get by anymore. But the P.I. doesn't know that, so I decide to have some fun with it.

"So, Devon Totman. What is it that you do?"

I almost feel bad when his face breaks into a celebratory smile. He thinks he's won. He has no idea that he's just become a pawn in my little game.

For the next five minutes, I let him talk all about himself. But I don't hear a word. The only thing I hear is Ethan's arms as they slice angrily through the water at a pace that grows faster with each length of the pool. It takes all my strength not to look over and see if he's watching me between strokes.

"So can I show you around?" Devon asks. "Maybe even tonight, after your swim?"

I reach my hand out of the pool again and offer it to him. "It's been nice meeting you, Devon. But I have to finish my swim and then I have other plans."

He grasps my hand, holding it far longer than necessary. "Another time then, Charlie."

I give him an award-winning smile that says the opposite of what I'm feeling—which is that he doesn't have a chance in hell. "I'll see you around the gym, Devon."

I watch him walk away, all too aware of the deafening silence that surrounds me. You could hear a pin drop in the massive room. Not even Mrs. Buttermaker's slow strokes reach my ears. I don't know where Ethan is, but I can feel the tension in the air. The heavy glass door slams behind Devon at the same time that arms cage me to the side of the pool. He's swum up behind me. His body doesn't touch mine, but there is a crackle of something between us. And it's more than the wave of water he brought with him.

I can feel his breath on my ear when he speaks. "Rule number three—don't talk to arrogant strangers who sleep their way through women at the gym."

Despite the heated water in the pool, shivers run all the way down my spine. Ethan's voice does things to me I can't explain. Devon's voice was nice. Jarod's rolls off his tongue like butter. But Ethan's—I can feel his voice all the way down to my toes. "I'm beginning to think you're making these rules up as you go along."

He swims away from me, leaving my body yearning for his touch as he dips under the lane dividers. "Steer clear of Devon Totman," he says, reaching his favored center lane. "He's trouble."

"I can take care of myself, Stone. But thanks for the head's up." I hear the beginnings of a snide reply but I cut him off, pushing myself off the wall, torpedoing myself under water to finish my swim.

A few laps later, I see someone standing by my lane at the head of the pool. I smile when I see Mrs. B drying off and I know what words will leave her mouth even before she says them.

"Will you be okay here, sweetie?" Her eyes flicker over to Ethan as she asks the same question she asked me yesterday.

I get the feeling I'm one of the only gym patrons to have given her the time of day. We talked for a few minutes that first night and now she feels like a mother hen or something. But it's okay. I like it. Not getting much in the way of mother-henning at my home growing up, I'm happy to accept it from just about anyone.

"I'll be fine, Mrs. Buttermaker. Enjoy the rest of your evening."

"Okay then. I'll just be on my way. See you Tuesday night, Charlie." She's known me three days and she already knows my workout schedule.

I smile. "Bye, Mrs. Buttermaker."

I finish up my swim, a little put off that Ethan hasn't paid me any more attention. I did, after all, wear my most revealing and boob-enhancing one-piece swimsuit for him. It's a bit old-school Baywatch, but it does the trick. Or so I thought. As I dry off, I watch his muscular body slice effortlessly through the water. I can't help but think back to last week in his office when that very same body was slamming into mine as I teetered on the edge of his desk. I remember his strong arms that carried me across the room. His shaggy hair that I ran my fingers through. His sexy tattoo.

I really want to know what the tattoo means. But that would involve asking a personal question. I don't do personal. *Then why did you let him kiss you that way?*

He pops up out of the water to catch me staring. "You done?" he asks.

I wrap the towel around my waist. "Yeah."

"Okay. See you next time." He turns around and continues his swim.

What the fuck just happened? No offer to walk me home. No more shit about Devon. No witty banter. Nothing. The man is more unpredictable than a PMS-ing woman.

I cross my arms over my body and stand there, watching him do a lap and waiting for him to swim back towards me. When he touches the edge closest to me, he doesn't even bother slowing down. He does his little underwater flip thing and keeps on going.

Ugh!

I sit down on the edge of the pool, putting my legs in the water where he does his turnaround. I scissor them back and forth so he won't miss them.

When he reaches my side of the pool again he grabs my feet, slowly walking his hands up my legs as he comes up for air.

"Was there something you wanted?" he asks, like he doesn't know his touch just melted my brain into a gooey mess, making it almost impossible for my mouth to form words.

He removes his hands from my legs, putting them on the edge of the pool next to me as he bobs up and down in the deep water.

I don't think I've ever wanted a man to put his hands back on me as much as I do this very second. I usually don't want a man's hands on me at all, but it's always been a means to an end. A way to thwart a brutal beating from my mother. A way to get a roof over my head. A way to forget reality.

"Uh . . ." I scramble for a reason to have interrupted his swim. Other than the obvious fact that I'm acting like an adolescent with a schoolgirl crush on a man who considers me off limits. "I just wanted to know what's taking so long. I mean, how hard could it be to find a few people? What the hell am I paying you for anyway?"

"Seriously?" His expression turns stern, making me further regret the off-the-cuff words I spoke. "First off, it's not just a few people, Charlie. It's a dozen."

I wince knowing all too well how many names are on the list. And I scowl at his use of my first name. It's all work and no play whenever he uses it. I guess I can't blame him. I did all but call him a bad P.I.

"Second, do you know how many John Taylors and Steve Smiths there are in New York? Even more if we expand the search.

It takes time to sift through all of them to find out which ones had a connection to your mom. And third, you haven't paid me yet."

I lower my head to my chest, feeling about two inches tall after the scolding he just gave me. "Sorry. I guess I'm just getting impatient. You don't have *anything* for me?"

"We've only found a few of them," he says.

"Can I get what you have or do you need a payment first? I don't get a paycheck until next week."

"It's fine. If you need the information that badly, I'll get it to you. Can you swing by the office on Monday?"

"Monday?" Now that I know he has some of what I need, I don't want to wait that long. "Couldn't we do it sooner?"

"I suppose I could bring it to you. Do you work tomorrow?"

"From ten to two," I say.

"How about I come in for a late lunch at two? I'll bring what I have so far. But don't expect much at this point."

I put my hands on either side of my legs, my upper arms squeezing my boobs together as I lean forward exposing even more cleavage. "Great. It's a date."

He gapes at my chest. He's a guy—of course he does. But the warming sensation I feel from the heat of his stare is short-lived when he rips his eyes away. "No, Charlie, it's not. I don't date clients."

Feeling rejected, I quip, "Right, you only fuck them."

He sighs. "No, I don't fuck them. I fucked *you*. *Before* you were a client I might add."

I lean back, removing my chest from his face. "Well, how long do you think it will be before I'm *not* a client?"

He laughs a deep resounding chuckle. Pushing off the wall, he says, "See you at two o'clock tomorrow, Tate."

So now it's *Tate*.

I stand up, shaking my head at the thought of the perplexing man swimming away from me.

Game on, Stone.

CHAPTER EIGHT

I didn't sleep much last night. And now I'm mindlessly going through the motions of my job. What will I do with the information I'm going to have at my fingertips later today? I know he said he didn't have much. But he has something.

God, it felt good to deck that Dewey creep. But is that all I want to do, I wonder? What if these lowlifes are doing that shit to other girls? What if they have families? I make a mental note to ask Ethan to find out for me.

Jarod has the day off and Piper is only filling in as needed now that I'm full-time. It makes for a boring shift. Mindy is here though. And while it's not the same as having my BFF here, I can't say it's not entertaining to watch her flirt with every heterosexual guy under forty that walks in—and maybe some gay ones too.

Mindy is Skylar's best friend and former roommate. She reminds me a lot of myself, only older. She doesn't take shit from anyone. And I admire the fact that even though she comes from money, she's working to put herself through school to become a physical therapist.

She's cool though, and our group of six girls that also includes Baylor and her bestie, Jenna, plans to have a girls' night tomorrow.

I'm not a big fan of girls' night but I agreed under Skylar's threat of working me every Saturday night for a month. I've never been one to get along with other women. Women tend to pretty much hate me. I get that the hair and the face intimidate them because of who my mother was. I get that I never really gave them a second thought other than what I could get out of their boyfriends or husbands. I get that I'm pretty much the opposite of what any girl wants to call a friend.

The Mitchells—they never gave a rat's ass what I looked like or who my mother was. But I think they were the only ones who didn't.

Maybe I could get along with Mindy and Jenna. Mindy doesn't seem to mind me that much and, while I've not met Jenna yet, I've heard great things about her.

As my shift is coming to an end, I stop by one of my tables where two guys are finishing their lunch. I'm surprised they haven't hit the bathroom yet; they've asked me to refill their drinks at least five times, flirting with me more and more each time I visit their table. I flirt back. Of course I do. Flirting equals great tips. They are both good looking. Not in a rugged-yet-clean-cut Ethan Stone kind of way, but head-turners none the less. And maybe a few weeks ago, I'd have taken it further. But now . . . everything has changed. I no longer have to wonder where my next meal is coming from. I no longer need someone else to provide a roof over my head.

That's it, isn't it? That's the reason I'm not carving notches on the bedpost that came from Baylor's guest room.

I shake off the thought and ask the decently-hot guys, "Is there anything else I can get you?"

The one with dark hair and bedroom eyes says, "How about your phone number?"

I roll my eyes. "Seriously? You New York guys have got to work on your pick-up lines."

"Who says we're from New York?" he quips. "And if I come up with something better, do you think I'll have a shot?"

"I don't know. It'll take me about sixty seconds to bring your check, so that's all the time you have." I walk away feeling slightly guilty that I gave the poor guy any sliver of hope.

I cash out another table along the way and when I return, Bedroom Eyes nods to something on the table in front of him. "Fifth row," he says. "We will probably be able to feel the sweat dripping off them as they play."

I look closely to see tickets for White Poison, a wildly famous band. Tickets that I know must've sold out within minutes. I'm not that into the concert scene, but even I have to admit, part of me would love to see them live.

His friend kicks him under the table. "Dude, Drew will kill you if you give his ticket away."

Bedroom Eyes flinches and rubs his shin "Shut up, Chris. Besides, I'm sure he'll forgive me when he sees why. I mean any man would be crazy not to do everything in his power for a date with" —he looks at my nametag— "Charlie."

I put their check on the table, next to the concert tickets, eyeing the face value on them. "You'd be willing to spend two hundred and fifty dollars on a woman you don't even know?"

I think back over the past five years. I've taken much more from strangers without a single thought. But then again, something was always expected in return. Suddenly, a sick feeling washes over me as I recall some of the journal entries I've read that were penned by my mother. And as if a freight train had hit me, I finally get it. I have pretty much become the daughter my mother raised me to be. Instead of her selling me for whatever she needed, I was selling myself for whatever I needed. I wasn't technically a whore, but I might as well have been. Just as my mom wasn't technically a pimp, but what she did to me certainly fell under the broad definition.

A familiar head of dirty-blonde hair scoots out of the booth behind this one. With a scowl on his face, Ethan leans over the table, pushing the tickets back to the man whose name I still haven't learned. "Sorry. She's already going, and with tickets far better than these."

He puts his arm around my waist and pulls me tightly against him, like he's claiming me as his. Like he's marking his territory against these would-be predators. Like he's the hot alpha male who fucked me quick and hard on his office desk.

I want to be mad at him, but I can't. When I turn to look up at him, he's brooding. And it's damn adorable.

He knows I'm new to the city. Is he just trying to keep me safe? Or is he jealous? Nobody has ever been jealous over me—is *this* what it looks like? This strong man, puffing out his chest to appear even larger than he is, staring down the schoolyard bullies that tried to take his lunch money.

I think back to last night, him warning me to stay away from Devon and then the way he ignored me after. Jealousy or protection? The signals he's sending are clear as fucking mud. One minute, he's shooing guys away, the next he's telling me he can't date me. Maybe it comes from being a private investigator. I'll bet he digs up some pretty twisted shit about people. People who seem normal on the outside but have major skeletons in their closet.

Fuck! What if he digs up shit about me? I mean, I just gave him carte blanche at the guys who all know the worst things about me. What if Ethan finds out?

I realize three pairs of eyes are staring at me, waiting on me to say something. I look back at Ethan, sweeping my gaze quickly up and down his body. It may be Saturday, but he's still wearing his usual linen slacks and crisp, clean dress shirt, although today he's minus the tie. Kind of a shame. He looks killer in a tie. I tighten my thighs just thinking about what he could do to me with one of his ties.

I look up into dark eyes that silently beg me to play along.

"Sorry." I shrug at the guys in the booth. "I guess I'm busy that night."

My would-be suitor's hand falls onto the tickets, sliding them across the table towards his wallet before he begrudgingly puts them in it. "Some other time maybe," he says, ignoring Ethan's punishing stare.

"Charlie's pretty busy these days," Ethan says, pulling me even tighter against him. He gives the guy a look. That guy look that says '*hands off.*'

Bedroom Eyes holds up his hands in surrender and whips a couple of twenties out of his wallet. "No harm, no foul, man. We'll just be on our way then."

We move aside so the two men can slip out of the booth. When they walk out the front entrance, I realize Ethan still has a grip on me. And his thumb is rubbing circles on the side of my ribs, burning a hole through the thin material of my shirt. I try to ignore the intensity of feeling shooting through me from that little, seemingly insignificant touch.

"What the hell was that?" I ask, prying my body away from his.

"Rule number four" —his eyes dart to the door and back— "don't play with fire if you don't want to get burned."

"Come again?"

"I heard you flirting with them, Charlie." He moves his neck from side to side, eliciting a cracking sound.

"I flirt with lots of customers, Ethan. You do realize I make a living off tips."

"Fire," he says. "Eventually you'll get burned."

"I'm a big girl, you know. I can take care of myself."

He stares at me thoughtfully, chocolate eyes carefully scanning every feature of my face as if he's memorizing it for future recall. He sighs, clearly wanting to get into it with me, but wisely choosing not to. "You look like a librarian," he says. "A goddamn sexy one."

I laugh. I've gotten so used to wearing the glasses and the bun, that I sometimes forget about the way I look.

I stop laughing when I see the intensity of his stare. Air crackles between us. The crowded restaurant falls silent to my ears that can only hear the pounding of my heartbeat under his heated gaze. As we stare into each other's eyes, something happens. Something I can't explain. It's like we can read each other's minds; extrapolate each other's thoughts.

He wants me. I want him. And it's written all over us.

"Charlie?" Mindy pokes me from behind. "Can you please finish up your tables before the eye-fucking going on here turns into a full-on porn show?"

Ethan rips his eyes from mine and I blow out a slow controlled breath. "Sit," I tell him, not able to look back into his eyes lest I be burned by the aforementioned fire. "Give me ten minutes."

I head to the kitchen wondering what the hell just happened. The way he looked at me, it was more intense than the sex we had on his desk. Another minute of that and I might have orgasmed in the middle of Mitchell's.

I wet a towel and run it over my face, hoping to tamp down the temperature of my scalding skin.

"Who on God's earth is that and how do I get one?" Mindy asks, brushing past me to pick up a food order.

"Don't you know him? That's Jarod's cousin. I thought he came in here all the time."

She raises her eyebrow, giving me a look. "Believe me, I'd know it if he came in all the time."

"But this is his fourth time here since I started the job."

"Well, there you go. Mystery solved. It's not the food he's coming in for, Charlie." She walks out of the kitchen with her tray piled high.

CHAPTER NINE

Standing stunned in the kitchen, I think about what Mindy said.

Not the food. Not Jarod. But he doesn't date clients. He's made that perfectly clear many times.

Ten minutes later, I sit down across from Ethan, placing a Reuben with a side of fries and water sans lemon in front of him.

He eyes it skeptically and then his gaze shifts to the empty spot on the table before me. "You're not eating?"

It takes me a second to catch on. "Oh, right." I shake my head in amusement. "Rule number two, if I remember correctly. But this isn't a date. You said so yourself."

His brow furrows into a scowl. "That doesn't mean we can't eat together, Charlie. You must be hungry after your shift."

I look at his food and realize he's right. It's after two o'clock and I haven't eaten since breakfast. I shrug. "I guess I could eat." I take my napkin and spread it out on the table in front of me. Then I grab half his sandwich and put it on the napkin.

A grin tugs at the edges of his mouth as he nods to his plate. "You want fries with that?" he asks like a seasoned waiter.

"That's my line," I say before taking a bite of my—uh, his— lunch.

I eye the folder on the table and almost lose my appetite remembering why he's here in the first place. "Is that for me?"

He puts a hand on it, holding it firmly to the table as if wanting to keep it from me. Then he opens it, retrieving the papers inside.

I remember the thought I had earlier of him finding out everything and it turns my stomach over. I quickly ask, "You didn't contact them, did you?"

"Of course not. You hired me to locate them, not contact them. We've found half of them so far." He hands me three pieces of paper, each one with a different name at the top. Addresses, phone numbers and other pertinent information line the pages. "Obviously the three who are celebrities have been easy to pin down. But none of them currently reside in New York. One still has a place in the city that he lives in part time, however, he's filming overseas for the next few months. The other two live in Los Angeles most of the year. You'll see their home addresses listed, but these are not places you can simply walk up to. You'll have to go through security to get in. It's also nearly impossible to get private numbers of these people. And they change often, so what we found may be outdated. Best to try and get in touch with them through their agents, whom I've listed for each of them. I'm sure if you tell them who you are and why you want to see them, it won't be a problem."

I almost choke on the corned beef in my mouth. If their agents knew why I wanted to contact them, they wouldn't roll out the red carpet, they'd secure a restraining order.

He pulls out another piece of paper. "This one, Peter Elliot, he's a small-time indie film producer. He lives locally, and although his address is confirmed, you won't find him there. He's in the hospital. Car versus pedestrian accident. The car won and he's been laid up in the intensive care unit at the hospital for six weeks now. You may want to wait on that one. I'm not even sure the guy can talk or have visitors."

I have to press my lips together to suppress a smile. Serves the bastard right.

"This one, Nick Dewey, as far as we can tell, he doesn't have a home address. He used to work for Grandiose Production Company as a camera operator, but lost his job almost a decade ago and hasn't surfaced since. If I find out anything else on the guy, I'll let you know."

Dewey. I remember how good it felt to hurt him at my mother's funeral. I know I didn't really need his information, but I thought, what the hell, I might want to send out a group text one day.

"The last one we've found so far is Milo McClintock, otherwise known as Clint. I'm not exactly sure of the connection between him and your mom, but because of the unusual name, and the fact he's local, he's most likely the one."

He scrubs a hand over his chin. "But, Charlie, call the guy if you need to talk to him. Don't go to his residence, it's not in a good part of town. We couldn't find a place of employment, either."

That's because he's a drug dealer.

"Even when you're in disguise" —he waves a finger at my hair and glasses— "you're still insanely beautiful and would be a target."

Insanely beautiful? Normally I might have a reaction to those words. But right now, I'm trying everything I can to keep it together and not lose my lunch, because my head is still stuck on

Milo McClintock. The first man who ever touched me. His name and his vile touch are ingrained in my memory for all eternity.

I rein in my feelings and reach for the folder, but he doesn't release it completely and we each have a grip on either end. Trying to keep my hands from shaking and giving me away, I silently count to ten, calming the storm that is brewing in my head. "Do you know if these guys are married or have children?"

Ethan studies me. He's always studying me. It makes me wonder if he's this way with everyone. Probably. He did say it was his job to read people.

"I can find that out." With his elbow on the table, his hand comes up to cover his mouth as he's deep in thought. He hesitates before asking, "Exactly what kind of message do you have for these men?"

"Isn't that beyond the scope of your employment?" I ask. "I pay you to find someone and you find them. No questions asked. Right?"

"For the most part, yes. But why ask for information on wives and kids? You said your mom was involved with these men. I refuse to be a party to you ruining people's families, Charlie."

"Really, Stone? Why so defensive?" I ask warily. "You don't even know these people. And what do you care about the sanctity of marriage, let alone having a child? From what I hear, you're nothing but a certified bachelor."

He locks eyes with me briefly, and then his gaze lowers to the table. I'm a bit taken aback, because in that moment I saw something in his eyes. Pain.

He recovers quickly. "Damn it, Charlie. Back off. I'm just not in the business of hurting people."

I grab one of his fries and pop it in my mouth, buying me time to think. "Oh, so you never follow cheating husbands and give their wives ammunition to obliterate them?"

"It's not always the husbands who cheat, you know."

"Whatever. Same difference."

"Those people who blatantly cheat on their spouses; I don't lose sleep over what becomes of them after my job is done." He nods to the folder that we're both still holding onto in what seems a stalemate tug-of-war. "But these men could have been your mother's lovers long before they were married. If you show up and open a can of worms, it could cause unnecessary strain on an otherwise good marriage."

"Relax. I have no intention of ratting out men for screwing my mother. I promise."

I will my eyes to appear sincere. I *am* telling the truth, albeit a twisted fucking version of it.

I must be as good an actress as my mother, because he finally releases the folder. "Fine," he says. "But I'm serious about this McClintock character. Call him. If you must make a personal visit, I'll go with you."

I grab another fry and swirl it into his ketchup. "I'm not sure I could afford your hourly fee."

"That one would be on the house, Charlie. Your safety is worth a lot more to me than a few hundred bucks an hour."

I look up from the food to see the eyes of a man who is being more than just chivalrous. More than just kind. These are the eyes of a determined man. A man with a mission.

And for the first time, I pray to God that mission is me.

CHAPTER TEN

I sit on my couch, arms crossed, staring at the folder on my coffee table while deliberating what to do with the information inside.

I reach out and flip the cover open. The paper on top of the pile is Peter Elliot's. Karma took care of that piece of shit. I move his paper to the bottom of the pile.

I peruse the information of the three celebrities, my skin crawling as I recall what each of them did to me. There's no way I could get close enough to them. But I could hit them where it would hurt the most—their livelihood. I wonder what reports of molestation would do to their lucrative careers. Surely I could get a reputable news magazine to listen to me considering who my mother was.

I decide to give it more thought. I would be putting myself in the spotlight and even if it means I'd accomplish my goal, I'm just not sure it's worth it.

I flip to the last page in the folder. My eyes burn with fury as I read the name. Milo McClintock. I had to contain my emotions and control my rage when Ethan uttered the scumbag's name at the restaurant.

I look at the last known address on the paper. The place Ethan warned me against. I enter it into my phone and map it out, getting a sick feeling when I see just how right Ethan was. Maybe this isn't a good idea after all. Maybe I should just stick to the ones who aren't so dangerous. Actors, producers, screenwriters—they are all perverts, but probably not as lethal as a drug dealer.

I lean over the couch cushion next to me and slip my hand between the cushion and the arm, retrieving my mother's journal. I flip through it until I find what I'm looking for.

February 21, 2008

If I had known mothering was such a thankless job, I never would have agreed to do it. All I ever hear from her is what she wants to do, which is mostly hang out with those Mitchell people who own some dive diner over on Main Street.

Do you think for one minute she even considers how hard I had to work to make this life for us? Not that George helps. Hell, they even made me pay him alimony after the divorce. In what world is that fair? I starred in those movies. I supported this family while all he ever did was write crappy screenplay after crappy screenplay hoping my celebrity status would get him noticed.

Not that Charlie ever realized he was dead weight. She still thinks he will come back one day. Come back for her. Sometimes I wish he would. It would get her out of my hair for sure. But he's never coming back. Not if he knows what's good for him. His empty threats bored me to tears and his cowardice was laughable. That man wouldn't know how to party if a party hit him in the balls.

Milo—he knows how to party. And he says he'll make sure it's worth my while if I let him party with Charlie.

I can't wait to find out what he can get for me.

I put down the journal, trying, but failing at my attempts to not think of that awful night.

"This is Clint," Mom says, indicating the man standing behind her in my bedroom doorway.

My stomach rolls. There is only one reason Mom brings men into my room.

"Please, Mom," I start to protest, but she raises her hand to me, making me flinch and sink back into my bed.

I should know better. I'll probably get a fresh burn for that later, or maybe a bruise. Depends on her mood. When she is high, she tends to favor cigarettes as her form of punishment. When she's drunk – her fists.

She leans down and whispers to me. "Listen up, Charlie. Do whatever Clint says or you'll be out on your ass faster than you can call your little Pied Piper friend. And if you think her parents will take you in, think again; they have three kids of their own and a struggling business. Your father left because of you. Just remember you are lucky you still have me to take care of you."

When she stands up straight, a trickle of blood escapes her nose and she pulls a blood-stained tissue from her pocket to wipe it. I'm young, but I'm not stupid. I know exactly what that means. And I'd be willing to bet Clint is helping her get it.

"I'll just leave you two alone then," she says, shooting Clint a look. "Just be quick about it, I need you."

She shuts my door and before my newest nightmare begins, I hear loud music blasting from the living room.

She always plays loud music whenever she leaves them with me. Maybe that's why I rarely listen to it myself. Books, that's my escape. Mysteries, sci-fi, action-adventure—those are what I seek when I need to turn off my reality.

"You are a pretty one, aren't you?" he says, taking a seat next to me on the bed.

They never sit on my bed. The chair across the room is where they always sit. My pulse shoots sky high and I think I might pass out when he reaches for me. I instinctively pull away and scoot back, hoping the wall will swallow me whole and protect me from this sick bastard.

He waves a scolding finger at me. "You wouldn't want me to tell your mom you didn't cooperate, would you?"

I turn my head away from him and stare at the wall, hoping the mural will protect me from him as it has all the others, but knowing this time it won't, because this time is different.

Unable to control the storm of resentment and the explosion of hatred I feel at the thought of him, I tuck my hair under a ball cap and add two layers of sweatshirts over my t-shirt, knowing a bulky coat will only get in my way. Then I head out the door, vengeance and wrath driving my actions.

CHAPTER ELEVEN

"Oh my God, Charlie! What happened to you?" Baylor asks, shocked when she takes in my red, blue and purple bruised cheekbone.

I tried my best to cover it with makeup, and I did a pretty good job of it, but not good enough to keep my friends from noticing.

Skylar looks me over from head to toe. Then she grabs my left hand, eyeing the healing cut on my knuckles. "What the hell, Charlie. Did you get into a fight?"

"It looks worse than it is." I walk further into Skylar's townhouse and put the bottle of tequila and margarita mix on the kitchen counter. Five pairs of eyes follow me.

Piper is not a stranger to my black eyes and bruised knuckles. I didn't always make the best choices in men when we lived abroad. Not to mention all the lovely marks my mother bestowed upon me. Still, she follows me step for step around the bar in the kitchen, her eyes burning into the back of my head. "Charlie?" she asks.

The tone of her voice tells me she's not about to drop this. So I shrug and tell them the story I made up on the way over. "The punk who tried to grab my purse is far worse off than I am, I assure you."

Gasps come from around the room.

"Someone tried to mug you?" Baylor shrieks.

"It's no big deal," I say, breaking the seal on the bottle of tequila. "Piper and I took self-defense classes in London. I think the kid will think twice before trying that again."

"What did the police say?" Mindy asks.

I'm well aware of Piper's laser focus on me, so I busy myself with mixing drinks so she can't see my eyes. She knows me. She knows my every look, my every nuance. She can read me like a book.

"I didn't bother," I tell them. "You know they can't do anything. I didn't even get a good look at the guy because he was wearing a hoodie."

I look up to see three sisters and their two friends staring at me in disapproval. "What?" I snap. "Don't worry, he got what was coming to him. I kneed him so hard I think I may have seen his balls come out of his mouth."

Mindy snorts her drink out of her nose.

Skylar pats me on the back and says, "Good girl."

The blonde who must be Jenna, says, "It sounds like you're a handy person to have around." She extends her hand. "I've heard a lot about you, Charlie. I'm Jenna. It's great to finally meet you."

"You, too," I say, shaking her hand. I nod to the drinks. "Margarita?"

"Hell yes. Long day," she says.

I laugh. "Are certain prima donna authors driving you crazy with their outrageous demands?"

Jenna is Baylor's agent and best friend. Baylor has written sixteen romance novels, one even based on her own love story with

Gavin. He was her college sweetheart and her first love. They were ripped apart by a betrayal only to find each other years later. It's the only one of her books I've read. I have to admit, she's good. But that sappy love shit doesn't do it for me.

"Hardly," Jenna replies. "Baylor is by far my easiest client. She is the opposite of demanding." She turns to Baylor. "In fact, you realize you could make a lot more money if you weren't paying your agent and publisher so much, right?"

Baylor takes a drink from me, shrugging. "I'm perfectly happy making what I make right now. Too much money can change a person, you know?"

Jenna leans across the bar and hugs her. "That's why I love you. You're so grounded."

Skylar looks around at the five of us and then to the drink in her hand. "I just realized we can all drink!" She glances over at Baylor. "Between pregnancies and nursing, it's been a while since either of us could partake."

Piper raises her drink. "A toast then. To none of us being knocked up."

"Oh hell," Mindy says. "Now you jinxed it." She eyes each one of us carefully. "Who's it gonna be? Which one of you will get knocked up next?"

All eyes turn to Piper.

"Whoa! Slow down, people." She puts her drink down. "I'm not even married yet. Plus, I'm still getting used to the idea of being Hailey's step-mom. She's only two-and-a-half. I believe that's quite enough for me to handle for a very long while. Not to mention I'm only twenty-two years old. What's the rush?"

"You tell 'em little sister," Baylor says. "Enjoy Mason. Enjoy that precious little girl. It all goes by so fast."

Jenna guffaws. "Says the old lady of twenty-eight. You know Jordan and Maddox would love a little sibling, don't you? And as you pointed out, you're not getting any younger."

Baylor plucks a grape from the bowl on the bar, pelting it at Jenna. "What about you? When is Jake going to put a ring on that finger and a bun in that oven?"

Jenna tips back her glass, emptying it in three swallows. "Seems like never. We've always said he should get a job that doesn't take him away so much before we get hitched. And being a batting coach for the Yankees has him on the road half the time."

"That never stopped us," Piper says. "If you really want it to work, it'll work. Mason was gone a lot in the fall." Her finger traces the rim of her glass as her cheeks start to pink up. "The Internet is amazing for long-distance relationships."

Everyone laughs.

"TMI," Skylar says.

"Just sayin'." Piper shrugs. "It's doable."

Mindy clears her throat loudly, getting everyone's attention. "I want to get the scoop on Jarod's hot cousin," she says, staring me down. "You know, the one who follows Charlie's every move at work and eye-fucks her every chance he gets."

Silence overtakes Skylar's townhouse as they all stare at me, waiting for a response.

"What?" I shrug.

"What do you mean, *what?*" Mindy says. "The guy comes in all the time. But only when you are working I might add. He's seriously hot and he's obviously into you. What's the deal?"

"There is no deal," I tell them. "He's working for me, actually. He's a private investigator and he's helping me dig up information about my mother."

"Private investigator?" Jenna says, fanning herself. "That's sexy."

"What's so sexy about being a private investigator?" I ask, as if I didn't very well know.

"I don't know. All those cheating husbands and lowlife criminals he must have to deal with. It's a risky job. That's hot. Don't you guys think?" Her eyes sweep the room to find four heads nodding in agreement. "Anyway," Jenna adds, "I'm just saying if I were you, I'd totally go after that."

"He works for me, Jenna. Kind of a conflict of interest, wouldn't you say?"

"He won't work for you forever," Skylar says. "How long can it take to find information about your famous mom?"

I shoot Skylar an annoyed look that Piper doesn't miss. Piper studies me. Hard. She scratches her face and runs a finger across the curve of her brow. Then after a long silence, she shrieks, "Oh my God, Charlie!" She turns to the others, pointing a finger at me. "This girl likes to talk about sex. In fact, I've heard every nauseating detail of every sexual encounter she had in Europe."

She turns her attention back to me. "I've never seen you so tight-lipped about a guy before. Why aren't you sickening us with tales of your sexcapades? That can only mean one thing—you like him. I mean, you *like* him, like him. So what's—"

"Wait a minute," Baylor interrupts. "You've had sex with him? With the P.I.?"

Heads snap in my direction, eagerly awaiting my answer as I shoot Piper a traitorous stare.

"I may have hooked up with him once."

"When?" Skylar asks.

"The day I met him."

Mindy shrieks. "And now he comes around almost daily just so you can serve him lunch? What—is your pussy made out of crack-cocaine or something?"

Jenna spews her drink all over the counter. "Mindy, you are so crude," she says.

Then, while the girls enter into a conversation about the animal magnetism of their vaginas, I realize that Piper may be onto something. I do like Ethan Stone. I like him a lot. But that very well may be my downfall.

CHAPTER TWELVE

"What the fuck, Charlie?" Ethan freezes in place when he sees me.

Although it's been a few days and my bruise has faded to something of a yellowish hue, it's still hard to completely hide it, even under makeup and my work glasses.

Ignoring his question, I pull my order pad from my apron and ask one of my own. "What can I get you gentlemen?"

Ethan has brought two men with him today. One of them shares a resemblance and is equally as gorgeous. The other is smirking as Ethan seethes in his chair, his stare burning into me.

I try not to think about what Piper said the other night as I put my pen to the order pad and ping-pong my eyes between the men, awaiting their orders.

Ethan refuses to even speak. I can see a vein throbbing at his temple as he continues to look at my bruised cheek. The wheels spinning in his head are more than evident. He's practically bursting out of his skin wanting to know what happened. The private investigator in him needs information. Information he's not going to get from me.

"What my very rude and socially inept brother is trying to say is that I'm Kyle Stone, Ethan's youngest brother."

Youngest. There are more? These are personal details I'd normally not care to know about a man.

But there's something about him.

Kyle holds his hand out to me and I try hard to suppress my smile as I shake it. Kyle has the same strong, angular facial features as his older brother, but that's where the resemblance ends. While Ethan has dirty-blonde hair and chocolate eyes, Kyle has what I'd describe as a darker honey-brown hair and eyes that can't seem to settle on a color.

"And this is Ethan's friend and co-worker, Levi Brandt." Kyle nods to the man sitting across the table who is offering me his hand.

I shake Levi's hand as he laughs, saying, "Co-worker my ass." Not releasing my hand, he tilts his chin to Ethan. "Boss here works me like a dog so he can stalk pretty girls." He winces. "Ouch, dude. Not cool."

I gather he just got a swift kick under the table from the mercurial man whose eyes are now focused on my hand in Levi's. I smile and Levi smirks, both of us aware of what our touch is doing to the eldest Stone.

I turn to Kyle. "So, what do you do, Kyle? Do you work for your brother as well?"

"This tool? Hell no. You won't catch me working for that tight ass with all his rules. I'm a med student at NYU."

"Is that so?" I glance over at Mr. High-and-Mighty. If he's not going to speak, why not see if I can rile him up a bit? "That sounds really interesting. So if I hooked up with a random guy and am now experiencing some kind of itchy rash, you'd be able to help me out with that?"

Vein. Throbbing. Harder.

Kyle laughs, his eyes quickly bouncing off Ethan's. "I'd have to see it first. But yeah, I could most definitely help you out."

I like him already. He's a smart ass like me. Nothing like his older brother. While Ethan dons his usual dress shirt, tie and linen pants, Kyle wears jeans and a t-shirt; one that's just snug enough to show off his muscles without seeming too self-absorbed.

Levi fits somewhere in between with a collared polo shirt and slacks. Also a handsome guy by anyone's standards, but unfortunately for him, he fades into the background next to the Stone brothers.

"We'll have waters, Charlie," Ethan says, pulling my attention from his tablemates.

"I'm on it." I raise my eyebrows at Kyle and Levi. "Lemon for you two, or is that a sacrilege?"

They don't even try to hide their amusement. "However you bring them is fine with us," Levi offers and Kyle agrees.

I turn around and head towards the drink station when strong arms pull me into the adjacent hallway. Ethan cages me in with his hands on either side of my head. My heart races being so close to him. I wipe a sweaty palm on my apron as I look up into his dark-as-night eyes.

He takes in a deep breath as if he's inhaling my scent. As if he's inhaling *me*. My skin breaks out in goosebumps.

"What . . . Happened . . . Charlie?" Each word comes out as a sentence punctuated by a blink of his eyes between the very deliberate syllables.

Despite blood rushing through my ears, throbbing so loudly it drowns out the sounds of the restaurant, I shrug, answering him calmly. "Some jackass tried to mug me the other day. Don't worry, he got more than he gave."

I concentrate on the pulsating vein at his temple, aware of how either our proximity or his anger has sped up the frequency of his heartbeat.

In my periphery, I see his hands come off the wall. I can feel the heat of them close to my arms, but I sense his hesitation. He wants to touch me. Protect me. Maybe he even wants to claim me.

But he doesn't.

And for the first time in my life, I want all those things. The realization pins me to the wall and I'm suddenly scared shitless.

Almost as if we can read each other's thoughts, he takes a step back and studies me. The air between us is thick with want and desire. Maybe even need.

I've needed men before. To provide for me. But I've never *needed* a man before. Not on the visceral level that is tugging on my insides right now. Not in the sense that I feel as if we were meant to cross paths. Not in the sense that has me believing that maybe my mother's death purposefully brought me to him.

Then again, that would make her death meaningful. There was nothing meaningful about that woman, except that I suppose she provided entertainment to millions and lined the pockets of thousands with her talent that simply wasted away because of her determination to stay wasted.

"I'll teach you how to shoot," he says. "A single woman in the city should know how to protect herself."

I'm reminded of the gun that was strapped to his calf when we had sex. I feel a wave of heat run up and down my spine thinking of it. I quickly swallow my emotions. "What makes you think I can't protect myself?"

He narrows his eyes at me. "This doesn't have anything to do with the information I gave you the other day, does it?"

"What? No." I scratch my head, then, realizing what I've done, I immediately put my hand to my side. Piper always says that's my tell. If he knew me better, he'd know it, too.

He eyes me skeptically.

"Ask Piper Mitchell if you don't believe I can take care of myself. We both took self-defense classes over in London."

"Good. That's good," he says, slowly backing away from me. "We'll take those drinks now." He turns to leave, hesitating as if he has something else on his mind. "Random guy?" he asks quietly over his shoulder.

"Just seeing if you were paying attention, Stone."

"I'm always paying attention, Tate."

I smile at what seems to have become our exchange of endearments.

"So, no itchy rash?" he asks.

"Not unless *you* gave it to me," I say.

Even as he walks away, I can see his triumphant smile.

I pour a cold glass of water but don't put it on my tray. I down it myself, drowning the fire that man set in my belly simply from his close proximity.

The rest of his lunch is spent with me making only quick visits to their table.

I make small talk with Kyle and Levi when I bring their food and the check. Each pass by the table, I sense Ethan's growing frustration over the fact I'm all but ignoring him. But he's too distracting. The way his eyes follow me around. The way I can feel his heated stare. The way my body reacts to him.

It's been one of the longest damn hours of my life.

Samantha Christy

CHAPTER THIRTEEN

Devon Totman. Mr. Tall-Dark-and-Endlessly-Cocky. The man does not take no for an answer. He sees me enter the gym and proceeds to follow me through the workout area. I make idle conversation with him, not wanting to piss off gym patrons since I'm here for free, but not wanting to lead him on at the same time.

As I reach the ladies locker room, he asks, "How about I join you for your swim?"

"That's okay," I say. "Mrs. Buttermaker is my swimming partner and I really don't want to offend her by replacing her."

"That old bat? She can barely doggie paddle from one end of the pool to the other."

"Yes. Well, that *old bat* is just about the nicest lady I've ever met. You'll do well not to piss her off or speak badly of her around me."

He holds up his hands in surrender, looking confused as I duck into the locker room without another word.

When I enter the aquatics area, I see Ethan helping Mrs. B out of the pool. I could swear I see her blush through her thin, wrinkled skin. She laughs, touching his arm as they have a conversation I'm too far away to hear.

She's flirting with him. And from the looks of it, he's flirting back.

She passes me by on her way out and it's obvious she's not sticking around for my swim. "That one's sweet as sugar, he is."

"If you say so, Mrs. Buttermaker. Did you have a nice swim? I'm sorry I'm late. My shift ran over tonight."

"Not a problem, dear. That yummy Mr. Stone kept me company. If I was forty years younger . . ." She giggles like a school girl.

I laugh. "I'm not sure Mr. Buttermaker would appreciate that."

"Oh, that old biddy wouldn't know the difference. Since the day he retired twenty years ago, he only makes love to his Lazyboy recliner."

"Mrs. B!"

"I'm old, dear. Not dead." She winks at me, slipping on her yellow flowered flip-flops before walking away.

I put my towel down and make my way over to my usual swimming lane.

Ethan watches me. Of course he does. I swapped out my one-piece swimsuit with a sturdy yet sexy bikini.

"Mrs. B likes you," I say.

His eyes rise from their survey of my body. But it's nothing he hasn't seen before—splayed all over his desk in fact. "Rule number five—be nice to little old ladies."

"I like that one." I give him a smile before diving in, hoping my bottoms stay on when I hit the water.

I swim for twenty minutes, the entire time acutely aware of Ethan's eyes on me from where he's perched on the side of the pool.

Finally, when I can't stand it anymore, or maybe because I'm simply too breathless to continue my swim under his heated perusal, I stop at the end of a lap and ask, "Something wrong with your legs? You forget how to swim or something?"

"I finished earlier," he says, sinking back into the pool and darting under the lane dividers separating us. He pops up before me, dripping wet and looking even sexier than he did at lunch when he had me caged to the wall.

"And yet you're still here."

Half of his face turns upward into a devious smile. "So I am."

Despite the warm water of the pool, my skin prickles as if a cool breeze is flowing over me when he inches closer.

"What did Devon want?" he asks, nodding to the clear glass separating the pool from the rest of the gym. I wasn't aware he was watching that exchange. I'm not sure if I should be mad or flattered.

"What does he always want?"

"That's what I was afraid of." His fist hits the water.

"I told you, Ethan, I can take care of myself."

"So you've said." His hand comes up to trace the faint outline of my fading bruise, more visible now that I have no makeup on. Feeling his light touch caress my face, a ball of need bursts to life in the pit of my stomach.

He frowns, studying my face. "Where were you when it happened?"

I try to remember what I told the girls. Did I give them details? "Uh, I couldn't sleep, so I went out and did some window shopping. It was stupid, I know. But like I told you before, I'm fine. Believe me, the guy looks much worse than I do."

Not wanting him to prod anymore, I ask, "What's your issue with Devon? And what does it matter to you who I date?"

Instead of an answer, he splashes water on me like an adolescent.

"Oh, you did not just do that, Stone."

"What are you going to do about it, Tate?"

"Nothing, you toddler." I climb out of the pool and then I turn around to face him, launching myself over him, doing a perfect cannonball in front of him, splashing him square in the face.

"Oh, you're gonna get it now," he says, shaking the water out of his hair.

I swim away from him, but he reaches me quickly under the water, jerking me back to him by my feet.

I come up for air. "Ouch!" I scream.

"Shit, Charlie. I'm sorry." Guilt overtakes his features as he releases his grip on me.

I smile and swim around to his back, jumping on it and dunking him under. He tries to buck me off, but I wrap my strong swimmer's legs around his torso and drape my arms around his neck.

He drags us both under water, twisting and turning in an attempt to dislodge me. I hold on for dear life, not budging an inch. He shoots us up out of the water and shakes his head from side to side, whipping his hair around. That's when I catch a glimpse of it.

His hair falls back against his neck and before he can swat my hand away, I push his wet locks aside and get a clear look at the tattoo at the base of his skull.

I let go of him instantly and climb out of the pool. Looking down on him, I remember the comment Levi said earlier about him stalking me. With accusatory hands on my hips, I ask, "Why the hell do you have my initials tattooed on your neck?"

He goes pale. "Your initials are C.A.T.?"

I shake my head at him in diffidence. "Like you didn't know that, Mr. Private Investigator."

"Charlie, I'm not investigating *you*. How would I know that?"

"Then how . . . why?"

He swims away, treading water more than a dozen feet from me, as if he physically needs the distance between us. "They aren't your initials." The words come out of his mouth, but it's almost like they aren't his words at all. They aren't the words of the strong, vibrant man I've come to know. They are more like the words of a broken one.

The resolve on his face tells me his declaration is true. And for one brief second, before I feel the wave of relief, I'm almost sad he hasn't branded part of me into his flesh. "Oh? Well, whose are they?" I ask boldly.

He looks forlorn at my question, but quickly recovers. "Rule number six—don't play your hand too soon."

"So, there's a hand?" I ask. "Some deep, dark secret about Ethan Stone?"

He ignores the question. "So what does the 'A' stand for?"

"Huh?"

"In your initials, what's the 'A'?"

"Anthony. As in my mom's last name," I tell him as I sit down on the edge of the pool.

"Charlie Anthony Tate," he recites my name and I find myself wanting him to chant it over and over again.

He swims closer, narrowing the space he'd put between us. "So you seemed very interested in my brother the other day."

I bite my cheek suppressing a smile. The formidable Stone has a jealous streak. "I was just making small talk."

"Right. Good for tips," he says.

"Something like that. But, now that I think of it, he is rather good looking. And a doctor—impressive."

"Med student," he corrects me. "And some people say we look a lot alike."

I giggle at his boyish remark.

"And he's named after a porn star," he says.

"Porn star? Really?" I laugh.

"Yeah. An unfortunate coincidence for him."

"I'll say."

"How about you, Charlie Tate? Were you named after the Hurricanes' football coach?"

I try to hide my surprise. Most people don't know who Charlie Tate was. He played football for a few years. He coached for a few years. But it's not like he was Peyton Manning or Bear Bryant or anything. For the first time in a long time, I think of my dad and how he loved football. How he would teach me what things like 'nickelback' and 'red zone' and 'safety' meant when we would watch games together. Football Saturdays are the only good memories I have left of the pathetic man who was my father.

I shrug. "My dad kind of had a thing for football."

"Sounds like he and I would get along then."

I ignore his statement completely. "So Kyle said he's your youngest brother? There are more?"

"Just one. Chad. He falls in the middle."

"Sisters?" I ask.

"Nope, just the three of us." He swims up directly in front of me. "Why are you suddenly so interested in my family?"

I slide my bottom down the edge, easing myself back into the pool. "You're the one who brought Kyle to the restaurant."

"For lunch. I am allowed to eat lunch with my brother, am I not?"

"Sure. It's just that you seem to frequent Mitchell's an awful lot these days."

"Well, yeah," he says. "They do have the best Reubens in New York City."

"They've always had the best Reubens." I raise my eyebrows. "But it's been brought to my attention that you've only been coming there for a few weeks. Why is that, Stone?"

His arms come up on either side of me, holding me prisoner against the side of the pool. "If you don't know that, you're not as bright as I thought you were, Tate."

Butterflies dance across my stomach. "I thought you couldn't get involved with me," I say, trying to keep the shakiness out of my voice.

"That doesn't mean I want you getting involved with anyone else."

His chocolate eyes burn into me. He picks up a wet chunk of my hair, working it between his fingers. I realize hair doesn't have nerve endings, but I swear his touch sends impulses through every synapse in my body.

"You can't have it both ways, you know." My chest heaves between words. Our close proximity has my pulse beating so hard I'm sure it must be echoing off the walls of the massive aquatics room.

Nobody else has come in to swim laps. It's late. Most of the gym patrons have gone home. A few stragglers remain in the fitness area, but they would be hard pressed to see us in the far corner of the pool.

I reach out and place my hand flat against his chest, right over his other tattoo. His heartbeat is in sync with the fast pace of mine, pounding heavily against his chest wall. Boldly, I run my hand down over his taut abs as his breath comes faster. He puts his hand over mine, halting my progress. I look into his eyes, clearly seeing the battle raging in his head.

I lean forward, letting my soft words flow over his ear. "What's it gonna be, Stone?"

Suddenly, his arms wrap around me, pulling me tight against his body so I can feel what our closeness is doing to him. One of his hands comes up and grabs the nape of my neck, and as he leans down, his heavy whisper resonates all the way through my body. "Fuck the rules."

His mouth comes crashing down on mine before my lips have time to break into a victorious smile. His hands are everywhere all at once, worshiping my thighs, my hips, my shoulders, as if he's a man deprived.

His large frame covers me, shielding me from prying eyes should anyone wander into the pool room.

He supports me against the wall, giving himself leverage while his lips lick pool water from my neck. He lifts me slightly out of the water with one hand, exposing my bikini-covered breasts as his pupils dilate and his eyes grow as hungry as his hands.

Slowly, his mouth works down my collarbone, across my shoulder, finally finding my breast as he pulls the fabric aside with his fingers to give access to his tongue.

Pulses of feeling bolt straight to my center as he sucks, swirls, and flicks my breasts in a way I've never experienced before. He blows air across my chest, puckering my nipples even further.

With one hand around his neck, supporting myself out of the water, I take my other hand and work it beneath his swim trunks, feeling him swell thicker at my touch.

His groans bounce off the walls, the sultry noises feeding my greedy desire to have him inside of me again.

My pants and moans match his, our arms and legs so tangled together it's hard to tell which limbs are his and which are mine.

When he slips a hand into my bikini bottom, grazing a finger across my clit, my back arches, scraping against the hard edge of the pool. He wraps an arm around my head, protecting it from the unforgiving concrete.

My eyes flicker open and I see the shadow of a person behind the glass walking across the fitness center. Realization of what we're doing and where we're doing it heightens my arousal.

Ethan, however, seems lost in the moment, oblivious to the world. Adrift to anything or anyone but me. I feel his focus, his passion. I feel like I'm the only person that exists to him—that has ever existed to him.

I moan loudly as his fingers enter me. I push his swim trunks below his erection and pull him towards me. He moves my bikini bottom to one side, allowing me to guide him to my entrance.

His eyes are ravenous—desperate with need as he enters me. Our simultaneous gasps are muffled when our mouths devour each other, our tongues mimicking the motions of other parts of our bodies.

I start to feel that sweet ache between my legs. I let it build, wanting for the first time to let it go higher and higher instead of settling for a quick release. I'm letting him take me where no man has. A place that now belongs only to him.

My thighs tighten. My back strains against the hard edge of the pool, most likely causing bruises up and down my spine. A painful yet pleasured burn coils in my belly and I bite down on his shoulder to silence the scream that begs to explode from me along with my powerful orgasm.

Then I watch his face as it contorts with his impending release. Suddenly, I feel vast emptiness as he quickly pulls out of me, finishing into the water between us as he shouts out my name.

We both sink into the water, our bodies languid as we chase recovery.

When I regain my ability to speak, I say, "You didn't have to do that, you know. I'm on the pill."

He looks around the vacant room, shaking his head in disgust as if he's just realized where we are. "What the hell are you doing to me, woman? I'm breaking all the rules with you."

"All the rules?" I ask, situating my bottoms back into place. "I thought it was just rule number one."

He raises a brow as if I've missed something obvious. "Rule number seven—no public displays of affection. We pretty much obliterated that one."

"I don't think anyone saw us, so technically it wasn't breaking the rule. Try again."

"Okay, how about rule number eight—wrap it before you tap it."

I laugh. "Oh my God. Do you have a list of these rules somewhere or do you just make them up as you go?"

He taps his temple. "They're all up here."

He climbs out of the pool, the veins in his arms bulging out as he pulls his weight up. Sitting on the side, he offers me his hand and then hoists me up to sit alongside him.

He heaves a heavy sigh. "I've never broken that rule, Charlie. I've never broken *any* rules before you."

I scissor my feet in the water, causing tiny waves to lap up onto the wall beneath us. "See, that's where we're different, Stone. I break rules all the time. What's the fun in life if you don't?"

He looks a little green and I realize what I said and begin to backpedal. "Except for that one," I say. "I've never broken rule number eight either, so you can relax."

His hands come up and scrub across his face, relief evident in his eyes.

"So, can I expect you to break rule number one again?" I ask hopefully. "I mean, now that you've done it, no sense in going back."

Ethan stands up and walks over to where we left our towels. He puts his around his neck and brings mine over, offering it to me. The fact that he didn't answer me straight away clues me in.

"Pfft . . . forget it. No big deal," I say, trying to sound unaffected by his impending rejection.

"I'm not the kind of guy who does relationships, Charlie."

That's the second time he's used my first name in the last thirty seconds. My heart sinks into my stomach before I even realize I'm feeling what I'm feeling. It takes my brain a second to catch up. My heart wants this man. My mind wants this man. My body wants this man.

Holy shit. Am I in fucking love?

CHAPTER FOURTEEN

I'm not the kind of guy who does relationships, Charlie.

His words echo through my head for the hundredth time since he said them.

Who does he think he is? *I* don't do relationships. I mean, other than Piper, my relationships consist of a mother who pimped me out and a string of mostly married men who, let's face it, used me as much as I used them.

Three days. That's how long it's been since I've seen him.

It bothers me that I'm counting. It bothers me that it bothers me. It bothers me that the way I feel about him is as close to a relationship as I've ever come.

This man is seriously messing with my head. And admittedly, my head's pretty screwed up already.

The way he looks at me, tries to protect me, touches me. It's all a contradiction to his declaration about not doing relationships. How can he act so jealous over ridiculous things like the guy at the restaurant who asked me out, or Devon at the gym? Even his brother seemed to rile him up. I'm no expert, but I'd say that is not the reaction of a man who 'doesn't do relationships.'

The buzzing of my phone in my pocket startles me. But not as much as the text I see on the screen. It's like the man has a direct line into my thoughts.

Stone: I have some more information for you. I'll bring it to the gym tonight.

I'm slightly amused that he didn't suggest meeting me at Mitchell's. He must know it's my day off. I can't help the smile that cracks my face at the thought of him knowing my schedule. I realize my heart is racing simply from getting his text and I try to sound casual in my reply.

Me: Sounds good. See you then.

I stare at the clock on my apartment wall. It's only ten o'clock in the morning. And it's my day off. That means I have to wait almost twelve hours for the information he has at his fingertips this very second.

That won't do. I put my coat on and grab my keys. The entire way to his office, I wonder which scumbag he found this time. Will it be J.T.—the one who was always so high he couldn't even get it up, yet he still got his kicks from seeing me naked? Or will it be Karl Salzman—the one who my mother let take my virginity at a mere fifteen years old? I feel nauseous thinking about the latter. I'm not even sure I'd want it to be him, because the truth is, I'm not sure kicking him in the balls and punching his face would satisfy me enough. More like water torture followed by castration.

I walk into the reception area to see Gretchen leaning over the counter, flirting with a man who's sitting on the white leather couch. When she sees me, her whole demeanor changes. Her smile fades into a frown and she quickly looks at the appointment book on the desk in front of her before making further eye contact with me.

"You don't have an appointment," she says, her cold blue eyes raking over my body, crudely assessing me from head to toe.

I follow her gaze, looking down at my clothes, realizing in my haste to get here, I didn't bother dressing up. In fact, I'm wearing sweatpants and an old UNC sweatshirt Baylor gave me when she quit going there. My hair is pulled up into a messy bun and I'm still wearing yesterday's eyeliner.

For a brief second, I contemplate walking back out the office door. But then I tell myself I don't give a shit, and then I pretend to believe it as I participate in a stare-down with Barbie.

"No, I don't have an appointment," I reply. "But I was hoping Ethan had a second to spare."

"Ethan?" she asks, questioning me with the raise of a thin, manicured brow as if warning me that only a select few have the right to call him by his first name.

"Yes, you know, your boss? The one who runs this company and calls the shots. That Ethan."

I don't back down. I'm pretty sure she gets the picture my eyes are painting. The picture that says she's not the only one in the I've-been-beneath-Ethan-Stone club.

"I'm sorry," she says, trying to sound professional and not like the colossal bitch she is. "Mr. Stone only sees clients by appointment."

"Okay." I try hard not to roll my eyes. "Then I'd like to make an appointment." I look at the clock on the wall next to Gretchen's desk. "How about ten forty-five?"

She snidely leafs through the appointment book in front of her without breaking eye contact with me. "I'm sorry," she repeats.

"It appears we don't have any openings today. Perhaps you could come back when we do?"

"And when might that be?" I ask in amusement.

"I might be able to work you in next week," she says. "But we usually reserve appointments for paying clients. My records show you haven't quite achieved that status yet."

Before I can censor my own words, I serve Barbie a cup of her own cattiness on a fucking platter. "Oh, I've made several installments," I say. "Just not with money."

Gretchen's jaw drops. The man on the couch snickers, further fueling Gretchen's fire. "Like I said, I can't work you in. You might as well leave."

I step away from the counter, pulling my phone out. "I'll just text him then. Mind if I wait over here?" I motion to the wall of family photos.

"Ethan doesn't answer personal texts during work hours. But whatever." She looks for imperfections on her long nails. "Suit yourself."

I walk over to the photo wall as I type out a text.

Me: I'm in your reception area. Can't get past the Gestapo. I was hoping you'd have a sec to give me the info you have.

I slip my phone back into my purse, hoping like hell he does in fact answer personal texts at work. The last thing I want to do today is give Barbie the satisfaction of watching me walk out of here with my tail between my legs.

A few long minutes pass without a reply. *What do you expect, Charlie—for him to drop everything and come running when you beckon?*

I busy myself looking at Ethan's family photos. Now that I know more about him, they've become more interesting. Like I am to my mom—he's a carbon copy of his dad. And if the photos are any indication, Ethan will be one hell of a looker as he ages.

I focus my attention on a picture of him with his brothers. Kyle looks to be about four or five years younger than Ethan with Chad falling somewhere in the middle. Now that I think of it, I'm not even sure how old Ethan is. Younger than most of the men I've been with for sure, but probably not over thirty.

Chad still looks familiar. I can't place him, but I know I've seen him before. I don't suppose he works for Ethan; I probably would have met him by now if that were the case.

The three of them together look like the Holy Grail of hotness. The genes it must have taken to create such a trifecta of perfection. It gets me thinking about what the children of Piper and Mason would look like. They have to be the best-looking couple I've ever seen.

I hear a door open behind me. I turn around to see Ethan and another man walking from the back offices into the reception area. He shakes the man's hand and looks back and forth between me and Gretchen, who is now seething in her skin-tight push-up-bra dress. Based on her reaction, I get the feeling Ethan doesn't often accompany clients out here, but that this is a direct result of my text. I mean, if looks could kill, I'd be flat-lining right here on the floor of this office.

"Everything okay out here?" he asks.

I feel my blood pressure spike when I hear his deep gravelly voice.

"Fine, Ethan," Gretchen says. "I was just telling um" —she looks at me snidely— "your name seems to have slipped my mind."

"Tate," I say to her, but I'm looking directly at Ethan.

He smiles that half-smile of his that could melt the panties off an Eskimo.

Gretchen's eyes dart between us and she puckers her full, fire-engine-red lips like she's eaten something bitter. Yeah, I'm pretty sure she good and well knows my name. I'm also pretty sure she hates that he is looking at me like this.

"I was just telling *Tate* how you were running behind," Gretchen says, motioning to the man on the couch. "I doubted we could fit her in just now."

He gives her an annoyed look. "You could've buzzed me, Gretchen."

He walks over to the man on the couch and addresses him. "Brad, a bit of an urgent matter has come up. Would you mind terribly giving me five minutes? Gretchen will be happy to fetch you some coffee or whatever else you need."

"Of course," Brad says, his eyes bouncing between Gretchen and me in amusement.

Gretchen's pout gives me more satisfaction than I'd like to admit, and I bask in silent victory as Ethan escorts me to the back.

"What's up with you and Gretchen?" I ask on the way to his office.

He shrugs nonchalantly. "We had a thing once. No big deal."

My good mood falters. *A thing?* What does that mean? A relationship? Were they fuck-buddies? Did they date in high school? I want to ask, but suddenly I'm not sure I want the answer. Maybe he just doesn't do relationships with *me*.

When I enter his office, I can't help but stare at his desk, remembering what it felt like when my naked behind was being pressed into it.

"Don't even think about it, Charlie. We've got two minutes."

"Yeah, well that and you don't do relationships."

I regret the words the second they leave my mouth. They make me sound like a bitter, desperate woman.

I could swear I see a hint of disappointment cross his face before he says, "You couldn't wait until tonight, huh?"

For a second, I forget why I'm here and his question confuses me as I think of him and the pool at the gym.

"Uh, well it's my day off and I had nothing better to do."

"Fair enough." He rounds the desk and pulls a folder from a drawer, handing it to me. "Anthony Pellman's information is in here. Turns out, his residence is just around the corner from where you work. He's probably eaten at Mitchell's before, maybe even with his wife of three years."

I don't miss how he stresses that last part, even as my body wavers between feeling numb and being swarmed with crawling insects at the mention of Tony's name.

"Kids?" I manage to ask through my disgust.

"Nope."

I breathe a sigh of relief.

He looks at his watch and I know that I've already taken up too much of his time.

I take the folder under my arm and head for his office door.

"Are you ever going to tell me why you are contacting these men?" he asks.

I hesitate with my hand on the doorknob. I turn around briefly. "What rule was it?" —I touch the back of my neck in the very same spot he has his CAT tattoo— "Number five? About not playing your cards too soon?"

"It was six actually." He gets up and walks me out. "Five was about being nice to little old ladies."

I stop walking and look up at him. "Seriously? Are you telling me you actually have rules? I thought you were making that shit up as you went along."

"Really?" He raises a brow. "I could have sworn the same thing about you."

CHAPTER FIFTEEN

November 13, 2010

Charlie better not screw this one up for me. She's become more argumentative lately. Being 16 does not suit her. If she runs this one off as she's done with some of the others, it could mean my career. Tony Pellman has connections. He says he's got an in with one of my former producers—the asshole who stopped returning my calls years ago. But the asshole is big time and he could get me back to being big time as well.

Standing in front of Tony Pellman's townhouse, I recall how he was the only one out of the dozen who ever apologized. After he'd had his way with me, he punched a hole in my wall, cursing himself between his sorrowful chanting.

I'll never forget that night. Not just because of what he did to me—which by then was nothing new. And not just because it was Friday the 13th. But because I truly believe it was the night my mother completely lost any shred of humanity she had left. After Tony ran out of the house without ever saying so much as a word to her again, she yelled at me so loudly that the neighbors called the police. But I never told them about Tony. About the others. About the fact that my mother had just hit me in the back of the head with her prized Oscar and blood was still trickling down the base of my skull as they questioned us.

Like everyone else, the police were romanced by the once famous Caroline Anthony. And I was too ashamed to speak up.

That day was my rock bottom. I had my suicide all planned out. She'd never even miss the powder. Or the pills. Or the alcohol. I'd done the research and knew just how much would kill me; and I planned to double it. Chances were, she wouldn't even realize I was dead for days. If it weren't for the Mitchells, I'd never have eaten a decent meal because my own mother would all but ignore me until she needed me to take care of one of *them*.

But I couldn't go without saying goodbye to my best friend. Piper had been sick for weeks, battling the flu or something, so I had barely seen her. When I walked the three miles to her house in the freezing cold and found out what had happened to her, my life changed on a dime and I knew I couldn't leave her. No matter what hell I was going through, hers was worse. It was that day we made a pact to leave the country after high school. To escape from her past and my present. To be there for each other. Cradle to grave we said. Nothing would stand in our way.

Seventeen months we'd have to wait until we had both turned eighteen and could get passports without our parents' permission. And since Piper's birthday was only a month before graduation, we promised each other we'd stick it out and get our diplomas. After all, what was another month of torture after enduring twelve years of it? Maybe my mother would come to her senses by then. Maybe she would overdose. Maybe I could slip her something and make it look like she did.

Yup – rock bottom.

But Piper was more important, so I vowed to remain among the living. And my mother never came to her senses. And I never killed her. But I dreamed about her dying every day after that. It only took six more years for my dream to come true.

I pull the strings of my hoodie tight so my face is pretty much hidden under the ball cap secured underneath it. I have no idea what I'll do if his wife answers. Will I tell her? Will I push her aside and hope that he's home?

Contemplating my options, I realize minutes go by and no one is answering the door. I'm not sure it's relief or frustration I feel. On a whim, I try the knob and my heart pounds into my chest wall when the knob turns and the door opens. I stand staring through the half-open door. Is this fate? Should I go in? I could wait for him. I could trash the place.

People pass on the street in front of the townhouse and I instinctively duck inside the front door and close it. There, I did it. I'm in.

Is it still considered breaking and entering if the door was unlocked?

I go to wipe my prints off the door handle but surmise it doesn't really matter since no one has ever taken my fingerprints before.

I wonder what the P.I. would say about this. Hell, he probably *does* this on a daily basis for all I know.

I look around the foyer and the first thing I see is a wedding photo starring none other than Tony Pellman. My stomach turns seeing him again. He's different. Not as skinny and strung-out looking. He looks healthy. Happy. But the way his bride is looking at him—I doubt she'd ever look at him like that again if she knew what he'd done six years ago.

As I stroll through the lower rooms of the home, I come across a study that boasts a wall lined with awards. 'Best Screenplay' is what's engraved into most of the various plaques. So he's done well for himself. Where's the karma in that?

I search his desk drawers for something to debase his precious awards with. In the bottom drawer, under a pile of file folders, I come across a small handgun. It looks like it's gone untouched for some time based on the amount of crap on top of it.

I pick it up and turn it over in my hand, studying it while musing over my choices. I've never held a gun before. It's heavier than it looks. I have no idea if it's even loaded. Without much thought, I raise it up and aim it at one of the plaques—a shiny platinum one. I put my finger on the trigger and dare myself to squeeze it. And damn it if I don't hear Piper Mitchell in my head telling me it'll make too much noise—draw unwanted attention. I push her out of my head. I don't want a voice of reason. I want to be unreasonable.

But my best friend is right, so I tuck the gun into the pocket of my hoodie and instead, I take the plaque off the wall and raise it above my head, intending to smash it on the hardwood floor, shattering it into tiny little shards that I'd like to use to stab the man in his tiny little heart.

Then something on the wall behind his desk catches my attention. In the most prominent spot on the wall, highlighted by a spotlight that sets it apart from everything else, is a large frame that holds about a dozen key tags of various colors. In the center of the key tags is a certificate. I step forward and read it.

Anthony Pellman
5 years clean and sober
Nov. 15th, 2015

That date. *Oh, God.* It's exactly five years and two days after he molested me.

I hear a noise and my heart rises into my throat. Female laughter echoes down the hallway as footsteps bound through the front door.

The laughter stops. "Baby, you really shouldn't leave the door unlocked," the woman says.

"We were just next door for five minutes," says a hauntingly familiar voice.

"Tony," she pouts.

"Okay," he says. "You're right. I'm really sorry."

Tiny hairs on my neck rise as that voice and those words take me back to my bedroom in Maple Creek. *I'm really sorry*, he said over and over, even before he was done with me. It was like his body and his brain were somehow disconnected.

"Thanks, baby," the woman says. "I love you more than the moon."

"And more than all the stars in the sky," he replies.

Their footsteps come closer.

What should I do? Different scenarios hastily shuffle through my head when I see a second door at the rear of the study. I step through it, away from their footsteps and into a kitchen. I spot a door to the outside and hope I can make it there before they discover me.

My sweaty hands slip on the handle of the sliding door, but I get it opened enough for me to sneak through unnoticed and I quietly close it behind me.

Shit. I'm on a balcony with no steps to the yard below.

I try to calculate the distance to the ground. Five feet? Ten? It doesn't look all that far, but then again, it might not matter either way. It's broad daylight and they could be in the kitchen by now, meaning I could be two seconds away from being thrown in jail.

I swing my legs over the wooden railing and jump.

Ouch! Son of a bitch, I scream in my head when my leg twists in a direction it shouldn't be twisting when it meets the hard, frozen grass.

I look back up at the deck. Ten—definitely ten feet.

I find a gate that leads to the alley behind the row of homes and limp through it. I remove the ball cap and lower my hood, trying to blend in with the mid-day pedestrians and not stick out like a thug on the prowl.

I stop walking when it occurs to me I have no idea what I did with the award I was holding when they came home. Did I put it back on the wall? Did I put it on the desk? Leave it on the kitchen countertop maybe?

Oh, my God. The desk. I pat my hoodie pocket, feeling the hard outline of the handgun I've now stolen from a man who once raped me.

CHAPTER SIXTEEN

Giving my sore ankle a rest, I let my arms do most of the work in the water tonight. I arrived at the gym earlier than usual, needing extra time to work out my frustration.

I wish I would have had a shift at the restaurant today. Maybe then I wouldn't have sat in my apartment brooding over what was and what could have been.

When I got home, I put the gun on my coffee table and stared at the cold hard metal for what seemed like hours. I had a deadly weapon in my pocket. One I forgot was there when the door opened and the voices startled me. Had I remembered it was in my possession, would I have used it? *Could* I have used it?

Maybe I should just leave town. Forget about this obsession with revenge. Throw away the diary and bury my past with my mother.

It would be easy enough to do now that the executor papers have come through. I could just put the apartment up for sale and live off credit cards until the insurance money and inheritance get sorted out.

Making my lap turn, I catch a glimpse of Ethan walking towards the pool. And all at once, my head, my heart and my body bombard me with reasons to stay. Reasons like his strong arms pressing me into the side of the pool. And his tongue, so soft yet demanding when it explores my mouth. And his fingers—holy hell what they can do to me with just the slightest touch.

But he doesn't do relationships.

I could just become my old self. The one who couldn't give a shit about things like hearts and flowers and stomach butterflies and voices that curl my toes. The one who could fuck for the simple sake of fucking. The one who could keep feeling out of it as I trained myself to do from such an early age.

I could be that person again. *Couldn't I?*

I think of something Jan Mitchell told me and Piper when we were young. She said you can't help who you fall in love with. That your heart makes decisions your head may not agree with, and sometimes you need to be smart enough to figure out which of them is right.

I spy three pairs of legs at my turnaround and look up to see Mason, Griffin and Gavin staring down at me.

For a split second, I fear they are here to kick me out unless I start paying to use the gym. Then I think better of it. After all, these are the guys who furnished my apartment when I had nothing. The guys who over the past month have accepted me as a third-wheel, a party crasher, and a meal poacher. The guys who would do anything for the women they love.

My eyes move from them over to Ethan, watching him as he swims through the water with the flawless form of an Olympic freestyle swimmer. And for the very first time, I'm jealous of the relationships my adoptive sisters have with these men. For a moment, I wonder why Ethan can't be more like them. Why can't *he* be the one who flies across an ocean for me? Who sings a song to me in front of friends and family? Who picks up his life and moves three thousand miles away from everything he knows just to be with me?

I quiet the voices in my head that want everything they can't have. I tell myself stuff like that doesn't happen to girls like me. I paste on a smile and pretend it doesn't hurt to look up at them.

"What's up guys?" I ask, holding onto the ledge by their feet.

"Who's your friend?" Mason asks, raising his chin in Ethan's direction.

I stare at him, wondering what this is all about. Then I think maybe one of the girls said something after our margarita night. "You're the owners," I say defensively. "Shouldn't you know him already?"

The three of them give each other a look. It's the same look I see on Baylor and Skylar's faces when they big-sister me.

"Everything okay over here?" A wave of water laps at my back as Ethan's protective words penetrate my ears.

He swims up next to me, eyeing the three men towering over us.

"You're a private investigator, right?" Griffin asks him.

"That's right," he replies, holding out his hand in greeting. "Ethan Stone."

"Griffin Pearce." He leans down to shake Ethan's wet hand. "And this is Gavin McBride and Mason Lawrence. We're the owners of this establishment."

Ethan shakes hands with the other two. "We met before," he says to Gavin. "When I used to run on the track before my knees went bad. I didn't know you were an owner."

"I remember." Gavin nods. "And I wasn't an owner then."

"Oh, well nice to meet you again," Ethan says. "Is there something we can do for you?"

The three men standing share that big-brother look again. Then they look down at me. And then at Ethan.

"As a P.I. surely you are aware we have cameras around the gym," Griffin says, motioning to a black opaque dome in the ceiling in a corner of the pool room.

There is a moment of calm, quiet contemplation before Ethan and I fully comprehend what Griffin is telling us.

I quickly run through that night in my head, surmising they wouldn't have seen more than the back of my head and maybe Ethan's elated face when he came all over the water between us.

I smile at the thought of being caught. And then I remember one of Ethan's silly rules about PDA. I turn to him. "There goes number seven."

He raises his brows at me, questioning me with his eyes.

"Rule number seven, right?"

He looks surprised.

I tap a finger to my temple. "Not as dumb as you thought, huh?"

He looks annoyed with me. "I never said you were dumb. Besides," —he touches my red hair, that when wet, extends to my lower back— "you don't exactly fit the bill."

"Are you saying only *blondes* are dumb?"

Well, he did sort of walk right into that one.

"Uh, no. Well, except for Gretchen. She's dumb," he jokes and I laugh with him.

Someone clears their throat and Ethan and I look up, having all but forgotten we had company.

"Yeah, about that," Ethan says, nodding at the camera. "Any chance you can conveniently lose that footage?"

I elbow him. "Or at least give it to *us*," I tease them with a wink.

I look at the stern expression on their faces and give them my best pouty face. "Oh, come on. That was funny."

Ethan climbs out of the pool and stands next to them. I get it. As a guy, he more than likely felt small down here with them towering over us. But damn . . . the amount of testosterone I see before me is astounding. The collective strength of these four men standing here could power a small town.

It's now when I realize just how big Ethan really is. I mean, Mason is a professional football player. The man literally works out for a living. But Ethan is just about as tall and almost as broad as he is. And although I've yet to see Mason without a shirt on, I'd bet this week's tips that Ethan's fine physique could give him a run for his money.

"We could probably lose the footage," Gavin says to Ethan. "How about you join us for poker night and we'll let you take care of it yourself. We play every Monday night in the gym office."

"You want me to join your *poker game?*" Ethan asks, like they just invited him to become a part of some super-secret man club.

"Charlie is like a sister to Piper, Skylar and Baylor," Mason explains to him. "That makes her our sister-in-law. And we protect our family. Anyone in a relationship with her needs to understand that. Well, that and we just lost our fourth player."

Ethan takes a step back as if Mason's words had physically pushed him off balance. "We're not in a relationship," he says, his eyes flitting over to me for a brief second. "But I'll be happy to take your money at poker."

I berate myself when I realize my heart just sank upon hearing that declaration. Again. *This is nothing new, Charlie.*

I shake it off and put my big-girl panties on. "I'll just leave you boys to it then." I swim to the other side of the pool and climb out to get my towel.

Faster than I can dry off, Ethan is in front of me again. "Is your leg injured?"

I look down at my slightly swollen ankle and then back up at his concerned eyes. I didn't think any of them were watching me get out of the pool with their looming poker game and all.

"It's no big deal. I went for a run earlier and twisted it." I shrug. "I guess I should just stick to swimming."

"You coming?" Griffin shouts from across the pool.

Ethan holds up his hand with outstretched fingers, never breaking eye contact with me. "Give me five to shower and change," he yells back.

"You were limping, Charlie. Maybe you should see a doctor."

"I'm fine. I'll go home and ice it. It's no big deal. Really."

He holds my stare. He's searching for the truth behind my eyes. I can see the questions. *Did I really injure it running? Is it really fine?* But I'm very good at hiding the truth. Just ask Jan Mitchell. Or the ten police officers who came to my childhood home over the years. Or any man who ever asked if it was *'good for me, too.'*

I walk towards the locker room, trying my best not to limp even though it hurts like hell. "Go," I tell him. "Have fun at poker night."

"I'll try," he says behind me, walking away.

I spin around and follow him. I should tell him he doesn't have to play along with their little game of luring him to poker night. He doesn't have to make nice with them. After all, like he said, we're not in a relationship.

But before I reach him, he runs a hand down the back of his head, grabbing his neck as he mumbles, "But it won't be the same as being with you."

I freeze. And he enters the men's locker room without realizing what I just heard.

Yeah, like I said—messing with my head.

CHAPTER SEVENTEEN

I was dying to hear how poker night went, but when I asked the guys, all I got out of them was that they invited him back because they liked taking his money. And apparently poker night is akin to fight club, because none of the girls could extract information either.

And my only contact with Ethan this week was the texts he sent me telling me he'd been called out of town on a case and wouldn't be back until Friday, so would I mind keeping Mrs. B company at the pool. He also asked about my ankle.

Now, I know I'm not an expert on relationships, but him texting me twice about personal stuff—does that not constitute one? Maybe he's just considerate that way and would have texted anyone who he swims with on a regular basis.

I wonder if he would text Gretchen to ask about *her* swollen ankle.

By the time Friday rolls around, I find myself missing him way more than I'd like to admit.

I've tried to become more attentive to other men. I've flirted with them. Engaged in witty banter. I even went so far as to give one of them my telephone number. But when he called me, all I felt was disappointment that it wasn't a certain private investigator.

"Charlie, someone is asking for you at table eight," Mindy tells me at the drink station.

"Thanks," I say, whirling around, happy to have a distraction from my thoughts. That is until I see who the occupant of table eight is.

Every bad thing I ever thought about this man comes rushing back in one large wave that almost knocks me on my ass. I spin around and duck into the kitchen, sinking against the wall as I hunch over and support myself with my hands on my knees. I try to keep myself from hyperventilating. I take deep, deliberate breaths as flashbacks from the past play out in my mind.

"Charlie, what's wrong?" Skylar asks, running over to me. "Are you okay?"

I can't yet speak so I shake my head from side to side.

She rubs my back in long, soothing strokes until my breathing settles enough for me to get out a few words. "Dad. Table eight."

She gasps. She knows good and well how wrecked I was when my father left me at the age of twelve. I think she was the one who even offered to share *her* father with me. It was then that I started spending more and more time with the Mitchells. My dad—who was the only parent who loved me, cared for me, and made sure I was fed and clothed—completely abandoned me without a word. Without so much as a goodbye.

Skylar walks over to the doorway and peeks around it into the dining room and then comes back to rest against the wall next to me. "I can call the police and have him escorted out. We could say he was harassing you."

I shake my head. "I don't want to cause a scene, Skylar."

She looks around the kitchen thoughtfully. "Okay, we'll simply shut down the restaurant. Claim a kitchen fire or something—anything to get everyone out of here quickly."

I look over at her, amazed she would even consider such a thing. Closing the restaurant. Losing thousands of dollars in revenue just so I don't have to face my father. And she didn't even hesitate. She is more family to me than the man sitting at table eight with whom I share DNA.

"No," I tell her. "I won't have you do that for me. Plus, he'll only come back some other time."

"So what are you going to do? Do you want to slip out the back? Hide in the kitchen? Whatever you want to do is fine. I'll cover your tables for the rest of your shift."

I stand up straight, wipe my sweaty palms on my apron, and gather all the strength I can muster. "I'm going out there. I won't cause a scene, I promise. I'll just hear him out and let him be on his way."

"Oh, Charlie, are you sure you want to do that?" She looks at me with the sympathetic eyes of a woman who never knew anything but a kind, loving father who would do anything to protect his daughter.

"No, I'm not sure. But I think it might be the only way to make him disappear."

Before I can talk myself out of it, I walk out into the dining room with purpose. He notices me right away. Our eyes meet. His are full of emotion. Mine are full of rage. I don't look away. I don't want him to see me back down. I want him to know I don't need him. I don't need a father who put himself before his own child. Who pretended to love a daughter and then destroyed her with his selfishness. Who left me at the most vulnerable time in my life.

Who I wish was dead and buried alongside my mother.

I scoot into his booth, sitting on the bench across from him.

He lets out a sigh, like he was holding his breath while waiting to see if I would come over. "Charlie," he says.

I have to keep my eyes from closing and remembering the voice of the protector he once was. From remembering how, when my mother would become mad at me, he would intervene and get her to walk away, thwarting what I feared would be another slap across the face. Or painful tug of my hair. Or deliberate push into a doorway.

But then I remind myself of what happened after he left. That's when the beatings really started. I don't know if she blamed me for his leaving or if she felt like without him around, she could get away with more. Whatever the reason, it's his fault. It's always been his fault. None of it would have happened if it weren't for him.

I take in his appearance. He's ten years older than when I last saw him. That would make him fifty. The sprinkling of gray hair along with the lines on his forehead and around his eyes speak to his age. But there is something else. Something behind his eyes that ages him even more. A tiredness that doesn't come from age alone.

I raise my brows at him, and without speaking, I question why he's here. With my eyes, I let him know I've no intention of talking. Only listening. I fear if I open my mouth, two things might happen. One: I won't be able to control my fury and I'll scream and yell and lash out at him in every way possible, causing a scene that would only hurt the people who truly love me, the Mitchells. Or two: I'll cry.

"Okay, you don't want to talk to me," he says. "I get it. I get that you hate me. I hate me, too. And I'm not here to try and change that." He rubs a hand over his jaw. "Well, maybe I am, but I know it may not be possible, certainly not after I stayed away so long. But I hope since you've come this far, you'll stay for a few minutes and hear me out. You don't have to say a word. Just listen. I know you don't owe me anything. But please, just give me a few minutes to try and explain."

Skylar comes over and places two glasses of water on the table. We make eye contact long enough for her to make sure I'm okay. I nod at her, assuring her I am.

I take a drink of water, wetting my bone-dry mouth. Then I look at my father, giving him permission to begin.

"I want you to know that everything I tell you today is not meant to take away from the hell you went through after I left. What I'm about to tell you pales in comparison to what became your life. But I hope it will at least provide you with an explanation. It may not be a good one. I failed. I failed as a husband. I failed as a father. I failed to do the right thing. I failed because of fear. I was a coward. And nothing I can do or say now can change that. But I'm going to tell you anyway."

I wring my hands under the table. And despite the cold March weather, I feel beads of sweat emerging on my forehead. But I keep my face stoic. I refuse to show him any emotion. There is nothing he could say that would make him deserving of my pity. I'll never feel anything but abhorrence for this man. I train my eyes on the table, refusing to even look at him while he talks.

"I don't expect you to believe me," he says. "But I truly had no idea your mother was hurting you in any way. I didn't know about any of it until recently. I just assumed you hated me because I left the two of you. And I let you hate me because I knew I deserved it. I knew I failed you as a father."

Anger climbs my backbone and I know I'm about to break my own rule about not speaking, but I can't help it. And it takes every ounce of self-control not to yell at him. "Liar!" I spit at him in a loud whisper. "I know you knew what she was doing. I heard you fighting about it before you left. I heard you specifically talk about how the hitting had to stop."

He nods. "I don't doubt what you heard, Charlie. We did argue a lot, but we argued about what she was doing to *me*, not you."

"What?" I ask disbelievingly.

"I don't know if you remember the day she cut off your hair when you were six," he says, nervously running a finger up and down the side of his drink. "But that was the day my life changed forever."

Spiteful words spill from my mouth. "*Your life?* You weren't even there that day."

He nods. "You're right. I wasn't there when she did it. But when I came home that night and saw what she'd done—that she'd cut off the hair I knew you loved to your very soul—we had a fight. I told her she had no right to do it. That she had to get over whatever she was feeling about getting older and not working. I had felt for some time that she blamed you for her lack of work. That somehow she thought it was *your* fault she was aging out of the roles she once coveted."

He sighs and looks around at the neighboring tables. Then with a weak voice, he looks directly at me and says, "I said those very words to her. I said them to her and then she hit me."

My eyes betray me as they look up to catch his.

He nods, his gaze falling to the table, as if embarrassed by what he just revealed to me.

"What?" I ask, again, not quite understanding what I think he is trying to tell me.

I think back to when I was younger and it dawns on me. I'm sure every girl thinks their daddy is a big strong man. I was no different. I mean after all, he would pick me up and twirl me around. He would carry me to bed when I would fall asleep in the car. He would scream and shout at the television when his team wasn't winning the game. To me, he was this larger-than-life alpha male. My protector. My dad.

But in reality, he couldn't have been more than a hundred and forty pounds soaking wet. He was tall, but impossibly thin.

"I was thirty-four years old when your mother started abusing me, Charlie." He clears his throat and takes a drink. "It started out as a slap here and a push there. But she was a woman and I wasn't going to fight back. She was frustrated about her job. She was under a tremendous amount of pressure to be this perfect person to everybody outside of her family. And I was blinded by her beauty. Her power. Her celebrity.

"She controlled everything about our lives. Our finances. My career. You." He shakes his head in shame. "I felt inferior to her in every way. And when the slaps turned into punches, that just made me feel even weaker. At first I wouldn't fight back. But then it got to the point where I couldn't fight back. I was ashamed. I was a man and should be able to stand up for myself. But I didn't."

My heart is pounding into my chest wall. I try not to show any emotion. Despite what he went through, he should have never left me there. With her. How could he not know?

"I had no idea, Charlie. No idea about any of it. I watched her closely with you. I never saw any aggression towards you. She was frustrated with you, yes, but what mother isn't frustrated with a rambunctious child?"

It's hard for me to feel bad for this man. He doesn't even know the half of it. I'm sure he thinks she just slapped me around a bit. Maybe I should enlighten him. "She hit me that day, too," I say. "The day she cut my hair—she slapped me. She slapped me and told me she didn't love me anymore and that you wouldn't love me either if I wasn't a good girl. After that, she didn't touch me much. A few slaps here and there. Until you left, that is. I guess when you left she lost her punching bag, so I became it."

I roll up my sleeves and display my forearms across the table. Anyone who looks closely at my scars can clearly see they are burns. And he knows my mom smoked like a fucking chimney.

"Oh, God," he says.

This is when it happens. This is when the tears start to fall. His—not mine.

"I'm so sorry." He reaches out to touch me, but I pull away before his hand can grab mine. "I'm so sorry," he repeats. "There is no doubt in my mind that leaving was the right thing to do. But I should have taken you with me, Charlie. I should have fought for you. I was weak. I had no idea she would hurt you. I had no idea what she was truly capable of. How can I ask you to forgive me when I will never be able to forgive myself?"

I take in a shaky breath. "No. You have no idea what I went through. You'll never have any idea of how your leaving ruined me."

I contemplate telling him. I contemplate telling him I could have lived with the abuse. The slaps, the punches, the burns. I could have even lived with the blows to the head from her precious awards. But what I can't live with is the fact that there are twelve names on the list I gave to Ethan. Twelve men who have seen me naked. Twelve men who have all done something to me against my will. Twelve men whose names, whose faces, whose vulgar touch will haunt me until the day I die.

Instead, I slide out of the booth to leave, but he grabs my arm. "Wait," he begs. He reaches into his pocket with his other hand and slides a business card across the table. "Take it. In case you ever . . ." He sighs. "Just take it."

I look at the card as if it could burn me. He knows I won't take it. He picks it up and reaches across the table to tuck it in one of the pockets of my apron.

"I've never been able to watch a football game without thinking of you," he says. "Without missing you so badly my heart hurts. Without regretting every decision I've ever made."

Then he lets me go.

And just like that, I walk away from the man who was once my whole world.

CHAPTER EIGHTEEN

I feel like I just ran a marathon. But I only walked to the rear hallway near Skylar's office. I slide down the wall until my butt hits the floor. Then I put my head between my knees and breathe.

"Sweetie, are you okay?" Skylar asks, having followed me back.

I nod even though I'm not.

She touches my shoulder. "Use my office. Go home if you like. Do whatever you need to do. I've got you covered."

I look up at her and give her a sad smile. "Thanks. I just need a few minutes. I'm not going home. The last thing I need to do is sit on my ass and think about what just happened out there. If I could just chill in your office for a few minutes, that would be great."

"Minutes, hours, however long it takes, Charlie." She hands me the key. "Let me know if you need anything."

She goes back out front to cover my tables.

As I enter her office, I look at the walls that are lined with family pictures. It reminds me of the wall in Ethan's reception area. It's such a novel thing to me—family photos. Maybe because I've never had one. As far back as I can remember, I can't think of one time we had a family photo taken when I was younger. Not. One. Time.

Who does that? What kind of mother doesn't hang pictures of her family on her walls? The only pictures I remember are pictures of *her*. *Her* winning awards. *Her* on a poster of movie promo. *Her* posing with other celebrities on the red carpet.

There is a knock on the door and then Jarod walks through, carrying a shot glass. I wasn't aware he'd started his shift yet. He puts the drink down in front of me. "Skylar said to give you this. She never condones drinking on the job, so you must really need it." He walks into the hallway and then turns around. "This doesn't have anything to do with my cousin, does it?"

My eyes snap to his. "Why would you say that, Jarod?"

"I don't know." He shrugs. "It's just that he's been in a really bad mood lately and now you're back here looking like this."

"Lately?" I ask.

"Yeah, like since he met you."

Oh? "I wasn't aware you two were close. I thought you said he was a pain in the ass."

"He *is* a pain in the ass. But he's my cousin and I still hang out with him. What's up with you two anyway?"

"Apparently, nothing," I say.

"Maybe that's why he's in a shitty mood."

I shake my head. "All the nothingness—it's *his* choice."

He nods his head like he understands. Then he gives me a sympathetic look. Before he walks away, he says, "Cut him a break, okay? He's been through some shit."

Some shit? I wonder if it has anything to do with the cryptic Chinese tattoo on his chest, or the CAT one on his neck. Or maybe it has something to do with Gretchen. But I'm too proud to ask. Or too scared. "Haven't we all?" I say. Then I raise my glass to him and throw back the brown liquid that burns my throat. "Thanks, Jarod."

I close my eyes and let the warm feeling of the alcohol wash over me. And before I know it, I'm fishing the business card out of my pocket. For a second I fear he's only given it to me in hopes I have contacts that could help him with his career as a screenwriter. But when I examine the card, I see he's not a screenwriter at all. I blink my eyes and re-read the card.

George Tate
Author of children's books

He writes children's books?

The card lists contact information with a website and email. I turn the card over to see he has hand-written his cell phone number on the back.

My curiosity gets the better of me and I lean over to use Skylar's laptop.

I've never once in ten years looked up anything about my father. I never wanted to know the first thing about him. I especially never wanted to know if he'd hit it big in show business.

My fingers shake as I open Google and type in his name. I'm directed to an Amazon page that lists all of his books. I count. There are nine of them. Upon further inspection, I see they are all short books illustrated by many pictures. The details in his bio say he writes the stories for young school-aged children to raise awareness of sensitive topics such as bullying, peer pressure and even abuse. The last line of his bio makes me pause.

George Tate writes these books in an effort to help the children of others, as he was never able to do with his own child.

It makes it sound like I'm dead.

I close the laptop, unwilling to read anything more about him. I don't want to know if, after he left me to the fucking wolves, he acquired redeeming qualities. He could be the king of fucking England for all I care. Nothing he has done or will ever do can make up for the fact that he left me. Abandoned me. Ruined me.

But all this time I thought he left because of me. Of course, now I realize my mother wanted me to think that. Hell, she started brainwashing me even before he left. Every time I misbehaved she would tell me he wouldn't love me. Every time she did something she didn't want him to know about, she threatened me that he might leave if he found out. So I never told him. I never told him about the drugs and the drinking and the men she would entertain when he wasn't home. I think maybe all along, deep down she knew he would leave so she set me up to take the fall for it.

She was jealous of our Football Saturdays. My dad was a big fan of college football and he raised me to love the game, too. The two of us even went on a road trip every year when his favorite team, the Miami Hurricanes, was playing within driving distance. Those were the only good memories of my childhood. Those trips were a thousand times better than meeting movie stars, going to premiers, or having lunch with big-named producers—all my mother's idea of showing me a good time.

Two months before he left, she ruined football for me, too. One Saturday when my dad and I were loading up the car to head four hours away to Pennsylvania to watch the Miami Hurricanes play Penn State, she stopped us at the last minute, telling my dad she was able to set up a meeting with a prestigious production company who wanted to look at one of his screenplays. But they would only see him *that* afternoon. We cancelled the trip, of course, and my dad waited three hours at a restaurant. He came home steaming mad. This was one of the fights I heard. He said he knew she was lying because he called the company and they had no record of anyone ever setting up a meeting. My mother made up excuses, telling him that his screenplays were shit and they must have decided at the last minute not to take the meeting. Producers do that all the time, she said. It's just the nature of the business. When he accused her of setting up the whole charade to keep us from our road trip, she laughed it off, telling him he was silly to even want to take a twelve-year-old girl to a football game. That others would think he's a dirty old man. I remember hearing a crash and running to my room.

The next day, my mother was complaining about how my dad broke one of her vases. My dad was complaining about how he hit his head on the bedpost in the middle of the night. I was too naïve to put two and two together. After all, women don't hit men. They only hit children, right?

And even though I work the rest of my shift, if only as a distraction, it doesn't stop me from thinking about a man who was once beaten by his own wife. A man who was once so ruined himself that he felt he had no choice but to leave his only child.

I hate him. But I hate *her* more. She broke him before she broke me. She's lucky she's already dead. Because if she weren't, I would fucking kill her.

At six o'clock, Skylar insists things are slow and that I should go home early. I don't fight her. Today has been emotionally draining and all I want to do is go for a swim and then pick up a bottle of tequila.

But as I exit the front door of Mitchell's, two things catch my eye.

A stretch limo.

And the gorgeous man standing beside it wearing jeans and a White Poison t-shirt.

CHAPTER NINETEEN

Stunned to see Ethan standing outside Mitchell's, and even more surprised to see him wearing something other than his regular attire, I fail to see what he's holding in his hands.

He waves something at me and I come closer to take a look.

Concert tickets to White Poison. I look up to question him.

"Rule number nine," he says, smiling down at me. "A promise is a promise."

I take them from him and examine them. I gasp. "Second row?"

"Yeah. We'll not only get to *feel* their sweat, we'll get to *taste* it."

He never misses a thing, does he? I remember the customer who hit on me saying something about being close enough to feel their sweat. But that was weeks ago, long after the tickets had sold out. "But they sold out in minutes. How?"

He shrugs. "I know a guy who knows a guy."

"And you just assumed I'd go?" I wave a hand at the limo. "And what's with all the pomp and circumstance?" I narrow my eyes at him. "And how did you know I wouldn't be working?"

I whip my head around to see Skylar standing in the doorway of Mitchell's. She winks and waves at me before turning around, disappearing back into the restaurant.

"A conspiracy?" I ask him.

"Something like that," he says. "After all, I'm practically part of the family now that I'm in on poker night."

I roll my eyes. Then I look at his shirt again. And then down at my uniform. "But I'm not dressed properly. I'll need to go home and change first."

"There's no time," he says, opening the door to the limo. "We've got it covered. Don't worry about a thing."

We? I eye the inside of the dark limo speculatively.

"Oh, come on, Tate. Where's your sense of adventure?"

I've never been one to back away from a challenge, so I give him a cheeky sneer and then duck into the limo. Inside, I slide along the long black seat, making room for him to scoot in beside me. I've never been in a limousine before. My mother never let me ride with her to premiers. It smells like leather and scotch and high-end perfume. If rich had a smell, this would be it.

When my eyes acclimate to the dark interior, I realize we're not alone. "Oh, hello," I say to the two people sitting along the seat that is perpendicular to this one. My eyes snap to Ethan in question.

"Charlie Tate, this is my brother, Chad Stone and his friend, Nicole."

"Nikki," she reaches over Ethan's brother to shake my hand. "Wow, you have soft hands for someone who does manual labor."

Manual labor? "Uh . . . thanks?" I say, still trying to figure out what is happening here.

I look at his brother, Chad. He's so darn familiar, I ask, "Have we met?"

He laughs and looks at Ethan.

"She's been out of the country for several years," Ethan says, as if that explains their amusement.

My eyes dart to Ethan's. "How did you know that? I never told you that."

"Poker," he says. "It's amazing the kind of information you can learn from a bunch of drunk guys at poker night."

My spine stiffens and a sick feeling worms through me. I don't know about Griffin and Gavin, but I do know that Piper shared my secrets with Mason when she was trying to hide her own. What if he told Ethan? *Oh, God.* I look at him and try to see if there is any hint of disgust over what he would feel if he knew.

"Relax," Ethan says, putting a hand on my thigh. "They just told me how you and Piper traveled overseas after high school. It actually sounds amazing. I'd like to hear about it sometime."

"Oh." I can't help the sigh of relief that comes after.

Chad holds his hand out to me. "It's actually quite refreshing to meet someone who doesn't know everything about me."

I shake his hand. "Why should I know everything about you?" I look between the three of them.

"Maybe it's the name you don't recognize," Nikki says, hanging all over Chad like a cheap suit. "Does Thad Stone ring a bell?"

"*Thad* Stone?" I ask. I turn to Chad, studying him. "*You're* Thad Stone?" Things start to make sense and my heart races. But not for the reason most women's hearts race when they meet him. My heart races because I hate actors. I hate everything about them. The way they think they own the fucking world and everyone in it. The way they look down on other people. The way they feel they are completely above the law.

He laughs. "Yes. But by the way you're looking at me right now, I'm not sure I want to be." He winces. "We didn't, uh . . . hook up or anything a few years back, did we? I'm pretty sure no matter how effed up I was I'd have remembered you."

My jaw drops and my eyes focus on Nikki, who doesn't seem to be the least bit affected by this conversation as she sips her glass of champagne.

"What the fuck?" I ask him, turning to Ethan because I'm completely confused.

"My little brother didn't handle his sudden stardom as well as we had hoped," he explains. "Chad went a little wild those first few years. I'm not afraid to say he scared the shit out of us with his reckless ways. But he's good now. Got it out of his system."

I eye his brother skeptically. No wonder he looked so familiar. I get it now, and it *was* the name that tripped me up. Thad Stone was the star of one of those high school drama series with a zip code or an area code or some stupid code. I never watched it, but even overseas, it was hard not to hear about all the hype surrounding the hottest new show to hit prime time television. It was cancelled a few years later and since then, I guess he's starred in a few movies. He's no Brad Pitt or Zac Efron, but he's certainly on the radar.

"There's always a price to pay when you become famous," I tell him. "I guess that was yours."

He and Ethan share a look and then Chad's eyes fall to the ground. "No, that wasn't mine." He quickly recovers and hands me a glass of bubbly. "But hey, let's not talk about shit in the past we can't change. Let's enjoy tonight. To new friends." He holds up his drink in a toast.

"To new friends," the rest of us say in harmony.

"You know, I'm familiar with you, too," Chad says. "A little more familiar than my brother here would want me to be."

"What the hell are you talking about?" Ethan shoots him a venomous stare.

"Oh, come on," he says. "You know—her *MM* centerfold."

Ethan slowly turns his head until our eyes meet. "You were an *MM* centerfold?"

I shrug and take a sip of expensive champagne. "Had to pay the bills," I say.

He chugs his drink and holds it out for more. Chad laughs and then tries to fill Ethan's glass without spilling now that we're winding through the streets of the city.

"I met your mom once," Chad says.

I was wondering if he would make the connection. All those Hollywood types seem to know one another.

"Splendid," I say, sarcastically.

"She was a grade-A bitch," he says, and I about snort my drink out my nose.

"Chad!" Ethan reprimands him. "Jesus, have a little compassion. The woman died not too long ago."

Chad's eyes go wide with regret. "Shit," he says to me. "I forgot all about that. I'm really sorry."

I try not to smile. He has no idea my initial impression of him just got a whole lot better.

"Thad, what's in the bag?" Nikki asks, eyeing it hopefully.

Nikki must not be a long-time friend of his. Either that, or he wants people to call him by his stage name.

"That's for Charlie," he says, handing it to me. "Ethan said there wouldn't be time for you to change so I picked up this shirt and had the guys sign it. It's probably way too big for you, but I didn't want to assume anything."

I smile. I'm actually impressed he didn't expect me to be a stick figure. More points for that. "The guys?" I ask, pulling a White Poison shirt out of the bag. Upon inspection, it has five signatures on the back. I don't recognize all of them, but you'd have to be dead not to recognize the name Adam Stuart, the lead singer. "You know them?" I ask, then roll my eyes at myself for sounding too fangirl. "Of course you do."

I unbutton my work shirt and take it off, revealing a skin-tight tank top underneath. I pull the t-shirt over my head, ignoring the stares I'm getting from everyone in the car. Then I expertly remove my tank top from underneath the oversized shirt without so much as a flash of my black lacy bra.

Chad raises his glass. "I like your date, bro. She's got spunk."

"This isn't a date," I tell him, gathering the extra material of the shirt and using my hair band to tie it off behind me, showing a small sliver of skin between the shirt and my pants. It'll have to do. "More like an obligation."

Ethan leans over and rubs my shoulder with his. "I prefer 'promise'."

"Whatever," I say.

"Oh my God, I loooooove your hair," Nikki declares, now that it's free from the bun I had it in. "Men must drool all over you with that gorgeous red color. Is it real?"

"It's real," Ethan says, sharing a fist bump with his brother that I wasn't meant to see.

"Toddler," I say.

"How much longer, Thad?" Nikki asks. "I have to pee."

"Just a few more minutes, Nik."

I look between them, wondering what the dynamic is there, but not daring to ask. For all I know, she could just be his arm candy for the night.

"So, should I call you Chad or Thad?" I ask him. "And would you mind if I ask why you made the change?"

"Chad is fine, Charlie. And my agent suggested I change my name. Back when I was starting out, there was already an actor by the name of Chad Stoner. My agent thought my name was too similar. I didn't really want to make the change, but he was pretty adamant. So I used the name Thad. It was actually what a childhood friend of mine called me because she" —he pinches the bridge of his nose— "well, it's a long story."

Ethan pats Chad on the shoulder sympathetically as they share a moment between brothers. *She?* I want to ask, but don't.

The limo comes to a stop and the door is opened from the outside. We pile out into a back alley that, in darkness, would scare the living shit out of me, but by the remaining few minutes of sunlight, appears to be a private entrance into the concert hall.

"Right this way, Mr. Stone," says a man with SECURITY written on his back.

We are ushered into a back door and through a maze of hallways and massive storage areas. The security guard hands us each a lanyard. "Make sure you have these on at all times. The band is right through those doors," the large man says. "Enjoy your evening."

"The band?" I ask Ethan with wide eyes.

He takes my lanyard from me and puts it over my head, carefully pulling my hair out from under it. He's so close I can smell him. I inhale his scent and it does things to my body that I'm glad no one else can see in the darkened hallway.

He holds the laminated card up in front of my face so I can just make out the bold white letters. "All access?" I ask, looking up at him. "Does that mean what I think it means?"

He laughs. "Come on, let's go meet the band." He pulls me by the hand through double doors into a huge lounge area with couches, chairs, a pool table, even a bar with attendants.

There are a lot of people in here. Dozens at least. Maybe more. It's not hard to spot the band. Although I've never seen them, it's obvious who they are based on the number of half-naked female bodies draped on and around them. To be fair, the girls do have clothes on, it's just that most of their skimpy tops seem to be suffering from wardrobe malfunctions at the moment. And from what I can tell, the bigger your boobs, the closer you get to the band.

I look down at my ample, yet clearly lacking chest, thinking I wouldn't get within ten feet of them even if I wanted to. Which I don't. I haven't met any famous musical groups before, but I'm sure they suffer from the same affliction as actors—self-absorption.

"Thad!" yells one of the men sandwiched in tits. "Hey mate, glad you could make it." He stands up, sending two girls tumbling off his lap without so much as an apology.

I'm a bit stunned by his British accent. Funny how when singing, most foreigners sound American.

He walks over and gives Chad a man-hug. Then he looks at me and Nikki. "And who are these lovely ladies you've brought with you?"

"This is Nikki and Charlie," Chad says. "Girls, this is Adam Stuart."

Nikki practically topples me over to get to him. Tugging her revealing shirt even lower before she shakes his hand, she says, "Oh, my God, you're Australian? But you sing American."

Chad and Adam share an incredulous look over the top of Nikki's head. "British, not Australian," Adam says. "And it took years of practice to learn your language." He winks at me and I roll my eyes.

Ethan leans into me and whispers, "Can I use the blonde joke now?"

I laugh.

Adam steps around Nikki and holds his hand out to me. "Charlie, it's very nice to meet you." He rakes his eyes up and down my body despite the fact I'm the most covered-up female in the room with the exception of the servers. "I dig your shirt," he says reaching out to touch it. "I'd very much like to see it on the floor of my room later."

Ethan's hand intercepts Adam's and he shakes it. "I'm Ethan, Thad's brother."

Adam looks between the two, taking in the resemblance. "No shit?" He shakes his hand hard. "Well any brother of Thad's is a brother of mine." He takes two steps back and nods his head at me. "Sorry about that, mate."

He calls the rest of the band over to introduce us. "Feel free to hang out in the wings during the show," Adam says to the four of us.

Ethan raises his brows and shrugs a shoulder as if asking me if I'm good with that.

"Uh, I don't know," I say. "This is my first concert and I think I'd like to experience it like everyone else." I look around at stunned faces. "I mean, if that's alright with you guys."

"For real?" Adam asks. "This is your first concert? As in *ever?*"

I nod, embarrassed that I've now drawn so much attention.

"That's unbelievable," he says. "But, wow. I'm honored you've picked us for your first. I hope we don't disappoint."

The lights flash and a big burly man gets up off his perch on a barstool in the corner. "Thanks for coming everyone. The band goes on in thirty. If you'd like to take your seats for the opening act, now would be the time."

I guess that's our cue to leave. They probably need time to practice or focus or meditate or whatever the hell they do to get ready for the show. Adam grabs a scantily-dressed blonde girl before she reaches the door. He whispers something in her ear that has her face splitting with a smile as she hangs back with him instead of being herded out with the rest of us. Okay, *whatever* it is.

As we exit the lounge, Chad tells us he and Nikki are going to hang backstage, and for a minute I feel guilty about asking Ethan to forgo that. I lean over to tell him, but before I can get the words out, he holds up his hand. "Charlie, no way. I know what you're going to say. But you must absolutely experience this like every other concertgoer. You're in for a real treat." He grabs my hand and tingles of sensation make their way up my arm.

Why is he holding my hand? This isn't a date.

I get my answer when we are escorted through a door into a mosh pit of people. There must be thousands of people trying to make their way to their seats. I almost lose Ethan ten times in the crowd, but he never once lets go of my hand. Not until we find our seats.

I turn around to take in the enormous crowd behind us. There must be hundreds of rows behind us. Thousands. I've never seen so many people together at one time before. And that's when I feel it. The energy. The excitement. The pure adrenaline.

Yes. This is exactly what I needed after the day I had.

CHAPTER TWENTY

The opening band comes out to cheers and applause.

I've never heard of this band before. But that's not surprising. I still don't listen to music all that often. I never got into it like most teens. I assume it's because of the negative association I felt with it. My mom would always play loud music when . . . well, she played it a lot. I'll never listen to music from the 80s or 90s. But White Poison is fine. They've only been around for the past four or five years, being catapulted to stardom thanks to the popularity of YouTube. They became popular by simply posting videos of themselves performing. They were offered a record contract without ever having played a live concert. Or so I was told in the limo on the way over.

It's hard not to get caught up in the excitement, and after a few minutes I find myself swaying my hips and tapping my feet to the beat.

I find it amusing that everyone is assigned a 'seat' when nobody actually sits down the entire time the band is playing.

There is a break when the first band leaves the stage. Being so close to the front, we can hear a lot of banging and moving as they presumably have to set up for White Poison to make their entrance.

The crowd is still buzzing with commotion, but at least I can hear Ethan speak when he leans his head close to me. "So . . . about this centerfold thing."

I shrug.

"I'm not sure I like the fact that millions of other men have seen you naked."

It's hard not to find his jealousy endearing. "I wasn't naked. I wore a G-string. Plus, it's a European publication. I hardly think millions of men have seen it. It's not like I posed for *Playboy* or anything."

"My goddamn brother saw it," he pouts.

"So what?" I ask. "I'm not your girlfriend, Ethan. You have no right to an opinion on those kinds of matters."

His hard stare burns down on me. "I still don't like it, Charlie."

"Then don't ever look at it," I say.

"Right." He laughs. "Kind of like telling a kid not to eat the cookie in the cookie jar. If he didn't know the cookie was in the jar, he wouldn't ever want it. And now that you've told him it's there, but that he can't eat it, it's all he can think about."

"So in this scenario, you're the kid and I'm the cookie?" I ask, amused.

He smirks at me.

"Nobody is saying you can't eat the cookie, Ethan. Eat the fucking cookie. I'm handing it to you on a platter."

"Are we still talking about the photo spread?" he asks.

I don't get a chance to answer him before deafening cheers, screams and cat-calls echo through the concert hall as White Poison takes the stage.

They start out playing a popular song I recognize from the radio. It may be one of the only songs I know of theirs since I'm not the type of person who buys music.

It's hard not to feel the pure energy around me, and before I even realize I'm doing it, I'm dancing along with the tens of thousands of other people in attendance.

The dancing. The energy. The sheer number of people in here. It's all contributing to the heat in the massive auditorium and I feel beads of sweat start to trickle down between my breasts.

Slowly, people work their way into every available square inch to get closer to the stage. Bodies are mashed together as we become one big sea of humanity. I scoot even closer to Ethan, trying to avoid being stepped on by the large man who's decided invading my personal space is his inalienable right. Ethan pulls me in front of him, caging me in his arms to protect me from the onslaught of fans edging closer to the stage.

The body heat we are both producing makes it even hotter, but I press myself into him anyway, loving the way his large frame envelops me.

After a few energetic songs, the band starts a slow ballad. Adam comes to the mic and says, "This one's for you, Charlie. Make sure big brother treats you right."

I crane my neck around and look at Ethan. He laughs and I can feel him shrug against me as if he had no idea that was going to happen.

The song is sad. The words tell a tale about a man who can't have the woman he longs for. Surely Ethan didn't tell him to dedicate it to me. I was with them the entire time backstage. Plus, Ethan doesn't do relationships.

No, I imagine Adam simply did it because it's my first concert and because he could.

The slow song has Ethan swaying his hips back and forth. And since his arms are still keeping me pressed against him, I'm swaying with him. Our bodies move in tandem, as if they are connected.

I think back to the two times they really *have* been connected and it makes me press myself harder into him. Suddenly, I wish all these people would disappear. I wish it was just the two of us, dancing back to front. Sweating, swaying, sighing.

His chin rests on the top of my head and his breath flows over my hair. No one has ever held me like this before. I've never felt more safe. More protected. More wanted.

My mind knows he's just keeping me from getting trampled. My heart knows it doesn't care why he's doing this, just that he is. My body knows he must be experiencing something because of the bulge I'm feeling when he leans into me.

Maybe it's only because of the friction we're creating. A physical reaction that any man would have in this situation, regardless of his feelings for the woman in front of him.

I reach up and put my hands on his arms that surround me and he gasps into my hair. He grinds his erection into my lower back and I know it can't be unintentional. I know he's reacting to my touch just as I'm reacting to his.

One of his hands finds the sliver of bare skin between my shirt and my pants. He plants it there, holding it against my sweaty skin, his thumb caressing circles into my burning flesh. I inhale a shaky breath. I've all but forgotten about the ear-splitting music and the mosh pit of people surrounding us.

Even when the song changes to a faster one, we continue the private dance we started. Sweat is pooling between us, drenching the back of my shirt and the front of his. It feels like we're skin to skin through the thin material of our soaked t-shirts.

We're invisible to those around us. Lost in a sea of fans who only care about the five performers on stage. Lost in our own world where we only care about each other.

Emotion overcomes me and I know if I don't tear myself from him, I could get lost forever. He feels me pull away, but his arms tighten, keeping me captive against his body. "Don't," he pleads the single word into my ear.

I obey his command. It's the only command I've ever wanted to obey. It's the only command I've ever *needed* to obey. And it's the moment I succumb. It's the moment I realize I'm head-over-fucking-heels for Ethan Stone.

We spend the rest of the concert joined this way. I'm afraid to move a muscle out of fear that he might remove his head from its perch on top of mine. He hums some of the tunes and I feel the vibrations throughout my entire body. My legs are almost numb from hours of standing in one place. But I don't care because the rest of my body is teeming with excitement. I'm about ready to explode from our constant connection. And if his breathing, his continued caresses on my skin, his constant erection are any indication—he's about to explode as well.

I can feel nothing but exhilaration when the concert comes to an end. I know nothing more about White Poison than the first few songs they played. The rest of the time, my mind was otherwise occupied with all things Stone.

"Let's get out of here!" he yells through the cheers and encore calls.

He takes my hand and plows a path through the sea of people until we reach the backstage door where a large man examines our badges before allowing us entrance.

As the band goes out for one more song, we find Chad and Nikki standing with some of the stage crew. Ethan shouts to Chad over the music, "We're taking off, can you call the driver?"

Chad whips out his phone and taps in a text. "Nik and I will head out too. We've all been invited to the after party at Vibe. Wanna come?"

Vibe is one of the premier clubs in New York. You get in by invitation only. I'm sure there are a lot of people there. Rich people. Famous people. People I don't care to have anything to do with. Plus, I'm wound up like a fucking clock. And based on the look Ethan and I are sharing, he feels exactly the same way.

"Nah, we'll skip the party if it's all the same to you," Ethan says. "Can you drop us off on your way?"

"No problem." Chad checks his phone. "The limo's outside. We can bounce."

The four of us make our way to the same door we came in earlier and scurry into the limousine under the protection of White Poison's security.

The driver lowers the partition. "Where to?" he asks.

All eyes look at me. I give the driver my address and then accept the glass of champagne being handed my way.

I look down at my shirt. It's soaked with sweat. It's a big shirt on me, but it's plastered to my body. "Oh, God, I need a shower."

Ethan leans over to me and whispers, "So do I, *Tate*. And I'm all about water conservation." His eyes burn into mine and the thought of us showering together almost makes me moan out loud.

Instead, I grab the champagne bottle from the ice bucket and hold it to my neck as he laughs.

Chad asks Nikki, "You need to stop at your place and get anything? We may be out pretty late."

She guffaws. "Lord, no. It's Laurie's night to have the little brat." She turns to us. "Laurie—that's my roommate—she has a two-year-old daughter who normally lives with her dad. But Laurie gets her every Friday night. I try my best to be gone, because, fuck, that kid is annoying. I mean some people just shouldn't reproduce, you know? I wish that child would just vanish into thin air and quit ruining my Friday nights."

Ethan chugs his drink and then slams the glass into the cup holder. "You are such a bitch, Nikki," he says, shaking his head in disgust. "Did you ever consider that maybe the so-called 'brat' acts up because her parents aren't together? I mean, I'm sure it's not easy having to share her time between two homes. How about a little fucking compassion?"

Chad looks at Ethan with sympathetic eyes while Nikki looks like she just ate a shit sandwich. I, on the other hand, am not quite sure what just happened here, so I just sink back into the comfy leather seat.

Chad breaks the awkward silence. "That *was* a pretty crappy thing to say, Nik. Why not just find a new roommate?"

"Are you kidding?" She laughs. "We have one of the best rent-controlled apartments in the city. I'm not about to let it go. Not all of us can afford to live in the Taj Mahal, you know."

"I don't live in the Taj Mahal," Chad says. "In fact, I live in a modest two-bedroom in the valley."

"Well, whatever," Nikki responds. "You *could* live in the Taj Mahal if you wanted to."

"Why would I want to live in India?"

"I didn't say you should live there; I was just saying you could live anywhere because you're so damn rich."

Chad sighs. "There's more to life than being rich, Nik."

I notice Ethan refilling his glass again when I've barely touched mine.

"Maybe," she says. "But being rich makes everything better. Rich people don't have problems."

I notice the three of us shaking our heads in disagreement of her statement. I'm not exactly sure why Chad and Ethan are doing it. But I'm doing it because this woman makes me want to scream. She is so goddamn superficial. Money does not equate to happiness. Just ask sixteen-year-old Piper Mitchell and her best friend Charlie Tate.

Ethan reaches into the limo bar compartment and pulls out a bottle of whiskey. He pours a couple of fingers of it into a glass and downs it.

I didn't know he was such a big drinker. He's obviously a good athlete and he keeps in such great shape, it kind of surprises me. Maybe he's nervous about tonight. We've had sex twice before, but neither time was as intense as what happened at the concert. Every time we are together, things just get better. More emotional. Scarier.

Maybe he feels this too and needs a few drinks to calm his nerves.

The limo comes to a stop and a few seconds later, the door opens. I thank Chad for the tickets and tell him what a wonderful time I had. I bid Nikki goodbye and exit the car.

Ethan gets out behind me, whispering something to the driver. He walks me up to my building but I notice the limo does not pull away from the curb.

I'm starting to put two and two together. "You're not coming up?"

He shakes his head in quiet confirmation.

"I don't understand. Am I missing something here? What about the water conservation? And the grinding at the concert? And the *Don't*?" Frustration spills out of me in a fiery sigh. "Is this about the argument with Nikki?" I ask. "She's a classless bitch, Ethan. She clearly hit a nerve, but there is no reason to let her ruin our evening."

He looks at the ground before he looks back at me. "Charlie, stop. I'm sorry. I just can't do this. I . . . I forgot about a case I need to work on."

"A case? Seriously?"

We stare at each other silently and I can see right through his bullshit like the clear glass shard he's stabbing in my heart. "What the fuck, Ethan? You have to quit messing with me. Do you want me or don't you?"

He runs two frustrated hands through his hair. "Yes," he says. "And no." He walks towards the wall and hits it with his open hand. "Fuck!" He grabs the back of his neck. "Go inside, Charlie. I'll see you tomorrow at the gym." He walks back to the limo and gets inside, but not before I hear him curse at himself one more time.

That's it. I'm tired of his hot and cold. His up and down. His on and off. I don't have to put up with this shit. I storm through the lobby of my building and go up to my apartment.

Then I fall on my bed and scream into my pillow. Because I've never been in love before. And it fucking hurts.

CHAPTER TWENTY-ONE

I return an order to the kitchen for the second time today.

"You're really not on your game today, are you Charlie?" Jarod asks.

I never get orders wrong. And the fact that I've screwed up two and it's not even noon yet, pisses me off. "I guess my mind is somewhere else."

"Does this have anything to do with that man who was in here yesterday? Or is it my asshole cousin?"

I take a minute to think about his question. I should be upset about my dad showing up. I should be upset about what my mother did to him. I should be upset that he didn't take me with him when he left. I should be upset about so many things. But why is it that when Jarod asked the question, there was only one thing that came to mind? "I'm going with asshole," I say, walking out of the kitchen with my new order.

I spend the rest of my shift worrying about tonight. I contemplate not going to the gym. I don't want to see him. It hurts too much to even think about him let alone have him in the same room with me. And I refuse to let him play this game anymore. But damn it, it's my gym, too. I'm not going to let him run me out of it. If anyone should leave, it's him.

I think back to last night at the concert. I never knew music could evoke such emotion. Maybe that was all it was. We got caught up in the music. The energy. It was like a drug and we were under its powerful influence. The high I got from it was unlike anything I'd ever experienced. It was perfect. Until it wasn't. Maybe once the dust settled, he realized I wasn't what he wanted.

Then I remember his plea when I tried to pull away. *Don't.*

It was one word. One syllable. But it said so much more. And the way he held onto me; the way he touched me—it was as if he was drowning and I was his life raft. I'd never felt anything like it before. I didn't ever want him to let go. Because even though he was the one holding on tight, *I* was the one who was being saved.

By the end of my shift, I make the decision that he's not going to break me. I've already been broken by my father. By so many other men. I've been broken so much, I'm not even sure all of my pieces will fit back together. I refuse to let him hurt me. I reach down between my legs and touch the unicorn tattoo on my inner thigh, hoping it will protect me from Ethan as it tried to protect me from all the others. Only this time, it's not my body that needs protection. It's my heart. My soul.

I go an hour early for my swim, hoping I will be done before Ethan arrives while still being able to see Mrs. Buttermaker. And for the first time since I've known her, she chooses the lane directly next to me, not at the other side of the pool. Even though she doesn't have any children of her own, she seems to have that sixth sense of a mother. Well, *most* mothers.

I complete my swim before she does, and I sit on the edge of the pool waiting for her to finish so we can talk. My conversations with Mrs. B have become one of the highlights of my day. She has this grandmotherly way about her. This worldly knowledge. This sophisticated wisdom that makes her one of the most interesting people I've ever met.

She's traveled the world and we've been to a lot of the same places. But she went to take in the sights, the beauty. I went to escape. And although our experiences were quite different ones, she has made me come to appreciate the places I've been and the things I've seen much more than I ever have.

However, before I get the chance to talk with her, Ethan comes out of the locker room, the look on his face clearly displaying his surprise that I'm already here. The look on my face clearly displaying why I am.

Mrs. B pops up at my feet, smiling her usual smile that adds even more wrinkles to her weathered face.

"I'm sorry. I have to go." I give her a sad smile as I quickly grab my towel and head for the shower without so much as an explanation for either of them.

When I pass Ethan, I try not to look at him. But it's as if his eyes have some magnetic force that draws me in. And that's when I see it. His apology. His desire. His pain. They are all rolled into one sympathetic stare that spears me like a flaming arrow. He reaches his arm out as if he's going to grab me, but then it retreats before his hand touches mine. Instead, he sighs and runs the hand through his hair.

I round the corner to the locker room so I'm out of their view. I lean against the concrete wall, sliding down until I hit the hard tile floor. I'm mad because he tried to touch me. I'm mad because he didn't actually do it. I'm mad because I let him get to me without even speaking a single word. But mostly I'm mad at myself for caring.

"Ethan Stone," Mrs. Buttermaker's raspy voice reprimands him. "What on earth did you do to that sweet little girl?"

"Nothing more than what she's done to me, Mrs. B. Nothing more than what she's done to me."

I hear a splash in the pool, putting an end to their conversation.

What I've done to *him?* I've done nothing to him.

I pick myself up off the floor and head to the shower, hoping to make a quick exit before Mrs. Buttermaker can corner me and be all motherly and shit. I don't need to talk about him. I need to forget about him.

On my way through the gym, I run into Devon getting on a treadmill, and just to spite Ethan—even though he can't see me do it—I say hello. "Hey, Devon."

He looks at me and then looks quickly around the gym. "Hi," he says, putting his earbuds in before turning away from me.

Okay then. Geez, I know I was kind of a bitch to him the last time we talked, but wow—that was cold.

Heading out the front door, I remember last night's plans involving something about swimming and tequila. Plans that were thwarted by he who will not be mentioned.

I stop at the corner store and pick up a bottle on my way home. When I get to the apartment, my door is unlocked. I cautiously open the door, relieved to see Piper standing in my kitchen. She walks out carrying two drinks. Margaritas.

I pull the bottle I just purchased out of the bag, show it to her and say, "Sometimes I swear we share the same brain." I laugh, taking the drink from her and downing half of it quickly. "How did you know I'd even be here?"

"Well, you know about two people here, me being one of them. All of my sisters are accounted for. And I called the gym to ask if they'd let me know when you left. They also happened to tell me that you didn't leave with the hot P.I., so I thought it was a good opportunity to come over and catch up. It's been days since we've spoken and I'm dying to find out what happened yesterday. Skylar told me about your dad showing up and then Ethan and the limo. So, come on, sister. Spill."

I take another drink of my margarita, wondering where to even begin. It's been a while since Piper and I have had a real heart-to-heart. I've missed it. I've missed her. But I'm not sure I'm ready to spill all my secrets about Ethan. About what he does to me. How I feel about him. How it hurts so badly.

She tugs on my arm, pulling me over to the couch. She points to an overnight bag on the floor. "I've got all night. I'm here as long as it takes. We can have a sleepover. It'll be just like old times."

I close my eyes and remember all the nights we spent talking until dawn. You would think even best friends would eventually run out of things to say after six or seven hours of talking. We never did. Not one time. I smile and motion to her bag. "Did you bring them?"

She rolls her eyes. "What do you think? Of course I brought them."

"Good," I say, bouncing up off the couch to go to my bedroom.

I rip off my clothes and dig through my dresser until I find what I'm looking for. Then I quickly put them on and join Piper in my living room.

We squeal in delight when we see each other wearing our matching long-john pajamas we bought from a street vender in Dubai about four years ago. That very same night, we put them on and stayed up all night talking. It was one of the best nights I'd ever had. We drank. We laughed. We dreamed. We may have even healed a little.

The next day, we surmised that the pajamas had magical powers, so from that day forward, anytime one of us needed to have a good talk, we'd pull them out and put them on.

My soul sister—the person who knows me better than anyone on this earth—she knew I'd need to talk after hearing about the visit from my dad. And she's the only one who really knows what happened to me, so she's the only one I can ever talk to.

Secrets are lonely.

I make us another round of drinks and then I tell her mine.

CHAPTER TWENTY-TWO

It's Monday and once again, I've got too much time on my hands. Yesterday, I went to brunch at the Mitchell's restaurant on Long Island. They have brunch together as a family every Sunday. I've begged off the past few, but as Piper did spend the night Saturday, I had no choice but to be dragged by her to this latest one. I was just glad it wasn't at the Maple Creek location. The original Mitchell's restaurant. The one where I grew up waitressing—in the town to which I vowed I'd never return.

Time is really not your friend when you have a lot on your mind. The idle brain has a way of taking small problems and turning them into big ones. Big ones such as what am I going to do tonight at the gym? It didn't go very well on Saturday. It hurts to see him. Physically hurts, like in the pit of my stomach and in the wall of my chest.

My phone pings with a text and when I look at it, the pain shoots through me like an arrow.

Stone: Can you come by the office? I have some more information for you. Or if you'd rather, I'll bring it to the gym.

Come by the office? Hardly. And I haven't decided if I'll be at the gym yet. I do know I need space. Space from him. Maybe he can just leave the stuff at the front desk and I can pick it up from Gretchen.

Ugh. The thought of seeing her makes me wince. Especially if she has any idea her boss bailed on me Saturday night. I'd never see the end to her gloating. No, that won't work.

He could leave it at the gym. I'm sure one of the guys or the front desk staff would hold onto it for me.

I stare at his text wondering what to say when it dawns on me.

Why can't he just email me the information? We are living in an age where meetings have all but become obsolete. In fact, why hasn't he just emailed me everything all along?

Me: Is there some kind of rule that says you can't email me this information?

Stone: Rule?

Me: Yes. Rule. And if there isn't one, why haven't you been emailing me this stuff all along?

Probably because he gets more billable hours if he takes meetings in person.

Stone: I prefer to meet with clients face to face for the most part. No, there's no rule.

Me: Then email it to me please.

There is a long pause before my phone pings again. I can only imagine what is going through his mind. Maybe that he won't be able to charge me as much. Maybe that I'm sick of him playing with me whenever it suits him. Maybe that he's an arrogant asshole who doesn't deserve a freaking girlfriend.

Stone: I'll have Gretchen send it right over.

Me: Thanks.

An hour later, I wonder what could possibly be taking so long. I pick up my phone to text Ethan when an email from Gretchen arrives, and suddenly I'm staring at the contact information for Morgan Tenney. Acid burns my throat when I think of what he did to me.

I know there is a journal entry about him. A detailed one that was so vile, I couldn't even read it in its entirety. My mother obviously wrote it when she was jacked up on something. *Didn't she ever re-read her entries when she was sober and realize what a monster she was?*

I don't dare read it now. I might be tempted to get the gun that is hidden under my extra bed sheets in the linen closet.

The gun that is part of the one secret I didn't tell Piper. No one knows about the list. No one except Ethan. And he doesn't *really* know about it.

I enter Tenney's address into my phone and I conclude it's not in such a bad part of town. I throw on my requisite hoodie and grab a baseball cap from my closet. Then I head to the subway. I'm so nervous, I get on two wrong trains before I get back on track and end up at the correct station.

For some reason, my skin prickles. It's been doing it the whole time. Like someone is watching me. I look around, half expecting to see Morgan Tenney, who's somehow figured out I was out to get him. Suddenly, I'm uneasy about what I'm doing. Maybe I'm not as safe as I think I am. Riding the subway, I take notice of everyone in the car with me. I once read that if you make eye contact with people, you are less likely to be accosted.

One man in the corner has on a baseball hat and sunglasses. Sunglasses—despite the fact that we are mostly underground. A few of the afternoon riders look like students skipping school. There are several young mothers with children in strollers who look like they are heading out to Central Park for the day. Businessmen and women intermingle, and there are a couple of homeless people in baggy clothing and stocking caps.

I reach into my pocket and pull out a few dollars to hand to each of them as I get off at my stop. I remember what it was like to be homeless. No, I never had to sleep on a train to get warm, but there were a few nights I wasn't sure Piper and I would have a roof over our heads. It came down to strangers lending a hand every time. So even if I can't afford it—even if I'm down to my last dollar—I'll always try to help those who are less fortunate. It's sad to even think about it. What I went through; what Piper endured— there will always be someone else who had it worse.

I walk a few blocks until I find the building I'm looking for. It's a secure building. One you have to get buzzed into by a resident. I know the drill. I start punching in apartment numbers until someone buzzes me in. Making my way up to the third floor, I hear someone else come through the front door followed by the yelling of several residents out their doors for people to quit fucking punching in numbers. Someone must have done it behind me. I used to live in a building like this for a time. It really does get annoying.

I arrive at apartment 318. I tuck my hair up into the ball cap and roll up the sleeves of my hoodie. I take a few deep breaths before banging on the door, and then I move out of the way of the peephole.

No answer. I bang again.

I think I see movement at the end of the hallway, scaring me half to death, but when I turn my head and stare, I see nothing. Now I'm just imagining things. I knock on the door one last time, this time not bothering to hide my face.

Frustration sets in. All I want to do is get this over with.

I hear a woman's voice as footsteps climb the stairs. "You shouldn't be here. Who let you in?"

I freeze. She's not talking to me, but to someone in the stairwell. My heart pounds. Is it Morgan? Does he know I'm here? Was he waiting for me to leave?

I race to the opposite end of the hall, find another stairway, and almost break my neck descending the two flights of stairs to the ground floor. I race across the street and duck into a coffee shop. I slip into a booth by the window and train my eyes on the two possible exits of the building I just vacated.

Not twenty seconds go by when a man exits. It's one of the homeless men I gave money to on the train. *What?*

He looks up and down the street and then pulls a cell phone from his pocket. *A cell phone?*

He makes a quick call and then removes his cap and fake beard.

Son of a bitch!

I storm out of the coffee shop and run across the street, narrowly escaping the bumper of a yellow cab in my haste to get there.

"What the fuck, Levi? Why are you following me?"

His head falls back in defeat and he looks at the sky, cursing silently.

"Did Ethan tell you to follow me?"

He gives me that look. That *I-plead-the-fifth* look.

"Shit," I say, storming off down the street. I hail a cab and am just about inside it when he calls after me.

"Charlie, wait!"

I give him a one-finger message to relay to his boss as my cab passes him by.

I angrily spew out the address to the cabbie and then apologize to him for my crassness before I ask him to please drive faster.

Arriving at my destination, I throw a twenty at him, leaving him way too big a tip, but not wanting to hang around for change. I run through the building and get a few nasty looks when I skirt by some people waiting to get on the elevator. "Emergency," I say, out of breath.

The elevator can't get to the ninth floor fast enough. I swear it stops at every goddamn floor. When it finally opens, I dart through the main door into the reception area. "I need to see him," I tell Gretchen. "Now."

She tilts her head at me and gives me an amused smile. "I'm sorry, do you have an appointment?"

"You know I don't, Gretchen. Just let me in, please. It's important."

"All of our clients are important," she says.

I walk over to the door and tug on the handle. It doesn't budge. I pound on the door.

Gretchen picks up the handset to the phone and waves it at me. "Do I need to call security?"

I close my eyes and breathe. "No."

Just as she puts the handset back in the cradle, the door to the back opens and a lady walks through. I don't even hesitate. I edge through the door before it slams shut and turn right to go to Ethan's office.

"You are so arrested," Gretchen barks at me before I hear her call security.

"Stone!" I yell before I even reach his office.

Several office doors open and unfamiliar faces peek into the hallway. Ethan appears in his doorway at the same time as Gretchen buzzes through a security guard. "That's her," she says, pointing to me with a sneer.

I look to Ethan. He shakes his head in disgust. At me for barging in? At Gretchen for calling security on me? At himself for having me followed? The possibilities are endless.

He holds up a hand, stopping the progress of the security guard. "It's fine, Harold," he says to the aging man who looks like he's held this job since New York became a city. "This is just a misunderstanding. There isn't a problem here." He turns to me. "Is there, Charlie?"

"Hmmpf," I rage at him. Then I turn to Harold. "No, no problem here."

"Thanks, Harold. You can go now," Ethan says.

"If you're sure, Mr. Stone."

"I'm sure. Thank you."

He turns back to me and steps into the doorway of his office, waving me by with a cautious arm. "Well?"

"Thanks, Gretch," I spit out at Barbie before stepping across the threshold.

Ethan shuts the door behind me. "Before you say anything," he starts. "I can—"

"*Say* anything?" I shout. "Oh, I'm not going to *say* anything, but I'm sure as hell going to *yell* shit, so sit the fuck down, Ethan Stone."

"Charlie, calm down. Please. People will hear and Gretchen might sic Harold on you again." He gives me a crooked smile.

"Ha ha," I say snidely. "I'm so glad you can joke at a time like this."

"So, Levi called me. He said you made him."

"*Made* him?" I ask.

"Yeah, you know, caught him following you." He sits on the edge of his desk. The same edge we had sex on a month ago. I wonder if he picked that exact spot on purpose. "I'm sorry. I was just trying to protect you."

"Protect me?" I yell. "Why the hell would you think I need protection? I'm not one of your cases, Ethan. And I'm not your girlfriend. You made that perfectly clear when you couldn't get away from me fast enough Friday night. Hell, we're not even in a fucking relationship according to you and what you seem to tell everyone who asks." I pace back and forth aggressively from wall to wall, trying, but failing to keep my voice at a respectable volume. "But what I can't figure out is what the hell you want from me. You have me followed? You warn men away" —he goes to speak but I raise my hand to shut him up— "don't give me any shit, I tried to talk to Devon at the gym the other night and he avoided me like the goddamn plague. And your own cousin seems to think you've been in a foul mood since you met me. If you don't want me, fine—but don't you dare presume to try and tell me whom I can and can't date. And call your damn lackeys off. I can take care of my own fucking self."

He watches my whole angry tirade without raising an eyebrow. He's casually leaning on his desk, arms crossed in front of him. The man is as cool as a cucumber and it pisses me off even more. I kick the leg of his couch in frustration.

"Tell me why you're having me track down all these men, Charlie."

"It's none of your goddamn business, Ethan."

He shakes his head, disagreeing with me. "I think you have some kind of score to settle with these men. The first time I gave you information, you turned up with a shiner. Then last week, the same day I gave you more intel, you limped out of the pool like a lame dog. And then today, you go dressed like a thug to Morgan Tenney's place. What would you think if you were me? Tell me, Charlie, did these men do something to hurt your mother? Are you seeking revenge against them?"

"No, Ethan. They didn't hurt my mother. Turn off your P.I. radar and quit messing with my life. I'm a big girl and I don't need you looking out for me."

"I'm not—"

"Don't give me that," I interrupt. "What about Devon? What about the guy with the concert tickets? Hell, what about your own cousin—you even warned me away from *him*. And let's not forget about your brother, Kyle. And then there's Chad's friend, Adam. Why did you step in when he propositioned me?"

"Why do you fucking think, Tate?" His eyes burn into mine and they are windows into his soul.

"And why do you call me Tate when you want to fuck me?" I yell, not caring who in his office can hear my outbursts. "If you wanted to just be my fuck buddy, you would have come up to my apartment on Friday. I thought you simply decided you wanted nothing to do with me. But now—the way you are looking at me. All doey-eyed and come-hither. It's obvious you want me. It's obvious to everyone in the fucking world except you, Ethan." I stop pacing and stand in front of him. "Why? Why are you so scared of relationships?"

He shakes his head. "I don't know," he says.

"The hell you don't," I say. "Why, Ethan?"

He sighs, scrubbing a hand across his face. "Rule number ten, that's why."

"Oh my God. You and your damn rules. Just tell me!"

He looks at me. He holds my stare with his eyes. He holds my heart in his hands. It's teetering on a ledge, about to topple over and splat all over the pavement below, or it's about to be pulled back, rescued from certain demise.

His hand runs through his hair and his eyes close briefly when he says, "If you don't have anything, you have nothing to lose."

His words slay me. But not in a *heart-splattered-across-the-pavement* kind of way. More like in a *he-wants-me-so-much-he-can't-bear-to-have-me* kind of way.

My breath catches. My chest heaves. My heart surges. And the moment he sees how his words affect me, his mouth comes crashing down on mine, claiming me so completely that not even my voice of reason has a chance in hell of stopping this freight train.

CHAPTER TWENTY-THREE

He bites down on my lower lip and then sucks on it before his tongue dives into my mouth, exploring every inch of it as heavy breaths come from deep down inside him. My tongue darts into his mouth, wanting to taste him just as much as he's tasting me.

I need to be pressed against him. My body remembers what it felt like at the concert and it craves more. I jump up into his arms, smashing our chests together. He holds me steady with his hands, caressing my butt as he walks us across the room.

He shifts my weight into one hand while he reaches the other out to his laptop.

My lips don't even leave his when I say, "Leave the camera on."

I can feel his smile against my mouth before he resumes the perusal with his tongue.

I don't even know how long he stands here, holding me, kissing me. His arms must go numb under my weight but he doesn't move. He doesn't put me down. His hands are all over my ass, rubbing, kneading, prodding.

I want those hands on other parts of me. "Touch me," I beg through our kisses.

He walks us over to the couch on the far wall of his office and carefully places me down on it. I rip my hoodie off, revealing an old tank top underneath. This was the last thing I expected today. I try to remember what bra and panties I put on this morning. I pray he's too worked up to even care.

I grab the hem of my tank but his hand comes out to stop me. "No," he says, removing my hand from the material. "Let me."

He carefully peels off my shirt like he's unwrapping a present. Slowly. Methodically. Almost painfully. I watch his eyes dilate when they fall to my breasts, still covered by the thin cotton material of my nothing-special bra. He pulls the cups down, exposing me to him, trussing my breasts up for his eyes to feast on. He reaches out both hands, giving equal measure to them and we gasp simultaneously when his hands meet my flesh.

One hand continues to explore my chest while the other comes up behind my neck. He tilts my head back, exposing my throat so he can press his lips to it. He works his mouth and tongue from collarbone to ear on one side, and then he does it all over again on the other. My body shudders. The sensations running through me right now are unlike anything I've ever experienced.

Finally, his lips find mine again and I moan into him as he claims my mouth once more. He kisses me. And kisses me. And kisses me. I've never kissed a man this long. Never had a make-out session with anyone. Never wanted to. Kissing wasn't necessary. It was a bothersome task that only got in the way of the quick release I wanted.

But, Holy God, the way this man is kissing me right now. I get it. I get what all the hype is about. He's not just kissing me; he's making love to me with his mouth. He's a starving man and I'm his dinner. He's a painter and I'm his canvas.

Is this what it's like for everyone? Surely not. This kind of kissing could bring about world peace.

I'm on the brink of detonation and he hasn't even touched me below the waist. I reach down and tug his shirt from his pants. I have to feel around for the buttons because my mouth is still held captive by his. I push the shirt off his shoulders and down his arms, his hands only parting from my body long enough to rid himself of it. I push his undershirt up, working my hands underneath it and up his taut stomach and strong pecs. He trembles under my touch and my heart surges. Everything about him wants this. He can't deny it any longer.

When he breaks our kiss to remove his undershirt, our eyes meet. We are both hungry with desire. Bursting with passion. Then we tear at each other's pants, our hands tangled and twisted until every shred of clothing we have is in a pile on the floor next to us.

I'm sitting on the couch and he's on his knees in front of me. I lean back and look at him through lidded eyes.

"My God, you're beautiful, Charlie," he says, as his gaze rakes over every inch of my body.

I take him in as well. His broad shoulders. The light fuzz of chest hair that trails down into a perfect V on his abs. His strong swimmer's thighs. His burgeoning erection that twitches under my perusal. "You are beautiful, too."

He leans over and kisses my stomach. And as he works his mouth down my body in slow ministrations, it dawns on me that he used my first name.

When his mouth hits the apex of my thighs, he inhales my scent, moaning in appreciation. When his tongue glides over me, I moan in ecstasy. He laves and licks and swirls his tongue around. Then he slides a finger inside me. Then two. "God, you're so wet, Charlie."

Charlie.

His tongue. His fingers. His words. They all come together to bring me to the edge of explosion. Then he pulls back right before I'm ready to come. My head rises off the back of the couch in surprise, and I look down at him, my eyes begging and my lungs panting. He puts his mouth to my tattoo and kisses it. "Rule number eleven," he says against my steamy skin. "All good things come to those who wait."

His fingers enter me once again and his tongue rubs slow, delicious circles on my clit, building me right back up. I want to touch him. I want to do to him what he's doing to me. I've never wanted something so badly in my life. I reach down and push his shoulders back until he's lying on the floor looking up at me in question.

"Rule number sixty-nine," I say with a sultry rise of my brow. "Give and you shall receive."

A low rumble of a laugh starts in his belly and erupts from his glistening lips. "I'm rubbing off on you," he says. "I think that might just be my favorite rule."

I reverse my position and climb over him, giving him full access to me as my mouth closes over him.

Sounds of pleasure echo through his office as we feast on each other. The erotic pressure between my legs builds up so much, I have to break my seal on him to gasp for air.

I feel his balls tighten. "Uhhhng," he murmurs before lifting me off of him. "I have to be inside you." He reaches for his pants, quickly pulling a condom out of his wallet. His voice cracks with need. "I have to be inside you *now.*"

His hands are shaking so badly, he has trouble opening the package. I take it from him and tear it open with my teeth. I rise to my knees, appreciating every silken inch of him as I roll it on.

My knees are getting sore on the hard floor, so I sit back up on the couch and spread my legs for him. He scoots towards me, his sturdy knees more able to withstand the pressure as he stares at what I'm offering him. He positions himself between my legs and as he enters me, our eyes meet, emotion flowing from them as if it were tears. "Jesus, Charlie," he says, not breaking eye contact as he glides in and out of me.

His eyes, they say so much more than the words leaving his mouth do. And in this moment, I realize why he's not calling me Tate. It's because we're not fucking.

We're doing something I've never done before. We're making love.

He threads the fingers from both of his hands through the fingers of both of mine. He stares at our entwined hands as his thrusts become more demanding. His eyes wander up my arms when suddenly, he stills, his focus trained on the scars that line one of my forearms.

I rip my hands out of his and put them on his hips, shielding the under part of my forearms from his view. "Ethan," I say, pulling his attention back to my face. "Don't stop."

I thrust my hips towards him, forcing him back into the moment. His eyes close briefly as he starts moving within me again. I grab his hand and shove it between us, not wanting to wait a second longer to reach the precipice of ultimate gratification. He rolls a slow finger across the place that will send me spiraling out of control.

"Oh, God," I murmur, pleasure coiling inside me.

"That's it, baby. Come with me."

His eyes never stray from mine as we fall down the rabbit hole together. My thighs tighten. My stomach clenches. Short spurts of air exit my lungs as an orgasm tears through my body, ripping it to shreds as no other orgasm has ever done before.

"Aaaaah, Charlie." He grits his teeth, his face contorting in excruciating pleasure as his cock dances inside my body.

He collapses onto me, matching the rhythm of my heaving chest, our bodies languid as our slick skin slides against each other. My aftershocks continue to massage him before he pulls out of me completely. He remains draped over me while we slowly recover.

When he pulls away, he looks down upon me in complete reverence, my body spent. Limp. Satiated.

"Wow," I breathe, once my brain connects to my mouth again.

He laughs. "Yeah. Wow."

The intercom buzzes. "Ethan," Gretchen's insistent voice says. "You're getting quite backed up out here."

Still naked, he walks over to his desk, pressing a button on his phone. "Five minutes," he says, removing the condom as he dismisses her. He comes back across the office, leaning down to rifle through our tangled clothes. He separates mine out and hands them to me. He motions to a door by the couch. "You can clean up in there. It's my private bathroom."

"Thanks," I mouth at him, still trying to recover my power of speech. I take my clothes and walk to the bathroom. As I dress, I realize how grateful I am that Barbie didn't interrupt us thirty seconds earlier. If she'd only known what she'd have ruined.

I look in the mirror, unsure of the person I see staring back at me. I'm different. Can one month; one man; one overwhelming emotion—change a person so completely?

I think of Piper and how much she's changed since meeting Mason. And I smile at the girl in the mirror. I smile because for the first time in my life, I think about the future. A future I thought couldn't exist for people like me.

CHAPTER TWENTY-FOUR

My body slices through the water, deliciously sore from the workout I had earlier. We didn't have time to talk after. I'd already caused one appointment cancellation, as Gretchen so crassly told me on my way out. Ethan gave me one last kiss before I left his office. He said we'd talk tonight, after our swim but before he plays poker with the guys.

Now they are *the guys*.

I ran into Levi on the way out. He apologized. I asked for my two dollars back.

I smile thinking about Mrs. B. She already finished her swim, but not before she lectured me on the ways of men and how not to get caught up in them. Never rely on a man for your self-esteem. Never rely on a man to put food on the table. Never rely on a man for an orgasm. That last one had me turning as red as her waterproof lipstick.

My mind wanders as I churn away the laps. I fantasize about what happened earlier. I wonder what it will be like to actually be someone's girlfriend. What a novel idea.

Before long, my arms tire and I realize I've been alone in the pool for some time. Too long. I glance at the clock. He's late. My heart beats faster thinking of all the possible scenarios. Accident? Disgruntled spouse of a client? Second thoughts?

Oddly, it's the last one that scares me the most.

It's also the last one that seems the most likely.

I get my answer when I see Mason walk through the door of the aquatics room. He addresses me with a sad smile. *Oh, God. What happened?*

I climb out and grab my towel. "What is it?" I ask.

"Ethan wanted me to check on you. Make sure you were okay."

I crinkle my nose at him. "Why wouldn't I be okay?"

He cocks his head and stares at me. "Uh, because he said you wouldn't return any of his messages."

"His messages?" I realize in my eagerness to see him tonight, I arrived earlier than usual so I haven't checked my phone for over an hour. "Did he get held up at work or something?"

"Well, shit." Mason pinches the bridge of his nose. Then he looks at me like he's about to tell me my dog just died.

"That son of a bitch," I say. "He didn't get held up at work at all, did he?"

Mason shakes his head and looks at his feet. "You should really be talking to Piper about stuff like this."

"Well, Piper isn't here now is she?" I huff out an angry breath. "What did he tell you, Mason? Like word for word—what exactly did he say?"

"I don't know, Charlie. He said something about how you are great but he can't be with you. He said it's him, it's not you. He said he knew you'd be pissed at him and wanted to make sure you were okay." He puts a sympathetic hand on my shoulder. "Maybe you should go listen to his messages. I'll send Piper over to your place. I'll stay home with Hailey. Poker night isn't happening anyway."

"So he bailed on you, too?" I say angrily.

He looks uneasy. "Well, not exactly. But he said he was going to skip tonight. Wait until the dust settles."

"So now I'm dust." I'm trying my best to hold back the tears, but I feel them coming. My chest is tight. My throat stings. My head hurts. My heart is in fucking pieces.

"Listen, Charlie, if it really bothers you, we'll ask him not to come back for poker night. Hell, I'll kick him out of the gym if you want me to. Just say the word and it's done."

"No. It's fine. He was here first anyway." I wrap my towel around me, hoping if I pull it tight enough, it will hold back the onslaught of waterworks about to erupt. "I'm gonna hit the shower. Piper can come over if she wants. Thanks, Mason."

I walk toward the locker room as Mason's words follow me. "I'm really sorry," he says. "But Charlie, if it's any consolation, he's a damn idiot and I don't mind telling you I let him know it."

All I can do is nod my head at him. Then I disappear into the locker room and stand under the shower until the tears stop falling.

~ ~ ~

"Here, drink this first," Piper says, holding out a shot glass full of tequila. "But then put the glass down so you don't throw it across the room." She picks up a pillow off the couch and puts it in my lap. "If you need to throw something—throw this."

I down the shot while staring at my phone on the coffee table in front of me. I know I shouldn't listen to his messages. I know they will crush me. I should delete them and not give him the satisfaction of having me hear whatever pathetic excuses he's come up with. But it's like he said—once you know the cookie is there, it's hard to ignore. Except it's *not* a cookie, it's more like a big roll of cookie dough—you know you will feel like shit after eating it, but it's too tempting not to eat the whole damn thing anyway.

"Just do it," I tell Piper, nodding to the phone I don't even want to touch.

She grabs my hand in hers and then taps on the screen to play the first message.

"Charlie," he says and then pauses. I close my eyes. The way he says my name says it all. It's not anything like the way it came off his lips earlier today, when he made my name seem more like a prayer.

Piper squeezes my hand.

"I'm so mad at myself," he says. "I never should have let that happen today." Another pregnant pause and I can imagine him running a hand through his hair as he does when he's frustrated. "I mean, it was great. *You* are great. But I can't let it happen again. I know I've said that before and that I'm a dick for leading you on like I have. And the reasons I have for not wanting this are all about me and have nothing to do with you. I hope you believe that, because it's true. And I'm sorry as hell, because I know I'm hurting you. Shit." He sighs deeply into the phone. "I really wish you would have answered the phone, because I feel like a bastard leaving you a message like this. But I needed you to know why I won't be coming to the gym tonight. The only way I know how to keep from hurting you again is to not see you anymore. But I hate leaving things like this, Charlie. Will you call me back and let me know you got this? I'm sorry. I really am. And you deserve better."

The message ends and I look down at the pillow, not knowing whether to throw it, or use it to muffle my cries.

"Sweetie, I'm so sorry," Piper says. I don't look at her. I can't. I know she's crying. She's feeling all of my pain as if our hearts were connected by a tether.

My chest heaves and my breathing is ragged as I try to hold it all in. My heart hurts so much I feel it might explode. I reach out and tap the next message, needing to get it all over with.

"Charlie, please call me back. You can yell at me. Call me names. But I need to know you are okay. I still care about you."

And then the last one.

"Okay, I get that you don't want to talk to me. But can you at least text me to let me know you're alright? Please, Charlie. God, I'm so, so sorry. You'll never know just how much."

I tap the screen a few times, deleting all three of the messages while my best friend pours us shots of tequila.

I throw back the shot. Then I break down in her arms. She holds me tightly against her as we both let the tears fall. And it takes me a while to realize this is the first time we've ever done this. We've spent countless nights together. Talking, commiserating, supporting. But we've never cried together. *Piper* never cried. After what happened on her seventeenth birthday, she vowed to never cry again.

Yet, here we sit, crying and snotting all over each other. She has changed. Mason has changed her. And the thought makes my chest heave even harder. My friend found a man she could trust enough with her heart, with her tears, with her horrible past.

But even though my heart is breaking, I know it was all an illusion. What was I thinking? I can't be anyone's girlfriend, fiancée, or wife. It was all a fantasy. Because deep down, I know I could never tell him—never tell anyone—what happened to me. How could a man even look at a woman the way Ethan looked at me today after knowing the things she'd done. Knowing the vile things that were done to her.

No. It's better this way. I've always known that. I just forgot for a little while.

CHAPTER TWENTY-FIVE

True to his word, Ethan didn't show up at the gym on Tuesday.

Or Wednesday.

Or Thursday.

Or Friday.

Well, he did show up, as I heard through the grapevine, just not when *I* was there.

And all week at work, even though I tried to keep myself from doing it, every time the door to Mitchell's opened, I'd look over to see if it was Ethan walking through it.

On Saturday, during a bathroom break, I find myself wondering where he's going for lunch if not here. Did another client walk into his office and take her shirt off? Did he decide to get back with Gretchen? They obviously have some kind of history.

I push up my shirt sleeves to wash my hands and it hits me. He saw my scars. Was he repulsed by them? I think back to the day that seems forever ago even though not a week has passed. No, even after he saw the scars, he still seemed interested.

Of course he did, his dick was inside you and you were making him come.

I shake off the thought. After all, now I don't have to try and explain the scars away. It's better this way, I remind myself.

Walking back out into the dining room, my heart takes a tumble when I see who's sitting at one of my tables. I quickly look at the front door of the restaurant to see if anyone else is coming. Then I make my way over to the table hoping no one notices my shaky legs.

"Hi, Kyle. Levi. How are you?"

The way they both look at me lets me know that, in fact, no one else will be joining them.

"Hey, Charlie," Kyle says. "You okay?"

I nod, pulling my order pad from my apron so I don't have to look at the man who shares a resemblance with the one who broke my heart. "What can I get you?"

Levi reaches out a hand and places it on mine. "We're not here for the food, Charlie. We wanted to make sure you were okay."

I look at him. "So, you're not ordering?" I snap at them. Then I realize I sound like a complete bitch. "Sorry. I'm not mad at *you*."

"It's okay," Levi says. "You have every right to be pissed. Ethan told us what he did and it was a real dick move."

"Yeah, um, seriously, are you eating? Because I have tables I need to get back to."

He nods. "Yeah. Bring us a couple of burgers and fries please."

"Water with that?" I ask.

"Please," he says.

"Coming right up." I stick my pad back into my apron and walk away.

I turn the corner and lean my back against the wall, breathing deeply. Seeing them is like seeing an extension of *him*. They see him every day. They talk to him. Maybe they even get to touch him. I don't want them here. I don't want any reminders of what I'm missing. And even though I've promised myself that there is no way in hell I'd give him another chance, part of me still wants him to try. But he had his second chance. And his third. Hell, no wonder he played me like a damn fiddle; I was a doormat.

I drop off their order in the kitchen, take care of a few tables and then return with their drinks.

"He's a damn fool, Charlie," Kyle tells me. "I'm not going to deny that, but there are things about him you don't know. Things nobody knows."

"We all have secrets," I say. "But that's still not a pass to be an asshole." I deposit their drinks on the table and then hand a check to a customer in the booth next to them.

I ignore Kyle and Levi until I have to take them their food. I know they love the guy, and of course they are going to try and defend his actions, but I really don't need to hear his excuses. "Enjoy your meal, guys," I say placing their plates in front of them, then turning for a quick getaway.

But Kyle grabs my arm, pulling me down into the booth beside him. "Just give me one minute, Charlie. Hear me out. I swear it's nothing you did. My brother has issues. Issues that keep him from having a relationship."

Before I can stop myself, my curiosity gets the better of me. "Does this have anything to do with Gretchen?"

"Gretchen?" he says incredulously. "No. Hell no."

"We would have warned you off sooner," Levi adds. "But we really thought you were the one."

"The one?"

Kyle nods. "Yeah. The way he talked about you. Looked at you. We really thought you were it for him. But we were wrong. He can't be with you. He can't be with anyone. He's broken, Charlie. We realize now that there isn't anything we or you or anyone can do about it. And I'm sorry as hell."

I motion to their food. "It's getting cold. You should eat." I scoot out of the booth, leaving their check on the table. "It was nice seeing you again. Good luck in med school, Kyle. Bye Levi." I make it sound final. Because it is. I know that now. They made good and well sure that I did.

He can't be with you. He can't be with anyone.

I hide out in the back until they leave, asking Mindy to cover a few of my tables. While I wait, I text Piper.

Me: I need a night out. You up for it?

Piper: Just tell me when and where. I'll always be here for you.

I smile. Who needs a man when I have my best friend?

~ ~ ~

Walking into the nightclub, everything feels familiar. Piper is on my arm and we're both dressed to kill. Kill what, I'm not sure, but we are.

Within minutes, we're given drinks compliments of some guys at the end of the bar. I lift my glass to them and toss it back quickly, knowing it won't be long before they come over and hit on us. This isn't anything new. I've done this dance before. In fact, it was pretty commonplace for the five years I was traveling abroad. When we were running low on cash, usually at the end of the month, Piper and I would head to a club. Men would buy us drinks. I'd feel them out to determine which one was more likely to let us crash for a few days. Piper hated those nights. She always stayed sober, hating the fact I was selling myself for a warm bed for the two of us. I never looked at it that way. It was only sex. A means to an end. Giving it away meant nothing to me. It would have been much harder to part with what material things I had of value. Like the platinum bracelet my only living grandmother gave me when I was seven, right before she passed away. Or the pearl necklace Piper's parents gave me for high school graduation. *Those* things meant something to me.

More drinks arrive, this time from a group of men sitting at a nearby table. Piper is still drinking her bottle of water. She never accepts drinks from anyone. And she's determined to be the 'designated driver,' even though we came here in a cab. I know it's her way of taking care of me. Making sure I don't do anything stupid. I'm not shy about taking up the slack, so I pull her new drink over to me and dump it into mine. I raise the empty glass to the men at the table. One of them whistles at me.

Piper eyes me skeptically. "We're here for us, right? Two girls having fun on a night out. We're not over there anymore. Right, Charlie?"

I take a slow swallow of my large drink. "Right, Pipes. No worries."

When one of the groups of guys comes over, we thank them for the drinks and politely decline their invitation to dance.

"So, is Mason pissed that I'm monopolizing so much of your time lately?" I ask her.

"What? No. Of course not. You are not monopolizing my time. He understands that best friends need to hang. He has nights he spends with the guys. Plus he—"

"Knows how fucked up I am so he feels sorry for me?" I say.

"That's not what I was going to say, Charlie. What I was going to say was that he looks forward to the nights he gets to spend with just him and Hailey. Don't get me wrong, we love hanging out as a family. But before I came along, he developed a really special bond with her. He just doesn't want to lose that. So it's good for them to have this time." She pulls me in for a hug. "And it's good for *us* to have this time. I've really missed you, Charlie."

"Well, don't get too attached," I say.

She pushes me away, holding me at arm's length as she scowls at me. "Charlie Anthony Tate, you are not leaving New York. I absolutely forbid it."

"You *forbid* it?" I ask, with a challenging rise of my brow.

While Piper goes into a tirade on how she just got me back and I can't possibly leave again, I can only think of one thing. CAT. What the hell does it mean and why did he seem so upset when I asked him about it? Is that why he can't be with me? Maybe he's still pining away over some other woman who wronged him.

I start thinking of the night in the pool when I saw the tattoo. It was the second time we were together. It was the first time I thought of him as more than just another screw. The first time my heart hurt over a man.

Shit. I have to get him out of my head.

More drinks are delivered by a waitress. This time, the men follow directly behind her, introducing themselves as soon as she puts the glasses on our table.

"I'm Zach and this is Kevin," the tall one says. "The drinks are from me. Kevin's married and he wants to make it perfectly clear that he had no part in this whatsoever other than being my wingman."

We laugh. You gotta admire the guy's sincerity. "Nice to meet you, Zach and Kevin. I'm Charlie." I motion to Piper. "And this is

Piper. She wants me to make it perfectly clear that she's engaged and is only here as *my* wingman."

"Well, now that we have all that out of the way, would you ladies like to dance?" Zach asks, holding his hand out to me.

I'm about to blow him off like the rest of the guys who've bought us drinks, but then I would probably just sit here and think of the P.I. all night long. And this night is all about *not* thinking about him.

Plus, Zach is funny.

I shrug and then raise my eyebrows at Piper, letting her decide for us. "Okay. It sounds fun," she says.

I quickly finish off drink number four and take Zach's hand as we get up to walk to the dance floor.

"So, how long have you been married, Kevin?" Piper asks.

"Four years," he says. "Married my high school sweetheart right after graduation."

"Aw, that's sweet," Piper says.

The closer we get to the dance floor, the less I hear of their conversation. Which is fine. Because it was already getting boring.

We work our way into the center of the floor. There are several circles of girls all dancing together, and some other co-ed groups like ours, with a few men and women hanging out on the floor doing what seems more like socializing than anything else. Then there are the couples who are doing more dirty than dancing.

We dance to a few songs as a group, and I'm all too aware of how Zach keeps inching closer to me. Before long, he has his hands on my hips, still standing a respectable distance away, but making it known he'd like to remedy that.

He leans in closer to speak in my ear. "So, Charlie, is that short for Charlene?"

Really? He's so original. "Nope, it's just Charlie."

"I like it. It's different. Your last name isn't Brown, is it?" He laughs at his own joke.

Yeah. Never heard that one either. "No. Not Brown."

"Well, what is it then?"

I stop moving and pull back to look him in the eye. "It's just Charlie. And I should tell you right now that I've no intention of seeing you after tonight, so last names really don't matter all that much, do they?"

He smiles. "Well, Charlie, with no last name, I like your style. Does that mean you're interested in seeing more of me *tonight*?"

I guffaw. "Hardly. Dancing is the only thing you're getting out of that drink."

He pulls me closer. "Well then, I'd better make the most of it." He smiles. It's mildly charming. I let him hold our bodies together and sway me to the music.

"Let's slow it down a bit," the D.J. says. "Let you crazy kids cool down for a minute, shall we?"

Piper motions to me that she's heading back to the table. I nod my head in understanding. Kevin shakes her hand and walks back over to another table. I can't imagine what that must be like. The two of them, being so secure in a relationship that they can dance with another person without it meaning anything.

The song starts and I freeze. Chills run up and down my sweaty back as Zach crushes his body to mine. I'm transported back in time, to the concert I attended last weekend. To when Adam Stuart dedicated this song to me. To when I was in the arms of another man.

I turn around to escape Zach's arms, but he pulls me back to him, caging me to him in the same way Ethan caged me against him that night. I get pulled into the song. Adam's voice caresses me with his words of love and longing. Emotion floods through me like a tsunami. I stop pulling away. I let his hips roll against mine. I let his body control our movements. I let his erection press against me. I let my mind pretend it's still that night and the man behind me is the only man I've ever let myself need.

"You feel so good," I hear a strange voice say behind me. My eyes fly open. Those aren't Ethan's words. It's not Ethan's voice.

My head is clouded with alcohol. My eyes are clouded with tears. I rip myself away from him and run towards the bathroom, passing by our vacant table, and noticing Piper vying for position at the bar.

I make my way down the hallway only to find a long line of women waiting to enter the bathroom before me. I turn the corner and see another door, hoping it leads to the outside because I need to escape this place so desperately I can't even breathe. I open it and find myself in a storage room, surrounded by cartons of toilet paper and straws. I shouldn't be in here. I spin around to leave only to find that Zach has followed me in.

He shuts the door behind him. Then he grabs me, pulling me towards him. He tries to kiss me, but I turn my head away and his lips meet my neck instead. He sucks and laves and licks the tender flesh beneath my ear. His hot breath flows over me as the ministrations of his mouth hypnotize me. His hands come up to grab my breasts. When I don't push him away, he moans excitedly and lowers a hand to raise the hem of my short skirt.

In seconds, his fingers are inside my panties, working my clit, entering my body. He rips my underwear in his haste to remove them. Then he unbuttons his jeans and pulls himself out, rubbing his erection along my slit.

"Hold on," he says, his raspy voice causing my eyes to snap open to catch him reaching down to his fallen jeans to get a condom. "Give me a sec." His voice grates in my head like fingernails on a chalkboard.

I look down to see a head of dark hair. I don't want to hear that voice. I don't want to see this hair. I don't want to be with this man.

Then, as I feel him push himself inside me, I close my eyes again and wish it all away. I conjure up a picture in my head. The mural on the wall I used to stare at when I was young. The painted unicorn that I begged to protect me for all those years.

But this time is different. I led him on. I let him touch me. I didn't ask him to stop. Unicorns don't protect those who bring it on themselves.

"Uhhhhhhh," he cries into my chest, achieving precisely what he came for.

As soon as he pulls out of me, I pull down my skirt and plow through the door, not even caring that my panties are in a shredded ball on the storeroom floor. I race down the hall to the bathroom, pushing several women aside to get in. A lady is exiting the handicap stall and I jump ahead of the line and lock myself in to the yells of a dozen inebriated girls.

I collapse on the floor and heave all of tonight's drinks into the toilet. Then I wet a paper towel and run it over my face as I look at myself in the old, cracked mirror. I stare at the woman's distorted reflection. Her hair is mussed up, her eyeliner smeared, her spirit broken.

And I'm totally sure of the person who is staring back at me.

Hello again.

CHAPTER TWENTY-SIX

It's been three weeks since I've seen his face. Three weeks of daily phone calls from Piper, talking me into staying in New York for one more day. Three weeks of forcing myself not to throw my clothes into a suitcase and leave everything behind.

Although I haven't seen his *face*, I did catch a glimpse of the back of Ethan's head last Monday as he was walking to the gym offices. Apparently poker nights are still a thing. But nobody talks about it. Nobody talks about *him*. Not even Jarod, and he's related.

I was too ashamed of myself to tell Piper what happened in the storeroom at the club that night. I cleaned myself up and found her sitting at our table nursing another bottle of water. She told me I looked like hell and maybe we should call it a night. I was grateful that I didn't have to explain why I wanted to leave. I was grateful that I didn't run into Zach on the way out. I was grateful that I could just go home and forget the horrible night ever happened.

So that's what I do with my days—try to forget. Forget Ethan. Forget Zach. Forget my mom and dad. Forget that appalling list.

The problem with trying to forget things, is that all you really do is remember them.

I reach over to my bedside table and grab my eye mask, putting it on to shield myself from the mid-afternoon sun shining through my window. No offense to Piper, but sleep has become my best friend. It's the one place I'm at peace. Unlike Piper, I've never had nightmares about my past, and if I dream, I don't remember.

My phone chimes, alerting me to an e-mail. Annoyed by it, but wondering who would be emailing me, because as Piper said, I know about two people, I grab it and tap the screen. When I see who the text is from my body tenses. The sender of the email is Gretchen. And the subject is 'Final list of names.'

Oh, God. I know what that means. It means they found the last four men. It means Karl Salzman's name will be among them. The thought of all twelve of them makes my skin crawl, but him— he's the one who took something from me I could never get back. It was his vile touch that stole whatever innocence I had left.

I say a silent prayer before I open the email. I pray he is dead. I pray he is dead and buried and being eaten by maggots and worms. That he is rotting in hell along with my mother where they are probably Satan's right hand man and woman.

I open the attached files and my heart skips when the word DECEASED is written in diagonal bold letters across the front of one of the pages. But upon further inspection, it's not Karl's name on it. It's Joe Mitchner's. I can't help but feel relief that one of these men is no longer walking the earth, but at the same time, I'm disappointed it's not Karl.

The second page details information on John Taylor. He's moved out of state and now resides in Utah. I find myself wondering if he's one of those men with ten wives and twenty-four kids. I cringe thinking about it.

Next is Steven Smith. The document says they aren't one-hundred-percent sure he is the right Steven Smith but that they've exhausted all avenues and this one came the closest to having ties with my mother. He also has moved out of state, but is at least more accessible, being in Massachusetts. Still, he'll have to wait.

I click on the last attachment, my heart pounding because I know whose it will be. When the name pops up, I wince. When my eyes fall to his last known address, I don't know if I should be upset or happy. He lives in White Plains, just a thirty-minute cab ride from here. Should I feel fortunate he lives close enough to confront him, or scared because of what I know I would like to do to him?

I pull my mother's diary from the nightstand and leaf through it until I find the page I'm looking for.

June 11, 2009

I have to up my game with Salzman. He's got even more clout than Morgan and J.T. combined. The man knows people. I've lost count of the number of times I've slept with him, and Dewey said he's going to cut me off if I keep giving away all the good shit he gets me. You'd think with all Karl's connections, he'd be able to score his own shit. The last time he was here, he promised me a sit-down with the producer of a famous book that was being made into a movie. Said they were looking for a mid-thirties female lead. So what if I'm not technically in my thirties anymore? I could pass for it and that's all that matters. Plus, with makeup and all the computer-generated technology these days, anyone can look ten years younger than they are. They'd be lucky to get me. Hell, with my resume, they should be begging me for the job. But my asshole agent refuses to book me any auditions that aren't within five years of my true age. I think it's time to look for another agent.

When Karl texted me he was coming over tonight, he asked if my daughter was going to be here. Damn Charlie, even the ones I want for myself seem more interested in her. She's grown so tall and developed so early. I thought I'd kept her hidden from Karl. I'm sick of all these guys paying more attention to a fucking fifteen-year-old than someone who's won not one, but two Oscars. Maybe if I just let him have her, he'd get it out of his system. You know, kill two birds with one stone—I get the part, he gets her.

My blood boils thinking back on that day. I throw the diary across the room and watch as it hits the wall and falls to the floor, all the while wishing it were Karl's head. Adrenaline is pumping through me when I slip into my jeans and t-shirt. Then I pull a hoodie over my head before I gather up what I need and head out the door.

I catch my reflection in the rear-view mirror of the cab, realizing I forgot the ball cap in my haste to leave. But at this point, I'm too far invested to care. I don't care if he knows who I am when he sees me. I would actually prefer him to be looking into my eyes when I do what I need to do.

The thirty-minute cab ride out of the city seems to take hours. All the while, I go over different scenarios in my head. All the while, I trace the outline of the hard metal in my hoodie pocket.

I have the cabbie drop me at the end of the street, not even asking him to wait. I still don't know what I plan to do or how long I plan to be here. I want to check the place out before I make any decisions. It's a private residence. This is White Plains, after all. Not a crack house, like Clint lived in. Not a townhouse like Tony. Not a busy apartment building like Morgan. No, this house is an affluent single-family home on a large lot surrounded by, of all things, a goddamn white picket fence.

I walk by the home, casing it stealthily. I can see beyond the fence into a backyard that has a swing set and my stomach clenches. Kids. *Fuck.*

I realize it's not quite five o'clock. The guy probably won't even be home. He has to have a good job to afford a place like this. I find myself walking around the block a few times, talking myself out of things then talking myself back into them.

The third time around the block, I see a car approach his house. It's a nice car. A Land Cruiser, I think. The garage door to the home opens and the car pulls inside. Then I have to keep myself from hyperventilating when Karl Salzman emerges from the garage, walking to the mailbox like he's Mister fucking Rogers. Like he doesn't have a care in the world. Like he's never raped a teenage girl.

He doesn't even notice me as I come around the bushes and walk towards him. He's too engrossed in opening a piece of mail. I almost make it into the garage behind him, but the garage door comes down before I can put my hand out to stop it.

My skin still crawling at the sight of him, I walk up the steps to his front porch and pound on the door. Moments later he opens it, the smile on his face falling faster than the time it takes me to reach into my pocket.

"Oh, God," he says, turning his head to look behind him.

When he turns back around, I have a gun pointed in his face.

"Wait, don't," he begs, holding his hands out to plead with me. "Don't."

Bile rises from the pit of my stomach, burning my throat. My hands are shaking so hard, I'm not even sure I could hit him with a bullet even though we're only feet apart. "Funny," I bite at him, "when I said those very words to you, you ignored me. Why should I listen when *you* say them?"

He starts to plead with me again.

"Shut up!" I yell, waving the gun at him. "And step the fuck back."

In this moment, I realize how poetic it would be to shoot Karl Salzman with Tony Pellman's gun. I let my finger caress the trigger, wanting so badly to pull it, but needing to give him a piece of my mind first.

Sweat dots his brow as he retreats a few feet, enough for me to walk through the front door. But then two things happen at once. A lady comes around the corner asking, "Honey, who's at the door?" And someone runs up behind me as I hear a familiar voice shout, "Charlie, NO!"

CHAPTER TWENTY-SEVEN

I can't even turn around to look at Ethan. I can't let my defenses down for one second or Karl could get away. I can't think about how Ethan probably just set me up, giving me this information so he could follow me. I want to be mad at him. But my anger is all directed at the monster in front of me.

But the thing is, he doesn't look like a monster. He looks like he could be anyone's dad. Anyone's husband. And he's scared. It's evident by more than just the look on his face. It's evident by the wetness spreading across the front of his pants.

I smirk at his crotch. Good. Humiliation from pissing himself is an added bonus.

"Charlie!" Ethan's words ring out from behind. "What are you doing? Put down the gun."

I shake my head fervently from side to side. "No," I tell him. "Not until he's paid for what he's done."

The woman who has now rounded the corner and taken in the full extent of the circumstances, screams. Karl reaches out to her, pulling her behind him, protecting her with his own body.

I hear a door close behind me and then I see Ethan carefully edge against the wall next to me. "Charlie, give me the gun. Please."

"No," I say, never taking my eyes off Karl. "Damn you, Ethan. You shouldn't have followed me."

"What's going on here, Charlie? What has this man done?"

"What has he done?" I ask, my voice cracking in agony. "What has he done?" I narrow my eyes at Karl. "Tell them, Karl. Tell them what you did to me."

I wince knowing that if he speaks, my secret will be revealed. But then I look at my hands, pointing the gun at Karl's head and I realize it doesn't really matter anymore. Nothing matters.

"Karl?" his wife asks. "What is she talking about? Why is this happening?"

"Natalie," he says, his voice trembling as he turns his head towards her. "Oh, God. I'm so sorry."

Fury radiates through my veins. "You're apologizing to *her?*" I yell. Then I motion to the woman. "Who are you? His wife?"

She nods and I shake my head in frustration.

"You married this sick bastard?" I ask. "Do you have any idea who you married?"

"Charlie, what the fuck is going on?" Ethan demands.

"Momma?" a soft whisper of a voice squeaks from the hallway. Gasps come from all four of us when a towheaded little girl walks sleepily out into the foyer, rubbing her tired eyes.

Natalie removes herself from Karl's protective stance, having no care for herself when running over to sweep the little girl into her arms. The child can't be more than two. I'm grateful for so many reasons. One: she's probably too young to remember any of this. And two: he most likely hasn't touched her. Yet.

"You have a daughter?" I ask, vileness dripping from my voice.

I lunge for him, but Ethan steps in front of me and I'm left pointing the gun at *him*. "Charlie, no matter what happened here, you don't want to do this. Talk to me. Tell me what's happening here."

"Move," I tell him. I take a step back, letting him know I won't advance further.

Ethan raises his hands in surrender as if he's the target of my aggression. Then he moves, but not back to where he was before. He walks over and stands next to Natalie and her daughter, protecting them in Karl's stead.

I look over at the child. "Is this your only child?" I ask.

"Yes," Natalie says. "Please don't hurt us."

"I'm not going to hurt *you*," I tell her. "In fact, you should be thanking me for this. It'll save you the trouble."

Natalie and Ethan both look in shock. Scared. Confused.

I'm glad the child is so young. Because what I'm about to say will have no meaning to her. But what I'm about to say could ultimately save her from a life of self-abhorrence. I look at her sweet, cherub face and it gives me the strength to do what I need to do.

There isn't a part of my body that isn't shaking when I tell them, "He raped me."

Ethan and Natalie both draw in sharp breaths. That's where the similarity ends. Ethan's eyes turn sympathetic. There is no question in my mind that he believes the words that just came from me. Natalie, on the other hand, tells me I'm mistaken. That he is a wonderful husband and father who would never do such a thing and I must have him confused with someone else. She said she's known him for four years and there is no way the man I'm pointing the gun at is the man who raped me.

"Charlie?" Ethan begs me with his eyes to explain.

I speak to Natalie. "Your husband. Your child's father. The man you love. The man you think you know. He raped me. Not last night. Not last week. He raped me seven years ago. When I was fifteen—when I was a virgin—he raped me in exchange for a favor."

I look at their stunned faces and then shock them some more. "And in the months after, he raped me ten more times."

I see Ethan's hands ball into fists. He's going to hit the bastard. Beat him to a bloody pulp if the look on his face is any indication. He lunges towards him, swinging at him with all his weight, making a loud cracking sound when his hand connects to Karl's jaw, sending Karl's body hurdling into the wall behind him.

"Ethan, no!" I scream, running over to pull him off Karl. "This isn't your fight."

Natalie puts her daughter down, joining me in my attempt to pull Ethan off her husband. Ethan stands over a fallen Karl, his arm snaps back, ready to deliver another blow when his elbow catches the side of my head, sending me toppling off him and onto the floor.

"Shit! Charlie!" He turns his attention from Karl to me, kneeling on the floor next to me, running his hands over my head to check for injury. "Did I hurt you?"

"I'm okay," I tell him. "You barely got me. Besides, I've had worse."

"Oh, God. Charlie." His eyes meet mine and all of a sudden it's as if he knows my pain. The pain of something being taken from you. Something you can never get back. And when he gently reaches out to take the gun from my clutches, I let him.

Natalie must have seen him take it because she whips out her cell phone and starts tapping on it. "All of you, stop it! I'm calling the police."

"Natalie, wait," Karl implores.

"Karl? What are you saying? I *am* calling the police . . . right?"

He gets up from the ground, rubbing a hand over his swollen jaw. He walks over and puts his hand on hers. The hand that was dialing the phone. "No, you're not."

"What? Why?" she asks. Her eyes snap to his and they have a silent conversation that only married people can have. Then her gaze drops to the floor and she takes in a breath as if she'll never breathe again.

"Oh, my God." She gasps, backing away from him to pick up their daughter. "Tell me it isn't true," she says, holding her daughter tightly in her arms.

Karl's knees give out and he falls to the floor, his head in his hands as he starts to cry. "I'm sorry," he tells her. Then he turns to me. "I'm so sorry." His chest heaves as his sobs become louder. "I was loaded. I didn't know what I was doing. I was different then. I . . . I—"

"Oh my God," Natalie says again in horror, her mouth agape as she looks at her husband in utter disgust. She holds onto her daughter for dear life. "We have a daughter, Karl. A daughter! How could I ever trust that you—"

"I would never," he says, holding his hand out to her.

She backs away. "Ten times, Karl?" she asks. "Ten times isn't being stoned. Ten times is being a psychotic pedophile. Ten times is . . ." She hands me the phone. "Here," she says, "*You* call the police." Then she disappears down the hallway with her daughter.

Karl tries to follow them, but Ethan gets in his way. "Sit the fuck down," he says.

219

Ethan turns to me and studies me. I can see in his eyes the moment he puts it all together. "Oh, Charlie," he says, closing his eyes briefly to sigh. "The list. Did they all . . . ?"

I shake my head. "No. They didn't all rape me, but they all did . . . something." I look away, not wanting to see the pain in his eyes when I say what I know will shock him. "My mother let them." I hear Ethan's fist go through the drywall as I look down at the sobbing man on the floor. "But he was the worst of them all."

He doesn't deserve to cry. He doesn't deserve to be sorry. He doesn't deserve to look like the broken, pathetic man he is right now. I lean over to grab the gun away from Ethan, but he quickly pulls it from my reach, tucking it into the back of his belt. When I lunge around him to try and get it, he envelops me in his arms, holding me tightly against him. "Look," he says, nodding to Natalie who is coming down the hall with the little girl in one hand and a suitcase and diaper bag in the other. "I know you want to kill him. I know how it feels to lose something and want to kill the person responsible for taking it from you. But, Charlie, punishment comes in all kinds of different ways."

Karl begs her to stay. Natalie tells him he will never see her or Kelsey ever again.

Kelsey.

I hope Natalie keeps her word.

She comes over to me and holds her hand out for her phone. I give it to her with a nod. She pulls me in for a hug. I have a feeling she wants to say something to me, but that she's in too much shock to have any kind of sensible conversation. My eyes connect with hers and we share a moment. A moment of shame. A moment of recognition. A moment that makes me wonder if something similar once happened to her. A moment she's saving her daughter from ever having.

"I'm going to my mother's," she tells Karl. "You will have your things out of here by dark tomorrow or I'll have you thrown in jail if Charlie doesn't."

Two minutes later, Natalie and Kelsey are out the garage door.

Ethan takes my elbow, escorting me out to the front porch, Karl's sobs echoing behind us.

We walk in silence to his car over on the adjacent street. I'm still shaking from the whole encounter. His strong arms are around me, holding me up. He opens the door for me, getting me settled into my seat before he walks around and gets into his.

He doesn't start the engine just yet. I breathe and breathe and breathe. I breathe so heavily, the windows fog up on this cool April afternoon.

"I wish you would have told me," he says.

I laugh. "Right. Because I go around telling guys I want to sleep with that a dozen people molested me. And I tell them it's because my mom basically sold me to them for blow. Or for the chance to revive her broken career. And I tell them she slapped me around just for the hell of it. Oh, and, news flash—now I can tell them she hit my fucking dad, too. She hit him so much he left me there to rot." I take a breath. "And let's not forget that I should tell them that thanks to Mommy Dearest and all her friends, I went on to sleep with guys for sport."

He cringes. "Shit, Charlie. I'm so sorry. I don't even know what to say." He runs his hands through his hair and as he turns away from me, I see him wipe a thumb under his eye as he tries to get his own breathing under control.

He reaches over and takes my arm in his, pushing up the sleeve of my hoodie. "And these?" he asks, his eyes bleeding emotion as they rake over my scars. "Was this your mom?"

I look at my lap and nod.

"When did it stop, Charlie?"

"When Piper and I left the country after graduation."

"My God," he says, looking repulsed.

I point to his face. "See that. That's why I didn't tell you. You're disgusted."

"I'm not disgusted, Charlie." He turns in his seat so that he's facing me head on. "I could never be disgusted with you. Quite the opposite, in fact. Those horrible things, they happened *to* you, Charlie. And the person you became after was a result of all those things. You shouldn't be ashamed of the way you are; you should be proud that you survived."

I nod, feeling tears burn the backs of my eyes. "Why did you follow me?" I ask.

"A hunch, I guess. You turning up injured. You wearing a hat and hoodie to Morgan Tenney's place. So I did some more digging into the names you gave me. Some of them were drug dealers. It scared the shit out of me to think of the danger you were putting yourself in. And after I saw the scars. I just knew something bad had happened. So today, as soon as I had Gretchen email you the names, I started following you."

I sigh. "I guess I should thank you for stopping me from killing him."

"I think you've had enough drama in your life. You don't need to add a prison sentence to it," he says.

I study him, thinking about something he said back at Karl's house. "You said you know what it's like to want to kill someone who took something from you."

He nods, bringing his hand up to rub the back of his neck. Right over his tattoo. "Do you have time for a ride?" he asks.

"A ride?"

"Yeah. I think it's time I introduced you to Cat."

CHAPTER TWENTY-EIGHT

Where is he taking me, I wonder? I'm curious. I'm terrified. I'm jealous of a woman named Cat that he loved enough to brand her name into his flesh.

Ethan breaks the silence. "You asked about the tattoo on my neck that day at the pool. But how come you never asked about the one on my chest?"

I think of the times I traced it with my finger, wanting to ask him about it, but not wanting to hear the answer. He knows everything about me now—the worst things about me. There is really no reason for anything but candor at this point. "I was afraid it might be a woman's name. And if it was, I didn't want to know."

He takes his eyes off the road for a second so he can look into mine. "It's not."

I let out a relieved breath. "Okay, then what is it?"

"It's the Chinese symbol for forgiveness."

I cock my head, staring at his profile. "Does this have anything to do with wanting to kill the person who took something from you?"

He nods. "It has everything to do with it."

"So, you just forgave him? Or her?"

"Well, it's not that easy, Charlie. Forgiveness is a long road."

We're heading back towards the city, but not into the city. He turns off the highway and we make our way through several residential areas. We pass a church. We pass a large cemetery. I'm hypnotized by watching the endless sea of headstones, but then I realize they aren't going by as quickly. We slow down and turn, driving under a curved wrought-iron entrance sign that reads: **Fairmount Memorial Gardens.**

I look over at Ethan but he is stoic as we drive along the roads that weave through the maze of headstones, grave markers and crypts. The car comes to a stop and he turns off the engine.

He takes a very deep, very long calming breath. Then he reaches over me to grab a small box from the glove compartment before he gets out of the car. I let myself out and join him as he walks along a paved path. I walk next to him in silence. With every step, I know what he's going to show me is horrible. With every step, I know he's trusting me enough to see it.

Ethan stops walking and sits on a concrete bench. I sit down next to him.

"When I was in high school, I got a girl pregnant," he says. "We'd only been dating for a few weeks. It was still casual. We weren't in love or anything. But we knew we were too young to become parents. Too young to make adult choices and live adult lives."

I nod in understanding. "I'd have done the same thing," I tell him.

"No," he says. "We didn't have an abortion. It was hard. Really hard, but we went through with it."

I gasp. "You have a child?"

He smiles a sad smile. "I do."

Another deep breath comes from far within him and I know he's about to tell me his darkest secrets. Just as I've now told him all of mine.

"My girlfriend's name was Cara," he says, pain evident in his voice as he speaks of her. I have the urge to look around us, look at the gravestones to find her name, but I keep my eyes focused on his.

"We tried to make a go of it as a couple, but we were just too young and we ended up fighting all the time. We had different goals. Different dreams. But what we did have in common was we both loved our daughter, so we put our differences aside so we could co-parent her. And before long we realized that although we didn't make a good couple, we did make good friends. In fact, she became my best friend."

He has a daughter. My eyes close as realization washes over me. It all makes sense now. His being uncomfortable giving me family information from the list. The fight with Nikki about her roommate's daughter. How he can't be in a relationship. Suddenly, all the pieces start coming together. He lost his best friend; the mother of his child. He has a daughter to raise. He doesn't want anyone getting in the way of that.

I don't know what to say to him. How do you comfort someone whose best friend died? I can't even imagine if something happened to Piper. And what he said about wanting to kill the person who had taken something from you? She must have died in a horrible way.

I put my hand on his knee, letting him know I'm here but that I just don't have the words.

He puts his hand on top of mine. Then he threads our fingers together and nods to the headstone to the right of us.

My heart stops beating and I die for a second. I die because what is etched into the gravestone kills me.

Catherine 'Cat' Grace Stone
November 2, 2006 – July 16, 2008
Beloved daughter and granddaughter.

Oh, God. His daughter died. I calculate the dates in my head. Not even two years old. I look for another headstone next to hers, one that would have Cara's name on it, but I don't see one.

The hand that is not entwined with his comes up to cover my sob. "Oh, Ethan," I cry, not even being able to come close to understanding what losing a child would feel like.

"It was the day before my nineteenth birthday," he says. "It was my day to pick her up from daycare. Cara hadn't gone on to college like I had. In high school, she'd worked at a department store, so when she graduated, she stayed with the store, becoming an assistant manager. My schedule as a college student was more flexible, especially being summer semester, and I was glad it afforded me a lot of time with Cat." When he says her name, he looks at the headstone lovingly.

He clears his throat and I know what he's about to reveal will gut him.

"When I got to the daycare center, they told me Cara hadn't brought her in that morning. They just assumed Cat was sick, or that it was another one of those days where I had a light schedule so I kept her with me all day. But I thought it strange that Cara wouldn't call me. She always called me when Cat was sick. It was much easier for me to miss school than for her to miss work.

"I knew something was wrong," he says. "I felt it. I ran out to my car, calling Cara on my way. When she answered, I breathed a sigh of relief. She sounded normal. Happy even. I'd never been so elated to hear her voice."

His hand starts to sweat in mine and he grips me tighter. He squeezes me so hard it hurts. But I let him. Because I know what he's about to tell me will hurt him far worse than he's hurting me.

"I asked her why Cat wasn't at daycare. Was she sick? Did she drop her at her mother's? Why didn't she call me? But the whole time I questioned her, she was silent. Then, just when I thought I'd lost the phone connection, I heard her scream into the phone, just before it went dead.

"I tried to call her back. I called her a hundred times as I raced through traffic to get to where she worked. But it was rush hour, and no matter how hard I tried, I couldn't get to her fast enough."

My heart is racing along with his. I know how hard his is beating because our hands are bound so tightly together, I can feel the throbbing in his wrist.

"By the time I got to the store, there were fire trucks and police cars everywhere. I tried to barge through the gathering crowd, but I was held back. I worked my way around to one side and spotted Cara on her knees, crying and screaming, blood coating her knees from the rocks in the pavement. Two firemen were holding onto her as she collapsed down onto her hands.

"Then I looked in the direction of the ambulance, over to the place Cara was reaching out to. Through the spectators and the flashing lights, I catch a glimpse of my daughter's small, pale, lifeless body on a gurney next to Cara's car."

"Oh my God," I cry out in horror, tears flowing from my eyes at his unbelievable, heart-wrenching words.

"I busted through the police barricade and ran over to the ambulance to see paramedics standing beside her body. They weren't doing anything. They weren't pounding on her chest or breathing in her mouth. They weren't hooking her up to an IV. They were all just standing there. Crying.

"I yelled at them to do something. To help my baby. A couple of the firemen came over, flanking my sides. One of them told me there wasn't anything they could do. She was gone. She'd been gone for some time because the heat in the car was just too much for her and she'd been in there for far too long."

That's the moment I realize what he's telling me. And suddenly everything I've ever been through pales in comparison to this man's pain. I always knew there were people worse off than Piper and me. I'd just never met any of them. Until now.

"They couldn't keep me from her," he says, his voice cracking in desperation. "I climbed over everyone in my way to get to her. I had to see her. Hold her once more. And they let me. They let me hold her until the coroner arrived. They let me hold Cat's frail little body and run my hands over her soft blonde curls for the last time.

"And after they took her away, there was another person I had to get to. I ran to her. I ran to Cara. She was broken, a shell of a girl being held onto by firemen twice her size. She saw me coming and held her arms out to me. I held mine out to her. But not to hug her. To kill her. To strangle the life right out of her because she'd taken the most important thing in my life away from me. And I hated her more than I'd ever hated any human being.

"The firemen pulled me off her before I could do any real damage. And we were both taken to the police station for questioning. But Cara was never charged with her death. It was concluded that it was an accident. That Cara had a lot on her mind that day because she was interviewing for a higher management position. That she'd simply forgotten to take our daughter to daycare."

He shakes his head and repeats, "Just forgotten to take her. How does that happen? How does a mother forget about her child?"

Then he turns to me, looking guilty. "Oh, Charlie. I'm sorry I said that."

"No, don't be. This isn't about me, Ethan."

"But it is," he says. "Your quest to find these men and hurt them the way they hurt you is understandable. But you have so much pain, so much hate within you that it's eating you alive."

"Don't you?" I ask. "You just told me you hated Cara more than you ever hated anyone."

"I did. And she had to get a restraining order against me. And I ended up in court-mandated therapy for PTSD. It was there that I learned about forgiveness."

"Forgiveness?" I ask. "How could you forgive her for that, Ethan?" I look deep into his eyes and see what he's getting at. "Uh . . . no. I know you aren't suggesting I forgive those bastards. I could *never* forget what they've done to me."

"Forgiving and forgetting are two different things, Charlie. Of course you'll never forget what happened. And I'm not saying you should show up on their doorstep with a plate of cookies or anything. I'm saying that before you can heal, you have to let go of the hatred. You don't forgive people for *them*, Charlie. You forgive people for *you*. Forgiveness is a gift you give yourself. With it comes peace and a renewed sense of freedom."

I sneer at him. "*You* have peace and freedom?"

"Yes."

"You could have fooled me," I say, looking down at our hands that are still folded together.

"I never said forgiveness would make a person perfect. *I'm* not perfect. I'm scared, Charlie. I loved that little girl more than my own life. I never thought it possible to feel that kind of love for another person. I'd seen it on TV. Read about it in books. But I thought it was all fantasy. Something made up by Hallmark so they could sell more cards. But the very first time I saw Cat, I knew it was real. I understood in a matter of two seconds, how one could love another so fiercely that they would give their own life for them."

He turns towards me, situating us so we are facing each other and not his daughter's grave. "It took me two seconds to feel that with her," he says. "With you, it was more like two weeks."

My mouth falls open at his words that I'm sure I heard incorrectly. I can't speak. I can't move. I can't even breathe.

"I swear to God, Charlie. It was like a punch in the gut when I met you. When I saw you that first time, something inside me shifted. And when you ripped your shirt off, I knew I must be dreaming. I tried to fight it. I tried to fight it every time I saw you. I tried to fight it every moment we were apart. I knew I couldn't fall for you. I couldn't risk loving someone again and then having them taken from me. But these past three weeks have been hell. You *were* taken from me. But by no one's fault but my own. *I* pushed you away. And the pain is excruciating. Knowing you are out there and I'm not with you is torture. I know I have no right to ask for another chance. I know I don't deserve another chance, but I'm asking anyway. Because if I don't, I'll never forgive myself."

I have to make a conscious effort to close my mouth that's been gaping at him for the past thirty seconds. Did he just forget everything he saw today? Everything he heard? "How could you live with what was done to me? With the things I've done?"

"That shit doesn't matter to me, Charlie. *You* matter to me." He takes both my hands in his. "I can't promise you anything. Except that I'll try. I'll try to be the man you deserve. I promise I'll spend every day trying to be that man. I'm going to fuck up from time to time. I'm not going to be perfect. But if you'll give me the chance, I swear I'll do everything I can to make you trust in me. Trust in us."

He wants me? After everything he knows about me. I take a minute to let it sink in. Everything he just said was perfect. *He* is perfect.

Alarms go off in my head and I can't help but think of Jan Mitchell and the talk she once had with me and Piper about our heart and our head. And right now, my heart wants him. My body wants him. I want him so badly it hurts. But my head reminds me of how hurt I was after that time in the pool. And the time at the concert. And the time on his couch. All the feelings I had those times come rushing back. All those feelings come back in this moment and trump the other feelings I'm having. The ones that want me to put my arms around him and throw caution to the wind.

"I'm not sure I can trust you, Ethan. You hurt me. You know I wanted you. I offered myself to you. I offered my *heart* to you. How will I know you won't just toss me to the curb again? How will I know you won't get scared? How will I know you won't break your promise?"

"Rule number nine, Charlie. A promise is a promise. And I won't break it. Ever. Please, give me another chance."

"Ethan . . ."

"I tell you what. You don't have to give me an answer right now. It's been an emotional day. Just let me start swimming with you again. Let me start building that trust. Let me take you to lunch, and to the movies, and on walks through Central Park where we'll talk about anything and everything. We'll do things friends do.

Because I want that with you, Charlie. I want so much to be your friend. I want that and more. But I'll take what I can get for now."

I nod. "I think I can do that. I can be your friend. But I can't promise you anything more than that right now, so you'll just have to be patient with me."

He smiles. "I'm not going anywhere, Charlie. Except maybe ten feet over there." He gets up, pulling something out of his pocket. "Just wait here for a few minutes, okay? There's something I have to do."

He walks over and perches himself on Cat's headstone, then he opens the box and pulls out a shiny metal harmonica and starts playing it. The song he plays is a lullaby. I can't recall which one because my mother never sang them to me, but I recognize the tune. And he plays it expertly, like he's done it a thousand times before this time. I stare at him, mesmerized by him. By his music. By his emotion. By his beauty.

He finishes the song and puts the harmonica back into the case. "I used to play for her when she was sad or colicky. Sometimes it was the only thing that would calm her down. So now I play every time I visit her. It makes me feel connected to her. And I like to think that somehow, she hears me playing and it brings her peace."

My heart leaps inside my chest. How can I not give another chance to a man who plays the harmonica for his angel daughter? A man who would put himself in danger to make sure I don't ruin the rest of my life. A man who not only accepted all of my secrets, but trusted me with his own.

And suddenly, I realize that I no longer have to envy Piper, Skylar and Baylor. Because, just as they found their knights in shining armor, perhaps I've just found mine.

CHAPTER TWENTY-NINE

I smile when Ethan walks toward me at the entrance to the park. This is our thing now, walking through Central Park on my days off. Well, that and swimming. And movies. And dinner. We've practically been joined at the hip—even though we've technically not been 'joined' at all.

The past month has been incredible. We've spent time together almost every day. But my favorite times with him are the times we just talk. Sometimes we can talk for hours on end, yet it seems like only minutes have passed.

He's told me all about his childhood and what it was like to grow up with two doctors for parents. He told me about the trouble he and his brothers would get into when they were young. He explained to me how his parents moved to California to teach young resident missionaries at UCLA Medical Center. He didn't go with them because of Cat, but it was there where Chad got discovered in the most random way.

We talk about everything. Even the hard stuff. And although he's never asked for details about my past, I feel comfortable sharing bits and pieces of it with him. And even though he'll never replace Piper, he's slowly becoming a best friend to me. Someone with whom I feel safe. Someone whom I can trust.

Our walk through the park starts out like every other. We meander through our normal pleasantries and recaps of what we've done since we've been together—which was only yesterday. Then, I close my eyes and gather the courage I need to ask him about the one thing we've not talked about. Gretchen.

"There is something I've been wanting to ask you for weeks now," I tell him.

He stops walking and crinkles his brow at me. "Anything, Charlie. You know that by now."

"Um, okay." I take a breath and prepare myself for what I may not want to hear. But then I chicken out and ask, "How old are you?"

He laughs, his smile revealing his gorgeous white teeth that complement his tanned face, a result of our long afternoon walks on my days off. "I'm twenty-seven." He nudges my shoulder with his. "But why don't you ask me what's really on your mind."

I roll my eyes at him. He's come to know me well. I start walking again, not able to look directly at him when I ask, "You once told me you and Gretchen had a thing. What exactly does that mean?"

Out of the corner of my eye, I see him nod his head. "I was wondering when this would come up," he says. "And I'm not sure how to say this without sounding like a complete douche and an insensitive prick considering your past, but, uh . . . guys have needs."

My mind goes crazy thinking about how Barbie satisfied those needs. And if she's still satisfying them.

He puts a gentle hand on my arm to stop my forward progress. "Charlie, I haven't been with her for a while now. It had been months since I'd been with her when I met you. And I promise you, it was just sex. Mutually consensual and totally unemotional sex."

He scrubs a hand across his jaw. "Shit. When I hear the words coming out of my mouth, I want to punch myself. But there's really no other way to say it. When she came to work for me five years ago, she was married. There wasn't even any attraction between us. But within a few months, her husband left her. He left because she couldn't have children. It was a low time for her. And I hadn't been with anyone since Cat died. I never wanted to risk a relationship, and I sure as hell didn't want to risk another pregnancy. So I stayed away from women entirely. But one night, everyone in the office went out for drinks, and at the end of the night, Gretchen and I were the last two standing. She was drunk and she broke down, telling me the details about a car accident that had left her unable to conceive children. She said she hated all men and never wanted another relationship, but that she missed sex.

"So there we were, two young single people, neither wanting a relationship but both having an itch to scratch. And the fact that she couldn't have children made her the perfect partner for me. So right then and there, we negotiated a deal of sorts. We would use each other for sex. No emotions. No relationship. No expectations.

"It worked out well for a long time. Years, in fact. Once a month or so, one of us would drop a key card off on the other one's desk for a hotel room at the place around the corner. It was an ideal arrangement, one that suited both of us perfectly. That is until she started to have feelings for me."

I knew it. I had suspected all along she was into him. The way she looks at me, like I'm the one thing standing between her and everlasting happiness. And damn it if currents of jealousy don't crash into me like punishing ocean waves. "She's in *love* with you?" I ask, my body stiff from the very thought of it.

"I wouldn't say love, but yeah, she made it perfectly clear she wanted more. So I broke it off. Ended our arrangement. But she had been the perfect assistant, so I didn't feel right asking her to leave. She's been nothing but professional. Well, except maybe for the times she tried to keep you from seeing me. But in her defense, she has been told that no one gets in without an appointment."

In her defense? He's defending her. My heart sinks low in my chest.

He must sense my reaction because, to my surprise, he grabs my hand and holds it tightly in his. We don't do this. We don't hold hands. We haven't touched that way since the day at the cemetery. Not one touch. Not one kiss. Not one embrace. He's kept to his promise. His promise to be my friend. Earn my trust. Protect my heart.

But my heart doesn't want to be protected anymore. It wants to be unleashed. His simple touch has me wanting to hold him. Kiss him. Claim him.

"Charlie," he says, turning to me, taking my other hand so that he's holding both of mine in his. "She's history. She's something that never was. The way I feel about you is unlike anything I've ever felt for any woman. Just spending time with you—swimming, walking, talking—just being with you, even without touching you, has been better than any time I've spent with anyone else.

"God, do you know how much I want you? Do you know how much I want to touch you? Kiss you? Every day is bitter-sweet torture. Every day I want to tell you how I feel about you. And every day I stop myself because I don't think you're ready. But, Charlie, you must know how I feel. I love you. I love you and I can't hold it in anymore." He pulls me against him. "I'm going to kiss you now. And I hope you'll let me. Because these lips are all I think about. All I dream about. And I will die if you don't let me have them."

He leans down slowly, gauging my reaction, looking for hesitation in my eyes that simply isn't there. I want him to kiss me. Of course I do. I've wanted it for weeks. Hell, I've wanted it my whole life. And when his lips meet mine, I know I feel exactly the same way—that I'll die if I can't have him.

He kisses me hard. He kisses me soft. He kisses me with every emotion inside him. He kisses me so long, my lips go numb. He kisses me so passionately, my knees go weak. He kisses me so publicly, people laugh and whistle and clap when they walk by us. But I don't care. He doesn't care. Because it's a kiss to end all kisses. It's a kiss to begin new lives.

We finally break apart when someone yells at us to 'get a room.'

I laugh. "I guess we broke rule number seven again."

"Yes we did," he says. "But rule number twelve takes precedence."

"Rule number twelve?"

He smiles. "Sometimes you gotta do what you gotta do."

"I like that one," I say.

"Come on." He takes my hand and pulls me down the path. "Let's go grab some food."

~ ~ ~

At work, I let my thoughts wander back to that conversation as I fill napkin holders and do other mindless tasks in preparation for the lunch rush. I try not to think about Gretchen and how she may or may not be head-over-heels in love with him. I try not to think about how they would slip away to the hotel around the corner and take care of each other's needs. I try not to think about how he sees her every day at work.

A sick feeling washes over me and I race back to the bathroom to splash water on my face.

The door opens behind me and Skylar appears in the mirror. "Are you okay? God, Charlie—you look green."

I grab a paper towel and dry off my face. "I'm fine," I tell her. "Just thinking bad thoughts."

She puts a knowing hand on my shoulder. Then she looks at her watch. "We've got some time before the lunch rush. Go in the back and sit down, take a few minutes if you need them."

"Thanks, Skylar."

She gives me a sympathetic smile as I exit the bathroom and head towards the back. I sit down and try to think about things that will keep my mind off Gretchen. Things like puppies and flowers and Reuben sandwiches with fries. Things like amazing kisses in the park. Things like Ethan telling me he loved me.

Things like me wanting to say it back.

CHAPTER THIRTY

Ethan is being very patient with me. Even after that incredible day together. Even after we shared that earth-shattering kiss. Even after he told me he loved me.

I've never said those words to a man before. I never thought I'd *want* to say them. But I do. I do so badly I can taste them on the tip of my tongue. But I can't. Not yet. Not until I'm sure he won't push me away again.

He's taking me to dinner tonight, after my shift. It will be our first official date. Yes, we've dined together many times. We've been to the movies. We've gone to a baseball game. He even dragged me to another concert. But none of those were dates. We were getting to know each other. Taking it slowly.

Tonight, however, is different. Last night at the gym, he told me he wanted to take me out. Wine me. Dine me. *Woo me,* I think he called it. And then he said he would walk me to my door and kiss me goodnight. No pressure. No expectations.

No pressure. *Right.* I think of all the things I should do before our date, but don't have time for. Pluck, wax, shave, moisturize. I know he said he would only walk me to the door, but I want to be ready. Ready for anything. Ready for everything.

Skylar watches me as Jarod and I roll silverware into linen napkins. She studies me so hard it starts to creep me out. "What?" I ask.

She walks over and pulls me by the elbow until we are alone in the kitchen, with the exception of Paul, the chef who is hard at work chopping and slicing. "You're looking pale. Are you okay?"

I inventory how I'm feeling. I guess I am feeling a little run down, but that's just because Ethan and I have been burning the midnight oil talking on the phone every night. "I'm fine," I tell her.

Paul excuses himself for interrupting our conversation. He holds out a tasting spoon for Skylar, asking her to sample the beef stew he's made for today's special. I get a whiff of it and my stomach turns.

"Uhhhhhh," I moan, putting a hand over my mouth as I dart out of the kitchen and run to the bathroom.

Skylar runs in after me just in time to see me puke into the toilet of the first stall. I didn't even have time to shut the door. She comes up behind me, rubbing my back until I'm done. Then she fetches me a wet paper towel.

I wipe my mouth as I shake my head in confusion. "I don't know what just happened," I tell her. "One minute I was fine and then next . . ." I go to wash my hands. "I feel better now, though. You aren't going to make me go home, are you? I'm sure it's nothing. And I promise not to touch any food today."

She eyes me up and down, chewing her lip the entire time.

"What?" I ask, worried she might make me leave and miss my shift.

"Are you pregnant?" she asks, looking me dead in the eye.

I guffaw. Then I shake my head in disbelief at her question. Then I guffaw again.

"What? I'm only asking." She looks at her watch. "Because, Charlie, you felt sick at this exact same time yesterday. And now this. When I was pregnant, I had morning sickness like clockwork."

"Morning sickness?" I look at her like she's crazy. "I'm not pregnant, Skylar. I'm on the pill for Christ's sake."

Her eyes scold me like a child. "The pill isn't always one-hundred-percent effective, you know. Do you have any other symptoms? Sore boobs, tiredness, missed period?"

"No." I roll my eyes. "Okay, yes, I'm tired, and maybe I've been a little sore, but it's only because I've been staying up later than usual. And I swim a lot. Sometimes things hurt. And I had my period a few weeks ago. Plus, I haven't had sex in months."

"Swimming makes your boobs hurt?" she asks.

"I don't know. Maybe," I pout.

She points to the chair in the corner of the bathroom. "Sit. I'll be right back."

"I'm *fine*, Skylar," I say, scooting around her.

"You just threw up, Charlie. Sit down for a freaking minute. Stay here, I'll be back in a flash." She pushes me down onto the chair and gives me that big-sister stare that says I'd better do what she tells me.

Not twenty seconds go by when she returns to the bathroom, locking the main door behind her. "Here." She shoves something in my face.

I take the box from her. It's a pregnancy test. "What the fuck, Skylar? I'm not pregnant!"

"Then you won't have any problem proving me wrong." She grabs the box back from me, opens it, tears the plastic wrapper and pulls a stick out. She takes the cap off. "Pee on this end."

I open my mouth to protest, but her hand comes up to silence me. "Just do it, Charlie. Humor me."

"Fine." I rip the stick out of her hand and open a stall. Then I turn around and narrow my eyes at her. "Why do you happen to have a pregnancy test here at work?"

She shrugs and then smiles. "Don't tell anyone, okay?"

"Oh my God, you and Griffin are trying to have another kid?"

"We're not trying, per se. But we're not *not* trying. We just decided to roll the dice and see what happens." She points to the stick in my hand. "Stick. Pee." She pulls the door to the stall shut to give me privacy.

It takes me a minute. After all, there is immense pressure to pee on demand. Especially when you don't want to comply with the order. There is no way in hell I could be pregnant. Skylar is delusional.

I finish my task and hand her the stick, not even the least bit embarrassed that I shoved something with my pee all over it into her hands. "Here, take it. See for yourself."

I wash up and watch her in the mirror as she studies the stick. A minute later, her eyes meet mine and if sympathy were a living, breathing being, Skylar just gave birth to it.

"Shut the fuck up," I say, reaching out to grab the stick from her. I read the word on the tiny screen. **Pregnant.**

"Oh my God," I say, looking at the stick. "Oh my God." I look up at Skylar. I sink to the floor, dropping the stick that just ruined my life onto the cold hard tile.

In an instant, Skylar is on the floor with me. "Charlie, it'll be okay. It could be wrong, you know. Hormones can get out of whack. Let's not jump to conclusions quite yet."

She pulls out her phone and taps the screen a few times. "Hey, Joanie, this is Skylar Pearce. Can you please tell Dr. Chavis I'm calling in that favor she owes me? I need an appointment right away. I'll be there in thirty minutes." She shoves the phone back in her pocket. "Dr. Chavis is my OB/GYN. I saved her ass last month when her caterer cancelled at the last minute. She owes me big time. She's also the best OB in New York. You'll be in good hands with her. No matter what happens."

~ ~ ~

"Relax, Charlie," Dr. Chavis tells me as she shoves a wand up my vagina.

I don't even remember getting here. I have no recollection of how we came. Did we take the subway? A cab? The entire time, all I could think of was what my life was like as a child. All I could think of is how people say we become like our parents. I can't have a kid. I could never be a mother. I wouldn't even know where to start. What if the kid made me mad one day, would I get so angry I would hurt it?

I feel sick again and want to jump off the table when Skylar squeals in delight. "Oh, Charlie. Look!"

I turn my head to the computer screen and the doctor points to something in the middle of it. It's a dark bubble with a blob in it. "There's your baby," the doctor says.

My entire body freezes. I stop breathing. The world stops spinning.

Some lines go across the screen and her machine beeps. She tells me she's taking measurements. "See this right here?" she asks.

I don't see it.

"That's the heartbeat." She hits a button on her machine and all of a sudden I hear "Whoosh, whoosh, whoosh."

It sounds really fast. But probably not any faster than my own heart is beating right now.

She presses another button. "One hundred and seventy-five beats per minute," she says. "That's perfect." She takes a few more measurements and then presses her finger into my lower tummy a few times. "Let's see if we can wake him up a bit, shall we?"

The blob on the screen wiggles around. "Oh, well hello, little one," she says.

I stare at the monitor, seeing little arm and leg nubs jerk around. I think I can make out its head, but it looks as big as the rest of his body and the picture is too grainy to see anything clearly. It's then I realize what she said. "You said him," I say. "Is it a boy?"

"It's too soon to tell. I tend to use 'he' when I refer to the little ones. Don't read anything into it." She pulls out the wand and wipes up the gel down there.

I feel a hand on my shoulder. I almost forgot Skylar was in the room. I look up at her and she's crying. "Welcome to the club, Mommy," she says.

"Skylar." I look at the ceiling, biting back my tears. "What if I can't?"

"You can," she says. "There are so many people who will help you. Me, Baylor, Piper, my mom, the girls. I promise, we will all help you. You will not go through this alone."

The doctor prints out a picture and hands it to me. "As best as I can tell you are nine weeks and two days along. That would put your due date on December 5th and your estimated date of conception on March 13th."

I ask Dr. Chavis for a calendar. She hands me a small one from the desk. I flip it back to the second week in March. For the hundredth time today, my heart stops beating. March 13th was a Wednesday.

Smack dab in between the dates I had sex with Ethan and Zach.

~ ~ ~

I sit on my couch, exhausted from crying. Exhausted from talking about this with Skylar and then Piper.

Ethan is going to be here in five minutes. I look at myself on my phone and laugh. I look horrible. This is going to be the worst first date in the history of first dates.

I debated calling it off, but he has to know. He'll leave right after I tell him anyway. He'll want nothing to do with me.

The knock on my door makes me jump. This is it. This is the last time I will ever see him.

I walk to the door and open it. Ethan takes in a sharp breath when he sees my appearance. He puts his arms on mine. "What's wrong, Charlie?"

"Come in," I say. "Sit down."

He hesitates before crossing the threshold. This was one of our boundaries. He never came to my apartment and I never went to his. He didn't trust himself to keep his hands off me. I didn't trust myself to resist him.

But he clearly sees I'm not in any shape to leave, so he steps into my living room and closes the door behind him. He walks me over to the couch as if I'm frail. "Are you sick?"

I have a quick debate in my head on how to answer that question. I think it's best not to beat around the bush. Just get it out there. Rip off the Band-Aid. After all, there's really no way to sugar-coat it.

"No, I'm not sick. But I will have to go to the hospital," I tell him. "In about seven more months."

I watch his face as it goes through a host of emotions. Confusion. Realization. Shock.

When I can't stand to watch it anymore, I close my eyes and wait for it. Wait for him to yell at me. Wait for him to get up and leave. Wait for him to walk out of my life.

I startle when he takes my hand. My eyes snap up to his and all of those other emotions are gone. All except one. The one I never expected. The one I wasn't prepared for. The one that has tears falling from my eyes just as they are falling from his.

"Marry me," he says.

A sob escapes me and my hand comes up to cover my mouth as I shake my head at him. "I'm so sorry, Ethan. I can't."

"Why, Charlie?"

The way he's looking at me right now tells me how much I'm about to hurt him. Two minutes ago I thought he would want nothing to do with me, and now he's proposing. Maybe he's doing it out of obligation. Maybe he's doing it out of love. Maybe it's a little bit of both.

But whatever his reasons, I know I'm about to pull the rug out from under him. Because for just a second, I saw a glint in his eye. A flash of hope. And I wonder if he's going to hate me as much as he hated Cara.

"Because it might not be your baby."

PART TWO

ETHAN

CHAPTER THIRTY-ONE

I let her words sink in. I feel like I was given everything and then left with nothing, all in the course of ten seconds. All these years, I was sure I never wanted another child. I never again wanted to be tethered so completely to someone that my happiness, my own sanity, relied upon another.

But in those few seconds, I felt something I never thought I'd feel again. In those few seconds, Cat's entire life flashed before my eyes and I realized that I wouldn't give up my time with her for anything. Not even to take away all the pain I felt when she died and all the hatred I carried around afterward.

And in those few seconds, I knew I wanted this. I knew I wanted it with Charlie.

"Fuck!" I shout. I get up from the couch and pace the room. I want to yell at her. I want to put my fist through the wall. I want to rip the throat from whoever else she's been with. But something deep down inside me keeps me from doing any of those things. She's been through hell. Every man she's ever known has let her down.

"Who is he?" I ask, in the calmest voice I can muster. I run a frustrated hand through my hair, hoping to God there isn't more than one.

She's still sitting on the couch, crying with a pillow pulled to her chest. "I don't know," she says, wiping a tear away. "It was only once, I swear."

"I guess once was enough," I bite at her. "Who is he, Charlie?"

"You were gone, Ethan. You didn't want me. You made that perfectly clear. And then when Kyle and Levi came to Mitchell's a week later, they made it clear as well. They said you couldn't be with me. That you couldn't be with anyone." She takes in a few ragged breaths, picking at the fringe of the pillow. "I was a wreck, Ethan. I did something stupid. I went to a club and hooked up with a guy. The song came on. The one from the concert. I thought it was you for a second. I tried to run away but he followed me and it just happened. And now this. What am I going to do? How did I get here?"

I lean against the wall of her living room, my hands balled into fists as I listen to her cry. I'm pissed as hell. But I have no one to be pissed at but myself. I pushed her away. I pushed her away right into the arms of another man. *Shit.* This is all my fault. "You didn't use a condom?" I ask.

"No, we did. I always did. Well, except for that time with you in the pool. But that's not when I got pregnant. The doctor told me when I had the ultrasound that I most likely got pregnant on March 13th. Ethan, that was right in between . . . Oh, God."

"You had an ultrasound?" I ask, upset that she didn't say anything to me sooner. "How long have you known about this?"

"Today. I just found out today. It was Skylar who figured it out. I got sick at work and she made me take a test. Then she got me in to see her doctor."

My head is spinning as I try to process all of this information. She did everything to prevent this. She was on the pill. We used condoms. I can see how distraught she is over this. I can see that she feels like she's in this alone. I want to support her. But I need answers. "Who is he, Charlie? I need you to tell me everything you know about him."

"I don't know anything," she says, shaking her head. "That Saturday after work, Piper and I went to Ganache—it's a nightclub over in SoHo. We met these guys, Zach and Kevin. Kevin was married and we joked about him and Piper being our wingmen. We danced. And then . . . " Shame and regret cross her face. "I don't know anything else. I never saw him again."

"Last name?" I ask.

She shakes her head reluctantly, looking down at the ground.

"Zach," I say, his name rolling roughly off my tongue as if I'd said the devil's.

"I'm so sorry," Charlie says. "I never meant for any of this to happen, Ethan. I've created a mess of things. Maybe I should just" —she winces as if she's in pain— "maybe I should just make it go away."

"No, Charlie." I finally go back to the couch and sit at her side. "You're not going to do that. *We're* not going to do that."

"What do you mean *we?*" she asks, looking over at me with red-rimmed eyes that match the color of her hair.

I touch her shoulder. "I never should have hurt you the way I did. I knew you had feelings for me. I knew we should be together. But I was afraid. And so I pushed you away. You had every right to be upset. You had every right to do what you did. How can I be mad at you when all of this is my fault?"

She cocks her head to the side, questioning me with her inquisitive stare. "You're not mad at me?"

I shake my head. "No. I'm not mad at you. I'm mad at myself for putting you in that position. And I'm not going to let you go through this alone." I'm bombarded with thoughts of what she must have felt at the doctor today. "Do you have a picture?" I ask.

"Picture?"

"Yeah, from the ultrasound. Don't they usually print out a picture when they do those?"

She nods, reaching in between the couch cushions to pull out the black and white photo. It's a bit crumpled. Not crumpled like she was going to throw it away; crumpled like she was holding onto it for dear life. I stare at it. I trace the tiny little body with my finger, and emotions besiege me. Emotions I haven't felt in over eight years.

I take her hand. It's so soft. So perfectly made to fit with mine. "Listen, Charlie. You don't know the guy from Adam. He's history. I'm here. I love you." I put a hand on her stomach. "And I want this. I never thought I would, but I do. I want this with you. This child can be mine. Even if it's technically not. We never even have to know. Marry me, Charlie. Marry me anyway."

She gasps, more tears flowing down her cheeks. It kills me not to know if they are caused by happiness or pain. The look on her face gives me my answer. She tries to smile. It's a sad smile. A broken smile.

"I can't, Ethan. Thank you for asking. For trying to do the right thing. But I just can't."

"Why?" I ask, searching her eyes for answers.

"You have blonde hair. I have red. But Zach—his hair was black. You say you'll try to love it, love us, but what if this baby is born with dark hair? What if every time you look at him, you feel betrayed?" She removes her hand from mine. "I know what it's like to be hated by a parent, Ethan. I won't let that happen."

"I could never hate it, Charlie." I put my hand back on her stomach and hold it there. "People raise children that aren't biologically theirs all the time."

"How can you even consider this?" she asks. "After what you've been through. After all these years of keeping yourself from relationships. What if something happens to this baby? What if something happens to me?"

I feel a stabbing pain shoot through me at the thought. And it hurts. "I know because the thought of losing you, or even this baby I've only known about for thirty minutes, hurts more than you can imagine. That's how I know this is right. That's how I know I need to do this. I need you. I need him or her. We can be a family, Charlie. We can have a great life together. All you have to do is say yes."

I see it in her eyes. On her face. I see the war raging in her mind. It gives me hope that she won't say no. I'm not sure I could take it after this past month. After getting so close to her, closer than I've ever been to anyone.

She sniffs and wipes her nose on the cuff of her shirt sleeve. "Can I say maybe?"

I look into her beautiful hazel eyes and hold her stare with mine. This woman slays me with her beauty. With her stubbornness. With her determination to break the cycles of her past. I laugh. "You can say anything you want, as long as it's not *no*."

She smiles at me. But it's not just a smile. It's a sign of hope.

"But I'm going to ask you over and over until the answer is yes." I grab her left hand and trace my thumb across her ring finger. "Rule number thirteen—some things are just meant to be. And I'm not giving up until you marry me. And I will work my ass off every day to make sure that happens."

She leans her head on my shoulder, a huge sigh leaving her body as she molds herself to me when my arm goes around her, securing her against me. And we stay like this for hours, both lost in thought. Thoughts of the future. Thoughts of the past.

Thoughts of the tiny human being growing within her that we both pray is mine. Thoughts that we will love it to the ends of the earth, even if it's not.

CHAPTER THIRTY-TWO

"The club is called Ganache," I tell Melissa. "Have you heard of it?"

"It's in SoHo, right?" she asks.

I nod. Melissa has worked for me for two years now. At twenty-six, she's older than Charlie, but can easily pass for a twenty-two-year-old if that's what the guy prefers.

I pass her a dossier on him, but it doesn't have much information. "All I know is that his name is Zach and that he has black hair. He has a friend, Kevin, who he was at the club with. Kevin is married. They went to the club on a Saturday night. In my experience, party-goers tend to hit the same spots. Go every Friday and Saturday night for the next few weeks and see if you can meet him. I don't think he's a threat, but use caution. Make sure you aren't alone. Any information you can get would be helpful, but all I'm really after is his last name."

"Seems easy enough," she says, standing and tucking the folder under her arm.

"And Melissa?"

"Yeah, Ethan?"

"This case is personal. Top priority. Whatever it takes as long as you aren't in danger, okay?"

"You got it."

Melissa closes the door to my office and I stare over at the couch. The couch that could have been the place my child was conceived. It hasn't even been forty-eight hours since Charlie gave me the news, but it's all I can think about.

I visited Cat's grave this morning. I told her she's going to have a little sibling. Cat would have been ten years old when the baby is due. I know she would have made a wonderful big sister. I told her how I want to marry the woman who came to visit her grave with me. The only woman I've ever brought to meet her.

After I played a song for her, I sat on the bench and thought about the night Charlie gave me the news. She fell asleep in my arms, exhausted from crying, from going through all the emotions she went through that day, from growing a child in her belly. I carried her into the bedroom and put her on her bed. I covered her with a blanket and then I removed my shoes and laid down beside her.

I held her all night. And in her sleep, she held me, too. It was incredible. It was exactly what I wanted my future to feel like.

And when she woke up in my arms, she smiled and thanked me for staying. Then she kicked me out of bed and told me to go make breakfast. While we ate, we talked. She said she didn't want to rush things. I told her I'd wait as long as she needed.

She agreed not to contact any of the men on the list without taking me along. I have to trust her with that. Just as I'm asking her to trust me with her heart.

I know she wants me. I'm pretty sure she might even love me. But every man she's ever known has failed her. Including me.

~ ~ ~

"How was your swim?" Griffin asks, dealing the cards for our first hand of poker.

"It was good," I say. "Uneventful."

They all laugh. I'm not sure I'll ever live down that video.

For several hours, we play poker and drink beer. It's the same routine we've followed for over two months. They've accepted me as their fourth. Their friend. And I've never been more grateful for that. Especially now.

Mason slams his beer down on the table, splashing some out of the top. "Are we ever going to talk about the elephant in the room? Because it's getting so fucking big I'm about to suffocate in here."

Gavin and Griffin give Mason a dirty look but then turn their attention to me.

"So," I say. "I guess you all know the news."

"Yeah." Gavin nods his head.

"Do you know *all* the news?" I ask.

"They are sisters, bro. What do you think?" Griffin asks.

It never ceases to amaze me how they, too, consider Charlie family even though not one of them shares blood with her.

"Um, so are congratulations in order, or what?" Mason asks. "We know what the girls have told us, but you know how chicks are. We wanted to hear it from you."

"As far as I'm concerned, you can congratulate me all you want. I'm in this for the long haul."

"Well then, congrats, man," Griffin says, reaching out to shake my hand. "Welcome to the club."

I guess they don't know I'd already been a member. Maybe Charlie doesn't tell them everything after all.

"Are you going to get a paternity test?" Gavin asks. "I think you can even do that before the baby is born these days. I mean, if it would make a difference."

I try not to get mad. After all, I'm their guest here. "Are you saying you think it would? That I would leave Charlie if it's not mine?"

"No," Mason says. "That's not what he's saying. We're just trying to look out for her. For them."

"Listen." I look each of them in the eye so they know I mean what I'm about to tell them. "As far as I'm concerned, this kid is mine. That asshole is out of the picture. We don't even know who he is. I don't need a goddamn paternity test to make me a father. Chances are it's mine anyway. I love her. I've already asked her to marry me. *Twice.* I'm not the one who has the issue with commitment here. I'm all in. And if any of you have a fucking problem with that, just tell me now."

Gavin raises his beer. "Okay then," he says. "To baby Stone. May he or she have his mother's gorgeous looks and his father's can of whoop-ass."

"Here, here," Griffin and Mason say, as we all raise our drinks.

"You're a private investigator, Ethan," Griffin says. "How hard would it be to track this other guy down? I mean just so you know he's not some kind of psycho."

I raise my eyebrows at him.

"Ahhh," he says. "Gotcha. You're already on it."

I nod. "Yeah, but she doesn't know. I don't want to upset her unless it becomes absolutely necessary. Are you guys okay with that?"

"Okay with you wanting to protect her?" Mason says. "Dude, this is fight club."

I tip my beer at the guys who have become my friends. The guys who would, like me, do anything for the woman they love.

CHAPTER THIRTY-THREE

After Charlie's examination, Dr. Chavis tells us, "It's safe for you to start making plans now because at thirteen weeks, you've started your second trimester."

"Are you still sure of the due date and um," —Charlie looks at me wearily— "the date of conception?"

Dr. Chavis looks at her chart. "Well, since we didn't do an ultrasound today, we have no new measurements by which to determine that. But nine-week ultrasounds are very accurate. I'm confident we have the dates correct. Do you have any reason to believe they wouldn't be?"

"No," Charlie says. "I guess not."

"Do you have any more questions?" the doctor asks.

"I have one," Charlie says. "We never got to talk about this at my last appointment because I was . . . well, I was freaked out. But how did this even happen? I was on the pill. I always use condoms." She gives me a look because she and I both know that's not entirely true.

"Well, Charlie," she says. "As a doctor I've seen a lot of things. Things that can't always be explained by science. And while

I don't really have an answer for you, I like to think that some things are just meant to be. Maybe this is just one of those things."

Charlie's eyes snap to mine and she smiles. She smiles so big it warms my heart. "Meant to be," she whispers so that only I can hear. Looking back at Dr. Chavis, she asks, "Are you two related?"

"Pardon?" Dr. Chavis asks.

"Oh, nothing," Charlie says.

"I do have one more question," Charlie says, looking at me with sympathetic eyes. "I've read about these paternity tests you can do before the baby comes. Do you do those here?"

The doctor looks slightly taken aback but recovers quickly. She looks at me. "Oh, so you aren't the father? Or you think you might not be?"

"I'm the father, alright," I tell her. "Just maybe not in the biological sense."

She nods and pulls up a chair. "I see. Well, yes, Charlie, to answer your question, there are a few prenatal paternity tests we do here. The only definitive one relies on amniocentesis which can pose the risk of miscarriage. It's not a big risk, but big enough that we don't like to do it unless there might be some genetic reason to perform the test. The other test is a simple blood test. Blood from the mother and blood or saliva from the potential fathers. It's accurate, but only so far as to be able to rule out a man as the father or to conclude that a man cannot be excluded from the possibility of being the father. There is always a chance both men could have the same result as far as not being able to exclude them as the father."

"We don't want the test," I tell the doctor. "We don't need it," I say to Charlie. "It doesn't matter," I tell them both. "If we don't have the test, can I still be considered the baby's legal father?"

"If you're married, and nobody is around to question the paternity, then, yes, you'll be considered the legal father and your name will be on the birth certificate."

I turn to Charlie. "This is when I ask you to marry me again."

Charlie smiles.

The doctor excuses herself, telling us to think about it and we can talk more at her appointment next month.

"I'm serious, Charlie. Do you want me to get down on one knee? Shout it from the rooftops? Hire a skywriter? Because make no mistake about it, I want to marry you."

She gets up from the examination table. "Maybe," she says to me.

"You heard the doc. This is meant to be."

"You and your silly rules," she says. "If it's meant to be then waiting won't change anything, right?"

"I guess not."

"Then how about we keep taking it slow, Ethan? These past weeks have been great. I love spending time with you. You have become another best friend to me. But I feel like I'm just getting my bearings straight here. I'm hormonal. I have a new emotion every five seconds. I'm not sure I can trust myself to make a life-long decision just yet."

I nod. How can I argue with that? "Then how about you just make an easy decision and let me take you on that date we never got to have?"

She looks at her watch and then she smiles up at me. "I work until seven. Pick me up at eight?"

A victorious grin threatens to split my face wide open. "I'll be there."

~ ~ ~

"What's it like?" Charlie asks me over dinner. "Watching a baby being born? I mean, if it's not too hard for you to talk about."

"I'll talk about anything with you, Charlie. But to answer your question, I don't know. I wasn't at Cat's birth."

"Oh, right, because you weren't married to her mom."

I shake my head, not overlooking the sadness on her face. "No, it wasn't that. I was going to be there. I had every intention of being at the delivery. I'd even taken those Lamaze classes with Cara. But Cat was born two weeks early and I was in school taking a test. Our professors had warned us early on that if we were caught using our phones during a test, it was an automatic fail. So it became a habit for me to turn it off and put it in my backpack. I had back-to-back classes that day and just forgot to turn it back on. So it was hours until I remembered to look at it. By then I'd received a dozen calls and texts. I headed straight to the hospital, but I was too late. Cat was born about twenty minutes before I got there."

"I'm sorry," she says.

"No, it's okay. I was seventeen. I'm not really sure I wanted to see all that stuff anyway, but I was trying to be supportive. And by the time I got there, Cat was all cleaned up. She was perfect." I smile remembering the first time I held her. It was awkward. I'd never held a baby before. I was sure I was doing everything wrong; that I'd drop her or make her cry. But at the same time, it was one of life's incredible moments; one I'd always remember.

"You don't have to be there, you know," she says. "I'm not going to make you. I don't really want to be there myself, but I kind of don't have a choice in the matter."

I reach across the table and grab her hand. "I'm going to be there, Charlie. I promise you I won't miss it. I'm not that squeamish seventeen-year-old boy anymore. This is the most important thing to me. I won't let you down."

"Okay, but make sure you stand by my head." Her body shivers like she's thought of something disgusting. She motions to her lower half. "I don't want you anywhere near there. After seeing something like that, you might never want to touch me again."

I smile. I smile big. She wants me to touch her again.

"What?" she asks, seeing the amused look on my face.

"Do you not realize what you just said, Charlie?" I lean over the table and whisper to her. "You want me. Quit trying to deny it."

A blush works its way across her fair skin. She's so damn beautiful. I love her creamy-white skin. Her freckles that go on for days. Her incredible red hair that frames her heart-shaped face in soft waves and falls down past her breasts.

My pants tighten and I shift in my seat thinking about her breasts. They were nice before, but now—Christ, they've gotten bigger and are stretching the buttons of her blouse. I long to touch them. See them. They are the center of my schoolboy fantasies.

"Excuse me." We look up to see an older lady standing at our table, staring at Charlie. Good, I needed the distraction. "I'm sorry to bother you while you eat, dear, but I just had to stop by and tell you I was a big fan of your mother. I was crushed to hear of her passing and wanted to give you my condolences. She was an amazing actress."

This isn't the first time this has happened. Charlie is the spitting image of her mom. She gets stopped all the time, especially on nights like tonight, when her hair is down. And tonight, much like every other time, Charlie's eyes glaze over and she forces a smile before simply saying, "Thank you."

"You're welcome, dear. I hope you enjoy the rest of your meal," the woman says before returning to her table.

"You are getting better at that," I tell Charlie.

"I know," she says, twisting the stem of her water glass. "It's because I stopped listening to them."

"Stopped listening?"

She lifts her chin at the lady across the room. "Every time someone does that, I tune them out. I think of a song in my head."

"Really? What song?"

"Um, it was the song you played on your harmonica. The one you played for Cat. You were right, it is calming. And every time I get upset, I think of it." A look of worry crosses her face. "Is that okay?"

"Of course it's okay, Charlie. That's all part of the process."

"What process?"

"Healing," I tell her.

She smiles sadly. "I'm not sure I'll ever be healed, Ethan." She looks down and touches her barely-there belly. "But somehow I think this helps."

"Yeah. Kids have a way of doing that. Especially when they are meant to be." I wink at her.

Her sad smile turns happy. Her beautiful face radiates with hope. And suddenly, the future looks brighter than ever.

CHAPTER THIRTY-FOUR

It's been three weeks since our official first date. Three weeks and nine dates. And each one has only gotten better.

I stare at a picture of Charlie in the new frame next to my laptop. She once said I needed more stuff on my desk, so last week on one of our walks, when the sun was setting over the trees of Central Park, I snapped a picture on my phone. It's true what they say about pregnancy. She was genuinely glowing and I've never seen her happier.

She hasn't mentioned the list in weeks. I know she hasn't forgotten about it. And I worry that one day she'll want to pick up where she left off. But I'm determined to keep that from happening. I've done more digging on the remaining eleven. I'm using every resource I have to keep tabs on them.

It disgusts me to think of those dirt bags living their lives as free men. I've had more than a few thoughts of how I could use my connections to take care of them. I've mentioned the word prosecution to Charlie a couple of times. But she's been through so much already. She wants to avoid what would be a lot of very public exposure considering who she is and who some of the men are. And she's not naïve, she understands the chances of conviction after all these years are slim. I'm not sure I could take watching her testify in eleven trials; putting her through eleven nightmares all over again.

There is a knock on my office door.

"Yeah, come on in."

Melissa walks into my office and sits down. She doesn't ever do that. I know she has information for me. "Tell me," I say.

"His name is Zachary Thompson. He's twenty-five years old. Single and not looking for a relationship. Although he did proposition me for a one-night stand. He wasn't very happy when I said no. He spent the rest of the night going from woman to woman until he found one who took the bait. He bought a lot of drinks for a lot of girls in the process. The guy is a certified asshole, Ethan."

"What makes you say that?" I ask. "I mean, other than the fact that he's just there to get laid."

"Well, he's a liar, for one. I was close enough to hear his conversations with several different women. He told each one a different story. That he was only in town for one night. Or that his grandmother just died and he's trying to get over the loss. Or that he's out celebrating getting hired as the youngest VP for some record company. One girl slapped him because she said he hit on her a few weeks ago and was too stupid to remember, and that he must have a lot of grandmothers."

"Sounds like a real winner," I say, shaking my head.

"He's a scam artist, too," she says. "Two times, with two different bartenders, when they handed him his change, he told them he gave them a twenty, when he'd only given them a ten. One of the bartenders called him on it. The other one fell for it."

"Wonderful," I say sarcastically. "Pictures?"

"Yeah, check your email, I sent them a few minutes ago. I did a little digging around online this morning and found him on Facebook. I sent you what I could piece together about employment, but if you run a background check, I'm sure you'll get more."

"Thanks, Melissa. Great job."

"No problem," she says, getting up to leave.

I open her email and immediately pull up his picture. He's built. Not like me, but he looks strong. Muscular. Black hair like Charlie said. Tanned skin, blue eyes. And even though I'm a guy, I can see why Charlie might have been attracted to him. It doesn't seem to me like he'd need much of a story to get women to go home with him. As far as men go, he's damn good looking. *Fuck.* My blood boils thinking of this asshole's hands on her.

I look over at the picture of Charlie. I want to be mad at her for hooking up with him. But I can't. None of this would have happened if it weren't for my sheer stupidity. I wouldn't be staring at the man who touched the woman I love. The man who could potentially be the father of the child I want.

I read over the information Melissa was able to extract from Facebook. His birthdate. His recent places of employment. Names of friends he's tagged with the most. Places he checks in at often.

I type what information I have into my source for background checks. I don't have a social security number or an address though, so I might have to call in a favor to get this one.

I pull up Zachary Thompson's Facebook page. Like anyone with sub-par intelligence, he doesn't have any privacy settings on it so I'm free to view all of his friends, all of his likes, all of his pictures. He posts a lot of pictures. Mostly selfies with beautiful women. Some while he's kissing them. I hold my breath as I scroll down through the hundreds of posts until I find the specific Saturday he was with Charlie.

I'm relieved to find there isn't a picture of her.

I know I'll need to tell Charlie about what I've found. Eventually, when I know everything there is to know about him, I'll tell her. But what she plans to do with that information scares the shit out of me. Every day since I put Melissa on task, I think that maybe I should have let it go. After all, we didn't know anything about him. He would have merely been a blip on the radar. A bump in the road. But in my haste to protect her, have I done nothing but open Pandora's Box?

No. She loves me. I can see it in her eyes. Feel it in her kisses. She doesn't trust men. She wouldn't risk telling him and putting her child in danger. I'm doing the right thing.

I check the clock, adrenaline shooting through me when I remember what tonight is. Tonight I'm making dinner for Charlie. Tonight she will come over to my place for the first time. Tonight I hope to do more than kiss those beautiful lips—the only part of her body other than her hands that I've had the pleasure of touching since the night I held her in her sleep.

I duck out early to hit the market. Being the boss allows that kind of schedule. When I tell Gretchen I'm leaving, she asks, "Are you sick? You never leave early."

I laugh. "No, I'm not sick. I just have something really important to do, that's all."

"Oh, well if it's that important, is there anything I can do to help you?" She flashes her teeth at me along with her cleavage.

Not a workday goes by where I don't get to see that cleavage. Not that I'm looking, but she just doesn't give up. It's hard for me not to feel a little bad for her, though. I can't imagine what it would feel like if Charlie had shut me out completely. But Gretchen is so obvious about it. Leaving me notes here and there. Baiting me with hotel room keys. Fucking me with her bedroom eyes. I really should put an end to it once and for all.

"Thanks, Gretchen. I'm good." I turn to leave, but then think maybe I can kill two birds here. "Actually, can you call a florist and have a few dozen bouquets of flowers delivered to my penthouse please? Roses and whatever other flowers girls like."

"Your penthouse?" she asks, her mouth full of sour grapes.

In the years that Gretchen and I, uh … helped each other out, I never took her to my place. Not once. I've never taken any woman there. Charlie will be the first. The only. And hopefully the last.

"Yes. My penthouse. Better make it six dozen, I'm going all out on this one. Thanks Gretchen." I turn and leave before I can see her reaction. I know I've hurt her. I know I probably should have ordered the flowers myself. But how many times do I have to tell her I'm not interested before she starts to believe that I'm really not interested?

I make quick work of picking out two perfect steaks at the market. Now that Charlie's morning sickness has passed, she's developed a strong craving for meat, and I'm all about satisfying her cravings. I grab the biggest strawberries I can find along with chocolate I plan to melt for dipping.

When I arrive home, the first thing I do is change my clothes. It's become quite evident to me over the past few months that Charlie much prefers me in jeans over my usual work attire. So I swap my linen pants, white shirt and black tie for blue jeans and a t-shirt that I bought because I think it's the exact shade of her eyes. I don't bother with shoes or socks. That's one more thing I've come to know about her, she thinks my bare feet are sexy. She's always staring at them when we get out of the pool.

Hell, I don't care if she thinks my bony kneecaps are sexy. Whatever turns her on is fine by me—as long as it's something. And I see it. I see it in her eyes every time we're together. She wants this as much as I do. But now she's the one who's scared.

It's all part of tonight's plan—to show her how serious I am about her. About us. About this baby whom I've considered my own since the moment she told me she was pregnant.

I busy myself with dinner preparations to keep my mind occupied. I told her I'd send a car for her but she would have nothing to do with it. So I texted her the address of my building and told her the doorman would be expecting her.

When my doorbell rings, my heart races like a goddamn teenage boy about to get a handy. I look around to make sure everything is in place. The flowers were delivered, and to my surprise, Gretchen did a great job on the order. I lit a few candles. I have soft music playing in the background. It's perfect. Well, I think it is anyway. I've never done this before. Maybe I don't have a fucking clue and I've just gone so overboard I'll scare her away. *Shit.*

But it's too late now, I've already spent so much time worrying over it, she probably thinks I'm not going to answer the door. I don't even have time to blow out the candles before I race over to let her in.

When I open the door, she sticks her head in before the rest of her body. She looks around and takes everything in. "The penthouse?" she asks. "You could have told me you were Richie Rich, Ethan."

CHAPTER THIRTY-FIVE

She looks down at the bottle of wine in her hand. "I feel really stupid bringing you a fifteen-dollar bottle of wine."

I laugh. "I'm not Richie Rich," I tell her. Then I take the bottle from her. "And I love this wine. You remembered?"

A few weeks ago we went to a hamburger joint because Charlie was having a craving. I rarely drink around her because I don't want her to feel deprived that she can't. But that particular night, someone was having a party and they were passing out wine so I accepted a glass. I told her how much I liked it.

And she remembered. I can't stop my boyish grin.

I kiss her on the cheek and invite her in. I follow behind her as she walks around the expansive open-style floorplan, taking in everything slowly. Her eyes rake over my brown leather sofas, my ten-seat dining room table that has never sat more than one, my chef's kitchen that usually gets used for microwaving frozen meals or reheating take-out.

She walks to the wall of windows, admiring the floor-to-ceiling panoramic view of the city. "You're loaded," she says, turning to me and swatting me on the arm.

"Me personally, no," I say, earning a *you're-full-of-shit* look from Charlie. "Okay, well, technically, yes. But I didn't earn it so I never look at it that way. My grandparents were very well off and when they died, they pretty much left everything to my brothers and me."

"They cut your parents out of their will?" she asks, surprised.

"Believe me, they didn't need the money," I tell her, reminding her they are both doctors. "When you put a neurosurgeon and a neonatal cardiothoracic specialist together, that makes for one hell of an income."

"When did your grandparents pass away?" she asks.

"My grandfather died about six years ago. He was eighty-one years old. He was sitting at his desk when he had a massive heart attack. When my grandmother found him, his glasses were still perched on his face. He died instantly. Peacefully."

"I'm sorry," she says, touching my arm, looking up at me in sympathy. I know she knows I'm thinking about Cat. Every time I think about death, I think about her. They go hand in hand.

I take the opportunity to put my arm around her as we both admire the view. "He had a great life and was healthy right up until the day he died. He was lucky."

"And your grandma?"

"She was lost without him. They had been married for sixty-three years. Got married as teens and never spent a day apart. I never understood how you could be with someone day in and day out and not ever get sick of them. Not until I met you, that is." I lean over and place a kiss on her head.

"You aren't ready to toss me to the curb yet?"

"Never." I run my hand along her jaw, wanting to kiss her, but needing to finish my story. "Anyway, my grandmother died on the day that would have been their sixty-fourth anniversary just ten months later. They said the sorrow of that day more than likely caused her own heart to simply fail. Tragic, but in kind of an awesome way if you think about it."

"Wow," she says. "I love that story. You should tell Baylor; she'd probably write a book about it." She motions around the penthouse. "So you inherited all this when you were only twenty-two?"

I nod. "Yes. And my brothers were pissed as hell because they were younger than me. They weren't allowed to touch their part of it until they turned twenty-one."

"And by that time, Chad was already into acting," she says, knowing pretty much everything about my family. "But Kyle still decided to go to medical school? Even though he had all that money waiting for him?"

"People who want to be doctors are a rare breed, Charlie. They don't do it for the money, yet most of them make bucket-loads of it. They don't do it for the glory, yet most of them are heroes. And Kyle is just like my parents. It didn't matter if he inherited two dollars or two million; he was going to become a doctor no matter what."

"I like Kyle even more now," she says.

My jaw tightens. "Just don't like him too much. I don't like to share, Charlie."

She laughs, pulling away from me to continue her perusal of the room. "I love the flowers." She walks over and smells one of the red roses. "The rest of the place is so masculine; they really soften it up."

"I'm glad you think so. Maybe someday, the entire penthouse will have a woman's touch." I raise my eyebrows at her so she gets my meaning.

"Hmmm." She walks over and runs her hands across the sleek quartz countertops, ignoring my insinuation. She looks at the oversized oven, double-wide refrigerator, and wine cooler that line one entire wall of the large kitchen. "Skylar would drool over this kitchen, Ethan."

"We should invite her over sometime," I say.

"We?" she asks.

"Hmmm," I respond, making her smile. "Are you hungry? I could throw on the steaks."

She licks her lips. "Steak sounds heavenly. I'll help. But can we wait a bit? I'd love to see the rest of your place. That is if you don't mind."

I was hoping she would say that. But at the same time, I'm terrified of what she'll think. "Right this way." I hold my hand out to her and she grabs it.

I'll never get tired of holding her hand. Charlie is tall. Much taller than Cara was, or even Gretchen. Taller than any girl I've ever been with. And because of that, her hands are longer, sleeker than the others, and they don't get lost in mine.

I take her down the east hallway first. It's the safest place to start. This is where I have my home office. Across from that is my workout room. And down at the end of the hall is a home theater.

"How do you live in such an extravagant place, yet you seem to live such a regular life? I mean, you take me out for burgers instead of Filet Mignon. You take cabs instead of having your own car and driver."

"Oh, I have a car . . . er, cars. I just don't use them much. I grew up with money, Charlie, as I'm sure you did before you left home, although I know you didn't get to see the benefits of it like I did. It's not a big deal to me. I mean, yes, it's great. And it makes life a lot easier. But—rule number fifteen—money doesn't always make life better."

She narrows her eyes at me, chewing on the inside of her cheek in thought. "What happened to rule fourteen?"

So she *has* been paying attention. "Oh, did I skip one?"

"Yes, you did."

"Hmmm." I shrug, leading her through the doorway into the theater room.

"You know, you'll have to deal with your own inheritance soon enough," I tell her. "Have you made any plans for that yet?"

"No. I'm not even sure I want her money, Ethan. The first life insurance check came a few days ago. I put it up on the refrigerator. I couldn't get myself to deposit it in the bank. I feel like it's blood money."

I turn her toward me and put my hands on her shoulders. "Deposit the check, Charlie. It won't do anyone any good if you don't, least of all your mother. You deserve it. You deserve it and so much more. If you don't want it for yourself, then donate it to charity. But don't not take the money just to spite her."

"You're right." She nods her head in hesitant agreement. "I know you're right. It's just hard that's all. I know I need to deposit it. How else am I going to pay you?"

"You're not going to pay me, Charlie. It's already off the books, so don't even try."

"But you used resources to help me, Ethan. It wouldn't be fair."

I motion my hand around the massive room we're still standing in. The one with the fifteen-foot projection screen. "Do I look like I won't survive if I don't get a couple of hundred bucks?" I ask her.

"That's not the point," she pouts. "I'm paying you. You can donate it to charity if you want."

"Touché." I laugh, knowing I've lost this one.

"Come on." She tugs on my hand. "Show me the rest."

We walk back down the hallway and through the living room to the west wing. I feel a little uneasy as we make our way towards the bedrooms. I show her the guest room my mother decorated. And then I take her to the master bedroom at the end of the hall. The master has the same view as the living room, looking out onto the city through a wall of windows.

She gasps at the view I wake up to every day. "How do you ever sleep with all the sunlight that comes in?" she asks.

I walk over to the bedside table and push a button on the remote. Room-darkening shades travel down the entire length of the windows, sealing at the bottom, making the room almost completely dark.

She's standing near the doorway, so she becomes this enchanting silhouette, shrouded by the dim light from the kitchen down the hall. She's turned slightly to the side and for the first time, I notice the distinct roundness of her baby bump and the sight of it takes my breath away. It takes every ounce of my will not to throw her onto my bed and claim her as mine.

"Can I see the bathroom, or is that too personal?" she asks, breaking my moment of magic.

I open the shades, letting light back into the dark room as I wave her into the bathroom.

"Holy shit," she says, when she sees it.

There are two separate vanities on either side of the bathroom, each end of which leads back to one side of a massive shower that meets in the middle and overlooks a sunken tub that sits in the center of the large room. The tub has pillars on all four sides, making it look like something out of a Greek play.

I've always thought the bathroom was a bit over-the-top, especially for a single guy. But the way she looks at it, like how a starving man eyes a steak, I realize I've never liked it more. I think about how much I would like to see her makeup on the vanity. Her shampoo in the shower. Her clothes in my closet.

"Just . . . wow," she says, admiring every inch of it the way I want her to admire every inch of me.

I'm jealous of a damn bathroom.

"Come on," I say. "There is one more room for you to see."

We walk back out into the hallway and I point to a closed door across from the master.

"Why is the door closed?" she asks. "And why do you look so nervous?" Her hand comes up to cover her mouth and she squeals. "Oh, my God. Don't tell me you have a playroom. As in whips and cattails and red leather couches with handcuffs?"

I laugh. "You read too much," I say.

"I didn't read it," she replies. "I saw the movie."

"No, Charlie. It's not a playroom. But now that you mention it, would you have been upset if it had been?"

Now both of us are laughing. And I'm glad, because the tension I'm feeling over what's behind that door was getting to be more than I could take.

"Go ahead, open it," I tell her.

She slowly steps towards the door, turning the knob carefully as if she's afraid of what's on the other side. When she sees the room, she gasps. She gasps harder and deeper than she did when she saw the view from the bedroom. And then she turns to me, tears pooling in her eyes. "You made a nursery?"

CHAPTER THIRTY-SIX

"Well, Dr. Chavis did say we could start planning. I'm planning."

I watch her look around the room that I decorated in yellows and greens. Although I hired someone to paint it, I did most of the decorating myself. I put together the crib, the changing table, the glider-rocker. I even had an artist paint a mural on the wall.

Charlie's hand comes up to cover her mouth when she sees it. I hope I didn't overstep my bounds on this one. We've talked a lot over the last few months. She told me about the mural painted on the wall in her childhood bedroom of the unicorn that protected her during those devastating years. The one she has tattooed on her inner thigh. I mulled it over for days. Would it bring back horrible memories, or would it inspire hope?

"I can paint over it if you want. I just thought—"

"That it would protect him," she says, tears streaming down her face.

"Yes." I nod.

She goes over to the wall to touch it, her hands shaking as her fingers trace the outline.

"Shit, Charlie. I'm sorry. I wasn't thinking."

She shakes her head, wiping her tears. "No. No. It's perfect, Ethan. But why did you do all this? Do you want the baby to stay here sometimes?" She motions around the room. "It's so much."

"Sometimes?" I say, my voice dripping with incredulity. *"All the time."* I walk over and turn her around so she's facing me. I take her hands in mine. "Him. Her. You. I want you both here. I want you to live with me, Charlie. I want us to live together as a family."

Her hands start shaking again.

"This is when I ask you to marry me again."

"But what if . . ." She looks around the room. I know what she's asking.

"Charlie, over the past two months, we've talked about every *what if* there could be. Don't you know by now how much I love you? How much I love this baby? And you can deny it all you want, but I know you feel the same way about me. I know you've felt it for a long time."

"How?" she asks. "I mean, if I can't be sure, how can you be?"

"Because it was all over your face the last time we made love, and pretty much every day since."

She looks up at me in disbelief.

"Don't believe me? I'll show you."

"Show me?" she asks.

"Yes. Come on." I pull her down the hallway, back through the living room and into my office. I sit down on my desk chair and pull her onto my lap. I use the mouse to click through a few screens on my computer and pull up a video.

When she realizes what I'm showing her, she looks at me with her jaw wide open and her face blazing with a blush. "Oh my God, Ethan. Have you watched this before?"

"I'm a guy." I shrug. "Of course I've watched it."

"But no one else has, right?"

"I've told you before, Charlie. I don't like to share." I pull her tightly against me, her back to my front. "Watch with me. I want you to see what I see every time I look at you."

She doesn't move a muscle as she watches the video footage from that day in my office. She watches herself beg me to touch her. She watches us kiss for endless minutes, clawing at each other to get as close as we can physically get. She watches us tear each other's clothes off and then she watches as I go down on her. And the whole time, I'm watching *her*.

I'm already rock hard and her sitting on my lap is making me throb painfully. The video is affecting her, too. She starts squirming around as she watches my tongue lash her, my fingers enter her.

I finally turn my eyes to the screen and we watch together as she implements rule number sixty-nine. "Still my favorite rule," I whisper in her ear. My hands come up to touch her. I can't not touch her when I'm watching us do this to each other. I want to do all that and more. And her body's reaction tells me she wants it, too. But I need her to see it. I need her to see what I see.

When we start to make love in the video, her breath hitches and I know she sees it. She sees her face the moment I enter her. And when we orgasm together, she sees our powerful connection. The undeniable force. The overwhelming love that passes between us.

"Oh God, Ethan," she says breathlessly, turning herself around in my lap so she's straddling me.

"You saw it, didn't you?" I ask. "You can't deny it anymore. That is the look I see every time I kiss you. Every time I walk into a room and our eyes meet. Every time we are together, that is how you look at me. You love me, Charlie. Dammit, why can't you just admit it?"

"Maybe because it's not just me anymore."

I put my hands on her stomach. "I love that it's not just you. I want this, Charlie. I want us. I want our family."

She looks down to see my hands caress her belly. "Are you sure, Ethan? I mean are you really sure? I need to know that no matter what happens, you won't leave. Because . . ." —her voice hitches and a tear escapes her eye— "Because everything you said is true. And I don't think I could take it—having you and then losing you."

"I'm sure," I promise her. "You could never lose me. No matter what."

She nods, her tears flowing freely down her face until I reach my thumb up to wipe them. "Okay. Then ask me again," she says.

It takes a second for my brain to catch up with her words, but when it does, a sense of elation washes over me. It's the purest form of happiness I've experienced in over eight years. I reach over into the top drawer of my desk and pull out a box. The box that has been sitting in there since the day after I found out Charlie was pregnant.

I open it and pull out the ring. It's big. It's over the top. It's ostentatious. And it's more money than I've ever spent on anything short of my cars and my penthouse. But I knew if I was lucky enough to have her wear it, I would want the world to know she was mine.

Her eyes go wide when she sees the massive sparkling diamond on the platinum band.

"I swear to you, you're stuck with me, Charlie. For better or worse. Both of you. And I'll spend the rest of my life making sure you don't regret it." I hold the ring out to her. "Charlie Anthony

Tate, marry me. Make me your husband and the father of our child. Say yes and make me happy beyond my wildest imagination."

She nods through her tears, licking them as they hit her lips. "Yes," she says. Her forehead comes down to meet mine. "Yes," she repeats, our lips so close they are almost touching.

"Say it, Charlie. Tell me you love me."

"I love you," she breathes into my mouth. "I love you so much, Ethan."

I close my eyes, savoring her words. The words I never thought I wanted to hear. The words I never thought I needed. I weave my hands into her hair, pulling her the last few millimeters until her lips meet mine.

And I kiss her. I kiss her with everything that I have. We taste each other's tears. We feel each other's love. It's a moment I know we'll never forget. It's a moment I hope to relive with her over and over again.

I realize I haven't put the ring on her finger yet. But before I do, I tell her, "This ring will protect you, just as I'll always protect you. Look inside."

She takes it from me, squinting her eyes to see the tiny engraving on the inside of the band.

Rule #14 – Forever

Next to the words is a tiny engraving of a unicorn.

"Oh, Ethan. It's perfect," she says. "So *that's* what happened to rule number fourteen."

I smile, taking the ring from her and slipping it onto her long slender finger. I admire it on her. "It looks good on you, fiancée."

She looks at the computer screen, laughing. "Did we really just get engaged over porn?"

I laugh along with her. "Yeah. I guess we'll have to change the story when it comes to telling our kids."

"Kids?" Her eyes snap to mine. "As in more than one?"

I nod. "I want as many as you'll give me, Charlie."

"What about what *I* want," she asks, looking down at me through lidded eyes, making my cock spring to life again.

"Anything," I say. "You can have anything you want. Name it."

"I want to watch the video again. And then I want you to take me to bed."

She doesn't have to ask me twice. I angle the chair so we both have a good view of the computer monitor. I have a feeling this won't be the last time we watch this. I have a feeling this is going to be the first of many memorable nights together. I have a feeling that despite the horrible things in our pasts, at this moment, we feel we're the luckiest two people on earth.

I smile and press play.

CHAPTER THIRTY-SEVEN

I spent this morning making phone calls. Phone calls that had nothing to do with work and everything to do with telling my brothers and my parents about my upcoming nuptials. I'd been keeping the news of Charlie's pregnancy pretty close to my chest. But now that we're engaged and she's showing more and more every day, it's time to spread the word.

As far as I'm concerned this baby is mine. And nobody else needs to know differently. I won't have them thinking about Charlie in a negative way. And I certainly won't have them looking at my kid as if it weren't truly a part of the family. I'm pretty sure none of my immediate family would do that, but gossip has a way of spreading like wildfire, so Charlie and I decided enough people know the truth already and the fewer people we tell, the better.

It's her day off today and I'm meeting her for lunch so we can take a walk. Between swimming and walking, she's determined not to gain too much weight. I could care less. She'd be beautiful if she put on fifty pounds as far as I'm concerned. But I'm being supportive. And I hate for her to walk through the park alone. So she agreed to use the gym when I'm not available to join her.

I find myself getting restless as the lunch hour draws near. We didn't get much of a chance to talk last night. We were . . . otherwise occupied. It had been so long since we had been together. Too long. I couldn't stop touching her. I couldn't stop staring at her burgeoning baby bump thinking of how it only makes her sexier. And then afterward, she fell asleep. Exhausted from our activities.

I smile thinking of how this morning I grilled our steaks for breakfast because the only food we managed to eat last night was the strawberries and chocolate. I get hard just remembering it. She said she loved me again. I told her I'd grill her steaks for breakfast every damn day if she would tell me that every morning.

I look at my watch to see it's almost time to meet her. I grab my gym bag and head into the bathroom to change into workout clothes. Although we're only walking, we do tend to work up a good sweat. And now that we're well into June, the weather can get downright hot at times.

I lock my office, slip my key and phone into my pocket and head for the door. When I near reception, I hear Gretchen talking to someone in the waiting area. She's raising her voice in anger and I wonder if we have the disgruntled spouse of a client trying to gain access. It happens from time to time. It's why we have bullet-proof glass and restricted access.

I freeze when I hear Charlie's voice. "Gretchen, this is getting a little old isn't it? Do we have to do this dance every time I come here? No, I don't have an appointment. Ethan was supposed to meet me downstairs, but I was early, and I really have to pee so I thought I'd come up."

I smile, ready to open the door and let her through when Gretchen speaks again. "You think you are so high and mighty, don't you? You think Ethan will just drop everything when you come around. Well, let me tell you something—he'll never change. He's not cut out for relationships. He likes to fuck. He liked to fuck me, and I guess now he likes to fuck you. But he'll tire of you and when he does, I'm the one who will be here. I'm the one he has leaned on all these years. I've put in my time and I'm the one who will eventually reap the benefits. So play your little game with him now. I'm not going anywhere."

I almost rip the door off the hinges trying to get out to the reception area. To Charlie. I quickly look around, relieved no clients are waiting because I'm about to tear into Gretchen like she's never seen. But before I can open my mouth, Charlie shakes her head at me. I'm confused. She doesn't want me to defend her?

"Oh, hi, Ethan," Charlie says with a huge smile. "I was just getting ready to ask Gretchen to calm down. All the anger coming off her is emanating so much heat in here, don't you think?" She fans herself dramatically. Then she proceeds to remove the jacket she's wearing over her track suit. And when she does, there is no mistake about it, she's either hiding a small cantaloupe under her tight tank top, or she's pregnant. By this time, some of my employees are peeking around the corner, having no doubt heard some of Gretchen's tirade.

I look over at Gretchen, whose jaw is so far open it almost hits the countertop. "What the hell?" she spits at Charlie.

Well, that's one way to break the news to the office. I pull my office key out of my pocket. I offer it to Charlie. "This is a master key that opens all the doors in the office. It's yours now." Charlie smiles and holds out her left hand to accept the key, making sure my big fat diamond is apparent to anyone who might be paying attention.

Gretchen's eyes turn dark when she sees it. "You have to be fucking kidding me," she pouts.

"Charlie is going to be the mother of my child," I tell her. "She's also graciously agreed to be my wife. And as such, she'll be entitled to half the stake in my company. That will make her your boss, Gretchen. So show some fucking respect or get the hell out."

"Ugh!" She looks around at the audience of employees. Then she straightens her pencil skirt and holds her chin high. She reaches down to grab her purse and a few things off her desk before she rounds the corner and comes out the reception door. "Good luck trying to replace me, Ethan. I'm the reason you get most of your clients you know." She adjusts her cleavage to reveal even more.

"If you really think that, Gretchen, you're dumber than I gave you credit for."

She parades through the room, not bothering to look at Charlie. I know it hurts her to see another woman pregnant when she can't have kids of her own. But she truly brought this on herself by being such a selfish bitch.

"Gretchen, wait," I say before she reaches the outer door.

She turns around, a glimmer of hope flashing across her face that maybe I've changed my mind. I hold my hand out to her. "I'm going to need your keys," I say.

She huffs through her nose as she reaches into her purse, retrieving her set. She throws them at my head, but Charlie reaches out and catches them just before they hit me.

"It goes both ways," Charlie says, smiling. "I'll always be here to protect you, too."

I take her in my arms to the cheers of all my employees. I barely even notice the door closing behind Gretchen on her way out.

CHAPTER THIRTY-EIGHT

"It's about time you fired that bitch," Melissa says.

"I didn't fire her. It was her choice to leave," I say. "But I'll tell you I'm not going to lose any sleep over it."

A look of guilt washes over Charlie's face. "Oh, Ethan. I'm so sorry. I should have just stayed downstairs. What are you going to do?"

"It's fine, honey. Levi will call the temp agency and get a receptionist here within the hour." I look at Levi. "You got this?"

"I'm on it," he says, walking over to shake my hand. "Congratulations, buddy." He leans in to give Charlie a hug. "I'm so happy for you, Charlie."

The rest of my employees wish us well before I escort my fiancée to my private bathroom.

"You look fantastic in that," I say, eyeing every amazing curve of her body. She's really carrying the pregnancy well. Some women tend to show all over. Not Charlie. She has this perfect little round belly. She's not one of those women who make you wonder if they are pregnant or just putting on a little weight. It's clear to anyone who sees her like this that she's expecting. And I love it. Just like the ring, it makes me feel like it advertises she's mine.

"Really?" she asks, looking down on herself and running her hands along her baby bump. "I think I look like a freak of nature."

"Are you kidding? Do you know how sexy you look right now?" I say. "In fact, how about we nix the walk and go for a repeat on my couch?" I wink at her.

She laughs, entering my bathroom. "I think you're a little biased," she says before closing the door. "You have love goggles on," she shouts at me.

I laugh, draping her jacket on the back of my chair. I kind of hope she will leave it here and her scent will permeate the leather so I can smell her for the rest of the day.

"Ready?" she asks, coming back into my office. She sees me situating her jacket on my chair. "If you really think I don't look hideous, would you mind if I leave my jacket here? It's getting warm out there and I already have an oven attached to me."

"You can leave anything you want here." I walk her back through the office and we make our way to the elevator. "And I'm serious about that key. Use it anytime you want." All of a sudden I have an idea. We ride to the ground floor in silence while I think of how to ask her what I want to ask her.

"Charlie, I don't want you to take this the wrong way. And this isn't about money, because I know you don't need mine, but do you plan to keep working through your pregnancy and after?"

She looks up at me in wonder, like she'd never considered this question before. "Uh, yeah. Of course I'm going to work. I don't know what I would do with myself if I didn't." She narrows her eyes at me and huffs, "If you think I'm going to stay home, barefoot and preg—"

I grab her hand. "That's not what I was saying at all. I would never ask that of you, although I would be okay with that if it's what you wanted. But I worry about you being on your feet all day long. Maybe you need a less demanding job, but one that still challenges you."

"What are you saying, Ethan?"

"I'm saying I know of a great job that just opened up. Good pay and great benefits—one of which is that you get to sleep with the boss."

"You want me to take Gretchen's job?" she asks, like it's the most unusual thing anyone's ever asked her.

"Well, sort of, yes." We walk across the street and head into the park. "I've actually been thinking of hiring a receptionist and separating Gretchen's duties. The job is getting too big for one person. She's been receptionist, bookkeeper, and office manager for five years. But I'm not sure the job would require someone full-time yet, so it might only be twenty or thirty hours a week."

"You want me to be your receptionist?" she asks. "But I don't have any experience."

"God no. I don't want you sitting behind that glass. We get some lowlifes in there from time to time and I wouldn't put you in that position. I want you to be my office manager."

"Your *what?*" She stops walking. "Ethan, come on. I have no management experience whatsoever. No bookkeeping skills. You are crazy. I'd run your business into the ground."

I laugh. "I was thinking just the manager part, not the bookkeeper part. I can find a receptionist with those skills. And you sell yourself short. I've been listening when you tell me about all the jobs you had overseas. You see yourself as a waitress, bartender, or shopkeeper's assistant. I see you as a problem-solver, an organizer, a peace-keeper. I need that in a manager. And there are plenty of people around who would be more than happy to show you the ropes. You'll need to learn the business anyway.

You're going to own half of it in . . . uh, when are you going to marry me?"

She starts walking again. "One life-altering decision at a time, Ethan."

"Okay, honey, but I'm serious. Just think about it."

"I will," she says. "It would be kind of nice not to be on my feet all day."

I smile. My plan is working. "So, what are you doing on your days off this week?"

"I'm not sure yet. Did you have something in mind?"

"Furniture shopping," I say.

"Furniture?"

"Yeah. I'd really like it if you would pick out some things that will make the penthouse yours. Like you said yesterday, my place is too masculine. You need to put your touch on it."

"I still can't believe we're doing this," she says. "It all seems so unreal. The baby, moving in with you" —she holds her ring out and stares at it— "this."

"Believe it, honey. It's happening."

"That's the third time you called me honey," she says, with a disapproving wrinkle of her nose.

"Don't you like it?" I ask. "I could always use sweetheart. Or maybe babe. Or darling?"

"Anything but honey, okay? It just reminds me of . . . stuff."

I cringe when I realize maybe some of the men who attacked her used that endearment. It makes my skin crawl thinking of the things that have been done to her. "I'm so sorry, Charlie. I promise I'll never use that word again."

She nods. "It's okay. You didn't know."

After a few steps of uncomfortable silence, she says, "So getting back to the furniture, what exactly are you thinking?"

"Bedroom and living room. And guest room, if you want."

"Oh, no, the guest room is lovely. I wouldn't dream of touching it."

"My mom decorated it. She can't wait to meet you, you know. But with their busy schedules, it may be easier for us to fly out to them."

"That might be fun," she says. "I'd love a beach vacation. But we'd have to do it soon. I don't want to fly in my third trimester."

"Right. That gives us about ten more weeks to get in the trip."

She looks over at me, seemingly impressed. "I can't believe you know about trimesters and stuff."

"When something is important enough, darling, it's worth knowing everything about."

She giggles. "You sound like a grandfather when you say that word."

I pantomime crossing something off a list. "No darling. Gotcha."

Halfway through our walk, we come across a group of guys playing football in the grass. "I can't wait to watch a football game with you, Charlie. That's okay, isn't it, us watching football together?"

"I'd like that a lot," she says. "It's been a while since I've enjoyed it. Plus, football wasn't the same overseas."

The ball gets overthrown and almost hits Charlie, but I reach out and grab it. I work it in my hands for a bit. It feels good there. I used to play for my high school team. I go to throw the ball back to them when I notice that one of the men is staring at Charlie. And Charlie is staring at him.

I look back at the guy and realization flows over me like hot lava, burning through me and eating me alive. I've seen that face.

I've stared at it more than I'd like to admit over the past twenty-four hours.

Zach Thompson.

I look at Charlie. She has fair skin, but in this moment, she is utterly pale, all the blood having drained from her face.

Zach walks over to us, sizing me up along the way. "Hey, um . . . Charlie Brown was it?" he asks her with a devious grin. His eyes rake over Charlie in a way that makes me want to tackle the guy to the ground and pound in his skull. His eyes bug out when they reach her belly. "Holy shit, you've been busy."

I put my arm around her, pulling her close. Then, instead of putting my fist through his face, I offer him my hand. "Hi, I'm Ethan. Charlie's fiancé."

He looks at my hand like it's a joke, but he shakes it anyway. "Zach," he says. He motions to Charlie's belly. "Dude, bummer for you. Kids—wouldn't touch them with a ten-foot pole. But hey, to each his own, right?"

By now, some of his friends are walking up behind us. "Zach," one of them says. "You plan on playing or what, man? We're down by one and we need you."

"I'm coming," he says, turning to me. "Do you mind?" He holds his hand out and I realize I'm still holding the football.

I toss it to him, relieved he's about to turn away and walk out of our lives as quickly as he walked in.

Then one of his friends has to open his big mouth. "Hey," he says to Charlie. "You look just like that lady who played Queen something-or-other in that movie." He turns to another one of their friends. "Trent, doesn't she look like her?"

The guy who must be Trent stares at Charlie. "Shit. She sure as hell does. It was Queen Dragonia, from that Enchanted Dragon series. When we were kids, my mom watched those videotapes so many times, it wore the damn things out and she had to buy them all on Blu-ray. What was her name?" he asks the other guy.

I can feel Charlie tensing up next to me. Then I see her eyes glaze over. It's almost hard for me not to smile, because I know she's thinking of me and the song I played for Cat.

"Catherine? Charlotte? Caroline?" he says.

"Oh, yeah," Trent says. "Caroline. Caroline Anthony." He turns to Charlie. "You look just like Caroline Anthony. She must be your mom. Is she your mom? Hey, I heard she died. Sorry about that." He says something under his breath, but not quietly enough that we don't all hear it. "Girl must be rich as shit."

Charlie must have been listening a little, because she looks up at me with that deer-in-headlights look.

"We'd best be going," I say to them before I pull on her elbow and lead her away.

"Wait," I hear from behind. And then Zach walks around us, staring at Charlie's stomach. "Exactly how pregnant are you?"

All of the oxygen is sucked out of the air surrounding me. I feel as if my world is about to crumble and there's not a goddamn thing I can do about it. *Helpless.* That's what I feel.

"That's a very personal question," I tell him.

"Maybe," he says. "But considering our *history*, I think I have the right to ask." He puffs himself out and stands tall, expecting a fight from me after those words.

"Let's go, Charlie," I say, keeping her behind me.

"How pregnant are you, Charlie?" he yells.

"Dude," one of his friends says. "What the fuck is it to you?"

Another one, I think it's Trent, says, "My sister is knocked up. She's about as big as her. She just found out she's having a girl with one of those X-ray things. I think she's like four months or something like that."

I see Zach try to do the calculation in his head. There is no way he could know when he and Charlie were together. Based on what Melissa told me, he's with a different girl every night.

Fuck. Based on what Melissa told me, the guy is a scam artist. And all of a sudden it becomes clear to me why he's so interested.

"We're leaving," I tell him. I pull Charlie along quickly, glancing back often to make sure we're not being followed. We aren't. But my heart is beating so fast I feel like I just ran a marathon. I also feel like I've just been kicked in the gut.

When we're out of their sight and far enough away, I find a bench and sit my panicked fiancée down on it. "It's going to be okay, Charlie."

She shakes her head over and over. "It's not. He knows. That was never supposed to happen. What if he—"

"No, Charlie. You heard the guy. He doesn't want kids. What was it he said? He won't touch them with a ten-foot pole? The guy was just freaked out. He's probably back there with his buddies saying how he dodged that bullet. I promise you. It'll be fine."

Her breaths come so quickly, I fear she's going to hyperventilate. "Charlie, look at me. Breathe slowly. This is okay. We're okay. It's just you and me. Don't worry about him. He goes through women like toilet paper. He's a liar. A nobody. He can't even hold down a decent job."

She lets out a deep breath, looking at me curiously. "How do you know he's a liar and can't hold down a job?"

I don't answer right away and she gets up off the bench, pacing the sidewalk in front of me. "Of course. You're a private investigator. It's what you do. How did you even find him? And why did you keep this from me, Ethan?"

I can see it in her eyes. I can see the trust she'd placed in me weakening. I stand up and stop her from pacing. I put my hands on her shoulders, forcing her to look at me. "The night you told me you were pregnant you gave me enough information to go on. His first name, his friend's. The name of the club. The fact he had black hair. It took almost two months, but Melissa finally met him and found out his last name. I only know what she told me and what I found on social media. I'm still waiting for the background check to come through."

"Two months?" she raises her voice at me. "You've been trying to find him for two months? When were you planning on telling me?"

"When there was something to tell, Charlie. Christ, I just found out the guy's name yesterday. Until then, I didn't know any more than what you told me."

"But you could have told me you were looking into it."

I nod. "Maybe I should have, but I didn't want to worry you for no reason. Once I had all of the information on him, I was going to come to you and tell you what I found. I promise, I wasn't trying to keep this from you."

"If you want me to trust you. I mean, really trust you, Ethan; you can't keep things like this from me. You have to treat me as an equal, okay?" Her eyes soften a bit and I feel myself take a deep sigh of relief.

"Okay. I will. I swear. But you have to understand something about me, Charlie. I will protect you and this baby at all costs. And I don't care how mad you get at me over it. There is nothing more important to me. I've failed in the past. I've failed to protect those I love. It's not going to happen this time."

"Oh, Ethan." She wraps her arms around me. "You didn't fail anyone. There is nothing you could have done. It's not your fault."

I nod into her hair, letting her scent distract me from the past. "I know that," I tell her. "Deep down, I know there isn't anything I could have done. But I'm telling you right now, I'm not going to apologize for trying to protect you." I put my hand on her belly. "Or him."

"Or her," she says, making me laugh.

"You're just going to have to put up with it."

"It's okay," she says. "I understand now. I'm not mad at you. I actually think it's one of the qualities I love about you. I grew up in a world where men didn't protect women, they only hurt them. So go ahead, protect me all you want. I'll take it. I'll take you."

I pull her as close to me as her growing belly will allow. "Well, you've got me, babe."

She laughs into my shirt.

"No?" I ask.

"No," she says, shaking her head and smiling. "Babe just sounds too cheesy."

"And another one bites the dust." I take her hand and start walking. "Come on, let's go feed the two of you."

CHAPTER THIRTY-NINE

"I really don't mind taking your shifts until Skylar finds someone new," Piper says to Charlie.

I'm glad Charlie decided to accept my job offer, but I really think it has more to do with her getting off her feet than anything else. I don't care about the reason, however, I'm just glad I will be able to keep her close. Her not having to flirt with men for tips is just an added bonus.

"I know, but you shouldn't have to do that," Charlie says. "You're volunteering at the theater and you have Hailey. I'm sure it won't be more than a few weeks until she finds someone as good as us."

I come up behind Charlie and place a kiss on her head. "She'll never find someone as good as you. I'm done in the living room. You need any help here?"

We're packing up Charlie's apartment. After a week of badgering, I finally talked her into moving in with me. She thought it was too soon. I thought nothing was soon enough. So today, we're loading up the stuff her friends gave her so we can return everything to its rightful owner.

Charlie is a minimalist. I guess it comes from living abroad all those years. She doesn't have any personal belongings other than her clothes to move to my apartment. And she doesn't even have many of those. I cleared out half my closet for her, but I doubt she'll use even a quarter of that.

"Can you hand me another box, please?" she asks, rolling up glasses in packing paper to return them safely to Jan and Bruce Mitchell.

I reach over to get the box and notice something conspicuously missing from the front of her refrigerator. "Uh, Charlie," I say, looking on the floor and in the opened boxes. "Did you pack that big fat check or did you rip it into shreds?"

She shrugs. "I deposited it," she says, not stopping what she's doing.

"You did?"

She nods.

"That's fantastic. I'm so glad you took the first step."

"Don't get your panties in a twist," she says, putting down a glass and looking over at me. "I haven't done anything with it yet, but I figure whatever or whoever I give it to should at least get the benefit of interest."

I hand her the box. "It's still fantastic."

"You can thank *me* for that," Piper says. "I dragged her ass all the way to the bank yesterday. It made me nervous to see that many zeroes just pinned right there on her fridge." She looks at me and rolls her eyes. "Well, it might not seem like a lot to you, Richie Rich, but to normal people like us, it's a lot of fucking zeroes."

I look at Charlie and raise my eyebrows.

"Best friends," she says, as if that explains everything.

"When will the guys be here?" I ask Piper.

She checks her watch. "They should be here soon. Mason said they were on their way over."

Good. I'm eager to get this stuff out of here and take her home with me so we can start our life together. So we can christen every damn room of the penthouse.

Charlie is worried about us living together and working together. Maybe it'll be too much togetherness, she said. I think she's wrong. My grandparents did it. My parents do it. We can handle it. She thinks we will run out of things to talk about and get bored with each other. I think we could be marooned on a desert island and that still wouldn't happen. We've spent hours together every day for months now. And even then, I could swear most nights when we part, one of us calls the other because we simply had more to say.

No, this is going to be great. I can feel it.

There is a knock on the door.

"It's open!" Charlie shouts.

Another knock follows.

Charlie gets up and opens the door. "You guys don't need to kno—"

"Charlie Tate?" the stranger at the door asks.

"Yes," she says.

He hands her an envelope. "You've been served," he says, before turning to walk away.

"Served?" She looks at what he deposited in her hand. She closes the door and walks over to the couch. "I wonder if this is more estate stuff or something."

She opens the envelope and pulls out the papers, but then she drops them on the floor when her hand comes up to cover her scream. "Oh, God, no!"

Piper and I immediately join her on the couch. "What is it?" Piper asks.

Charlie grabs her belly protectively and my heart lunges into the pit of my stomach. I pick up the papers, hoping I'm not going to see what I think I'm going to see. Only when I do see it, it's even worse than what I was imagining.

"That mother fucker," I say, not even bothering to read it all before I pull out my phone and make a call. "John, this is Ethan. I'm sorry to bother you on a Sunday, but I've got a real problem here." I walk into the bedroom and shut the door so Charlie doesn't have to hear me. "The short of it is, there is a very small chance that my fiancée is pregnant with another man's child. I'm not going to get into specifics, but the asshole just served her papers demanding a paternity test. It says he'll be suing for full custody if he's the father. There is a bunch of other legal crap I haven't read through yet. Can you help me?"

"Of course, Ethan. Jesus, I can't imagine what you guys must be going through. If you can snap pictures of the pages and email them to me, I'll take a quick look and call you back with my initial thoughts. Tomorrow I can get some of my people on it to help us fill in any blanks."

"Thanks, John. I owe you one."

"No, you don't. Your office has helped me out on several occasions. This is just payback. I'll call you back as soon as I've read through everything."

I take careful pictures of the six-page document and send them to John. Then I head back into the living room to find two teary-eyed women being consoled by Mason and Griffin.

From the looks on their faces, they already know the gist of it. "I was just on the phone with my attorney. I sent him a copy of the documents. He will call me back within the hour." I get on my knees in front of Charlie. "This is not happening. Do you understand me? I don't care what that asshole says, he is not getting custody of this baby."

The entire time I was on the phone with John, I was wondering why a jerk like Thompson would even bother. But I remember what Melissa told me and it all makes sense. "He's after money, that's all. He's a scam artist, Charlie. I saw it in his eyes last week at the park when he found out who your mother was and when his friend made a comment about how rich you must be. That's all he wants. Either he's looking for a payoff or he's going after the baby so he can get child support. Either way, he's looking at this as a meal ticket."

"You saw this guy in the park?" Griffin asks.

"Yeah. Last Monday," I say. "He was playing football and the ball almost hit Charlie. It was so random I can't even believe it. Over eight fucking million people in the city and we have to run into *him*."

"You guys have enough to deal with, Ethan," Mason says. "Why don't you pack up whatever clothes Charlie needs and head to your place. We can take care of this."

I look around at all the furniture and then I look at Charlie. I know she needs me more than the guys do. "Yeah. Thanks."

~ ~ ~

An hour later, when we're unpacking her suitcase in our bedroom, my phone rings. I look at the screen and answer it. "Hey, John, do you have anything for me?"

"Yeah, but you might not like it."

I'm thankful Charlie is busy hanging her clothes in the closet. I'm not even sure she heard my phone ring. "Tell me," I say, sitting on the bed.

"The papers are all legit. But the attorney he used to prepare them is an ambulance chaser. It looks to me like this guy is after money, Ethan. Everything points to it. It even states that if he's awarded full custody, he intends to sue not only for the maximum child support allowed by law, but punitive damages as well."

"Punitive damages?"

"He claims Charlie fraudulently withheld information about the pregnancy from him and that he has suffered emotional trauma as a result."

"That's bullshit, John," I whisper into the phone so I don't alarm Charlie. "They hooked up one time, in the storeroom of a bar. They were drunk. All she knew was his first name. There would have been no way to contact him even if she wanted to." I realize how that makes Charlie sound, so I add, "Uh . . . Charlie and I were on a break at the time."

"Hey, no explanation necessary," he says. "But Thompson claims she knew who he was and how to contact him. He claims she deliberately withheld this from him."

"He's lying, John. But I guess we've no way to prove that, do we?"

"Exactly. And I was able to contact a buddy of mine who is an expert on family law." He pauses. "This is the part you might not want to hear."

"Oh? Because everything else you've told me is all peaches and fucking cream?"

"I'm sorry, man. But someone has to break the news," he says, sympathetically.

"I know, just lay it all out on the table."

"Well, I guess his lawyer is smart enough to know they can't force Charlie to take a paternity test if she refuses. So they've given her up to one week after the birth to have the baby tested. But, Ethan, honestly, the best way to get this guy off your back if you really think he's not the father, is to go ahead and have her take the test now."

"I was afraid you'd say that. Tell me the ramifications if we don't."

"If she doesn't do the test, he could argue she is continuing to withhold information. He could argue she is trying to keep him from the unborn child. He could sue her, and maybe even you, for more pain and suffering. In addition, as the potential father, he has every right to try and gain access to medical records associated with the pregnancy. Tests. Ultrasounds. Due dates. Whatever."

"Not that it'll be easy for him," he says. "He'll have to get a judge to sign an order. But if his attorney is good, he'll know exactly who to use for an order like that."

"Shit." I rest my elbows on my knees and stare at the carpet.

"Ethan, be straight with me. What are the chances he's the father?"

I blow out a deep sigh into the phone. "About fifty-fifty."

"Whoa," he says. "That's a little too close for comfort."

"Tell me about it."

"You said she's your fiancée, so I'm assuming you love her and you really want this child, am I right?"

"It goes without saying."

"I think the lesser of two evils is to wait on the test until after the baby is born."

"And let him have access to her records?" I argue.

"Yes. Think about it, Ethan. If the test comes back showing him as the likely father, he'll have more ammunition, more rights, more reason to be in your life. Right now, he's just a *potential* father."

"Okay, so we hold off on the test. What else can we do?"

"It's what you *shouldn't* do," he warns.

"What do you mean?" I ask.

"Do not try to pay this guy off. I mean it, Ethan. As your attorney, I know almost as much about your finances as your accountant does. I know how easy it would be for you to write a check and try to make this all go away. I know you must be pissed and hurt and wanting to protect what's yours. But that is the worst thing you could do. Even if *he* comes to *you*, he could later say you were the one who tried to bribe him. And even if you did come to a financial arrangement, if he is the biological father, he can still veto the adoption up to six months after the baby is born."

"So I could pay him off and he could still end up having parental rights?"

"Exactly," he says.

"Fuck!" I yell, punching my fist into the bed. "So he's got us by the balls."

Charlie comes out of the closet and sees me on the phone. She sits next to me on the bed and takes my hand.

"John, I have to go. Charlie and I have to talk about this. I'll get back with you tomorrow. Thanks a lot for getting on this so quickly."

"Anytime, Ethan. Good luck."

It'll take a hell of a lot more than luck to hold me back if I ever come face to face with this asshole. It'll take a fucking miracle.

CHAPTER FORTY

It only took the bastard two days to get an order allowing him access to any pregnancy-related medical records. Since then, it's been a week without any further word from Thompson or his cronies. But I know better. He's scum. A bottom dweller. He will sit back and attack when he knows it'll hurt her the most.

It makes me sick to think about the kind of man he is. When I read his background report a few days ago, everything I thought about him was confirmed. He's been arrested on several charges of fraud and identity theft. He was once arrested for scamming an elderly lady out of thousands of dollars, but the charges were dropped because she passed away and her surviving children decided not to pursue it. He's spent a few nights in jail here and there, but for the most part, his punishments consisted of financial retribution or community service. It seems there isn't anything this guy wouldn't do for money.

That's the very reason I made sure Levi came with us today. He's sitting in the lobby of the building, ready to intervene if anything should happen. I don't know what to expect from the dirt bag and we need to be prepared for anything.

Charlie has been tense all week. She hasn't been eating right or sleeping well. The stress of this is really taking a toll on her. And the only reason I've not insisted she quit her job at Mitchell's immediately is that work is one of the only things that seems to distract her. However, I insisted on hiring private security to sit outside the restaurant in case Zach Thompson decides to make an appearance. She didn't fight me on it. She was grateful I discussed it with her before actually doing it. She's come to accept the fact I will do anything to protect her and the baby.

As we approach the doctor's office, I grab her hand. "Whatever happens, it'll be okay."

There is a window into the reception area and we look through it before opening the door. It doesn't take us long to spot the only man sitting by himself. The man who looks like he'd rather be anywhere but in a reception area with pregnant women and babies. He's going through a pile of magazines, shaking his head when he can't find one to suit him. A baby starts to cry and we can hear its high-pitched wail through the glass. Zach looks at it with disgust and puts his earbuds in.

"Oh my God," Charlie says, moving away from the window and backing up against the wall. "We should leave. We should change doctors."

I shake my head. "He'll use it against us, Charlie. And he will still be able to get access to your records. Dr. Chavis's office knows what's going on. I called them earlier to prepare them for the possibility of him being here. They assured me that if he was here, they wouldn't make us sit in reception. As soon as we check in, we'll be allowed through to the back."

She looks up at me with appreciation. "You did that?"

"Of course I did."

Before we go in, I send Levi a text letting him know Zach is here and to stand by. Levi is carrying, so he can't come into the medical building because of the metal detectors. Luckily for us, the doctor Skylar set Charlie up with has some very high-end clients. Famous athletes, celebrities, wives of Wall Street moguls. Security is high in this building. For which I'm grateful. Still—doesn't mean I don't want to have my own guy.

"We've got this," I say. We lock eyes, and for five whole seconds, I make sure she sees how much love I have for her and this baby.

She nods and I open the door. I stare the asshole down as we make our way to the reception desk. I tell the young lady behind the counter, "I'm Ethan Stone and this is Charlie Tate. We have an appointment with Dr. Chavis. I called earlier and we need to be taken in the back right away."

"Yes, Mr. Stone, I've been waiting for you. I'll buzz you back immediately." She points to the door on her left. "Please come on through."

"Want to make it a threesome?" I hear behind me.

I turn around and face him, wanting in the very depths of my soul to punch the smirk off his snide little face. I see we have an audience, as he didn't even attempt to lower his voice as he baited us.

"Do you want me to call security, Mr. Stone?" the girl behind the desk asks.

I shake my head. "Not unless he tries to follow us into the back," I say, looking directly at him. I gently push Charlie through the door and pull it closed behind me.

We are escorted into Dr. Chavis's office and told to wait here while she finishes up with another patient.

I hear Charlie breathe when she sits down. I think it's the first breath she's drawn in minutes. I reach my hand over, pulling hers into my lap. "That was the worst of it. He just wants to intimidate us, you know. He'll either be gone by the time we leave, or he'll demand to see your records at the front desk. Either way, we shouldn't have to deal with him. Okay, Peaches?"

Her face breaks out into a smile right before she mimics sticking a finger down her throat.

"No?" I laugh. She shakes her head laughing. Mission accomplished.

Dr. Chavis walks in and closes the door. She greets us and sits behind her desk. "So I hear your lives have gotten a lot more complicated."

"To put it mildly," Charlie says.

"If there is anything I can do, please let me know," she says.

"Thank you," I say. "That means a lot to us. The man who is filing suit against her is a scam artist. He's using this baby as leverage. We'll take all the help we can get."

Dr. Chavis nods and makes a few notes in Charlie's chart. "I want to assure you both that Charlie and this baby are our top priorities here. We will comply with the order to release medical information, but rest assured, it will be the bare minimum. Have you thought any more about the paternity tests we discussed?"

I squeeze Charlie's hand. "We've decided against that until the baby comes. We don't want to risk him having any more access than he already does."

"I understand," Dr. Chavis says. "Well, I'll have a nurse take you back and gown you. We'll do an ultrasound today to get a good look at the baby's heart."

"Heart?" Charlie asks.

"It's standard procedure around this time. Also, if he or she cooperates, I should be able to tell you the baby's sex, so think about whether or not you'd like to know that." She stands up and leads us to the door. "I'll see you in a few minutes."

A nurse has me wait outside while Charlie changes. Then she takes her vitals and situates Charlie on a table before she wheels in the ultrasound machine. "The doctor will be in soon," she says, leaving us alone in the room.

"We've never really talked about it, have we?" Charlie asks. "In the thousands of hours we've spent talking, we've managed to completely avoid this one topic."

"What topic?"

"Whether the baby is a boy or a girl," she says. "Do you think you'd be upset if it's a girl?"

"Upset? Why would you say that? I don't care if it's a boy or a girl as long as it's healthy."

"I just thought you might want a boy is all." She gives her belly a rub. "You know, because a girl might remind you of Cat."

I give her a sad smile. "Charlie, *any* baby will remind me of Cat. Every time I look at our child, girl or boy, I'll think of her. But that's okay. I loved her very much. I like to think about her."

"What if *I'm* the one who doesn't want a girl?" she asks, guilt washing over her beautiful features.

I feel my forehead crinkle as my eyes question her.

"I mean, I love little girls," she says. "Hailey and Jordan are wonderful. But, I'm just not sure *I* want one. Look at what happened to me. To Piper. What if that happens to *our* child? The Mitchells loved their daughters more than any parents I've ever seen, yet they couldn't protect Piper. I don't know if I could take it, Ethan. It would kill me."

"The odds of that happening are—"

"One in four, Ethan. One. In. Four. That's a twenty-five percent chance our daughter will be raped. Molested. Assaulted."

I can see she's getting worked up. I step behind her and rub her shoulders. I can feel her relax under my touch and it makes me smile. "Charlie, we can't live our lives in fear of that," I tell her. "We could get hit by a bus on our way home from this appointment. We can't live in a bubble. We have to live our lives to the fullest and hope for the best."

She cranes her neck around. "Why do I feel there is a rule coming?"

I laugh. "Okay, how about this one. Rule number sixteen—carpe diem."

"Doesn't that mean 'live for today' or something?"

"Technically, it means 'seize the day,' but yes, you've got the right idea. We can't control tomorrow. We can't change the past. All we can do is make today the best we can make it, and go on from there."

She pulls me around her so I'm standing between her legs. "I knew there was a reason I loved you. You're just so . . . reasonable."

"Reasonable?" I make a sour face at her. "I'd rather you love me because I'm charming. Or sexy. Or an incredible lover."

"I love you for all those things, too. But right this second, I love you because you're reasonable."

I kiss her on the tip of her nose. "I guess I can live with that."

"So, are we going to find out the sex?" she asks.

"If you really want to we can. But there are so few true surprises in life anymore. If it were up to me, I'd wait."

"Then we wait," she says.

"Really?"

"Of course. You're his daddy," she says. "Or hers."

My smile splits my face in two. "Say it again," I beg.

"You're his daddy," she says.

"Or hers," I add, and we both laugh.

~ ~ ~

While I wait for Charlie to dress, I stare at the ultrasound photos Dr. Chavis printed off for us. Turns out, baby Stone was not cooperating and we wouldn't have been able to find out the sex anyway. His or her legs were so tightly crossed it's as if he or she were in on the surprise.

Charlie emerges from the room and I tuck the pictures into my pocket. If Thompson is still outside, I wouldn't want him to see them. I grab her hand and escort her quickly through the waiting area, not looking around to see if he's still here.

As soon as we're through the door, someone comes out into the hallway behind us. "So, am I going to have a son or a daughter?" Thompson asks. "I really hope it's not a girl. Girls are more trouble than they're worth. Of course I'm not sure I want it to be a boy if he's going to be some pansy-ass ginger."

I pull Charlie behind me and turn around. "What you're going to have is my fist in your nose if you don't walk away right now."

He holds up his hands in surrender. "Geez. Aren't we touchy? Just trying to get the information I'm entitled to. I guess I'll have to go ask the office whether I should get pink or blue shit." He grabs the door handle, but then he spins around and looks right at me. "Oh, and I'd think twice about threatening me. You have no idea how much power I really have over you, do you?"

I'm in front of him in two steps, Charlie begging me back. I get in his face. "I'm not threatening you," I say. "I'm telling you there is no fucking way you will ever touch me, Charlie, or this baby. I know exactly who you are and what you've done. Apparently you don't know the same about me. In the future, I'd be careful who you fuck with."

He doesn't seem as affected by my intimidation as I'd hoped. He simply says, "You two have a good day. Be sure to feed that kid of mine, okay?" Then he disappears back into the office.

Levi comes barging through the stairwell door, out of breath after apparently running up eight flights of stairs. He looks at the hallway that is now empty but for Charlie and me. "Shit. Sorry I took so long, I had to leave my gun with security."

I raise my eyebrows at Charlie. "You called him?"

"It was a text," she says, not looking apologetic in the least. "I couldn't have you and Zach killing each other."

"Is this you protecting me?" I ask, taking her hand in mine.

"It goes both ways," she says.

"What happened?" Levi asks, his eyes bouncing between us.

"Pissing contest, I'd say," Charlie tells him.

"Who won?"

I shake my head. "I'd have to call it a draw."

I look at Charlie, pale and frazzled from the confrontation. I decide to take the rest of the afternoon off, telling Levi to handle things in my absence. Charlie is under a tremendous amount of stress and I need to make sure she's okay.

"Let's get you home."

Thirty minutes later, she's sitting on our new couch as I'm drawing her a bath. I think the oversized sunken Jacuzzi tub is her favorite thing about the penthouse. Well, that and the view. She will sit and stare out the windows for hours. But whenever I ask her what she's thinking about when she does it, she clams up.

Sometimes I think she's wondering where all the men from her list are. Other times, maybe she's wondering about her father.

Days like today, when I catch her staring out the windows while rubbing her belly, I know she's thinking about the future. Wondering if the plans we're making are just pipe dreams, or if they could be our happily-ever-after.

I fetch her when her bath is ready. She brings her phone so she can call Piper. I give her some privacy to talk with her best friend. But not five minutes go by before I hear her heart-wrenching cries while I'm preparing her a snack in the kitchen. I run in to see what's the matter, fearing she's tried to get out of the tub and slipped on the tile.

She's still sitting in the tub, her legs pulled up and her arms wrapped around them. "What happened? Are you okay?" I ask, looking her over for signs of trauma.

She looks up at me, tears rolling off her cheeks and into the water. She nods to the phone clutched in her hand. "She's dead."

My heart thunders. "Who's dead?"

"Mrs. Buttermaker."

"Mrs. Buttermaker died?" I ask. "How do you know?"

"Piper told me. Mason told her. When she didn't show up for her swim last night, the girl at the front desk got worried and called her house. Mrs. Buttermaker hadn't missed a swim in five years." She closes her eyes, shaking her head. "It's not fair, Ethan. That woman was in better shape than most forty-year-olds. She exercised every day. She exercised while her deadbeat husband wasted his life away in his Barcalounger. How is it that she's the one who died from a stroke and not him?"

"Oh, no. She had a stroke?" I sit on the edge of the tub and take the phone from her, placing it on the vanity.

She nods, her chest still heaving with each breath. "It's not fair, Ethan. She was so nice and good. Why do bad things happen to good people?"

All of a sudden, I know we're not just talking about Mrs. B.

Charlie's sobs come so quickly, I fear she might become hysterical. In record time, I remove my clothes and slip into the tub behind her, wrapping my arms tightly around her.

"Why, Ethan? Why is all this happening?"

I embrace her until she settles down, then something on the floor catches my eye. The ultrasound pictures are sticking out of my shirt pocket. I dry my hands with a towel and reach over to get them. I hold one of the pictures up in front of her. "Look at this," I say. "It's amazing. We can see his fingers. His toes. He's still got so much growing to do, but he's already perfect."

She takes the photo from me, tracing his tiny little feet. "Or she," she says, leaning back into me.

"Or she," I say.

We stare at the pictures until the water cools.

"We need to get out of here," I say.

She nods. "Yeah, the water is too cold."

I laugh. "Well, that, too. But I was thinking we should get away for a few days. Take a vacation before the baby comes. Let's fly out to California and stay at my parents' house. It's right on the coast. We can go for long walks on the beach. We can lie in bed all day. We can fatten you and Junior up with my mother's cooking."

"Junior?" she asks.

I shrug. "It could be gender neutral."

She laughs and it's music to my ears. "A beach vacation sounds heavenly, Ethan. I just need to see if I can get the time off."

"Somehow, I don't think that will be a problem." I wink at her. "I know people who know people."

CHAPTER FORTY-ONE

Our long weekend in Santa Monica has turned into a ten-day vacation. I've never seen Charlie more relaxed and carefree. And watching her with my mom—it's everything I didn't know I wanted.

Dad and I are sitting at the bar in the kitchen watching Mom and Charlie prepare tonight's dinner. Chicken Piccata I think they said. It's amazing witnessing the bond she has formed with my parents in a mere eight days. From the moment they picked us up at the airport, they welcomed her as part of our family and doted on her like the daughter they never had.

Of course, my mother is over the moon about becoming a grandmother. Yes, she's been one before, and although my mom was a great Nana to Cat, I think she and I both know this time will be different.

My mother pulls Charlie into a hug. "I'm going to miss you so much, dear."

"We still have two more days, Jackie."

My mother gives her a stern look so Charlie adds, "Sorry . . . *Mom.*"

My mother's smile lights up the room. She insisted Charlie call her 'Mom' the instant they met. I can see Charlie isn't completely comfortable with it yet, but she's indulging my mother. My mom is not an easy woman to turn down.

"With our hectic work schedules, and the few hours we get to see you each night, it feels like you just got here," Mom says. She turns to my dad. "Marc, when are we going to retire so we can move back to New York and spoil our grandchild?"

He laughs. "Tomorrow," he says with a wink to Charlie. My parents often joke about wanting to retire. But the truth is, nothing could pull them away from the jobs they love. My parents *are* their jobs. When they can no longer hold a scalpel, they will no doubt teach. I'm pretty sure they will work until they drop dead like my grandfather, hopefully at ripe old ages.

"Am I doing this right, Mom?" Charlie asks her, looking down at some kind of butter sauce.

Dad knocks his shoulder against mine and whispers, "She's a keeper, son. Well done."

I smile at him. He hasn't known her long, but I can tell he thinks she's *the one*. Just like my mom is for him and his mom was for my grandfather.

I hear the front door open and then footsteps echo through the grand parlor and get louder as they come closer to the kitchen. My brother appears in the doorway. "Smells good, I didn't miss dinner, did I?"

Chad has stopped by several times this week while we've been here. Charlie even convinced me to go out with him one night for what she called 'brother bonding.' But truthfully, I think she just needed a night off from all the sex we've been having. Another bonus of being here and so far away from our problems.

"Hey, Chad," Charlie greets him. "No, you didn't miss dinner."

He walks around the massive center island, kissing both Charlie and my mother on the cheek.

"So, how's everything in the world of Thad Stone?" my father asks.

"Good," he says. "We're finishing up re-takes for *Defcon One* this week. I'll be glad when *that's* done." He rolls his eyes.

Defcon One is the movie he's been shooting for the past several months. It was one of the reasons he was in New York back in March. He's had some trouble with his co-star. Let's just say she's Gretchen-esque. I can relate.

"When will the movie be released?" Charlie asks.

"Probably not until early next year. The time it takes to produce a film from start to finish is about twelve months. Sometimes longer."

"Well, I can't wait to see it," she says.

"You guys should come out for the premier," Chad says.

Charlie looks down at her belly. "I don't know, Chad. Depending on how early next year, we may have a newborn."

"Nonsense," Mom says. "You'll come and I'll babysit. I hate those premiere things anyway." She winks at Chad. "We won't want the baby picking up any germs on a commercial airplane so Ethan will charter a jet."

"Charter a jet?" Charlie stares at me suspiciously.

I shrug. She's seen my penthouse. My cars. But she hasn't seen my bank account yet. I may have downplayed my net worth just a tad.

"Let's play it by ear, okay?" I say. "Who knows what will be going on then." Charlie's eyes turn sad. She and I both know that if things don't go our way, our lives may be filled with restrictions where the baby is concerned.

Just as we're sitting down to eat, my mother's pager goes off. She looks at it and sighs. "Sorry, guys," she says. "Nature of the business." She gets up and takes her plate to the counter where she wraps it with tin foil.

My dad gets up and hands her his plate, too. "I'll keep you company, sweetheart. There are some patients I'd like to check on myself."

She smiles at him and wraps up his plate of food. I smile at Charlie. We lock eyes. I know we're both thinking the same thing. That we hope after we've been married for thirty years, we won't mind skipping meals just so we can be together.

"Don't wait up!" Mom shouts on their way to the garage.

Halfway into our meal—that's been prepared to perfection by Charlie under my mom's tutelage—my phone pings with a text from Levi. There is a case he's working on that needs my immediate attention.

"Charlie, I'm sorry, I have to make a couple of calls. Do you mind if I leave you in my brother's capable hands for a little while? I promise to make it up to you later," I say with a devious grin.

"Bro, I'm sitting right here," Chad says. "Please stop giving me visuals."

She laughs. "It's fine. Go take care of your work thing."

"Thanks for a wonderful dinner, sweetheart," I say.

I immediately look for her reaction.

She wrinkles her nose and gives me a small shake of the head. "Makes you sound like your dad," she says. "I'm pretty sure you don't want me thinking about him when—"

"Enough said," I tell her, holding out my hand to stop her words. I mentally cross that one off the list.

"Jesus, will you just go already," Chad says. "You two and your dinner foreplay are killing me."

~ ~ ~

Two hours later, I crawl into bed next to Charlie. She's sleeping, but still she gravitates over to me. When she places her head on my chest, I inhale her scent. I swear since she's been pregnant, she smells even better than she did before.

In the moonlight, I watch her sleep. She's so peaceful. More peaceful than I've ever seen her. It makes me wonder if being in New York is part of the problem. Even if the Zach Thompson issue goes away, will she ever be comfortable living so near the place of her childhood nightmare?

She seems to love it here in Santa Monica. We've gone for long walks on the beach every day. I've taken her to see the sights. We even went up to the Wine Country. She insisted we go even though she was unable to partake.

I think she's even put on a few pounds which is a good thing. I was beginning to worry, as was her doctor, that she wasn't gaining enough weight. Everything feels better here. Lighter. Happier.

But I know leaving New York right now isn't really an option. And I'm not sure I could ever tear her away from the Mitchell clan. They are all so close. They seem to be making up for all that lost time together when Charlie and Piper were traveling abroad.

My family is here. My parents. Chad. Everyone but Kyle. They could be her family. I think about how well she's gotten along with them. How close they've all become in a few short days. I sense Charlie loves the parental attention she has been missing all these years.

It makes me think of her dad. She's told me a lot about him. And although he's not going to win any Father of the Year awards, I'm not sure he's as bad as she makes him out to be. The guy was being abused by his controlling wife. Charlie was so young, only twelve, when he left. She could be confused about things. He could have had every intention of taking her, but maybe her mom threatened him. Maybe there were circumstances she didn't know about. He claimed he didn't know she was hitting Charlie. I'm willing to give the guy the benefit of the doubt until I hear otherwise.

I'd like to meet him and see for myself. But I won't. I promised Charlie I wouldn't do anything like that again without consulting her. She trusts me now. She loves me. And it's the best feeling in the world knowing she will put her life in my hands, her child's life, and know I will always take care of them. It's taken a long time to get to this point and I'm not willing to jeopardize that for anything.

Before I know it, the sun is coming up. I think I've watched her all night without sleeping.

She makes an adorable squeaky yawning noise and then she opens her eyes to catch me staring. She smiles, but then she narrows her eyes at me, looking worried. "You look tired," she says. "Were you up late working?"

"I was up late," I tell her. "But I wasn't working. I was watching my beautiful fiancée sleep."

"Oh, God," she says, throwing an arm over her face. "I hope I didn't snore. Or drool."

I laugh. "There is nothing you could do that would turn me off, Charlie. But no, you looked like an angel. So peaceful. I wish I could bottle it up and take it with us back to New York."

"Me too," she says. "Everything just seems . . . better here."

I smile wondering if maybe in the future, we could make a life here. A life with our child. I push the thought of moving here aside for now, thinking I'll bring it up again if we really do get to come back here for the premier of Chad's movie.

"Everything?" I ask, pulling her so close she can feel what lying next to her does to me.

She reaches down, touching me through my boxer briefs, making me even harder. Needier. "If I recall," she says with a wry grin, "you promised to make something up to me. I'm curious as to just how you plan to do that, Stone."

"Unnngh," I growl through her long strokes across the thin fabric separating us. "Any way you want me to, baby."

She stops stroking me.

"What, not 'baby' either?"

"Nope." She thinks on it for a second. "I actually don't mind it when you're deep inside me, about to come. And now that I think about it, I really don't care *what* you call me during those times. As long as it's not Gretchen."

I cringe. "You had to go and ruin a perfectly good erection by bringing her up."

She slips her hand under my boxers. "I think we can still salvage it."

I tug them down to give her full access. Her eyes go wide and hungry as she stares appreciatively at my naked body, making me want to pound my chest.

"I thought this was about *me* making it up to *you*," I say, perfectly happy to have her fondle me, but at the same time, needing to put my hands on her.

"Just let me play for a little bit," she says, looking at me through lidded eyes. "You got to watch me all night. Now it's my turn."

Who am I to argue with that? I latch my hands behind my head and enjoy watching everything she does to me. Every touch. Every stroke. Every light tickle she feathers over me. It doesn't take long for her to work me up into a frenzy. And right before I topple over the edge, she pulls back. She knows I only want to come inside her. She knows that since we don't have to use condoms anymore, I want to be deep within her, sharing our release together.

She climbs up my body, taking time to explore every ridge and ripple. I've never felt more revered in my life. What did I do to deserve this? To deserve her?

She kisses the underside of my left bicep. "Mmmm," she says. "I love this."

I have a birthmark there. She thinks it looks like a banana. I always thought it looked more like a fingernail moon, but after the first time she said it, I examined it with a magnifying glass and damn it if she wasn't right. One edge of the birthmark sticks out like the stem of a banana. Twenty-seven years I went without knowing that. She knows me better than I know myself.

She licks it and I shiver. When I can't take not touching her anymore, I reach around her and pull her on top of me so she's straddling me. She pulls her sleeping shirt over her head, leaving her clad in only her underwear. My eyes rake over her body, her magnificent full breasts, her perfectly round belly, her soaked-through panties.

I put my hands on her breasts, giving her nipples a pinch. They pucker and harden under my touch. She gasps at the sensation. She's gotten so much more sensitive there since becoming pregnant. I've been able to make her come just by playing with her nipples. It's fascinating to me that the same part of her body that brings us so much pleasure will also be used to feed our child. He's not even here yet and already I'm jealous that he'll get more access to them than I will. "Mmmm," I mimic her. "I love *these*."

She giggles, pushing her chest further into my hands.

I'm growing painfully hard beneath her. "I need to be inside you. Right now."

I don't want her to move off me, so I reach down with both hands and rip her panties right off her body.

"Hey," she pouts. "I liked those, Ethan."

"I'll buy you a hundred pairs. Every color you can think of."

She smirks at me. "Will you have them delivered by charter jet?"

I put a finger inside her, feeling how ready she is for me. "I'll deliver them by submarine if you want, just let me make love to you, Charlie."

"Do you really have enough money to buy a submarine?" she asks.

I add another finger and press my thumb on her clit. She gasps. "Do you really want to talk about this now?" I ask.

"Noooooo," she responds breathily. "Oh God."

"Are you okay like this?" I ask. I love the fact that her belly is getting bigger, forcing us to get creative with all kinds of positions. But her being on top is probably my favorite. It gives me the best view of her face when I make her come. And being so up close and personal with her chest isn't that bad either.

She answers me by lowering herself onto me. She sets the pace, working herself slowly up and down at first. She threads her fingers through my hair. She loves to grip my hair when she rides me. I put my hands on her hips, urging her to increase her pace as I thrust into her from beneath.

Our lips come together as we kiss and breathe and pant into each other, each of us wanting to find release. Each of us wanting to stretch this out as long as we can.

She moves herself back and forth and in circles on top of me, driving me to the edge of insanity. I want to take her over the cliff with me so I work a hand between us and find her slippery nub. My other hand I use to pinch and twist one of her sensitive nipples.

She rips her mouth from mine. "Oh, yes . . . Ethan!"

We lock eyes as she begins to shudder. Knowing she's right there. Feeling her start to pulsate around me. Hearing her shout my name. It all comes together at once and my body stiffens as I thrust into her one last time, emptying myself into her as her spasms milk every last drop from me. "Charlie!" I hear myself shout without any care of who might hear.

She collapses onto me, her body molded against mine as we regulate our breathing and regain our bearings. Then she sits up suddenly and squeals, "Oh my God!"

"What is it?" I ask, not knowing if she's in pain or having a second orgasm.

"I just felt the baby move," she says, putting her hands on her stomach. "Oh, Ethan. Oh my God. I felt him move. Oh my God. Oh my God."

I put my hands next to hers and try to feel something, but I don't. That doesn't stop me from sharing in her excitement, however. Seeing her experience this for the first time is beyond wonderful. The baby inside her is alive. *My* baby is alive and moving and kicking. If I thought she was beautiful before, that pales in comparison to how she looks right now. She is a goddess. My love. My everything.

"What does it feel like?" I ask, needing every detail of every feeling.

"It feels like little bubbles," she says. "Or maybe like a butterfly flapping its wings. It's so soft." She concentrates hard. "I can't feel it anymore. But, God, Ethan. There is really a baby in there." A tear escapes her eye and I kiss it away with my lips. "I mean, I know there is a baby in there, but now . . . it's just so real." She puts her hands back on her stomach. "I want him to do it again."

I remove her from my lap and position myself over her, using my elbows to keep my weight off her belly. "It was the orgasm," I tell her. "I've read about that. Your uterus contracts and it causes the baby to move around."

I kiss her and then work myself down her body, past her breasts, past her belly. I look back up at her. "Give me five minutes and I'll have Junior doing somersaults."

One hour and two orgasms later, she's exhausted. I'm exhausted. But mission accomplished. She felt him move two more times. And seeing her that happy makes me want to give her a hundred orgasms.

I lay with my hand on her stomach, longing for the day I'll get to feel his movements along with her. I can't believe I'm going to be a father again. I'm excited. I'm terrified. I'm so fucking grateful.

I swear to myself right here and now to be the best father I can be. To always be there for this child. To never ignore her because my favorite television show is on. To never be too busy to throw a baseball with him. To love his mother so much, he has no choice but to find the woman of his dreams and do the same.

I think of all the fathers in the world who don't do any of those things. I think of all the fathers who are missing out on the best part of life. I think of George Tate and the mistakes he made that ruined his relationship with his only daughter.

I prop up on an elbow and stare at Charlie until she looks over at me. "What?" she asks. Then her jaw drops. "I don't think I could do that again, Ethan."

"That's not what I had in mind," I say, laughing. "But can I ask you to do something for me when we get back to New York?"

"Of course. Anything." She smiles at me, running a finger across my three-day stubble.

"Would you take me to meet your father?"

CHAPTER FORTY-TWO

It took almost four weeks, but Charlie finally caved in to my pleading to call her father. If there's even a small chance to salvage their relationship, I knew I had to try. As the father I once was and the father I'm about to become, I'm not sure I could live with myself knowing there is a man out there who loves his daughter but can never know her. Not if there's something I can do about it.

She's nervous. She didn't eat breakfast this morning. I've already got a catered lunch on standby, hoping all will go well and she'll want to eat after our meeting.

George Tate.

I've stayed up many nights wondering about him. I've investigated him with Charlie's approval. It was one of her conditions of meeting with him. The other conditions were that it was here, at our offices, and that I be in the room. She didn't have to twist my arm on either of those points.

Having Charlie work right down the hall from me is even better than I thought it would be. I gave her the largest unoccupied office, thinking we could stick a crib in the corner and bring the baby to work with us. Unless she wanted a nanny, of course. But the day we had the decorator come to put her office together,

Charlie told her she wanted a rocking chair instead of a couch. That's when I knew. I knew she wanted exactly what I wanted.

It amazes me every day how the two of us found each other. If I searched the ends of the earth, I wouldn't find a woman more perfect for me than Charlie.

We have settled into our new routine since coming back from California. We come in to work together each morning. She works until noon and then I walk her home and we have lunch together before I return for the rest of my day. She will rest, or do something with Piper, or shop for baby clothes. And after I get home we will go for a swim and then cook dinner together.

After Mrs. Buttermaker died, neither of us wanted to swim late at night anymore so we changed the time of our workout. In some strange way, it just wasn't the same without her.

And thanks to my mother's crash course in cooking, Charlie has become pretty good at it. We muddle through together and have found it to be the best part of our day.

Charlie isn't the only nervous one today. I found myself picking at my breakfast as well. After all, I'm the one who demanded this meeting. I'm the one she'll blame if it goes south. I'm the one who will have to deal with the fallout.

As if on cue, Brittney, our new receptionist, buzzes me telling me there is a Mr. Tate here.

"Please tell him to have a seat and we'll be with him in a few minutes," I say into the intercom.

I head down the hall to Charlie's office. She always keeps her door open in case anyone needs anything. She has fit right in as our new office manager. She's proven to be even better at scheduling, coordinating and problem-solving than I thought she would be. Everyone is impressed with her professionalism, her candor and her quick wit.

That's my girl.

I stand in the doorway for a minute before she notices me. She's hard at work transferring our files to a new system she found that will handle the needs of our agency much more efficiently.

"Hey," I say.

For a split second, she smiles at me. For a split second, she forgets what day it is and thinks I'm here to walk her home. But then her face falls and she leans back into her chair. "Is it too late to change my mind?"

I walk over and rub her shoulders. "You can do this, Charlie. If it doesn't work out, I'll take full responsibility and you can punish me however you'd like later at home." I lean down and whisper in her ear. "*However* you'd like."

I feel her relax a little and she reaches up to touch my hand.

"If he turns out to be the bastard you've always thought him to be, he'll be out of your life in thirty minutes. But what if the opposite happens, Charlie? What if he turns out to be the father you never knew you had? The father you never knew you wanted? It's worth a twenty-minute conversation, right, snookums?"

"Oh, my God." She spins around in her chair. "That's even worse than 'peaches.' If you ever call me that again, I won't do that thing you like me to do. You know, that thing I did last week that drove you—"

"Got it," I say, interrupting her. "Never again." I hold my hand out to her. At twenty-four weeks, she's starting to get big enough that getting out of chairs is becoming a little more difficult. "Let's do this."

Forty-five minutes and one very needed late-morning scotch later, I'm still trying to wrap my mind around what George has told us. He went over everything that he told Charlie a few months ago. He went over all of it in painful detail. As a man, I was a bit skeptical about another man being abused by his wife. But listening to his story, I get it. I get how it started out as Caroline being a controlling woman. She had him over a barrel with his career. With their finances. As he tells it, the abuse started out slowly. Months would go by between instances, so he thought maybe she had changed. By the time her attacks came on a more regular basis, she'd already worn him down so much he didn't think he had a choice but to be with her. He loved her. Despite what she did to him, he thought he loved her. But now he knows he was really only in love with the women she would portray on the screen.

His red-rimmed eyes look at Charlie as she sits beside me on the couch, holding onto my leg for dear life as he pours his heart and soul out to her from the chair across from us. "You will never know how sorry I am for not taking you with me. For not coming back to get you. I have no excuse for not fighting for you, Charlie. All I can say is that she was rich and powerful and I thought there wasn't a chance in hell she'd let me have you. I knew no judge would give a child to an unemployed screenwriter whose only source of income was alimony from his ex-wife. If she'd had her way, I never would have gotten that, either."

He takes a drink from the bottle of water I'd offered him, declining the stronger route I'd taken myself. "If I had known what she did to you after I left, I'd have found a way, Charlie. I would have kidnapped you. I would have figured something out. But I had no idea. I swear I had no idea she hurt you. I had no idea she . . . let *men* hurt you." He looks physically pained when he reveals that, like I'd punched him in the gut.

Charlie stiffens beside me. I know this is news to her. She told him about the hitting, the burns, but not about the men. But before either of us can ask him about it, he says, "I know about the men,

Charlie. Or more specifically, one man. I can only assume there were more."

"How?" I ask, squeezing Charlie's hand to remind her I'm here for her.

"It was last December. Before your mom died. Before you came back to New York. I was sitting at a bar watching a football game when I overheard a drunken conversation at the table next to me." He shakes his head in disgust, rubbing a hand across his jaw. I can tell he doesn't want to say aloud the words he's about to speak. "The men were comparing their sexual conquests. They were trying to one-up each other. It was an interesting conversation to say the least, so I found myself eavesdropping. One of the men said he'd not only slept with a movie star, but with her lookalike daughter. He told the other man if he'd never had a" —he looks at Charlie with tears pooling in his eyes— "sweet young girl, he needed to try it sometime. He said all he had to do to get the daughter was guarantee the mom an audition for his upcoming film. He said it was like taking candy from a baby."

George looks like he's going to hyperventilate, and as a father, I feel every emotion I see cross his broken face. "When his friend asked him who the movie star was and he said your mother's name, I had to run to the bathroom and throw up."

Charlie is pale. I make her drink some fruit juice while George gathers himself.

"When I was cleaning myself up, I looked in the mirror, disgusted at myself for not protecting you. I knew you left home when you were eighteen so I knew it had to have happened before that. This guy was in his forties. It didn't take much to put two and two together. I punched my reflection in the mirror, sending shards of glass to the floor. One of the pieces was jagged and in the perfect shape of a knife. So I rolled up some paper towels and bunched them around one end so I wouldn't slice my hand open. I put it under my coat and walked back out into the bar. I wanted to kill him right then and there, but I knew his friend would jump me, so I went out front and waited for him to come out. I knew he would. The guy had been going outside to smoke every twenty minutes. I stood outside, planning his death. I saw it play out in my head, right down to the number of times I was going to stab him in the chest. I was insane with fury that just seemed to burn deeper every time someone walked out the front door.

"When he finally came out, I watched him for a minute. I watched him light a cigarette. I watched him lean against the building. I watched him stare at women walking past the bar. All the while, my hand working itself around the makeshift handle of my knife.

"I walked over to him and told him who I was and that I was Charlie Tate's father. He had no idea who I was or what that should mean to him. Then I told him I was Charlie Anthony's father and that I was sitting behind him in the bar ten minutes ago. Then I told him I was going to kill him.

"Before I could even pull the knife out, he pushed me down and started running away, turning around to see if I was following. I was still trying to pick myself up off the ground when he ran right out into traffic and got hit by a car."

"Oh, God," Charlie says. "Peter Elliot."

My jaw twitches at the revelation and for a moment, I find myself admiring the father sitting across from me.

George nods. "I didn't know his name until days later when I'd read about the accident in the paper. I read that he'd drunkenly stumbled into traffic, being struck by a car that caused massive damage, putting him in intensive care. I remember being upset the accident hadn't killed him. I didn't have one ounce of guilt that he ran into traffic because of me. I still don't. He deserved that, Charlie. He deserved that and more.

"I have a friend who works in the hospital so he was able to find out about his recovery. He's still in rehab for his spinal injury and the guy may never walk again. He must have never told the authorities about me, because no one ever came around asking about him."

He lowers his head, resting his elbows on his knees as he slowly breathes in and out. He makes eye contact with Charlie. "I take it he wasn't the only one, Charlie. How many of them were there? How many men did she let use you?"

Charlie closes her eyes, a tear escaping one of them as she says, "Twelve."

George puts his head in his hands, sobbing quietly as he realizes the full extent of her nightmare. "I'm so sorry," he chants over and over.

I feel bad for the guy. What happened to Charlie is not his fault. He wasn't the one who hit her, burned her, molested her. He didn't even know it was happening. But I also know he'll never look at it that way. He will blame himself forever.

What if I'd taken Cat to daycare that day instead of a distracted Cara? What if I would have skipped class and spent the day in the park with her as I'd often done. What if I'd called Cara earlier in the day?

I want to tell him it's not his fault. That his only mistake was leaving without Charlie. That he had no way of knowing what would happen. But it's not my place to offer him forgiveness.

Charlie doesn't say a word. Her body is frozen to mine as she stares blankly at the wall. I want to know what she's feeling. What she's thinking. But with George here, I know she won't tell me.

"You need to give her time" I say, standing up to dismiss him. "It took a lot of guts for her to agree to this meeting. And now, after hearing all this. Well, you just need to give her time."

He nods, getting up off the chair to make his way to the door. But before he leaves, Charlie surprises us both by speaking. "I've read your books," she says.

We both whip around and look at her. This is news to me. I had no idea she had done that.

"You have?" he asks, a glimmer of hope shining through the pain in his eyes.

"They're good," she says. "But I have a question."

"Anything. Ask me anything," he says.

"You claim you didn't know I was being abused until I told you earlier this year, and you say you didn't know I was molested until last December. But how is it then, that you wrote all these children's books about those very subjects?"

"The books started out to be more about helping myself than others," he says. "I knew that as a man, if it was that easy for me to live with and deny being abused, that it must be even worse for women and children. So I wrote a book about abuse, only I geared it towards children. I wanted them to know it wasn't okay. None of it—the yelling, the slapping, the controlling. I thought that maybe if someone had educated me on the subject as a child, I'd have never gotten myself in that situation. Or at the very least, I never would have allowed it to continue.

"Writing that book was therapy for me. So after that, I researched other issues that might help children. Bullying, peer pressure, divorce. And I just started writing, making it a complete series, funny and interesting enough for kids to follow, but with clear messages about the sensitive subjects I wanted them to learn about."

"But you named your main character after me," she says.

He nods. "I did. I guess it was my way of keeping you with me somehow."

She looks down at her stomach, rubbing her hands over it. "I'll read them to him someday."

"Or her," I say, helping her up off the couch.

Tears fall from George's eyes and for the first time, I think they might be happy ones.

She walks towards him but still keeps her distance. "Ethan is right. I still need time. I'm not sure what to do with all this information. So please give me some space. Someday, I might be ready to talk more. Someday I might be ready to see if we can be more than strangers. But please don't ask me to call you Dad."

He sighs, relief rolling across his body from head to toe. "Okay," he says, offering her his hand. "How about we just start with George."

She reaches her hand out to shake his. My own hand comes up to cover my heart, or more specifically the tattoo etched over the top of it.

CHAPTER FORTY-THREE

I look at my stunning fiancée as we ride in the cab to dinner. She is dressed to the nines for our night out with the guys and their Mitchell ladies. Even as big as her belly has gotten, she'll still be the most beautiful woman in the room.

Charlie is breathing a bit easier these days, which is ironic considering she's thirty-two weeks pregnant and the baby is taking up a lot more room in her body, pressing up against her lungs.

We haven't heard from Zach Thompson or his attorney in three months. The hope is, he's given up and moved on to some other scam. The nagging feeling in the back of my mind tells me differently. This guy wants money, and he'll do anything to get it. And I'm sure his attorney has been able to estimate how much Charlie is worth by now. She's sold her mom's apartment, received another life insurance payout, and the estate has been closed, with all money and future royalties put in her name. In the past eight months, she's amassed her own small fortune, albeit one she never wanted. Add that to mine and Thompson is probably drooling all over himself.

When we arrive at the restaurant, the girls hug and kiss and fawn over each other's dresses and shoes while the guys stand back and watch in amusement. You'd think they haven't seen each other in years, not days.

Over dinner, I catch up with the guys to find out what's happened since last Monday's poker game. Gavin's production company just contracted with a popular Iraqi author whose memoirs of the war have become a best-selling novel. He's excited to get the opportunity to produce something other than chick flicks. He started Mad Max Productions by producing a movie based on one of Baylor's romance novels. I felt obligated to watch it after Charlie and I got together. It earned Gavin some high-fives, but I couldn't look Baylor in the eye for months. The movie he produced was based on their own story. And it was very, very, um . . . R-rated.

Griffin tells us about his latest photo shoot, and Mason is still on a high from getting to play more than half of the game last Sunday after the starting quarterback got injured. They won, largely because of Mason's performance, and we all secretly hope Johnny Henley's days as starting quarterback are numbered. Henley is good, but he's getting up there in years. Mason is young and strong and has paid his dues.

Charlie and I have gone to every home game, and it's nice to see her enjoy football again. She's even started to open up to me more about the times she and her dad bonded over the sport.

Although she hasn't seen George since that day at the office, they have been corresponding by email. Emails she shares with me, and I'm more than delighted to see a relationship blossoming between the two of them. My hope is she will see him again soon. Maybe even when the baby comes.

"Are you guys up for some drinks?" Griffin asks after dinner. "I know a great club down the street. That is if Charlie isn't too tired."

"I'm not," she says. "That sounds fun." She rubs her belly. "Obviously, I won't be drinking though."

"Well, if Charlie's not drinking, neither am I," Skylar says. "You shouldn't have to be the only sober one there."

"I'm with you two," Baylor says. "It'll be fun watching everyone else make asses out of themselves."

"Did you just call us asses, darlin'?" Gavin drawls.

"Not you," she says, laughing. "Everyone else at the club."

"How about it, Piper," Skylar asks. "Are you with us? You know, one for all?"

"Are you seriously putting peer pressure on me *not* to drink?" she asks, looking at each of them.

"Looks like we may all have our designated drivers," Mason says.

"You are the only one who drove, Dix," Griffin says. "The rest of us took a cab."

"Oh, right," Mason says, turning to his fiancée. "Have I told you how much I love you?"

Piper rolls her eyes. "Fine. I won't drink. But you owe me one, babe."

When we get up to leave the restaurant, Charlie asks me a question only I can hear. "Did Griffin just call Mason a dick?"

I laugh and explain, "He called him *Dix.* It's a nickname, because his name is Mason. You know, Mason Dixon?"

"Do *you* call him that?" she asks.

I shake my head. "No. I'm not into nicknames, except with you, darlin'."

"*Darlin'?*" she looks up at me with disapproving eyes.

"What?" I say. "Gavin pulls it off."

"That's because he's from Texas," she tells me. "There is nothing southern about you, Ethan."

We walk one block over to the club and are ushered through the main door in front of everyone else who is waiting. I'm not sure if Griffin knows the owner, or maybe it's Mason's recognizable face that gets us in. Either way, I'm glad Charlie didn't have to wait in that long line in those heels she's wearing. And she hates it when I use money to 'make things happen,' so I'm glad this special treatment has nothing to do with me.

We get escorted to the top level of the club to a special VIP area. There is a couch, a few lounge chairs, a table, a big-screen television and a private waitress all at our disposal. Charlie shoots me a questioning look. I hold my hands up. "Don't look at me," I tell her.

"The owner is the guy who hired me for a private shoot this week," Griffin says. "His wife just had a baby and they wanted pictures that are going to be released in next month's *People Magazine.*"

"*People Magazine?*" Piper asks. "Wow, he must be famous. Who is he?"

"I'm sworn to secrecy," he says with a smirk. "Not many people know he owns this club."

Skylar swats him. "They are family, Griffin." She turns to Piper and whispers the name.

I can't hear it, but it makes Piper's eyes bug out. Piper tells Charlie and Charlie tells Baylor and then they all giggle and swoon over the discovery. I know it's not a movie star. Charlie would never swoon over a movie star. In fact, I don't think she's ever swooned over anyone but me. Damn it. Now I'm jealous of the guy who owns this club. But I'm too stubborn to ask who it is.

We spend the next few hours drinking, laughing and talking. I even managed to get Charlie on the dance floor, but she went barefoot because the high-heels had taken a toll on her feet. So instead of enjoying the dance with my future bride, I worried the whole time that someone would step on her feet.

Around eleven o'clock, I can see her begin to fade. "I think Charlie and I are going to call it a night," I tell the group. "You guys stay and enjoy the rest of the evening."

The girls say their goodbyes, hugging like they aren't going to see each other tomorrow or the next day. I look at Charlie's round belly, thinking we should have more children right away. I want our kids to be close, not only in age, but emotionally, like Charlie is with her adopted sisters. Like I am with my brothers.

Plus, I'd have the added benefit of Charlie being pregnant all the time. Pregnancy for Charlie is like having a sex kitten on steroids. Even as big as she's getting, she's still horny all the time. All. The. Time.

I'm the luckiest bastard alive.

But the best part is getting to feel the baby move inside her. I've been able to feel it for a few months now and it's incredible. Cara and I never had that kind of relationship. Even though we became friends after our breakup, we weren't the touchy-feely sort of friends that would go around feeling each other's bellies.

We're walking through the club, trying to make our way to the front door. It takes time. The club is really crowded, even more so than when we came in. It takes us several minutes to navigate through all the drunken party-goers without getting trampled.

Just as we're about to make it to the front door, I hear Charlie's named being shouted. We turn around to see which one of the guys called out to her. Maybe she forgot her purse or something. But it wasn't Gavin or Griffin or Mason who had shouted her name. It was Zach fucking Thompson.

I grab Charlie, pulling her in front of me as I turn us back around and push our way through the door. He was twenty feet or so away from us, so I'm hoping we have time to get around the corner and into a cab before he can follow us.

We don't. I hear his voice call out behind us. "Wait."

I pull her close to me and we keep walking.

"Aw, come on, I just want to talk, Charlie," he says, still following us.

We turn the corner and I look for a cab.

"You're not scared of me, are you, Stone?"

I swear to God that is probably the only thing the asshole could have said to make me turn around. I've got to hand it to him, he's a good manipulator.

"Turn around and walk away right now, Thompson, or I will call the police on your ass faster than you can steal quarters from that parking meter. You are harassing Charlie."

"You can't call the police on me. I haven't done anything. This is a public sidewalk and I have every right to be here. And as far as I'm concerned, I was just the one who was threatened here."

I don't want to take my eyes off him for a second, not even to hail a cab.

He eyes Charlie in her form-fitting maternity dress. "Holy shit, you're fat," he says. "You must be feeding my kid well."

I lunge forward, but Charlie puts a hand on my arm. "Don't, Ethan. He's not worth it."

I take a step back and he laughs.

"Don't Ethan, he's not worth it," he mimics in a high-pitched voice. "Do you always do what slutty bitches tell you to do?"

Faster than Charlie can try to hold me back, I have him turned around and pinned against the building, holding both his hands behind his back as I press the side of his head hard into the brick wall. "Don't you ever talk to us again, you piece of shit. You may think you have something on us. You don't. This kid isn't yours and you won't get a goddamn cent out of us."

"If you were really sure about that, she'd have taken the test," he says into the wall. "You may have me against this fucking wall, but I'm the one with the upper hand here."

"Ethan!" I hear a male voice shout. I turn to see Mason, Griffin and Gavin surrounding Charlie, ready to pounce on Thompson if I give the word. "Everything okay?" Mason asks.

"Fine," I say. "I was just nicely asking Mr. Thompson here to stay away from Charlie."

"You know, there's an easy way to make all this go away," Zach says.

"And I suppose you're going to tell me how much I should write the check for."

"It's probably not as much as you'd think," he says. "A couple mil is chump change to you. But it will get me off your back. I don't want a snotty-nosed kid. But I'll take it if it means the money will follow. And believe me, I have a pretty good idea of the money that will follow. But, hey, I should look at the bright side; I can always bang the babysitter I'll hire with it."

The thing that pisses me off the most right now, other than the fact that this asshole's dick has been inside my fiancée, is that if John hadn't warned me about this, I'd probably be whipping out my checkbook right now. And it scares me that I'm this worried about him being the biological father.

"You can take your bribe and shove it up your worthless ass," I tell him. I give him one more push into the wall so he's sure to feel it in the morning. Then I step back and release him. "Now get the fuck out of here before I make it so you can't walk away."

He walks to the corner before he turns around and stares me down. "I may have dipped my stick in your girlfriend, but you're the one who's getting fucked, Stone."

He disappears around the corner and Charlie runs over to me, wrapping me in her arms. "Are you okay?" she asks.

"Me?" I run my hands over the outline of her face. "What about you? Are you okay? Do you need to sit down or something?"

I notice she's not pale. She's not panicking. She's not even shaking.

"I'm good," she assures me with a smile. "I've thought about this a lot these past few months. And I'm not going to let him get to me anymore. Whatever happens, happens. As long as you and I are together, we can get through anything."

"Charlie." I smile down at her. "You just made a rule."

"What?" she asks.

"Rule number seventeen—whatever happens, happens. I must be rubbing off on you."

She laughs, pulling me tighter against her. "Have I ever told you how much I love your rules?"

"No, but now that you have, I'll never stop making them."

CHAPTER FORTY-FOUR

Once again, I catch myself watching Charlie sleep. She fell asleep on the couch after we got home from Sunday brunch with the Mitchells. I can't take my eyes off her stomach. Through her tight, thin shirt I can see the baby kick and it's fascinating. A hand, foot, knee, or elbow works its way across the left side of her belly. I put my hand on her lightly so I can feel it. I wonder how she can sleep through this. I wonder how it must feel to have something growing inside you.

I wonder how a woman can experience this and go on to hit the very child she gave life to. How she can loathe her own flesh and blood to the point of becoming her child's worst nightmare.

I look at the journal lying on the coffee table. The journal I found when I was looking for something in our closet. It fell on the floor and as I was picking it up, I caught a glimpse of what was written. Vile words from a woman so selfish, she would sell her own child's body to get what she wanted.

Out of respect for Charlie, I didn't read any more words than what my eyes caught when I leaned down to retrieve it. But I need to let her know I found it. I need to let her talk about it.

"The baby is really active today," she says, startling me.

"How do you sleep through that?" I ask.

"Sometimes I don't. But most times, I'm so exhausted that he could be kick-boxing in there and I'll sleep right through it. I think I've just gotten used to it."

I keep my hand on her and lay my head down on her stomach to talk to the baby. "Listen up, Junior. You need to let your mom get some sleep. Save the kick-boxing for later, say seven weeks or so from now."

Charlie runs her fingers through my hair. "Seven weeks," she says. "I can't believe it. On the one hand, it can't get here soon enough, but on the other . . ."

I look up at her. "On the other, what?"

She sighs, looking slightly guilty. "I like our life, Ethan. Things have been so great the last few months. Once the baby comes, I feel like everything will change. Not just because of the Zach thing, but because it won't be just us. What if everything changes?"

"The only thing that will change is that I will love you even more," I assure her. "Charlie, this baby will only bring us closer. No matter what. I promise."

"You don't know that. Having a baby can change people, Ethan. What if it changes me? What if I become someone you can't love?"

I know she's thinking about her mother. "That won't happen. You aren't her, Charlie. You could never be like her." I reach over and pick up the journal. "You are nothing like the woman who wrote this."

Charlie gasps, her hand leaving my hair to cover her mouth. "Oh my God. Where did you get that? Did you read it?"

I drop the journal and sit up. I take her face in my hands, forcing her to look at me so she knows I'm sincere. "No. I didn't. I was in the closet looking for your sweater—the soft one you love so much— I was going to cover you up with it after you fell asleep. But when I pulled it from the shelf, the journal fell to the floor. I only caught a few words of what was written before I closed it up and brought it out here. But those few words were enough for me to know who had written them. I don't want to read it, Charlie. And neither should you. Why are you torturing yourself by keeping it?" I pick up the journal and slam it back down on the table. "The woman who wrote this is dead. She can't hurt you anymore. The only one who can let her continue hurting you is you."

She cocks her head to the side, studying me.

"What is it?" I ask.

"Nothing," she says with a sad smile. "It's just that I think I remember saying something along those lines to Piper last year when she was running away from Mason."

"I knew I was marrying a smart woman."

She shakes her head. "You might not want to marry me if you knew what was in that journal."

"There is nothing in there that would change the way I feel about you, Charlie. I know everything I need to know about your past. And that's just what it is, the past. As far as I'm concerned that damn thing should have been buried with your mother."

She looks down at the journal, studying it. Then she looks at me and something happens. Her eyes go from being dark and guarded, to shining bright with hope. "Will you help me do it? Will you help me bury the past?"

"I'll do anything for you, Charlie. You know that."

She gets up and walks back to our bedroom. A moment later, she returns with a file folder. "In here are all the files you gave me from the list. I want it all gone." She slams it on the table next to the journal. "I want it gone before the baby comes. I want it gone

351

now, this second. I don't want any more reminders of her. Of them. Let's bury it with my past, Ethan."

I think about what she's telling me. This is it. This is the moment I've been waiting for. But how do we do it? I was being metaphorical when I said the journal should be buried with her mother. But I feel like that's what she needs. A burial. A funeral. Closure on her past so it can't haunt her anymore.

I stand up and wrap my arms around her. "I don't think I want to risk you getting thrown in jail for desecrating your mother's grave. How about cremation?" I ask. "We can burn it. We'll burn everything right here in the fireplace."

She looks at the fireplace. Then down at the journal. Then up at me. "I'll get the matches," she says.

I bring the file folder and the journal over to her, but I don't put them into the fireplace. That's for her to do. I lay some kindling and start a fire with the matches she hands me. We watch it for a minute to make sure it catches. Then she holds her hand out and I give her the documents.

She opens the file folder and takes out the piece of paper on top. She glances at it and then crumples it up into a ball. "Fuck you, Karl Salzman," she says, throwing it into the fireplace.

She takes the next paper and does the same thing. "Rot in hell, Joe Mitchner," she says.

And another. "Karma's a bitch, Peter Elliot."

I can't help but smile as I stand behind her and watch this cathartic moment in her life. As she throws each piece of paper into the fire, I can almost see the healing. I can hear it in her voice. I can feel it radiating from her.

When she's done with all the papers from the folder, the only thing left is her mother's journal. She stares at it for a long time before speaking. "Thank you, Mother," she finally says. "Thank you for showing me the kind of mother I don't ever want to be. For showing me how ugly life is without love. But most of all, thank you for dying, which brought me back here so I could meet Ethan."

She tosses the journal into the fireplace and we watch it burn. We watch the edges curl and blacken. We watch the ashes swirl up the chimney. And along with them, I watch Charlie become free from her past.

I stand behind her and wrap her in my arms.

"Not exactly forgiveness," she says. "But it's the best I can do."

"It's everything, Charlie." I hold her tighter. "Marry me," I say.

She leans back into me. "I already said yes."

"I mean marry me today."

She laughs. "We can't get married today. We have to get a marriage license first. Plus, I'm not ready, Ethan. One big thing at a time, remember?"

"Fine." I blow out a breath into her hair. "But let's at least get the license. That way I can ask you every day until you cave."

"I'm not going to cave. Not yet. But if it makes you happy, we can get the license."

I kiss the top of her head. "*You* make me happy."

She turns around after every last paper has been reduced to charred ash and soot. "You make me happy, too. Thank you for this."

The intercom buzzes, alerting me I've got a visitor downstairs. "Way to ruin a perfect moment," I say to no one. Charlie laughs into my shoulder.

I walk over and push the button on the intercom. "Yes?"

"Mr. Stone, there is someone here to see you," Frank, the doorman, says. Then he lowers his voice, sounding like he's cupped his hand over the phone. "It's a policeman. He's got some official-looking papers, Mr. Stone. Says he needs to give them directly to you. What would you like me to do?"

"I'll be right down, Frank. Thank you."

"Policeman?" Charlie says. "Official papers?"

"Stay here," I tell her. "I'll see what this is all about and be right back."

On my way down the elevator I call my attorney. "John, I'm on my way to the lobby of my building. There is a policeman who has papers for me that he says he can give only to me. Do you know anything about this?"

"Sounds like you're being served, Ethan. I can be at your penthouse in an hour," he says.

"While I'd like nothing better, I hate to ruin your Sunday, John."

He laughs. "Ethan, you pay me enough that I'd let you ruin my wedding anniversary."

"I'm not sure how your wife would feel about that," I say.

"She'd probably divorce me. But she'd get a hefty settlement because of how goddamn much you pay me. See you in an hour?"

I laugh. "Sure. Thanks."

~ ~ ~

John puts the papers onto the kitchen table, having read over them carefully. "Basically this is an order of protection. A restraining order. He claims that you physically harmed him and threatened to do more harm. Is that true?"

I look from him over to Charlie, cursing myself for letting Thompson get to me last weekend. "Yes," I tell him. "He approached us at a club. He said some very unpleasant things about Charlie. I told him to stay away from us."

"Told him?" he asks, raising his eyebrows.

"I may have had him pinned up against a brick wall when I did."

"Shit, Ethan. Witnesses?" he asks.

I nod. "Yeah. Charlie and three of our friends."

He shakes his head. "Okay. Well, let me lay it all out for you. This is just a temporary restraining order. There will be a hearing in thirty days to determine if it will become permanent. But I won't sugar-coat it, Ethan. The guy has a case against you. And he has witnesses to prove it. Even though they are your friends, they can still be called to testify for him and I'm sure you wouldn't want to put them at risk by asking them to lie under oath."

I sigh. "I would never ask them to do that."

"Given the circumstances," John says, looking at Charlie's pregnant belly, "you may find a judge sympathetic to your situation. Honestly though, it could go either way. But for now, this order is a 'stay away' order which means you can't go to his residence, his place of employment, or any other location that would put you within a hundred yards of him."

"That won't be a problem," I tell him. "I don't want to be anywhere near that asshole."

John looks at me in sympathy. "Ethan, you don't understand what I'm telling you. You can't be where he is. If you are, he can have you arrested. You can't be *anywhere* he is. That includes the hospital if he chooses to be there when the baby comes."

Charlie gasps and touches my hand before getting up to pace the room.

"What? That's crazy," I tell him. "Do you mean to say he can keep me from watching this baby being born? From supporting Charlie through it? From witnessing one of the greatest things a man can experience?"

He nods. "That's exactly what I'm saying."

"Fuck!" I slam my palm on the table.

Charlie walks over and rubs my shoulders. "Ethan, how will he ever know when the baby is coming if we don't tell him?"

"You are required to tell him," John says. "That was in the original court papers you got served. You are required to tell him about all things related to the baby, including when you go into labor. If you don't, you could be brought up on charges for withholding information. That will not help your case against him if he turns out to be the father."

"So, what do we do, John?"

"What's your due date, Charlie?"

"December 5th," she says.

"That's about seven weeks." He looks at the restraining order again and thinks for a minute. "Honestly, if it were me, I'd get that paternity test."

"Get the paternity test?" I ask. "Now?"

"Yes," he says. "The guy pretty much has you over a barrel, Ethan. And you are close enough to her due date that it doesn't really matter anymore. I mean, the way it is now, he can prevent you from being at the birth if he gets the permanent order. If it turns out he's the father, he can make things very difficult as well, even if a judge doesn't award him the order. But you seemed to indicate to me there is a fifty-fifty chance this child is his. And as I see it right now, fifty-fifty is the best shot you have to get him out of your life. How long does it take to get the results of the test back?"

"I think Dr. Chavis told us it would take two to three weeks."

"Good, so you'll have the results back before the hearing. Get the test. We'll deal with the rest later. Until then, stay away from him. Don't give him any more ammunition."

"Thanks, John," I say, shaking his hand and walking him to the door.

I join a very somber Charlie on the couch. "We will get through this," I tell her. "Together." I touch her engagement ring. "You are so strong, Charlie. Look at what you did today. You just need to be strong for a little longer. Can you do that?"

She nods, giving me a barely-there smile. "As long as I have you, I can do anything."

"That reminds me, I guess now we'll have to take two tests this week."

"Two?" she asks.

"Yeah. The paternity test and the marriage license test."

She laughs and the sweet sound permeates my ears and goes all the way to my heart. "There isn't a test for a marriage license, Ethan."

"There's not?" I say, playing along. "You mean I don't have to prove to anyone how much I love you? I'm really good at tests, you know."

She giggles again. "Thank you," she says.

"For what, dear?"

She laughs, snorting through her nose. "For making me laugh when there isn't anything to laugh about. And don't call me 'dear'."

"Okay. How about 'Buck'? 'Fawn'? 'Moose'?"

"If you call me 'Moose,' I'll spit on your dinner."

I pretend to pull a pen from behind my ear, dab it to my tongue and write on my hand as I say, "Do not call pregnant fiancée 'Moose'."

"I love you," she says, still laughing.

"I love you, too, Buck," I say.

"You're hopeless." She swats the back of my head.

"Hopelessly in love with you," I say. And while I realize that might have just been the cheesiest line in the history of all cheesy lines, it earns me a long, wet, erection-producing kiss, so I really don't give a shit.

CHAPTER FORTY-FIVE

I lie in bed next to Charlie, listening to her toss and turn. Wanting to believe it's because she's thirty-six weeks pregnant and uncomfortable. But knowing it has more to do with the stress she's under.

Two things should happen this week. We should get the results of the paternity test. And I have my hearing for the restraining order.

Damn Zach Thompson for doing this to her. Just when she had let go of the past, he had to go messing with her future.

As I promised John and Charlie, I've kept my distance. Even though I want more than anything to ruin him. But that doesn't mean I haven't had a team of people working around the clock to dig up anything we could use against him.

She cuddles into my side. "Can't sleep either, huh?" she asks.

"Nope." I put my arm around her and mold her body to mine.

"The baby is really kicking tonight. And I've been having more Braxton Hicks."

"Do you need me to calm both of you down?" I ask.

"Would you?" She smiles at me in the moonlight.

I love to see Charlie in the moonlight. The curves of her body, the nuances of her face. And the sun comes up late enough in the morning this time of year that I can leave the shades up. Not to mention she loves to look at the nighttime view with the twinkling city lights and the luminescent skyline. And who am I to deny her anything?

I reach over and pull the box out of my nightstand drawer. I now keep one box here and another in my car. I pull out the harmonica and start playing a soft melody I know she loves. I've been doing this a lot lately. It calms her. It calms the baby. It makes me feel closer to Cat, as if it somehow makes her a part of all this.

"Better?" I ask, putting my harmonica away after the song.

"Mmmmm," she mumbles sleepily into my chest.

I smile, knowing I can help her relax when there is so much to be tense over.

But then she draws in a breath and sits up as fast as an eight-month pregnant woman can sit up. It scares me so I reach over and flip on the light. I look at her and she looks terrified. "What is it?"

"Ethan." She rubs a hand over her belly. "I think my water just broke."

My eyes widen in surprise and my pulse rate shoots through the fucking roof. I try to remind myself that I'm the one who's supposed to remain calm here. "Are you sure?"

She shoots me a look of annoyance. "I haven't wet the bed since I was four, Ethan." Then her face goes back to looking terrified. "Oh my God. It's too soon."

"Charlie, you are close to thirty-seven weeks. Dr. Chavis told you last week that even if you delivered at thirty-six, the baby would most likely be fine. That's what she told you, right?"

I try not to think about the fact that I wasn't at the appointment. That it was the only one I'd ever missed. I wasn't there because Thompson's asshole attorney called John and told him his client would be showing up and wondered if he should bring the police with him to escort me from the building. I almost lost my shit then, but Charlie assured me everything would be okay. She took Piper *and* Skylar *and* Griffin with her. I also insisted Levi go and sit in the waiting room to keep an eye on the manipulative prick.

"Yes." She nods. "But that's not what I'm worried about, Ethan." Tears pool in her eyes and spill over as she breaks down in hysterics. "I can't do this without you. We don't have the test back. Your restraining order. This can't happen now."

I look at the rather large wet spot on the bed. "Oh, this is happening now," I tell her. I take her hand. "Everything will be okay."

"How? How will everything be okay if I have to deliver this baby alone? If I have to go through labor without you, knowing *he* is in the next room?"

"Let's make something clear. You are not going to have this baby without me, Charlie."

"But what about the restraining order?"

"Fuck the restraining order," I say. "I'll deal with the consequences later. We don't have to let him know. He's not expecting the baby this early anyway."

She grabs a hold of her belly and her face scrunches tightly.

"Are you having a contraction?"

She nods, breathing through it. "It's not that bad."

I rub her shoulders until her face goes back to normal. "Come on," I say, getting out of bed and offering my hand to her. "Let's clean you up and head to the hospital."

She looks up at me. "Maybe I could have the baby here. Surely you wouldn't have to leave your own home, even with the restraining order."

I realize going into labor might cause some women to make unreasonable demands, so I try not to look at her like she's said something really ridiculous. "Charlie, I'm not risking the health of you or the baby over a stupid piece of paper."

"That piece of paper could have you ending up in jail, Ethan."

"Not if Thompson doesn't know the baby is coming."

"But what about the other order, the one that says I'm required to call his attorney when I go into labor? When he finds out we didn't comply, it will give him ammunition to fight for custody."

I sit back down on the bed next to her and cup her face with my hands. "Charlie, listen to me. No judge is going to give this baby to that dirt bag. Especially not now with all the information my team has found on him. The guy is grasping at straws here. He wants money, not a kid. Let him sue me for emotional trauma or whatever the hell they call it. And if by some strange twist of fate, he is the biological father, I'll make sure he signs his parental rights away, no matter how much it costs me. I don't give a shit about the money. All I care about is the two of you."

She grabs her stomach again, wincing.

"Unless you are serious about having that baby right here on this bed, we'd better get going," I tell her.

Ten minutes later, I've gathered the things I need along with Charlie's overnight bag and we're in my car calling all of the Mitchells. I smile when I back out of my parking space, seeing the car seat that's been in my back seat for over a week now. The next time I drive this car, a baby will fill that seat. *My baby.* No matter what any goddamn test says.

~ ~ ~

Four hours later, the sun has come up, the Mitchells have all arrived and Charlie is dilated to a seven. They just gave her an epidural, so she's no longer feeling the contractions with a lot of intensity.

Now's the time.

I'm hoping the whole being unreasonable during labor thing will work in my favor.

When the nurse finishes looking at the baby monitor stats, she exits the room, leaving us alone. I wait for the current contraction to pass. I'm relieved she's no longer in excruciating pain with them. Both the lines on the monitor and the decreasing pressure on my hand alert me to the end of this one.

I lace my fingers with hers and sit on the edge of the bed, looking deep into her eyes.

She holds a hand up in front of her face. "Stop looking at me like that, I must look hideous."

I pull her hand away from her face and kiss the back of it. Then I brush a lock of red hair behind her ear. "I've never seen you look more beautiful," I say.

She smiles at me. "It's the love goggles again."

"If that's the case, I never want to take them off. Because I love you. I love you more than I ever thought one person could love another. And I don't want to spend one more second without you being my wife."

"What?" Her eyes widen with surprise. "What do you mean by that?"

"I mean I want you to marry me. Here. Now. Today—not tomorrow."

I've asked her every day for the past few weeks. Every day since we got our marriage license. But I've never asked her like this. We'd pass in the hallway and I'd ask her if today was the day she was going to marry me. She'd always say 'not today, maybe tomorrow.'

She waves her hand at our surroundings in her hospital room. "I can't marry you today, Ethan. We're having a baby."

"That's exactly why you should marry me today," I say. "Hospitals always have clergy around to do this sort of thing."

"We don't have our license," she says. "And there is no way I'm letting you leave to go get it."

I pull a folded piece of paper out of my pocket and show it to her.

"You brought it?"

"Of course I brought it. I need you to become my wife, Charlie."

She studies me. "Why, Ethan? Why do you need it right now? What's any different about today than tomorrow, or a month from now?"

I put my hand on her stomach. "Because if this is my baby, I want him born bearing my last name. And if it's not, I want him to know I loved him enough to marry his mom regardless."

"Or her," she says. A tear falls from her eye and I catch it with my thumb. "Well, why didn't you just say that before?"

I laugh at my stubborn fiancée. "I've been saying it for months, Charlie. Maybe you just didn't hear it until today."

I pull a small box out of my other pocket and open it to show her the wedding rings I had made for us.

She looks at the rings, identical platinum bands embedded with diamonds. She goes to pick the smaller one up, but I stop her.

"I want to see the engraving," she pouts when I swat her hand away. "I know you put a rule in there."

I shake my head. "Not until you are my wife."

She shifts in the bed and I glance at the monitor to see another contraction starting. "Then you'd better get someone in here quickly," she says. "Because I don't know how much longer we have."

In short order, the room is filled with everyone we love. The Mitchells were all in the waiting room, so that was easy enough. Kyle was in the hospital shadowing a doctor today, so he's able to be my best man. And we've got my parents and Chad on Facetime.

I'm not sure how many people get married sitting on a hospital bed. But frankly, I wouldn't care if we were married in a garbage dump as long as it means this woman is mine.

Jan Mitchell scoured the hallways, finding a pastor who was willing to marry us, so a mere thirty minutes after Charlie succumbed to my pleas, he pronounces us husband and wife. I kiss my bride to the applause and whistles of our impromptu audience.

Somehow, Kyle was able to scrounge up a bottle of champagne and a bunch of those put-together plastic champagne glasses. He's handing them out to everyone, but Skylar declines.

Charlie laughs. "It's okay, Skylar, you don't have to refrain because of me."

"It's not because of you," Skylar says.

Skylar and Charlie share a moment where they stare at each other and then Skylar gets a big smile on her face. Charlie squeals in delight. "Oh, my God, really?"

Skylar nods.

Mason asks, "What am I missing here?"

Skylar looks at Griffin and he smiles. She says, "We were going to wait until you delivered to tell everyone, but I guess now is a good time. We're pregnant!"

Everyone in the room cheers again. Everyone but Baylor. She looks at her younger sister in utter disbelief. "You have got to be kidding me," she says.

"What?" Skylar asks.

"I'm not drinking champagne either," Baylor says.

"Oh my God!" Skylar squeals as they run to embrace each other.

"So, last month at the club, you knew?" Baylor asks Skylar.

"Yup. You?"

"Yup. When are you due?" Baylor asks.

"May 22nd. You?"

"June 3rd."

They both turn to look at Piper and then the rest of our gazes follow. Piper holds up her hands. "Don't look at me," she says. "I'll drink the whole damn bottle."

Mason comes up behind her and wraps her in his arms. "Now will you consider it?" he asks.

Piper cranes her head back at him and then looks at all the faces in the room. "Are you all seriously peer-pressuring me into getting knocked up?"

Everyone laughs, including Piper. "Okay," she says. "I might be willing to consider it."

Mason lifts her into the air and spins her around. Then he says, "Let's go home and consider it right now."

She swats him. "I think I'd like to hang around until my niece or nephew makes an appearance."

Mason looks at Charlie. "Do you think we could hurry this along?"

Dr. Chavis comes into the room, smiling at the festive atmosphere. "I hate to break this up, but somebody is about to become a party crasher," she says, walking over to place a hand on Charlie's belly.

Everyone comes over to kiss Charlie and wish us well. Bruce Mitchell shakes my hand, pulling me into a hug. "Welcome to the family, son."

I can barely control my emotions when I see my mother crying happy tears over the video stream. I know she never thought this day would come. The day when she would see her son experience pure joy again. I tell her we'll call her back after the baby arrives. Then I shut the lid to the laptop and turn around to face my bride.

She too is crying, because she has removed the ring and is reading the inscription. "Rule number eighteen—forever isn't long enough." She looks up at me, eyes glistening. "I love you so much."

I take her in my arms. "Right backatcha, Mrs. Stone."

"Charlie Stone," she says, pondering over the name. "I think that has a nice ring to it." She frowns and I wonder if another contraction is starting. "I just wish we could have said vows and stuff. There is so much I want to say to you."

"We will have sixty or seventy years to say all the things we want to say to each other," I tell her. "And believe me, the vows I want to say to you, are for your ears only, Tate."

Her eyes snap to mine and she smiles. She smiles big.

"That's the one?" I ask.

She nods. "That's the one," she says. "That's *always* been the one."

Dr. Chavis clears her throat. "Is there anyone we need to be calling?"

I know what she's asking, but I don't let the thought put a damper on this incredible moment. I shake my head. "No. Everyone who is supposed to be here is here."

Dr. Chavis smiles. "That's what I thought. Now let's have this baby, shall we?"

CHAPTER FORTY-SIX

I look down into the baby-blue eyes of our day-old son. I've counted every finger and every toe a hundred times. They are all still there. And they are perfect. He is perfect.

Charlie comes up behind me to catch me staring again. She wraps her arms around me. "All babies have blue eyes, Ethan. It doesn't mean anything."

I nod my head. I know that. And I know that whatever the test says and whatever happens, he will be as much my son as Cat was my daughter. But I was hoping for some kind of sign. Blonde hair maybe; or his second and third toes being slightly webbed together as mine are.

But Eli is completely bald. He's the cutest bald baby I've ever seen. I love it when his little face scrunches up right before he cries. I love it when he grabs my finger and holds onto it for dear life. I love it when I watch him feed from Charlie's breast. I love it when I look at him and think of how it felt to hold Cat in my arms.

I'm only human, though, and I know if he's not my biological son, it will devastate me. I won't love him any less. I won't be any less of a father to him. It shouldn't make any bit of difference in the world. Except that I know it will.

I stare at him, unable to pull my eyes away from this little miracle swaddled in the hospital blanket they wrapped him in. I have the car seat all ready to go. I've long since loaded all of the flowers, cards and teddy bears into the trunk of my car. And Charlie is getting his going-home outfit out of her bag.

I almost dread leaving the hospital. It means we have to go home and face reality. The reality of us not informing Thompson. The heartbreaking task of being forced to do it now. The consequences of what will come after.

But when I look down into Eli's face, I know it was all worth it. Watching him come into the world; sharing that moment with Charlie; having her become my wife. Nothing and no one can ever take those moments away from us.

"Let's get him changed," Charlie says. She picks him up out of the hospital bassinette and lays him on the bed. I help her as we carefully, and somewhat awkwardly, remove his blanket and try not to break him as we dress him in his very first outfit.

I'm working on getting his little legs into it, while she works on his arms. She gasps, putting a hand over her mouth to muffle her cries.

My heart slams into the front of my chest. I quickly look him over to see if he's hurt and to make sure he's still breathing. "What is it?"

Through her tears, she says, "I didn't notice it before. Oh my God, Ethan. Why didn't we notice it?"

"Notice what?" I ask.

She holds up his tiny left arm, pointing to the underpart of his bicep. I squint to see what she's showing me. As it comes into focus, my heart stops and then starts again. The rug I thought was coming out from under me is now securely in place under my feet. The future that was uncertain is now entirely ours to navigate.

Tears stream down my face, matching those on Charlie's when I see his birthmark. The tiny brown marking that to me still looks more like a fingernail moon than a banana. But I realize now might not be the time to argue the point.

Charlie touches my left arm, running her fingers over the very same place the birthmark is on my skin. "He's yours, Ethan. He's yours," she cries.

I reach over and pick up my half-dressed son. I hold him securely in my arms. I place kisses on his soft bald head. I thank God for giving us this sign. "He was always mine," I tell Charlie, leaning down to kiss her.

"I don't think I've ever been as happy as I am right now. Right this second." She touches Eli's cheek.

"Get used to it, Tate. I plan on making the two of you happy every day for the rest of our lives."

The nurse comes in asking if we're ready to go.

"Just about," I say, wiping what's left of Charlie's tears.

While Charlie finishes dressing Eli, I send a text to Skylar, letting her know we're on our way. She and Baylor and Piper have been decorating the penthouse for our arrival. And Skylar has been there all day, cooking enough meals to last us two weeks. I smile knowing my son will never know a family without love. He will never know parents who wouldn't die for him. He will live a life surrounded by cousins, siblings, aunts and uncles.

Before I put my phone away, it pings with an email. When I see who it's from, the only thing I can do is smile. It's not the reaction I would've had ten minutes ago. Ten minutes ago, if I'd seen this email containing the results of the paternity test, I would have fallen to my knees, praying the results would go our way. But now, even before I open the email and see the results, I know what they will say. I also know that both Charlie and Zach have gotten the same email.

Charlie finishes securing Eli into the car seat. "Check your email," I tell her.

She gives me a strange look. "Now?"

"Yes, now."

She pulls out her phone and opens up the email. Fresh tears stream down her face as she reads it. She throws her arms around me and hugs me. "It's over. It's really over," she cries. "He's out of our lives." She looks up at me with red eyes. "I'm so sorry I put you through all this, Ethan."

"I forgive you," I say, knowing there is nothing to forgive. "But I'm the one who's sorry. I never should have pushed you away back then."

She puts her hand on my chest, right over my tattoo. "I forgive you, too."

I smile down at her. "It feels good, doesn't it?"

"What?" she asks.

"Forgiveness," I say.

She looks over at Eli, now fast asleep in the car seat. Then she looks back at me. "I think I'm ready," she says. "I'm ready to talk to my dad again. Maybe we could have him over to meet Eli."

I nod, holding back more tears because as a father, I know just how much that will mean to him.

"Come on," I say, gently picking up the car seat. "Let's take our son home."

She gathers her overnight bag, but before we leave the room, she stops, turning to me. "There is one stop we need to make on the way."

I look down at our day-old son, wondering what on earth could be so important. "Where?" I ask.

"I want to introduce Cat to her new brother."

If love were tangible, I would be suffocating in it. This woman never fails to surprise me. She never fails to become even stronger than she thought she could ever be. She never fails to make me love her more deeply than the moment before.

I look down at my son in one hand, and then I take Charlie's hand with my other. "Let's go, Mrs. Stone. Let's go see what amazing things life has in store for us on the other side of that door."

She smiles. Then she opens the door and we walk through.

THE END

GLOSSARY

Stone's Rules

Rule #1 – Don't get involved with clients

Rule #2 – Don't take out a woman who won't eat

Rule #3 – Don't talk to arrogant strangers

Rule #4 – Don't play with fire if you don't want to get burned

Rule #5 – Be nice to little old ladies

Rule #6 – Don't play your hand too soon

Rule #7 – No public displays of affection

Rule #8 – Wrap it before you tap it

Rule #9 – A promise is a promise

Rule #10 – If you don't have anything, you have nothing to lose

Rule #11 – All good things come to those who wait

Rule #12 – Sometimes you gotta do what you gotta do

Rule #13 – Some things are just meant to be

Rule #14 – Forever

Rule #15 – Money doesn't always make life easier

Rule #16 – Carpe diem

Rule #17 – Whatever happens, happens

Rule #18 – Forever isn't long enough

And let's not forget about Charlie's

Rule #69 – Give and you shall receive

Book 2 is Chad's story

Stone Promises

If you've enjoyed Stone Rules, I would appreciate you taking a minute to leave a review on Amazon. Reviews, even just a few words, are incredibly valuable to indie authors like me.

ACKNOWLEDGEMENTS

All good things must come to an end. It's hard saying goodbye to the Mitchell sisters, but I've had so much fun introducing you all to the Stone brothers. I hope you will love them as much as I do and want to stay with them through their journeys.

This book was difficult to write. Charlie's story was traumatic, and although this book is purely fiction, I know there are people out there who have suffered similar pasts. My heart goes out to you. May you have the strength and courage to find the peace that you deserve.

Thank you to my editors, Ann Peters and Jeannie Hinkle. You've been with me since the beginning—for all seven books. I keep expecting you to tire of me, yet you keep coming back for more.

To my beta readers, Tammy Dixon, Laura Conley, Heather Durham and Angela Marie: you guys each have different qualities in a beta reader that all seem to come together and make my book a better read. I couldn't do this without you.

The life of an author has many ups and down. My family gets to celebrate my highs with me and support me through my lows. None of this would be possible without them.

ABOUT THE AUTHOR

     Samantha Christy's passion for writing started long before her first novel was published. Graduating from the University of Nebraska with a degree in Criminal Justice, she held the title of Computer Systems Analyst for The Supreme Court of Wisconsin and several major universities around the United States. Raised mainly in Indianapolis, she holds the Midwest and its homegrown values dear to her heart and upon the birth of her third child devoted herself to raising her family full time. While it took time to get from there to here, writing has remained her utmost passion and being a stay-at-home mom facilitated her ability to follow that dream. When she is not writing, she keeps busy cruising to every Caribbean island where ships sail. Samantha Christy currently resides in St. Augustine, Florida with her husband and four children.

You can reach Samantha Christy at any of these wonderful places:

Website: www.samanthachristy.com

Facebook: https://www.facebook.com/SamanthaChristyAuthor

Twitter: @SamLoves2Write

E-mail: samanthachristy@comcast.net

Printed in Great Britain
by Amazon

84252858R00221